I0690761

VALIANT

CORINA ZURCHER

NeverMore Publications, LLC ®

Text Copyright © December 2023 Corina Zurcher

Cover Art and illustrations by Scott Edward. Copyright © NeverMore Publications, LLC

All rights reserved. Published by NeverMore Publications, LLC

Publishers since 2013

NEVERMORE PUBLICATIONS and the RAVEN LOGO are trademarks and/or registered trademarks of NeverMore Publications, LLC

Library of Congress Cataloging-in-Publication Data Available

Library of Congress Control Number: 2023952309

ISBN-13: 979-8-9887502-1-5

Printed in the U.S.A.
First American edition, January 2024

"Seeing the sun, the moon and the stars, I said to myself, 'Who could be the Master of these beautiful things? I felt a great desire to see him, to know him and to pay him homage'."
– Saint Josephine Bakhita

I

"Bring me the Tablet of Destinies."

Tick-Tock vaulted across the old toad chief's abode and into a darkened cavern without making a single sound. Chief Netapheha was kneeling over a small pool of water that led to his domain, studying it with a deep frown on his face. Narrowing his bulbous eyes as he looked down into its depths, he was deeply troubled. "What...what...what should I see deep within thee..."

Tick-Tock returned, landing down beside the chief carrying the old stone tablets in his birdlike arms. Chief Netapheha took the first one from him and quickly scanned its markings; his webbed fingers roaming rapidly over the ancient symbols. He tossed the tablet aside and grabbed for the second one. His entire body froze the moment he found what he was searching for. He quickly looked back at the water; his frown now gone, replaced by a look of disbelief. "Whoever rules the sea, rules the realm...it cannot be...*banished*...driven to a land far beyond, yet it is he..."

He held the stone tablet close to his chest as he continued to stare down at the pool of water, trying to decipher this new revelation. As he continued to stare, the water began to slowly move back and forth until tiny waves formed from the stillness. The emerald stone hanging around Tick-Tock's neck flickered and came to life as a deep glow illuminated from its center. The feathers and fur on Tick-Tock's body rose straight up as the waves continued to rise and fall; he growled lowly.

Water slopped back and forth, spilling up onto the landing where Chief Netapheha and Tick-Tock were leaning over. As the waves continued to rise in height, gaining momentum from an unseen force, the old toad chief neither flinched nor took his eyes from the pool — not even when it began to freeze over, turning into a jagged pile of black ice.

He leaned in closer.

From the unseen depths below, a clawed hand suddenly rose up, smashing through the ice, viciously swiping at Netapheha's head. Tick-Tock immediately grabbed for him and pulled the old chief backward before he could be

1

assaulted; a loud roar rose up from the pool of water and echoed throughout the small cavern. And just as quickly as the water turned to ice, the ice rapidly melted, leaving the pool of water as still as it was moments before.

The old toad chief and totem sat in silence staring at the tranquil water until Netapheha said, "He is coming…"

Tick-Tock slowly turned his large head toward the chief.

"The king…the king…is coming…his army living in the dark. No light amongst his kind. No balance to weigh the mind over the heart…the eagles were mistaken." He looked at Tick-Tock. "Wise was the wolf king. Foolish was the bird king." Netapheha looked down at the emerald stone hanging from Tick-Tock's neck; it was no longer glowing. "The time has come for you to become. Go…go…go now….the three will need you…not just she."

And with no further prompting, Tick-Tock lunged forth on his hind legs and dove into the water leaving Chief Netapheha still clutching the single tablet close to his heart. "The sea, the sea, that is the key…they do not know but will soon come to know of thee…guardian created for she and the three…yes, yes…to protect them from he…"

As if in reply, another roar rose up from the depths of the pool of water just as a sudden burst of wind blew through the cavern, sweeping all around Chief Netapheha like a tornado, blowing past him and out toward the lion's den.

II

The wind glided all throughout the den, searching down its long stone hallways, along its stairwells, past the Great Library, down several corridors, until finding its subject. The wind softened to a gentle breeze and seeped through the tiny crack under the door, winding through the darkened room, until rising above the large canopy bed. It hovered for a moment before descending onto the sleeping form of the lion king. Blowing through his wavy brown hair, the wind whispered its message softly in his ear.

The king stirred in his sleep, the wind continuing its whispers before quietly dissipating, until only a small bit of moonlight trickled through the curtains, giving a sliver of light to the darkened room. Daniel slowly opened his eyes, taking in his surroundings. He had heard the silent whisper while he dreamt but could barely remember it as the sluggish fog on his brain refused to lift in order to allow him the full clarity of what had been communicated.

It was a single phrase — not quite an order or a command — but it escaped him — like most dreams forgotten upon awakening. He knew it would eventually come to him but gave it no further thought as he slowly rose from his bed. Stretching his limbs, he yawned deeply as he crossed the large room toward the covered windows. He threw open the heavy drapes, flooding the room in moonlight as the fog on his brain finally lifted.

Just before the dawn.

Daniel looked out across the den and breathed it all in: the serenity, the stillness, the peacefulness of his slumbering home before anyone in his kingdom awoke to the busyness of another day. He exhaled deeply, relishing in the stillness of the hour. He was just about to turn away from the window when he caught movement out of the corner of his eye.

In the shadows...

He narrowed his eyes, watching as a large being crept silently along the wall of the surrounding den gate.

The creature stopped, sensing someone's eyes on him. Daniel crossed his arms over his muscular chest, continuing to watch the shadowed being's movement. Bold for a creature to venture inside the den. Disturbing that whatever it was had not been seen by any warrior or guard; he wondered what it could be.

The lion king continued to watch as the creature began to move once more. From the shadows, a dark claw extended out from the darkness and reached out to touch the ground — a raven. A second claw followed suit — an eagle.

Tick-Tock.

Daniel narrowed his eyes, watching the totem move further into the moonlight, its head dipped low. He could see Tick-Tock's owl eyes on all three heads suddenly close; all three heads slowly began to turn. One by one the snow owl shifted to barn owl and then slowly to horned owl.

As Tick-Tock did so, the lion king watched as the wind began blowing gently around the totem. The ground swirled beneath the guardian's touch just as the light from the moon cascaded down upon him. Even the air seemed to cool a bit as the lion king watched Tick-Tock's movements.

Daniel stood there spellbound. With his clawed hands extended over the earth, it appeared to the king as if Tick-Tock was communicating with the elements. But as Daniel watched this private action more closely, it seemed more like Tick-Tock was listening instead.

A still small voice.

The owl eyes snapped open in unison and, without skipping a beat, Tick-Tock suddenly leapt up and over the den walls, vanishing from sight.

Daniel looked up at the full moon and back down to where Tick-Tock's talons had touched the earth; a perfect spot to feel the ray of light pouring down from above. The lion king could not help but wonder what the significance of that moment meant and how often the totem must seem to do it.

Daniel suddenly thought, *I wish they would speak to me...*

It was then that Daniel suddenly remembered his dream. It was one he had many times before, but one he had not had in quite a while. It was of Rebekah. Queen Rebekah dressed in the color of the darkest night, dancing in the moonlight. Shadows of large creatures dancing beside her moving and gliding to the sound of the lone beat of a drum. They danced side by side, dancing as one, dancing before the fire that blazed red like the sun. And rising from the shadows on her right and on her left, there came an eagle and a raven...followed by the phrase...

Remember...remember...

"My king..."

Daniel's thoughts shifted from his unconscious memory to the warrior at his door, snapping him back into the present moment, reminding him that today was no ordinary day.

"Cheetah."

His guardian solemnly entered, fully dressed, carrying his king's royal attire in his long arms. The warrior walked stiffly inside, his shoulders tense, his gaze held low.

"You look awful."

Cheetah laid his king's clothing on a nearby table. "I have not slept, my king. My mind has been consumed with many thoughts." He turned and stood erect. "I wish to speak freely."

"This sounds serious."

"It is, my king."

"I'm listening." Daniel watched as his guardian struggled to find the words as Cheetah's body seemed to constrict and tense all over.

"I have been and always will be…your guardian." Cheetah exhaled slowly, "Years ago Princess Tara came to see my family to find a protector for her son. She chose *me*. It was the greatest honor my family had ever received, as you were and are the heir to the throne and the lifeline of our existence. No one from my tribe had ever been tasked with such a request before. And as much as it meant to my family, it meant more to *me*…that your mother found me worthy. It brought great pride, not just to my tribe, but to my entire family. We relished in such an honor knowing the responsibility laid at our feet. And from that day, I vowed to my princess — your mother — that I would guard you with my life."

He knew where this was going. "Cheetah…"

Cheetah placed his paw up in the air. "*Please*, my king." Daniel paused. "I have been lax in my guardianship…because…most of your life we stayed here. These walls were more of a shield than I ever was. But where I did not stand before you, I have watched beside you: where you go, the path you take." He paused, struggling to find the words. "That day, when you snuck out of the den, I watched you do it. I didn't stop you because…because I *knew* it was you. I knew you were the one…the Noble Heart…the Noble One. I'd always known it. And I was *proud* when I saw you climb over the walls that had been holding you back for so long. It was your time to do. It was your destiny to be. And it was you alone, my king, that changed the realm forever."

Cheetah's fur was raised straight up as he continued pouring his thoughts out to his king. "I made Reginald swear to me that when the falcons came to take you to Bird Kingdom or Wolf Lair that they be champions, warriors he could trust. I always knew their flight path and never worried, for I trusted the old captain. I never lost sight of where you were or where you were going. *Never.* But today…today my heart is filled with a deep unrest. I don't know the path you are taking. I won't see what's before you or behind you because you have commanded that I remain here, severed from your side. The walls will be harder to climb, my king. The sunrises will be over different hills, and they will speak to your days with different messages than the ones you find here." He inhaled sharply, clenching his clawed hands into tight fists before exclaiming, "I *must* go with you, my king! If you perish, we are done for! And it will be my fault! SinJin failed Prince Marcus and the den has never forgiven him for it! *I* will *not* break my promise to your mother, my king! I will not disgrace the clan! I will *not* fail you! Take me with you!"

Daniel was taken aback by Cheetah's emotion. He had never seen him like this before. The lion king had known his guardian was distraught over having to stay behind, but he thought Cheetah understood the reasoning behind it.

He paused, trying to think of the right words he knew his guardian needed to hear. "Cheetah, I have the chance to seek the Creators — the ones who deemed me worthy. It's as you say…they chose me as the Noble One. The one to shift our realm back into a place of prosperity. They have guided my steps in all of this, and I have no reason to believe they would bring me harm now. I'm not afraid of what's out there. I'm only afraid of what will happen if I stay here and don't keep trying to change the odds that continue to be stacked against us. I want to finish what I started."

Cheetah's eyes were tiny slits, "It is the good that perish first, my king. It is the honorable whose light is extinguished before the candle burns out. There is a specific time allowed for us all, and however long we think it may be, the world has other ideas. You did your duty once before. Let the others pick up where you left off. If I'm ordered to stay here, so must you. You are the only king who could lead the other clans to build that dam. The amphibian king does not lead!"

"He is a king of this realm."

"Who has yet to earn the title! The den will not listen to him! You *know* they won't! He is a king of a *lesser* clan!"

"*I* have commanded it! By my order the den must obey!"

"You don't know what's out there!"

"None of us do! But I'm going all the same!"

They stared at one another for several moments. Daniel grabbed Cheetah by the shoulders so that they were eye to eye. "You *are* my guardian. You *have* protected me…in more ways that I've ever known. And to keep on protecting me is to champion all that I have done and all that I am about to do. You *must* stay to guard my orders, Cheetah. *You* must see it through on my behalf, just as you would if we were standing side by side. I need you to do this. I need you here to help King Sebastian with the den. If he fails, with or without that stone, all of our time is up."

Daniel could feel his warrior's shoulder drop in silent resignation. The moment he saw Cheetah's fur relax and his warrior's breathing fall into a calmer rhythm, he knew he had succeeded in keeping his champion home.

He let go of his guardian's shoulders and quickly dressed as he said, "And never forget, Cheetah, I'm not without a guardian. I have Tick-Tock."

Cheetah's fur shot straight up again. Daniel saw his face darken, quickly realizing he should have stopped while he was ahead.

"It is unnatural, my king. Dark magic. *Old* magic. A guardian, yes, but meant for only one clan. This creature resembles none of the living. He is a reminder only of the dead. You don't know what he really is."

"And what is he?"

"Dark…and light."

Daniel could not help stopping the chill that suddenly ran down his spine the moment Cheetah spoke the words. He felt his mouth go dry as he said, "Well then, I think I need my own light to shine right now."

Cheetah reluctantly nodded and followed his king out the door, knowing what his king meant and needed, but not before looking back at the shadows in the room.

It was just before the dawn.

III

*"W*arrior, is that where the lion prince was found?"

The falcon looked down toward Wolf Lake. "Yes, king."

He felt the cool wind on his face as he stared up at the moon. He was flying over Wolf Lair. He shifted his eyes to survey the landscape, catching a glimpse of the lake. It was beautiful.

"I'd like to take a closer look."

"My queen commanded that I take you directly to her kingdom. It is not safe here."

"I just want to…"

"Tok…tok…tok…"

And all went black.

Byron shouted and bolted upright from the chair he had been sleeping in. He was breathing hard; sweat had drenched his brow and clothing as his body trembled. The gorilla king lowered his head in his hands and tried to calm himself.

"Another nightmare?"

Byron looked up at the sound of Minotauro's voice. The bull king stood in the doorway just inside the library.

"I can't get him out of my head. It's maddening." He turned and looked out at the darkened window to the jungle beyond.

Minotauro studied the look on Byron's face. Not only did the gorilla king look pale and exhausted, but he also looked incredibly sad. He had looked that way every day since Queen Rebekah had died.

Minotauro moved across the large library and leaned against the bamboo railings near one of the bookshelves. The bull king was pensive, feeling a deep tension in his shoulders as he studied his best friend's demeanor. It pained him to see Byron look this way, watching him mourn silently during the day, only to be found sleepless and distraught at all hours of the night.

"My bulls hated that raven." He looked out one of the windows into the night sky. "Actually, my clan always hated the ravens…and the crows. They could never see them coming at night."

"I know I didn't. I just wish I could remember the moments after instead of

8

the ones before. Then I would sleep easier knowing that my life was spared for some greater purpose."

Silence filled the room until Minotauro turned to the gorilla king and said, "You deserve to be here."

Byron turned from the window and looked at him; he swallowed hard, clenching his jaw, trying to hold back the pain that longed to expunge itself from his heart. He remained silent, holding it in, merely shaking his head in disagreement.

"There *is* more for you to do…and you haven't done it."

Byron exhaled, "Whatever I'm supposed to do, Minotauro, I don't have the energy to even try. I'm tired. And I'm tired of being tired." He grabbed Rebekah's medallion hanging around his neck and looked down at it. "Kings are supposed to have boundless energy and passion for purpose at all times, aren't they?" Minotauro did not reply. "It's a cruel joke sometimes, this world. I've gone through the hard times…many times…seeing a light at the end of the tunnel. And I start to relax, feeling the weight of my soul begin to lighten. And then…another blow, and I have to find the energy and motivation to keep going." He looked out the window once more. "Today, although we are about to leave our kingdoms in search for what we hope exists, one would think my spirits would be rallied and my heart thundering with the anticipation to see it through." The gorilla king shook his head. "I can't find it. I have no energy. I feel no hope. I just see the raven's scarlet eyes burning into me, reminding me that the last time I had such hope…that it was all for naught." He let go of the medallion and rubbed his head. "I can't keep living like this…always on the defensive of the unknown. I want to lower my shield for once, Minotauro…and simply *be*."

"We've had our share of pain, haven't we? Every day feeling like a sunrise of suffering. And each night, a pitiful, monotonous sunset of woe. But you know what got me through it and keeps me getting through it?" Byron peered up at him. "You. Your friendship…and Sebastian's. You're the brothers I never had. The best friends any king would envy. The raven is dead, my friend. And you are in the realm of the living. So live."

"I'm trying to. I'm just…"

"Grieving."

"Yeah."

"And the world won't let you. It never does. Especially when you are king."

Byron stared absently across the room; his fingertips gently touching the medallion hanging from his neck. "Or a queen. I keep thinking about Rebekah and how she chose to help us all when none of us deserved it. I never told you this, but when I had heard she had awoken, I was terrified and excited at the same time. I wasn't sure what kind of queen she would turn out to be: vengeful, cruel, or kind." He turned to look back at Minotauro. "She was more than what I could possibly have imagined: passionate, brave, loving, and yet could be fierce…she loved her clan. *Loved* them, Minotauro. I cannot imagine what she must have been thinking when she saw them destroying all the good she had

9

sought to sough in this world.

"First, the realm tried to destroy her. Then her clan tried to annihilate everything she was trying to build up. And all she was ever after was to leave this place better than what she was born to, living well within the beauty she imagined. And she failed."

"Did she?"

"She never got to see it through."

"But she tried. She laid a path for us to follow. The energy it must have taken her to rally her spirits day after day is likened to our own. She lost much in this world, Byron. And there is no doubt in my mind Queen Rebekah knew that her actions were a risk. A risk to engage with this world to do an impossible thing. And she did it in anyway. She chose. As have we.

"Since we were children, we've always been haunted into being too afraid to believe we were meant to be happy in a world filled with so much despair and desolation. Get your hopes up one day, only to be reminded the next that tragedy is the brand of your existence. Yet, we continue to master the blows that keep coming our way, strengthened by our suffering. This moment, too, shall be mastered, for it is the dawn of a new day, my friend, and hope is on the horizon."

Byron sat back in his chair and inhaled deeply; the tense look on his face slowly subsiding. "And the sun is about to rise…to rally my spirits once more."

"It is."

The gorilla king nodded, understanding his friend's full meaning. "Time to go."

"The heartbeat of passion must beat on, so we can truly *be*."

And with that, Byron rose to his feet, rousing his energy once more. The kings walked out the door and to the jungle grounds beyond. From the shadow in the room, two scarlet-colored eyes illuminated in the darkness.

"Tok…tok…tok…"

IV

Daniel was standing atop the hill in Bull Valley waiting for the sun rise over Bird Kingdom. He wondered how long it would be before he stood atop this hill again — or if he ever would. Looking out toward the castle, he remembered the first time he ever saw it.

The Noble One.

It was a little over a year ago, yet it seemed so much longer. Standing on the hilltop, he could not help but think of his grandfather Nathan, wondering what he thought of all this now — an Element Fortress, a stone that might help bring the rain. He even remembered their last conversation about Mariner Sea. *"It would take a miracle to resurrect that sea, Daniel. The rain would have to fall for years. And if it did, flooding and mudslides would destroy the surrounding landscape. There's no way it can be done."* His grandfather was probably right. This trek they were about to go on might all be for naught. But Daniel was a man who believed in miracles; he had seen them come to pass. And he knew another miracle was due — especially for those who were about to risk their lives to help the entire realm find the hope it so desperately desired.

Daniel inhaled deeply, watching as the sky shifted from darkness to light. He never got tired of such a moment. It was almost as if he was watching the stripping of the stains of sin that wanted to bind the world to desolation as the shadows vanished, replacing them with the colors illuminated by the sun, consoling it, making everything new. There were sunrises where he missed the moment — that sudden shift in light. He wondered if that split second when it changed was a lot like life and death. He wondered if that was what it was like when one's life ended and moved on to the next phase. Daniel did not know if there really was a next phase, but he believed there had to be, or how else how would a being like Tick-Tock exist or even make sense? And had the totem never existed, there was a part of Daniel that believed there was something beyond this life anyway. There had to be or what was the purpose of existing if nothingness was the result of your time in this world?

He wondered if Nathan thought the same thing. He wondered if his grandfather pondered the Old Ones, the Creators, the Elements of this world.

11

He wondered if all his thoughts were dreams of his life unlived or of his life to live when Queen Rebekah arose. How long he had waited for her to rise again. He even wondered if Nathan ever had doubts that he would ever see her again before he died as he watched the sun rise day after day, shifting the darkness to light. It made him realize he had missed so many opportunities to ask his grandfather...*anything.*

Thoughts like these were the reason he came to this small mound every day. It was a moment when he rose to witness the dawn of a new day, knowing he had been given the chance to be in it. It was a moment when he could be alone with his thoughts, reflecting on the days past and the days to come before turning to the noise of the present and the reality he faced as king of the den.

And even though Cheetah came with him every morning, standing side by side with him now, he knew that even his warrior understood the need to stand still, to watch before moving, to relish in the silence.

He was thinking about what Cheetah had said earlier that morning. Thinking about the possibility of his demise triggered the thought of death. It was a lot to think about so early in the day, but it was probably a good thing to ponder, as his warrior was right to be concerned. If he perished, his entire clan would cease to exist. And what then? What did it mean to die? And in the grand scheme of things, would it matter in the end? Did the realm need the den? Aside from an heir, did the den really need him?

What part of this world would collapse if I were missing?

His thoughts of the afterlife were suddenly interrupted by Cheetah's growl.

"Clear skies...it's going to be a beautiful day today."

Daniel turned to find Byron and Minotauro climbing the hill toward him along with a band of their warriors. Byron carried a book in his hand. "It's a good sign, I'd say."

Daniel was glad to see them. It snapped him back into the world of the living. "Where's Sebastian?"

"He wanted to watch the sun rise from a different angle."

"What for?"

"He needs time by himself. He's trying to comprehend his new normal as leader of the realm."

The three kings stood side by side looking out at Bird Kingdom; a myriad of thoughts and emotions were running through each of their minds as they looked out toward Rebekah's kingdom. No one said a word as the sun continued to rise. No one could, for they were stunned when they saw it...that sudden shift in the light...*and the color of the rising sun.*

The fur on Cheetah's body stood straight up the moment it came into view — it was the hue.

12

"Whoever controls the sea, rules the realm."

He had heard the saying once before, but he could not remember when or how. All he knew was that there was no sea — just a stunted body of darkened water — a mere portion of its prior, massive, and powerful existence. And now he was supposed to build a dam around it. And not just any dam, but an entire irrigation system to the other kingdoms like the way it was before the shockwave demolished it all. Worst of all, he had to build it with *all* the other clans.

His head already hurt just thinking about it: the challenge and chaos that was about to ensue.

This...is going to be impossible.

Sebastian was tight all over, feeling the tension in his neck and shoulders as he tried to relax.

It was true that he had broken ground at the dam months before. It was also true he had been working on a design to rebuild the irrigation canals to the five kingdoms with bamboo from his swamps. What was not true was that he had the ability to command members from the other clans to carry out his orders on their king or queen's behalf.

Breathe...

Sebastian had seen old paintings of what Mariner Kingdom looked like after the Old War. He remembered one of his frog warriors telling him the story of the shockwave decades later; how it pulverized Mariner Tower, destroyed the dam and flooded the kingdoms. It was a good thing he was king of the swamps — a water world was where he was born to survive. But it was when the waters receded during his lifetime due to the drought, that Sebastian's world began to change. Instead of swamps to play in, it was the trees he sought. It was the only place he knew he could hide and feel safe.

As Sebastian stared up at the old treehouse from his youth, he longed to be inside it once more. So he climbed the gnarled branches of the ancient tree and opened the bottom latch to the inside.

The treehouse was smaller than he remembered, yet there was still plenty of room for him to fit inside. He moved to one of the corners and sat, stretching his legs out, crossing his arms across his chest as he took it all in. His eyes scanned the small room. He could still see the carvings etched on the interior wooden panels: drawings, initials, dates...it calmed his mind just looking at them. This was the sanctuary of their youth — Minotauro's, his and Byron's. A place they could come to escape the violence of the world beyond and be shielded from the sound of the cries that never seemed to stop. And it was a place he needed at a moment like this to gather his thoughts in complete solitude.

He rested his head against the splintered wall and cringed. He was still angry with his own chief, Netapheha, for selecting him to remain behind. It seemed neither fair nor logical. Daniel was the more natural choice amongst them. Even Byron would have been the better option if any other king were needed to stay, for he had always been the leader in their small trio.

And to make matters worse, Sebastian had not been sleeping. All he could think about was how this would be the first time he would do anything on his own. His greatest friends would not be there with him to support him, to give him advice or encouragement. They would not even be there as sounding boards for ideas or offer solutions to challenges he knew he was going to face. There would be no one now with whom he could rely on...no one but himself. It made Sebastian's insides turn. He begrudged the entire thing. King or not, all he knew was that he wanted to stay inside this treehouse and never come out again.

"I don't like it when my daughter cries. And I don't want her to be afraid."

Sebastian's head snapped up. He looked out the small window, having sworn he heard...*no...it couldn't be.* There was no one there. Several moments passed before he sat back against the wall, remembering that night when the wolf king found them inside their treehouse. It was the most terrifying night of Sebastian's childhood. Everyone was at war with one another. He thought it was the end of the world.

Even now, his people were worried yet hopeful. As their king, he wanted to give them a sense of peace and make them proud. He remembered that night when King Alexander found his way inside their treehouse. The king of the wolves had come to tell him, Byron and Minotauro that the terror of the night would soon be over.

How wrong he was. It had only just begun. The lions and other den warriors would feast on his own soldiers for years. But Sebastian remembered that moment; he *believed* the wolf king. He believed him because he saw the determination behind the king's eyes. He heard the conviction in the tone of his voice. He remembered King Alexander climbing down from the treehouse and running toward the battle before him. Sebastian never forgot the image of the wolf king facing the battle ahead instead of turning away from it. He ran first...and his pack followed.

Sebastian sat there, digesting this new revelation. And as it sank in, a new image began to take shape. The amphibian king envisioned himself with his warriors behind him, overlooking the dam they would build together to keep the realm alive and thriving. He imagined the clan warriors listening to his commands as he spoke with authority and strength. The image he was seeing in his mind's eye was giving him the courage and confidence he needed to climb down from the treehouse — a boy prince who was now a man and a king.

"You may fail, prince...but the better question to ask is...what if you win?"

Now he knew he was not imagining things.

Sebastian looked down from the small treehouse once more and saw Tick-Tock on the ground below peering up at him. They stared at each other in silence for some time before Tick-Tock dropped down to all fours and ran toward the direction of the Wolf Lair, leaving the amphibian king to ponder that last question.

What if you win?

Sebastian looked up at the rising sun. He slowly climbed down from the treehouse, still looking skyward as he took in the color of the fiery orb as it rose from the darkness. He turned toward the direction of the den and broke out into all-out run. From the trees around him, his toad and frog warriors emerged and followed.

V

Alexandra was sitting down with her back against a tree, staring up at the fading moonlight. The sun would soon rise, reminding the wolf queen that today was another day of change. It seemed as if change never ceased. And today, she wanted it to. She wanted a moment to pause. A moment where she could just…breathe. There was so much to do, yet she did not have the strength to do it. And although she had been sitting against the tree for several hours, alone and in complete silence, it was not the kind of pause she needed. She needed days, weeks even, to filter through everything that had come at her so quickly and all at once, just to collect herself and reset, refocus, absorb, and re-energize. But that moment was not going to be coming any time soon, making her wearier just thinking about it.

Wolf Lake rested a few yards in front of her, as still as a sheet of glass. Everything around her was silent. If any of her pack was around, she would have known. Had they been watching her, they would have thought she was sitting there thinking — perhaps about her father, maybe about her life, and just possibly about the road ahead. But Alexandra was not thinking about anything at all.

Even as Tick-Tock arrived and watched her from the shadows of the trees, her mind was a blank. Her body was numb — and not just from sitting against the tree. It had all been too much. In a single day, her entire world had been turned upside down. The birds attacked the clans; the crows had tried to kill her. And then Rebekah sacrificed herself to stop her birds from murdering them all. And now the bird queen was gone — Reginald too. Until the final blow came: the death of her father.

She never saw it coming.

Alexandra continued to stare blankly at the fading moonlight.

"Do you think Queen Rebekah can see you right now?"

"I don't know, princess. There are times when I can feel her heart. I can sense when she

16

is sad or angry. But so many days and nights have passed where I hear nothing but silence. I yearn for a stirring to feel her presence."

The wolf queen yearned for that stirring now. Loneliness was a word she understood, for she had always felt that way since she was a little girl. But now the word "alone" took on an entirely new meaning. Since she was little, her father was her world — her champion, her confidante, her protector — her best friend. As she grew, Reginald became her mentor. And by the time Rebekah showed up, she had a real family. But now, they were all gone. All three wiped out in a single day.

Just.

Like.

That.

Alexandra still could not wrap her head around it. She had cried the last few weeks without ceasing, unable to eat or sleep. How she was supposed to go on a quest to help the realm survive, she could not even comprehend. She could barely even move. The only thing that got her out of bed each morning was the arrival of Daniel's letters. Although he was busy prepping the dam with the rest of the kings, he had written her every single day. He had...great words — something Rebekah had called them once.

Rebekah...

She inhaled sharply, suddenly seeing the image of Rebekah in her mind as the bird queen fell from the sky. She still could not even fathom what the bird queen had done. To die. To know that your death was the only way others could live, and to choose to do it.

Alexandra lowered her head, looking away from the changing color of the sky. She began to cry; she could not help it. Her sobs were so devastating, she could barely breathe as the grief spilled out from the well of pain deep inside her heart.

As she wept, a wolf howled mournfully in the distance. Followed by another. Then another.

It was her pack.

She tried desperately to control her tears, knowing full well she was causing them pain, but her tears would not stop. She looked out at the lake beyond.

"I cannot take this anymore...please...help me..." Alexandra's head slowly lowered. She had no idea who she was speaking to, but felt the need to speak to someone, to something, all the same. She continued to stare at Wolf Lake for what seemed like hours until her attention was drawn to the silver medallion resting in her hands; it suddenly began to glow.

The wolf queen narrowed her eyes, thinking it was a trick of the light. But it was no trick. She looked up at the rising sun as if its light was causing the metal to illuminate brightly. She ran her silky fingers across the metal that formed the shape of a moon itself, suddenly looking out across the lake, remembering the night it slowly washed up onto her shore. It was after her father's death when it appeared. A gift — almost as if someone had heard her cries and wanted to remind her that as alone as she felt, she wasn't.

Alexandra looked down at the silver medallion once more, touching the wave etched across its orb. The light reflecting off it had suddenly turned a shade of red. Her head snapped up.

Crimson.

The color of her roses.

"It has the autumn tint of gold…"

Without turning her head at the sound of her father's voice, she simply said, "Yes, Tick-Tock, it does."

And as she stood in the lake looking up at the sun, Alexandra did not realize she was no longer crying…and neither were her wolves.

VI

"The realm was created in a single day when time and space held no existence. How it came to be was not as important as to why it existed. When man and beast were created, there was an immediate divide severing its intended unity as the kingdoms within the realm rose and fell. Clans formed against one another, separating man and beast by boundaries and borders, forming armies and fortresses to show who exuded the greatest power and influence over the weak, creating an even larger divide amongst themselves.

"And this was not how it was meant to be. That is not how the Creators, the Old Ones, intended for it to be. And so, Wind, Fire, Ice and Earth watched the beauty of their creation be dismantled piece by piece, person by person, clan by clan, as the need for power grew more important than how power was meant to be used." He stopped reading, "What is all this?"

Sebastian, Daniel, and Cheetah were looking at a map on the lion king's desk. Sebastian looked up at Minotauro, "I didn't know you knew how to read."

"Ha-ha."

Byron replied, "Keep going."

He huffed and then continued, "So they continued to watch and wait, knowing that the world they influenced was bound by rules no master or beast could ignore. Such rules could mend and fix the problems of the realm; they could bring peace to the hearts of men and calm the fire in the hearts of its creatures. They could provide balance and peace. For from the beginning, a blood bond had been forged between man and beast. One could not live without the other, and only defined masters would rule over all." Minotauro paused, "Who wrote this?"

Byron replied, "A scribe from my clan...many centuries ago. I thought I'd give it to Daniel to add to his collection on the histories of the clans."

"Do you believe all of this?"

19

Byron shrugged, "I never really thought about it. I've just always accepted our way of living as the way it was always meant to be. It's as natural an exercise to me as breathing."

Minotauro closed the book and dropped it back onto Daniel's desk. "What I don't understand is how every generation before us seemed to know about the Creators, the Elements, the Old Ones, or whatever they're called…yet none of them decided to share that knowledge with us."

Byron answered, "I think a lot of that had to do with King Luther and the rest of the den after the Old War. The king, from what I remember, had wanted to banish the worship of nature and anything else so long as the devotion was reserved for the kings and queens on his side of the realm. He simply didn't believe in the beliefs of the clans that there was anyone or anything more important than serving the king or queen. A clan's sole existence was to work to the benefit of the kingdom they belonged to. And every creature's purpose was solely to make it thrive. After his death, the lion queen carried out his wishes. At least, that's what my father told me."

Cheetah suddenly growled.

The room went silent.

Byron and Minotauro suddenly realized how freely they had been speaking in front of Daniel.

"Daniel…I…"

But Daniel interrupted him, "Your scribe was correct."

Minotauro tried to change the subject. "Too bad your scribe never wrote about how to bring water to a dam, Byron. Then we wouldn't have to go on a trek to nowhere."

Byron studied his friend's body language, knowing what was on his mind the entire time he spoke. "Daniel seems pretty confident in his uncle's findings."

"That's because Daniel has faith in the unknown."

"I'm still in the room, you know." It was Daniel.

"Miracles do happen, Minotauro."

"Of course they do. Who would have ever thought we would join with the Lion's Den. Our master becomes our friend."

"Still here!"

"Daniel, your stairway…"

The kings immediately rose and bowed the moment they heard Alexandra's voice. As she walked inside the room with Tick-Tock and her wolf captain Hood beside her, Daniel's face broke out into an enormous smile. His eyes almost seemed to dance the moment he saw her.

Alexandra stood in the center of the Great Library gaping up at the ceiling; it was covered with hundreds of maps. Her eyes moved all along the walls seeing design after design layered over every square inch of the room. Tick-Tock's three heads examined all corners of the room. Turning away from the maps covering the library walls, his eyes fell onto the portraits of all the lion kings stacked in a lone corner of the room. Atop of the pile was King Nathan's portrait. Hood's eyes seemed to glow silver the moment he saw it.

Tick-Tock moved toward it, swiveling his head to snow owl — the voice of the past. He looked at the painting for a long while before saying, *"My love is just as new as the night our hands touched on that dance floor long ago. His eyes...his heart...they are the same to me now as they were then."*

Daniel stared at the totem in disbelief. He remembered that conversation as if it were yesterday. He moved closer to Tick-Tock. "How did you know...how can you..."

Tick-Tock turned his large bulbous eyes toward him. Alexander's voice replied, *"Bring my daughter back in the same condition you took her, and...protect her...at all costs...there are many enemies waiting in the shadows who would love to do me and my pack harm..."*

Hood let out a low growl.

Alexandra's eyes filled with tears upon hearing her father's voice. She moved closer to Daniel and wrapped her arms around his waist, resting her head against his shoulder as the tears continued to silently fall. "He does this all the time...speaking with the voices of the past."

Daniel lowered his head, resting it against hers, holding her close. "Who is out there, Tick-Tock?"

"Others." His eyes suddenly glowed scarlet. *"Thisss isss not one of theirsss...it isss larger in size."*

Hood stopped growling.

All five remnants stood there in stunned silence. Minotauro glanced at Byron; less because of what the totem had just said, and more out of concern for his friend's state of mind as Poe's voice echoed forth from the strange creature.

Daniel spoke, "What memory is this? What are you talking about?"

Tick-Tock walked across the library, taking in all the mismatched maps that covered it. *"I sssaw a place...a mountain larger than any I had ever ssseen. I sssaw land made of ice and snow....there wasss a footprint on our land from a creature that doesss not live on our side of the realm. I went to find it."*

Daniel swallowed hard as he asked, "And did you?"

Tick-Tock stopped moving and looked at the lion king. *"No. I found something else..."*

"What?"

"Purpossse..."

No one said a word for several moments. Both Cheetah and Hood's fur were standing straight up.

Byron asked, "Daniel, what is he talking about?" His body was visibly trembling.

"I don't know."

A cold breeze suddenly blew through the library giving everyone the chills. A shadow seemed to cast itself across each of the remnants' faces as they stood in silence.

"Why is everyone so gloomy?"

Alexandra jumped.

Minotauro turned, "Lydia!" He moved swiftly across the room, a wide grin plastered across his face as he scooped up the beautiful Cheetah clan woman in his strong arms. He kissed her, holding her close. She laughed, filling the room with a sense of joy and lightness it needed just at that moment. Minotauro lowered her to the ground and knelt in front of her, kissing her small belly.

Byron smiled to himself, remembering the day at the den not so long ago when the bull king first spotted the blonde beauty with almond-shaped eyes. It was the day when all the clans had gathered at the den to forge a new way of life and agreed to rebuild the dam. Minotauro had spotted her from his seat inside the forum. She was Daniel's cousin. The moment their eyes met, it was all over. Within a month, Lydia and Minotauro had wed and were now expecting.

Byron was reminded of what his friend had said earlier about the dawn of a new day. He began to feel a sense of peace, knowing how right the bull king was about believing in hope of a better tomorrow. Looking at the two of them in love, how could one not only hope…but believe.

Lydia looked up at the ceiling in awe. "King Daniel…did Prince Marcus do all this?"

Daniel pointed toward one group of maps. "He did. And there's no method to the madness, Lydia. Most of the maps don't even match up."

Byron asked, "So which way do we go?"

Daniel pointed to one of the maps beyond the Wolf Lair and Bird Kingdom. "North."

"Why north?"

"The queen watched the sun rise every morning, not from her kingdom…" He turned to Alexandra, "But yours."

Byron nodded. "I think it's a good bet that the Element Fortress resides north of Bird Kingdom and the lair. The tallest mountains reside there. If I were an element, that's where I'd be."

Alexandra added, "So as not to be disturbed."

"Or to watch for anyone coming." Daniel turned toward the rest of the group. "We set out at dawn. Our cheetahs have your rooms ready for whenever you choose to retire."

Minotauro looked at Byron, "You see, another miracle, Byron. We're having a sleepover at Daniel's house tonight."

Daniel shouted, "Never left!" as he turned toward Sebastian. "Sebastian, you have a heavy task of ruling our kingdoms for us. I'm apologizing now for the lack of manners in my lions and tigers." He placed his hand on Sebastian's shoulder. "And I thank you."

Minotauro patted his friend on the back. "Lion, this king here won't tell you to your face, but he's secretly harbored the idea of being sole emperor of the realm since he was a wee tadpole."

Sebastian corrected him, "Actually…since I was an egg." Sebastian looked at Byron and Minotauro. He grabbed them both by the backs of the neck and pulled their heads together. "You are my greatest friends, my family." He looked them in the eyes. A deep understanding passed between them as they nodded to one another. "Whatever these brother elements are, they undoubtedly lack the one thing that sets us apart…we kings…are all heart. I'll finish the work here, brothers. And if it exists, get that damned stone and come home soon."

Minotauro moved from his friends and back over to Lydia. He laid his strong hand against her belly one more time. "I don't want to miss this."

She ran her fingers through his dark hair. "We'll be with you every day." Lydia tucked a handful of hand-written letters inside his shirt pocket.

"Stay close to the den." He kissed her good-bye.

"Only if I have to. The valley is my home now. Your bulls and my cheetahs will keep me safe."

"As will my warriors." Sebastian extended his arm to her. She took it as he escorted her out.

Minotauro called after them, "Sebastian…" Sebastian stopped and turned. "Take good care of them."

"Always." Sebastian nodded and left with the bull queen. As Minotauro watched them go, a sharp pain formed inside his chest. He did not know why, but the image of Sebastian and Lydia walking away from him suddenly made his heart hurt.

Byron patted Minotauro's shoulder, "Sebastian will take good care of her. And by the time we get back, your son or daughter will be born, and you'll be a father."

"And I aim to be one completely different from my own." He looked directly at Daniel when he said it. An understanding passed between them as he and Byron headed out the library doors.

Daniel and Alexandra walked hand in hand across the den. Too much time had passed since they had seen each other. No matter how many letters had been written between them, there was nothing like being with each other in person.

They walked in silence, stealing shy glances at one another as if it were the first time they had ever met. It made Alexandra feel lighter, younger, free. She could not explain it, but she was even a tad bit nervous. Daniel felt the same way, but he was not about to admit it out loud. He was simply happy she was there. He did not realize until the moment she walked through his library doors how much her presence affected him and how much he missed her. His strength felt renewed. There was a lift in his step, and he could even breathe easier, feeling at peace with her beside him.

"What are you thinking about?" she asked.

"My grandfather." Daniel pulled her hand closer toward him and held it close to his heart. "So much has changed since he died — and so quickly. It doesn't seem that long ago. Yet, at the same time, it feels like years…" He kissed her hand.

She loved it when he did that. "I'm sure King Nathan and Prince Marcus are looking down at you now, proud of what you've done and what you're about to do. Your mother and father too."

Daniel pondered the idea for a moment as he looked skyward, "You think they can see us?"

"I do." She laid her head against his shoulder touching the silver medallion resting gently under her shirt. "Did you ever wonder how they were going to make it work?"

"Hmm?"

"King Nathan and Queen Rebekah. Their kingdoms were clear on the opposite sides of the realm — like ours."

Daniel pulled his head back and peered at her. "Those two could have made anything work — so can we."

She lifted her head and looked at him. "I meant…the living arrangements."

"Oh." Daniel blushed. "My grandfather mentioned they would take turns living in the den and then at Bird Kingdom."

"And you? You would live in the lair?"

They had not talked about engagements or marriage before, but alluding to the idea of it made Daniel smile. "I would live in the lair."

"Even though it's dark and creepy."

Daniel laughed. "I never said that."

"You don't have to. I've watched you when you've arrived. Your eyes grow wide like a scared kitten as you take in the shadows of the trees looking all around for my pack."

He laughed nervously. "You're right on one hand. Your pack doesn't scare me, but your lair is pretty creepy. And what about you? You could live inside the den?"

She looked around as they passed the thatched homes that surrounded Daniel's castle. She nodded and smiled. "It's brighter here. And warmer. It would be a good change of pace from time to time as the seasons shift."

He stopped walking and turned to face her. He moved a strand of hair from her face as she continued to smile at him. She was beautiful. Seeing her smiling up at him took his breath away. "I love you, Alexandra."

She inhaled quickly. It was the first time he had ever said that to her. As she looked deep into his turquoise-colored eyes; she knew he was terrified the moment he said it. "I love you too."

Daniel extended his left hand under her head and his right arm to embrace her. He kissed her.

A growl immediately sounded nearby.

They both turned and looked at the source.

Daniel asked, "Was that Hood or Tick-Tock?"

"Does it matter?"

They smiled at one another as Daniel kissed her again.

VII

The night sky was darker than he had ever remembered. He could barely make out his own hand as he held it in front of his face, waiting for his silver-colored eyes to adjust to the midnight hue. But they never did. Shadow shrouded his every movement; darkness covered him like a hooded cloak. A simple reminder that it was better to have it be this way, for what he was attempting to do, he desired no other witness. The path he was now taking was a guarded one, but he knew the way. He had taken this path many times before. So, where his eyes could not see, he listened to the wind in the trees instead. Lowering his hand, he moved on.

No owl could be heard as he walked through his own crooked forest, out past the desert sands of Reptile Lands and into the Amphibian Swamps. He listened ever closer for the padded footsteps of his alpha, Garm, but heard nothing. The realm was uncannily silent.

He turned and looked back. No eyes mirroring in the darkness. No shadows crouching among the trees.

Good.

That meant no one had followed him; and they always followed him. His pack...they knew his scent. They heard every fly buzzing, every twig cracking, every step walking. The fact that all was silent meant only one thing: *they knew.* They knew what he was about to do and were not going to try to stop him.

With a sword at his side, the only other item he carried with him was a small satchel he clutched tightly in his strong hand. He moved through the dark still waters and on through the bamboo forest. He knew he had all that he needed, as he had heard of this ritual only once before. He was not even sure that it could be done. It may have only been a rumor written down or even a bit of lore meant to assure the realm that there was always a way to do what must be done for one's clan. A fool's errand or not, he was willing to try.

"Why would anyone do such a thing?" he had asked.

"Kings and queens before us, apparently. And they didn't find it an unusual act in the slightest. As a matter of fact, the bloodline could be protected if a guardian could be summoned when an heir was in tremendous danger. They didn't look at this ritual as being something disturbing...or dark."

"I don't believe you."

"I wouldn't lie to you, Feyedor."

The gorilla king Brock strutted across the room and pulled a velvet-covered book from a secluded shelf in his enormous library, turning to the exact same page the story had been recorded. It was then the wolf king knew this was no ordinary fiction.

"Even though it was written in the darkest purple book I've ever seen, hiding in a shadowed corner of your library while we speak in whispers."

The gorilla king paused. Several moments passed in complete silence until the king broke out into a loud, raucous laugh. Brock took the book and moved it over toward a section of the room that held less of a mystery and a lot more light. "There. Out in the open."

"I'd leave it where it was. I'm no fan of alchemy or the joining of elements to forge a new way of life."

Brock looked up from the book, his face severe. "Even after all that's happened? Palimus is dead. Gunthar murdered. Our kingdoms divided amongst themselves. A new world has split us apart." He laid his hand over the over the book, considering the words within. "What would this mean to us kings, my friend, to have an opportunity to protect the last of our clan...from beyond the grave?"

Brock continued to ponder the book beneath his palm as Feyedor digested the words the gorilla king had just spoken. The realm was still reeling from the war and the loss of the bird and lion kings. No one had ventured outside their kingdom door anymore for fear of being attacked — all except him. He still could not accept that he had lost his greatest friend in all the realm and that with this visit to the gorilla king — he was about to lose another.

The gorilla king tilted his head to the side, still looking down at the book. His eyes seemed to darken until they almost glowed. "What if...what if we really could create the ultimate warrior — the greatest guardian — for one of our heirs?" He looked up at the wolf king. "What if the legend in this book is true?"

"What are you talking about?"

Brock finally removed his hand from the simple binding and sat back against his chair, taking a long sip from his goblet. "Tomorrow, another war may start, another battle we don't see coming." He set his goblet down. "It is our children we must think of as we weigh all of our choices." He looked directly at Feyedor. "What if tomorrow the sun does not rise? What if the vision Palimus had foreseen really does come to pass?"

"We don't know that what he saw was true."

Brock studied the wolf king. "Part of you believes it. Always has. Which tells me I should always be prepared." He downed the rest of his wine, leaving the two powerful kings sitting in silence.

27

"IT ALL BURNED TO THE GROUND! ALL OF IT! THE REALM! THE SEA FILLED WITH BLOOD! THE LAND BARREN! THE BIRDS WERE GONE! BONES LINED THE VALLEYS! ONLY REMNANTS SURVIVED!"

He could still remember Palimus' dark, wild eyes filled with fear and rage as he shouted the words. He had never seen the king in such a state before, and it was the bird king's last statement that haunted Feyedor, for the vision Palimus foretold, had not come to pass. Brock was right. A war could arise at any moment. Time in this world was not guaranteed. And if tomorrow Feyedor's time was up, what could he do today to protect the future legacy of his clan for tomorrow?

"The circumstance would have to be grave." It was Feyedor who spoke. "A remnant."

The gorilla king nodded, "Yes. One who had no other means of survival."

"Alone and without his pack."

"Or hers."

"The cornerstone."

The idea started to make sense.

"I would do it," said Brock. "If there was no other way, I would."

"But what is the greatest warrior? What is the fiercest guardian made of?"

Brock thought for a moment before replying, "The wisest and strongest amongst us."

"The light and the dark within the clan."

Brock nodded, "Yes. One would need the balance of the two. One with the wisdom as to know when to protect. And the other with the ruthlessness to know how. A being without fear. A guardian whose only purpose is to guard what is left of us for the clan to live on."

For the clan to live on…

That was the last time Feyedor had stepped foot inside Gorilla Jungle — almost a decade ago. And yet, that conversation had haunted the wolf king over thousands of moonlit nights until he found himself standing in front of a large bamboo gate in Amphibian Swamps.

The circumstance would have to be grave…

But it was not grave. There was no war. There was not even a hint of a battle on the horizon.

With the realm split in two, life had settled into a new rhythm, shifting trade and resources in half, leaving the kings and queens on his side of the realm to limit themselves to what one side provided. Less luxury and supplies from what the other side of the realm had to offer, yes, but nothing that had caused catastrophe. Nothing that had caused suffering or even pain.

It had been ten years since he had told Damon, the raven assassin, that he was going to see the old toad chief — but he never made it there. He had talked himself out of it, for there was no need. But there was now.

My son.

Yes, the wolf king had a son. Feyedor's whole world shifted the moment his heir was born. He had not anticipated how the centering of his purpose would shift by the birth of a child. But it had.

Night after night as he watched his son sleep soundly, he began to understand Palimus a little bit more; and something deep within him stirred. At first it was sorrow, for he felt more mortal as he looked at his son's tiny body. And the longer he memorized the changes in his son as he grew day after day, the wolf king's sorrow turned to a fierce desire to shield his heir from any storm he knew he could possibly face. But the shield would not be just to protect the prince, but for his son to protect the clan he would rule as he moved against any force that dared come against it.

He needed wisdom.

And so Feyedor and the Wolf Pack had dedicated their lives to educating and training the prince that would rule the lair one day. And what they were doing...*was working.* The young wolf prince was now ten years old; strong, witty, resourceful. His son could hunt, gather, read the moon and stars, understand the tide, and strategize need based on the changing of the seasons. He was the best of the king and his queen. Should anything happen to either of them, their son would survive and live on — leading while others followed.

But was it enough? What about the heirs in the generations to come? *One who had no other means of survival...*

It mattered to Feyedor to think beyond the family he had to the one that would live generations beyond him. It mattered to the wolf king that the future heir be protected, for he trusted no one — not even his own pack; he never had. For Feyedor never believed the bloodline between Man and Beast was equal. Man could reason. Beasts survived. And if a remnant was in dire need of help, what if the warriors in the clan refused to provide it the way they should? What if the king or queen was despised amongst the clan? What then? And even worse...what if Palimus' vision finally did come to pass?

His pack never made him feel this way. There had never been a pack in the history of the lair who had challenged his king or queen. But there was something deep within Feyedor that gave him pause. He watched his pack...*always.* And they followed the alpha. The alpha in the pack, and the alpha strength they recognized in the king or queen. But what if the king or queen was not so fierce? What then? It was in the wolves' nature to challenge rule to keep order. And there was no doubt in Feyedor's mind that they would challenge any rule that led to a downward spiral that could lead toward their demise. They would never stand for it. They would overthrow that king or queen.

And if that king or queen was a remnant? Who knows what they would do to them until an heir was born.

That was what kept Feyedor up at night, wondering about what more he could do for the family he would never know. Was there something more that should be done? Was there something more that could be?

What is the greatest warrior?

Feyedor looked down at the small satchel clutched in his clenched fist, thinking he had found the answer. And if there was one last thing he could do to ensure the survival of his clan long after he was gone, it was this.

Standing before the bamboo gates, he did not know what he was supposed to do next. He was not even supposed to be here. It was forbidden to cross the borders since the war, and he had not traveled past his own in almost ten years. But no one had stopped him. He kept reminding himself that he had not even been followed. But then, he felt it. He felt the sense of someone watching him…and it was not coming from the bamboo trees.

The wolf king slowly lowered his silver eyes and looked down at the darkened swamp before him. There was something in the water. Feyedor slowly moved his free hand to the hilt of his sword, readying himself for any sign of attack. His eyes scanned the swamp. There was no movement, but he sensed someone's presence all the same.

It was then he saw it.

It was only for a split second, but he caught sight of a man's face. Golden hair. Turquoise-colored eyes that illuminated against the night sky and blackened waters. The only true image he had seen all night. And then it was gone. Feyedor had not blinked the entire time, yet he knew he saw it. And for a split second, he doubted he had, thinking it must have been a trick of the moonlight, and all he had really seen was his own image reflected in the water. But he knew it was no trick. It *was* a man. Who, he did not know. So, he kept his hand on his hilt, shifting his eyes to the surroundings all around him, listening to the sounds of the night.

But he heard nothing. He could not even feel the lurking presence he had felt only moments before. He looked back down at the water, knowing the amphibians were down there. But how deep did they guard the gate? He did not want to dive under to make himself known; he hated water. Ironic that his lair was surrounded by it to the north. He and his pack only went into Wolf Lake for fishing and bathing and nothing more.

He continued to stare at the swamp, willing the amphibians to rise from its depths so he could do what he came to do. He crouched down and touched the crystal liquid, trying to gauge the temperature. If he had to swim, he would.

He looked up at the moonlight, wishing for a different option when the king felt a gentle breeze on his face. He looked down and saw vines rising up from the water. He watched as they continued to move, gathering around the bamboo gates as if they were arms and hands. They wove all around them, gripping onto them, pulling them apart. The wolf king gazed in awe as the earth shifted beneath his feet and the gate was opened by the force of the vines. Looking down at the darkened marsh before him, the wolf king was bowled over the moment he saw the water disappearing, sinking, watching as the massive maze of caves down below emerged as a spiral staircase appeared. That was when he heard the sound of their ribbits.

Lining the staircase was a squadron of toad warriors. Their bulbous eyes stared at him until the leader of the group finally spoke, "King…he's been waiting for you."

VIII

The remnants walked through the woods in Wolf Lair in complete silence. As Alexandra looked around at the landscape to her fortress, she had to admit...pack or not...it was pretty creepy. No wonder everyone was quiet. Since she was queen of this domain, she was head of the group, leading them past Wolf Lake and out toward the land beyond. It was Daniel who finally broke the uncomfortable silence, "My uncle Marcus told me he ventured into these woods when he was a young boy."

Alexandra scoffed in disbelief, "Why would he do something so foolish! He's lucky the pack didn't rip him to shreds!"

"They almost did. He told me Queen Rebekah found him and saved his life. My grandfather came after him as well with a few of his warriors. She saved them too; she sent Reginald to protect them and carry them home."

Byron was suddenly very silent.

Minotauro studied him, "What is it?"

"The trees...bad memories."

SNAP!

Byron whipped out his bone scepter, Bane, and swiftly swung his body up onto one of the branches; his heart thundering inside his chest.

Minotauro looked up at him gripping tightly onto the tree, "Overreacting a bit?"

Byron had already broken out into a cold sweat. "Not in the least." His eyes continued to search the trees.

"It was only Tick-Tock stepping onto a dry branch."

Byron was breathing hard. "Are you sure?"

Alexandra agreed. "It was. I heard him clear as day."

Byron finally rested his eyes on Tick-Tock. They drifted down to his raven claw. "I haven't been in these woods since that night."

Minotauro saw what Byron was looking at and tried to reassure him, "The

32

raven is dead, my friend. He can't harm you anymore. Tick-Tock is our buddy." He patted the totem on the back. "Our guardian, not our assassin."

Byron looked into Tick-Tock's eyes; he wasn't so sure. There was something there, deep inside those eyes that gave Byron no comfort. "I'll be glad when we're out of these woods. No offense, Alexandra."

"None taken."

Byron jumped down from the tree and moved swiftly ahead.

Minotauro looked back at Tick-Tock, wondering what his friend had seen behind the totem's eyes. "Hey, buddy. You're awfully quiet."

Tick-Tock merely looked at Minotauro and walked on, leaving the bull king to stare at the back of one of his heads. Minotauro watched as the totem moved along behind Alexandra. It was then that he noticed his breath fogging on the air. *Strange.* The night was warm, even as they continued north. The king suddenly stopped dead in his tracks. He lowered his forehead like one of his bulls, lowering his hand to the hilt of his sword. He felt it.

Someone was there.

Up ahead, Alexandra tilted her head to the side. She had heard something. She slowly turned back, looking around. She saw Minotauro surveying the landscape realizing he had sensed it too. Byron and Daniel slowed their step.

"What is it?"

Alexandra continued listening, watching Minotauro.

Minotauro moved slowly forward, "We're being watched."

Daniel turned to Alexandra, "Someone from your pack?"

She shook her head, still listening.

Byron began to sweat again. He looked at Tick-Tock and could see the emerald stone hanging around his neck flickering slightly. The totem was crouched low beside Alexandra but remained completely silent.

Minotauro came closer. "Tick-Tock, bring up the rear. Alexandra, if you don't mind, I'll take the lead." Without waiting for her reply, he moved ahead of the group, still clutching his hilt tight.

Daniel looked at Tick-Tock. "Do you know what's out there?"

Tick-Tock's head swiveled to barn owl as he growled lowly — the voice of the present. *"The creators do. Especially the one who spoke to the raven."* The moment he said the words, Daniel's entire body went cold.

Minotauro asked, "Which element was it?"

But Tick-Tock did not answer.

Daniel replied, "I didn't think the Elements spoke to us."

Tick-Tock stood up, "They speak to us all…"

IX

Alexandra watched the flames as they flickered back and forth in the small campfire, studying their movement as they moved softly against the night sky. She could not stop staring, mesmerized as the flames danced before her eyes, calming her, filling her with a peace she had not felt in a long time.

Alexandra watched Byron as his body twisted and turned; he was dreaming. She could hear his sharp breaths, wondering what it was he saw in his subconscious. Thinking about his reaction in the woods, no doubt he was thinking of Poe. She could only imagine what he must have seen behind those scarlet-colored eyes.

They had traveled the rest of the day, never encountering that feeling of being watched since leaving the lair. The air had cooled as they trekked north, but not as cold as earlier in the day when everyone was on edge.

Strange.

They had found a place to camp for the night. Minotauro and Byron were fast asleep, having fallen into a deep slumber the moment their heads hit the ground. Alexandra had never been able to do that. She envied their ability to drift into a deep slumber so easily — especially in an unknown territory so far from home.

Alexandra sighed softly as her eyes drifted over to Tick-Tock. He too was staring at the fire when Poe's voice emerged, *"We ravensss cherish Fire…"*

The wolf queen observed his demeanor. The totem seemed almost peaceful as he watched the flames flickering in the darkness.

"Ravens were never evil, you know."

"Hmm?" Daniel's head was resting in her lap as she stroked his wavy, brown hair. Tick-Tock turned his head and looked at her.

"They were protectors of the Bird Clan — the guardians at night — just like the wolves. Kin clans. That's why the ravens lived in the woods near the lair. Together, they kept everyone safe — all the kings and queens of the realm — before the Old War."

Tick-Tock turned his attention back toward the fire as Daniel followed

34

Alexandra's gaze over to Byron. "I don't think you could ever convince Byron of that…or me."

Alexandra looked down at Daniel's solemn face, remembering that it was Poe who had killed his uncle Marcus. She ran her fingers through his wavy hair, "It makes me wonder."

"What?"

"What Poe thought he was protecting."

Daniel continued to watch Alexandra's face as she continued to ponder her thought.

"You think he was protecting the clan?"

She looked down at him. "The realm."

Daniel's demeanor shifted.

Alexandra glanced back at the fire. "My father told me a story once about the bird king Palimus. He had a vision when he looked into the fire. He saw chaos…bloodshed. That's why they say he betrayed the old lion king."

"King Luther."

She looked down at him again and nodded. "My father told me King Palimus believed the bloodshed would come from the lions." Alexandra could immediately feel Daniel's body tense. "But his vision never came to pass. It makes me wonder…did Poe see something when he awoke…when he looked into the flames?"

Daniel slowly sat up and looked at her. "What are you talking about?"

"I saw a large fire one night. It was after Queen Rebekah had awakened. It was a massive glow coming from somewhere deep inside my woods. I asked my father about it. All he said was that it was an old ritual between the ravens and the wolves. It hadn't been done in over seventy-five years; not since the bird clan disappeared. We assumed it was Poe."

Daniel was trying to decipher her meaning. "You're saying that Poe saw what Palimus saw?"

"I don't know. I don't even know if it was Poe who started the bonfire. But if it was him, I believe he saw something. I don't think it was just vengeance he sought. I've thought about it over and over again. The only answer I've come to is thinking that he believed he was doing what he thought he should. I'm just wondering what it was and why."

Daniel shook his head aghast, "Poe was mad. Mad with vengeance. Whatever happened to him when he slumbered across time, Alexandra, made him insane the moment he awoke."

"How do you know?"

"Byron is not the only one who saw deep into the raven's eyes or been the target of his wrath. I've been up close and seen the look behind them…"

Memories of Poe descending upon him as he and Cheetah raced across bird clan gardens flashed across his mind.

"And what he did to Marcus…" Images of Prince Marcus' body floating in Wolf Lake filled his thoughts. Daniel tried to shut them out. "No, I don't believe he thought he was doing anything good, Alexandra. No matter what he saw in the fire. He tried to annihilate us all. He wanted to."

Alexandra tenderly took his hand. "Perhaps you're right. It wouldn't have helped his mindset then when he saw that footprint on bird clan grounds. Maybe that's what caused him to attack us all at the den. It roused his passion for vengeance. It spurred his desire to wipe out all those he deemed 'enemy'."

"And don't forget…it made him want to capture his own queen so she could not deter him from what he aimed to do that day at my den." He remembered hearing Poe's shout to the crows. "No, Poe had much to do with why we're here now. And I don't blame Byron one bit for being suspicious of Tick-Tock when Poe speaks through him from the dead. It's odd that he does. Of all the voices to allow to speak…"

Tick-Tock continued to stare at them in silence.

She looked at the totem thinking about what Daniel had just said. He was probably right, but something deep within Alexandra gave her pause. There was something she felt when she looked into Tick-Tock's eyes that meant something more than what the other kings perceived. She could not explain it. But then again, she *was* the wolf queen. She knew the dark nature of her clan and that it could easily be misinterpreted. She also knew that the ravens were kin clans with hers for a reason. There was something in her blood that seemed to understand the nature of the wolves and ravens that others could not when they looked into the fire and into the dark — and even into Tick-Tock's design. Whatever it was, she decided to keep her thoughts to herself for now, knowing how Daniel and Byron felt about Poe.

Byron stirred again.

"We should wake him."

Daniel leaned over and shook him. "Byron."

Byron's eyes snapped open. He immediately sat up, completely drenched in sweat. He looked around, trying to gauge his surroundings. "You're still awake?"

Off of Minotauro's snore, Alexandra replied, "*Wide* awake. He could wake the dead with that snore of his. Poor Lydia…"

Byron saw Daniel and Alexandra looking at him with deep concern. Slightly embarrassed, he smiled slightly and scratched his head. "I must have been dreaming again."

"Your clothes are soaked through."

Byron's smile faded. He inhaled slowly, "I don't remember it. I never do. Whatever I see in my dreams, the moment I wake, it's gone."

"You can trust us, Byron. You must see something."

He glanced at Tick-Tock; his eyes falling on the raven claw. "All I see is Poe's scarlet eyes." He swallowed hard. "All I hear is his raspy warble. And then all goes black."

Daniel glanced at Alexandra.

She replied, "Perhaps Poe is trying to tell you something."

"Or maybe it's just my subconscious reliving my darkest moment when he tried to murder me."

Daniel tried to help the conversation along. "I used to dream of Rebekah. For years it was the same one. Rebekah dancing before a large fire."

Alexandra tilted her head to the side. "You never told me that. I only thought you dreamt of her once...before you awakened her."

"It didn't seem significant until now."

All the while, Tick-Tock watched the three remnants, listening to their discussion in complete silence.

"I haven't had that dream since I found Marcus' book on the elements, but I'm having the same dream now."

Alexandra asked, "Why? What would be the reason? Rebekah is dead."

"I don't know." Daniel looked back at the fire, "I guess it's like the bonfire in your woods...all the things we don't know that lie just beyond our reach."

They all sat in silence.

Minotauro snored loudly again, breaking the silence. Byron sighed deeply. "Well, since most of us are up, maybe we should get moving." Byron nudged him. "Minotauro..."

Minotauro's arm reached up automatically. He pulled Byron into him. "*Lydia...*"

Byron struggled to get out from under his grasp. "Minotauro...let go." He was finally able to pull himself free and sat back next to Alexandra and Daniel. "Or not." He continued to look at Minotauro, shaking his head, "I still can't believe it."

"What, that he's going to be a father?"

"No...that somebody actually married him." He stared at his long-time friend feeling a pang of happiness for him and a pinch of envy that his friend had found someone to love. Byron suddenly felt lonely. He shrugged the feeling off, knowing deep down that envying another's season of joy would bring him no further comfort. Besides, of all the kings that deserved his season, it was Minotauro.

He looked at his friend's sleeping face, "I've never seen him so happy. It's been a long time since he could lift his head and not be ashamed of who he was, and not be afraid of being who he wanted to be." Byron looked back at Daniel. "Even now he has a hard time being around you, lion."

Daniel looked at Byron, knowing full well what he meant by that statement. It was Minotauro's father, Rom, who had killed the lion prince Matthew — the father he had never known. It was a battle with the bulls that had brought about his mother's death as well.

Daniel shifted his attention toward the fire, trying to avoid the conversation. There was nothing more to say. Daniel never spoke about his mother or father; he barely remembered them. And remembering that they were killed by the father of his newfound ally was not something Daniel wanted to think about so late in the night.

Byron looked at the fire, attempting to change the subject, "My father may have been a brute, but he loved many women. Minotauro's father...he had no love in him at all."

"You remember him?" Alexandra asked.

"Rom? He was hard to forget. None of us ever wanted to be around him; Minotauro most of all. He was a hard man. Cold. Even the bull and buffalo warriors feared him. There was no dissension under his rule. If there was anyone who hinted at disobedience, they were punished severely. Some were hung from the trees in the old forest. Others were whipped and beaten. And some were even banished from the clan."

Alexandra and Daniel sat in complete silence.

"When Rom was killed, Minotauro became king overnight. We all did."

Alexandra was bewildered, "But you were just children."

Byron nodded.

"How did Rom die?" she asked.

Byron looked at her, almost confused by the question. "Your father killed him. Beheaded him."

Alexandra's face went ashen. She was stunned, "I...I had no idea." She looked down at Minotauro's sleeping face.

Byron reached for his bone scepter, Bane, and held it gently, "That night, Sebastian, Minotauro and I became kings to our clans, and our warriors have protected all three of us ever since."

"Remnants." It was Daniel.

Byron nodded. "It changed everything. Our bond with each other and with our warriors was and is...rock solid. We are family. There is no fear of punishment, no cause for dissent. Just a fierce loyalty to one another. We protect one another." Byron threw another branch into the fire. "It's still strange sitting here with the two of you — a king to a clan who ruled us and a queen to a pack we never knew."

"How do you think Sebastian's doing?"

Byron paused, staring at the fire before answering. "He's never had to lead on his own. There's always been power in numbers with we three kings. But...funny enough...he's the perfect person to build that dam and lead the clans to do it. Sebastian feels things very deeply, which makes him intuitive to the needs of others. It allows a humility to dominate over the boastful. In truth, Daniel, he is loved. Our three clans will support him against the den and lair if he runs into any trouble." Byron smiled as he looked back at the fire. "And man, does Sebastian hate trouble."

X

"*BREAK IT UP!!!*"
The wolves and lions were at it again. It had only been a day and a half, but they were at each other's throats, threatening to battle it out amongst each other as if a war were still going on. The amphibian, bull and gorilla clan warriors surrounded Sebastian as he jumped into the fight between Hood and Chester — the alpha from the lair and the captain from the den. They were grappling viciously with one another; Sebastian bounced right off of them. Bull, amphibian, and gorilla clan warriors were immediately at his side. They tried to help him up, but he threw their hands off of him.

He was pissed.

He immediately pushed himself off the ground and pulled his two short swords from their sheaths. He rushed toward Hood and Chester again, diving between them until slicing his swords straight up between them. The tips of both swords were touching each of their jugulars. The two warriors froze, seething at one another as the swords remained in place. Lion's Den and Wolf Pack soldiers growled and barked at the king, moving in closer to defend their leaders. The gorilla, bull, and amphibian clan warriors, however, moved in between them, outnumbering the Wolf Pack and Lion's Den.

Sebastian could feel the heated energy coming from all sides, but he stood his ground keeping his weapons in place. "I'm going to remove my swords. If either of you attack me or each other, the warriors surrounding you will end you. Is today the day you wish to die?"

Both leaders shifted their eyes to the gorilla, amphibian and bull warriors surrounding them. Sebastian removed his swords from their throats but held them ready in case of attack.

Hood lowered his head in a challenge, never taking his eyes off of the lion. "The *cats* are trying to steal from our ration of food and water!"

Chester's mane stood even higher. "There are fewer *dogs* than lions, and

39

yet they still get the same supply!"

The roars, cowls, barks and growls immediately followed.

"*SILENCE!!!*"

No one listened.

Sebastian's voice was no match for a cacophony of clan warriors. It was not until the gorilla, baboon, bull, buffalo, frog and toad warriors weighed in, drowning out the lions and wolves, that the den and pack quieted down — especially the lions. They hated the sound of baboons.

"What would your king and queen say if they saw this today?"

"Our king would be angry."

Everyone turned and saw Cheetah standing there amongst the den warriors. He was looking directly at Chester. The moment their eyes met, Chester's breathing began to slow and the hair on his mane lowered down. Chester turned back to Sebastian. "We only tolerate you by command of our king." He looked at Hood. "Tell the dogs to stop stealing what is not theirs to own...or there will be a battle only the den can fight...and we will win." His cat eyes shifted to Sebastian. "We always do."

Chester and the den warriors stormed off; only Cheetah remained. Sebastian turned to Hood. "Is the pack stealing other rations?" Hood remained silent. "You have enough."

"Says the king who has more." Hood's eyes seemed to glow even brighter. "Our pack has learned to store up for other seasons and sacrifice for the day-to-day. 'Enough' is not a word in our vocabulary, king. We take what we are given and take a little bit more. It's how we survive — even our queen. In that, we are justified." Hood turned with the remaining pack members and returned to their side of the dam.

Sebastian put his swords back in their sheaths, realizing how foolish it was to jump in between the two captains. He was a remnant. He should be protecting himself. But he also realized they did not attack him. A small victory if anything. Sebastian looked at Cheetah. "You look like you have something more to say."

"King, you are trying to lead us all, thinking we are all equal. Only in birth and death are we the same. Our circumstance and perspectives shape the way we live. It cannot be easily changed — even if there is a greater good at play."

"What are you suggesting I do? Let them fight? Kill themselves? Our time is not guaranteed, Cheetah. It may end sooner than we think. We have to use what time is left to do what must be done for the realm."

"Perhaps. But you will never get the clans to see that if they have no say as to how the hours and days are spent. Consider the leaders. Use their knowledge and influence. Get them to buy in. Let them tell you what they think about the time that is not guaranteed, for it is theirs to weigh, they may have grander ideas." And before Sebastian could respond, Cheetah nodded in respect and ran back to his side of the dam.

Amun spoke, "He's right, my king. The lions have never taken orders from anyone. They give them. And the wolves…their nature is to dominate their territory to protect it."

"As do the bulls and gorillas. There is no difference there. But you are right. The lions have ruled our side of the kingdom for centuries and have answered to no one." Sebastian turned to his warriors. "Gather up all the rations and supplies. A new base camp is to be built where everyone goes to get what's needed. Ram, Amun, send your men to do it. From now on, there will be one line for food and one line for water."

Ram, a Black Angus warrior, snorted and said, "The lions and wolves will not like this."

"You will be responsible for divvying out the rations every day, just as you did before the bird clan fell. Everyone will get their fill. Whatever their issues are with each other, they need to put their rage to the task, siphon the anger and focus on the work."

The warriors nodded and walked off leaving Sebastian to stand there looking out at all the clans. He knew it was going to take more than an assembly line of supplies to create a new order. But at least it would give him time to think about what Cheetah had said. He knew the warrior was right. They were completely siloed, only focused on building the side that was designated for their own kingdom — and it wasn't working. He knew they would have to work together to build the dam the way it should be done for the entire realm, but seeing how the warriors could barely stand beside each other, let alone build together, he knew it was going to take a miracle to get it done.

XI

Byron and the rest of the remnants had been traveling through a thick forest since sunrise. The leaves were lush and green; something none of them were used to seeing, as most of the landscape in their kingdoms had been affected by the drought throughout most of their lifetime. Alexandra took in the sight of the trees. They had to be over one hundred feet tall. "These are the tallest trees I've ever seen. My pack would love this."

Tick-Tock's head swiveled around as he looked up at the trees. Their trunks were thick, expanding at least thirty feet wide. His head kept shifting, trying to find the right head to get the best view. "The horses don't mind it either." His head swiveled around again.

The remnants slowed their step and turned around to look at Tick-Tock.

"*Horses?*" Byron looked at the totem.

Tick-Tock tilted his head to the side; his bulbous eyes appearing to stare at them with wide-eyed innocence. Minotauro's face looked grave. "The *horse* clan."

Byron asked, "Huh?"

Alexandra spun around and whipped out her sword, crouching in a protective stance as she stared out at one area between the trees. Daniel came up beside her, "What is it?" The remnants pulled out their weapons as well.

Alexandra's eyes rapidly scanned the trees. No one moved; not even Tick-Tock. A gentle breeze moved through the trees, winding softly around and into Alexandra's ear. "It's here."

Daniel pulled his sword and whispered, "What?"

Silence.

Suddenly, a white beast raced past them. It sped around the trees, winding through them like a flash of light before disappearing out of sight.

Alexandra shouted, "*THERE!!*"

As if in reply, the beast rode swiftly through the woods, racing past them so quickly, none of the remnants could make it out before it disappeared once again.

All was silent.

Daniel scanned for movement. "Do you hear it?"

Alexandra looked for movement as she listened closely for any sound. "No."

Daniel whispered to the totem, "Tick-Tock...are horses friendly creatures?"

His head swiveled to the barn owl of the present. "The beasts or their queen? Two separate questions with two different answers."

Byron scoffed, "Great. A vicious queen or killer horses — whatever those are." He tucked his scepter in his belt and began to climb a nearby tree. He swung from branch to branch, climbing higher and higher until he was completely covered from view. Tick-Tock watched him with curiosity until finally deciding to follow suit.

Minotauro whispered up to Byron, "Do you see anything?"

"*GET DOWN!!!*" Alexandra whirled around, shouting as she dove for cover.

The ivory-colored stallion warrior charged from around the tree closest to Alexandra. It leaped over her and raced straight toward Daniel and Minotauro. Daniel dropped to the ground, but Minotauro was not fast enough. The bull king turned only to receive the full blow of the stallion's impact. It drilled into him and rammed him into a nearby tree. Minotauro slammed into the trunk and dropped to the ground just as the stallion wound around the trees once more; it turned and stood directly across from Minotauro. The warrior smirked and stomped his hoof-like fist into the ground.

Minotauro pushed himself up and glowered at the horse — his eyes almost turning red. "You are not fit for this game, *horse!*"

It was on.

They charged toward one another. Minotauro lowered his head and collided into the stallion warrior, knocking the warrior in the forehead.

CRACK!

The stallion warrior's head snapped back; his neck broken upon impact. The warrior's body smashed to the ground.

But the bull king was not done.

Minotauro grabbed the horse by the neck, spun around like a cyclone, and off his momentum, hurled the stallion into a nearby tree. It smashed into the trunk, causing a thunderous sound that echoed across the forest. The stallion's body collapsed limply to the ground, while the tree itself was uprooted, falling on impact. Daniel and Alexandra stared at Minotauro in disbelief. They had neither seen him fight like that before, nor had they ever seen him so angry.

Alexandra got up and walked over to the stallion, never having seen a warrior such as this. It was strong. Alexandra could clearly see the large muscles exuding power from the warrior's thighs. His long mane was shiny, beautiful, as it glimmered in the sunlight. "Well, if the horse queen wasn't evil before, she will be now. You just killed, what was probably, her best scout."

Minotauro brushed the dirt from his forearms. "That was no scout. She knows we're here. She was sending us a message. And she sent a pretty strong one." He rubbed the grass off his massive arms and looked up at the trees, "Nice warning, Byron!" He glared at Tick-Tock, "Hey, buddy! Any time you want to use that future head of yours, *bird*, would be a good one!"

Tick-Tock's head peeked out from the foliage above, "I am not a bird, I'm…"

"I know! A totem or whatever that is…"

Daniel crouched down over the stallion examining it. "So this is a horse. What an amazing animal."

Alexandra was not amused. "Sure. Amazing that he tried to run us down and kill Minotauro."

"Thank you, Alexandra. I was beginning to feel a bit unloved."

Alexandra's head shot up, "They're coming!"

Daniel stood, "Who?"

Tick-Tock's head peeked out again, "She's coming! The horse queen is coming!" He jumped down beside Alexandra.

As if on reply, the ground began to shake violently as a stampede of horses thundered throughout the forest.

Byron descended a few branches, swinging from the trees above them, rapidly moving across each branch. He shouted to the ground down below, "Follow me!"

While he swung from above, they ran below but they were not fast enough. Alexandra looked back and saw the horde: zebra, donkey, Clydesdale and other horse warriors — and they were all gaining on them.

Alexandra shouted, "They're too fast!"

The stallion warriors split and took to the outsides of the trees. Alexandra, Daniel and Minotauro watched as the horses wound around the foliage, closing the distance, surrounding them on all sides. Riding on the fastest black stallion of them all was a woman. Her wild raven-colored hair matched that of her warrior's.

She wound around the trees and turned to face the remnants. Her stallion warrior reared up as a wall of horse clan soldiers surrounded the remnants. Minotauro, Daniel, Alexandra and Tick-Tock skidded to a halt. Under his breath, Minotauro grumbled, "Nice going, Byron."

The horse queen jumped off her stallion's back. Her warrior rose up from all fours, standing on his two hind legs. His height was almost nine feet tall. Her other clan soldiers followed his lead. Daniel was staring at the queen. With her long, wild raven hair, olive skin and athletic physique, she was beautiful.

Alexandra caught him staring. "Hey."

Daniel shifted his gaze.

The queen looked at Tick-Tock, taking in his peculiar form. "I've never seen anything like you before."

Tick-Tock's head swiveled to horned owl. "I am...*beyond this world.*"

The horses snorted, shifting uneasily. It was then the queen noticed the emerald stone hanging around his neck. She quickly looked at her black stallion — their unknown thoughts communicated between each other. She stepped back, shifting her attention to Minotauro. She looked him up and down before slamming him in the face with her fist. "You killed one of my best warriors."

Minotauro rubbed his jaw off her blow. He looked at Daniel, "Question number two answered."

She tried to punch him on the other side of his face, but the bull king grabbed her fist before she landed her blow. She was fast, however, and slammed her other fist into the same side of his jaw instead. He roared in pain and clenched his fist as if about to strike. The horse queen's warriors immediately armed themselves with their bows, aiming their arrows at Minotauro; he lowered his hand. The queen turned her attention to Daniel and Alexandra. "Where's the other one?"

Daniel answered, "There's no one else."

She looked Daniel in the eye. "You're a bad liar."

The horse queen noticed the satchel and metal chute strapped across his chest. She opened the chute and pulled out the maps.

Alexandra growled threateningly. "You raise a hand to him, *I'll bury you.*"

The queen eyed Alexandra. "For a man to lie badly, it means he has honor. You should be proud. Is he your mate?"

"Stay away from him."

The queen smiled knowingly. "So, he's not. Which means...he is still free to choose another." She eyed Daniel. "An impressive specimen. I can see why you desire him. He'd be good to ride." She tossed the maps to one of her warriors. The queen's stallion dropped to all fours. She mounted him, "Bring them to the village."

Most of the warriors dropped in unison, riding off behind their queen. Five of her warriors remained. They were still aiming their arrows at the remnants. A zebra warrior commanded, "Move."

The remnants walked side by side, the horse soldiers behind them. Minotauro looked at Alexandra and slowly smiled. "Alexandra, I had no idea you were so territorial. You grow more and more alpha every day."

"I know, I kind of liked it." Daniel grinned proudly. "I *would* be good to ride."

Alexandra was not smiling. Daniel's grin immediately disappeared the moment he saw the look on her face. "Or not."

From behind them, the horse soldiers were knocked down one at a time as a bone scepter swung down, smashing their heads one by one. Alexandra, Daniel and Minotauro ignored all the action behind them and continued walking.

"So would I. I don't know why she thought you the better of us two."

Alexandra answered with disdain, "You're a bull. She knows better."

The remnants continued walking as Byron dropped down from the trees. He raced to catch up with them. "Hey! We're not going to let her get away with this, are we?"

Minotauro kept looking straight ahead, "Alexandra, did you hear something?"

"Not a thing."

Daniel added, "What?"

Byron stopped walking. "Very funny. Look! I just took out the soldiers! Hey! Where are you going?"

All he could see was the back of one of Tick-Tock's heads as he said, "Up to no good. Going to get even. Walking off the beaten path for no greater purpose."

Byron nodded, "Well, all right then."

He raced to catch up. Behind the gorilla king, the trees shifted and moved, creating an alternate landscape with a different path. Not even Alexandra heard it.

XII

"No sign of them, my queen."

The horse queen Diana looked out at the forest beyond. Night had fallen and there was no sign of the remnants or her soldiers. Her face was set as a black stallion warrior named Knight walked up beside her.

"It was that other king. I know it."

"Are you sure he was a king?"

Diana looked at her warrior. "They all are. The woman is the queen of the wolves."

A shadow seemed to cast itself across Knight's face. "Then they are the dark ones from the southern realm." She nodded. "Why are they here?"

"I don't know, but if the stories about them are true, I don't want them finding the village now that they're roaming free."

Diana turned and looked out at the people inhabiting her clan: children, farmers, hunters, and gatherers living alongside one another in peace. There was no way she was going to let outsiders corrupt or harm her people. "Have the herd keep extra watch on the borders tonight. Send a squad to hunt the kings and queen down. Tell them to take them to the waterfall when they find them. I'll meet them there." She handed Daniel's maps to Knight. "And burn these." Knight bowed to his queen and neighed to his herd of assassin black stallions. They dropped to all fours and rode out into the darkened forest.

Diana was deeply troubled.

What were the kings and queen from that cursed realm doing here — and without a band of warriors to protect them? Were they that powerful? That invincible? And now that they had escaped, where were they?

She walked slowly through her village and toward a large tree, leaning against its trunk. Diana reached her hand up to the medallion hanging around her neck; she clutched it tight. That was when she felt another hand reach up from behind her and grip her throat.

"Do not scream, queen." He was behind her, hiding in the trees. *"You are remnant to your clan, are you not?"*

The other king.

Diana could barely nod her reply; his grip was tight. She managed a slight jerk to her head to acknowledge his question.

"Good. Then you know I could crush your throat before you could utter a single sound. My friends and I...we wish to speak with you...*alone*."

He moved his hand quickly from her throat to the back of her hair and pulled her up the tree swiftly before anyone saw her disappear. Once up in the tree, Byron pressed her body against his and whispered in her ear from behind. "Try anything funny, and the wolf queen will burn down your village. She likes to do things like that."

Diana tensed. She could not see his face nor he hers. "Hold onto me. And do not scream." He swung in front of her onto the branch of the tree. She wrapped her arms around his shoulders; she could tell they were muscular — strong. Diana did not know what was going to happen next, but her question was answered the moment they took off through the trees. The king swung fast and furious from branch to branch as he flew across them and between them. Diana held onto him tightly.

As they swung through the forest, she took in the sight of her kingdom. It was the first time she could see it from this angle. Homes made of thatched roofs connected by wooden bridges and staircases built between the trees; torches softly lighting the pathways, hearths lit and glowing warmly from inside the homes — it was beautiful.

The fires lighting her domain slowly dimmed as they made their way higher up the treetops. Diana looked up and saw the stars — there were so many. As she gazed at them above, she could feel the wind on her face. It was just the surge of confidence she needed to regain her senses to do whatever it was she needed to do — no matter where this king was taking her. And although she should have been terrified, she was not. Whatever was about to happen next, she told herself she would be ready.

Byron leaped through the forest with ferocious speed, clearing a large distance between the trees. Diana could see a clearing up ahead. Byron made one last lunge as they swung down from one of the branches, dropping down to the ground in the middle of nowhere. She let go of him and stepped back. It was then that Byron turned around to face the horse queen.

The moment their eyes met, the furious look on his face slowly subsided. She sized him up, looking at him from head to toe.

Byron said, "Come here." He motioned for Diana to move toward him. Without hesitation, she moved slowly toward; something she had never done for any other. *It was his voice.*

And not just his voice. The gorilla king was devastatingly handsome, and he exuded authority and strength. With his dark hair, olive skin and dark eyes, followed by his muscular build — Diana could not be help but be deeply attracted to the king.

She was standing in front of him, toe to toe. They continued to stare at one another in silence. It was then that Byron reached his hand out and took her by the waist pulling her even closer. She did not even try to stop him. Their faces were inches apart; she could barely breathe as his dark eyes looked directly into hers. He moved his hand to her side and slowly pulled her sword from her sheath. "You don't need this." The moment he spoke, the wind blew gently through the trees. Diana saw the branches gently sway as he backed away from her.

They continued to stare at one another.

"Oh, please."

They turned and saw Alexandra standing a few feet away from them, her hands on her hips. She turned away from Byron and Diana in disgust. Byron and Diana looked at each other once more, barely able to tear their eyes away from each other. It was Byron who finally broke the spell, "Follow her."

Diana walked toward Alexandra while Byron followed. The two women glared at each other as they moved through the fields. It was then that the open clearing shifted, and a multitude of trees sprang up from the ground — and no one heard a thing.

XIII

Alexandra led Diana and Byron down a hilly path toward a small pool of water beside a massive waterfall. Alexandra suddenly stopped and listened. Byron saw her reaction and motioned for Diana to halt.

"What is it?"

She listened more closely, looking back at the trees. "The trees…they weren't there before."

Byron looked around. "You're sure?"

"It was flat ground."

"It's Agoura." They turned and looked at Diana. "Sister Earth. She shifts the landscape, so you never walk the same path twice."

"She knows we're here?" Alexandra and Byron exchanged looks.

Diana looked back at him. "They *all* know you're here. I should warn you, my clan is protected by Wind. That's why my horses can ride faster than you and your lion, *wolf*. Oh, wait…he isn't your lion. My mistake."

Alexandra slowly stepped toward Diana and looked her dead in the eye. "I'm not in the mood, *horse*. You're lucky you didn't inherit your clan's looks. Your teeth would be the end of you."

Byron burst out laughing. Diana glared at him. "She gave you a compliment. What is your name, queen?"

Begrudgingly, she turned to him and answered, "Queen Diana."

"Keep walking, Queen Diana."

They moved down toward the waterfall where Minotauro, Daniel and Tick-Tock awaited. Minotauro was reading a letter from Lydia. The moment Tick-Tock saw Diana, he jumped down in front of her. Startled, the horse queen moved away from him, backing into Byron. She was surrounded with nowhere to go as Tick-Tock examined her from head to toe. His head swiveled three times speaking in Rebekah's voice, "*The eagle represented wisdom to rule, and the raven cunningness to protect.*" His head swiveled to barn owl. He looked directly at Byron. "She rules with wisdom. She protects her clan, this queen does."

Diana whispered, "Old magic..." She looked deep into his bulbous eyes. "You are not what you seem..." Diana and Tick-Tock continued to stare at one another. She looked at his body, noticing the different pieces put together that made him whole.

How had this been done?

It bewildered her and terrified her all at the same time. Her eyes zeroed in on the raven and eagle feathers on each of his arms.

"Birds..." Diana looked between them. "I've heard of you and your kingdoms. The amphibians. Wolf. Lion. Gorilla. And Bull. But...there are no more birds..."

Daniel asked, "I don't understand. How have you heard of us?"

"Whispers on the wind..."

Byron could see the disturbed look written all over her face. He moved toward her, speaking gently. "We are remnants, queen, like you."

Daniel noticed the queen's demeanor change as well; he could see the tightening of the muscles around her neck. He saw her shift her body position in such a way that he could tell she was preparing herself to either flee or fight. He tried to reassure her, "We aren't here to harm you or your people, queen. We had no idea your clan even existed until we saw your horse warrior."

"You mean when her horse attacked," added Alexandra.

Minotauro, all the while, remained unnaturally silent — still reading his letter.

"Then why have you come?" When no one answered her, she answered for them, "Your famine. Your drought." The remnants looked at one another, shocked that she knew even this detail. The horse queen glared at them, "*I know*...I know all about how you eat your own kind!" She spat the words, making her disgust clear.

Handsome or not, the queen could barely stand to look at the gorilla king or the other remnants. She focused her attention on the wolf queen and lion king.

Alexandra reacted, "What?!?"

Minotauro lifted his head and stared at the queen; his face seemed to darken the moment he caught sight of her. Daniel remained silent, while Byron winced at her words, knowing full well his and Minotauro's warriors were the ones once feasted upon. He clenched his jaw in anger, he was about to retort when the queen shouted, "You're liars! And now you're here to find another clan to feast upon!"

Byron had enough; he shouted back, "Queen, we aren't here for that!"

"I don't believe you!"

"*I don't lie!*" Byron looked at Minotauro to jump in, but the bull king did not say a single word. He simply continued to stare at the queen.

The gorilla king continued, "It's true that there was a famine! It's true there was a drought. And it's also true that the generation that ruled before us did terrible, horrific things, but *we* do not! We have vowed amongst each other to never have that kind of atrocity in our realm again!" He exhaled slowly, softening his tone. "That is why we are banded together."

But Diana was not listening. She backed away from Byron, searching for an opening; she saw it. She suddenly raced for the other side of the pool and began to climb the rock wall. Byron ran up the rocks behind her. She turned and kicked him in the groin; he immediately went down.

Minotauro was still sitting on the rock, returning to his letter. "I know...she's stronger than she looks. She's got passion, that one."

Alexandra leaped past them and climbed swiftly up the wall after the queen. She was a foot beneath Diana. Diana saw her and kicked at her but missed. She kept climbing. Alexandra waited for Diana to get higher before she leapt again. She vaulted up and over the horse queen so that she was on top of the cliff. Alexandra crouched down and put her hand up. "Stop! We're not going to eat your clan! We seek the elements. We seek the gift of rain — an answer to our famine and drought." The horse queen, out of breath, stared at her. "*Rain,* Diana!"

Alexandra was breathing hard as well. "I have never and will never eat a member of my clan or any others — bull clan warriors most of all. They smell. They piss all over themselves and don't bother to clean up."

Diana looked deep into the wolf queen's eyes. The wind blew gently passed her, speaking to her.

Believe her.

She did not want to. But when Wind spoke, the queen listened. Several moments passed before Diana looked down at Minotauro, finally deciding. "They do smell." She looked at Daniel; he was staring up at her with pleading eyes of understanding. She shifted her gaze back to Alexandra. *"Rain."*

Alexandra nodded, "Rain." The wolf queen extended her hand. Diana reached out to take it when she suddenly lost her footing. Before either queen knew what was happening, Diana slipped off the rocks and fell backward.

Diana's scream was joined by Alexandra's shout as the horse queen plummeted down toward the rocks below. Diana saw them rapidly coming into view as her body was about to crash down upon them. She closed her eyes, bracing for impact, when she suddenly felt her body rising into the air. She opened her eyes to find Byron holding onto her, swinging her to safety as he hurled their bodies away from the rocks and onto the ground below. He was clutching onto a vine hanging from one of the trees as they hit the ground hard. Byron was on top of her, staring into her dark brown eyes; he looked angry.

She did not blame him. She had kicked him pretty hard, but she held his stare. His face seemed to soften as he held her in his muscular arms and said, "Bulls do stink, but not gorillas."

"It's called *pheromone*. It's how we woo our women."

Byron looked back at Minotauro. "Oh, that's how you wooed Lydia? Pheromone? And here I thought you actually had a strategy." He stood and pulled Diana back off the ground.

Alexandra leaped down from the waterfall as the bull king attempted to defend himself, "I was referring to my herd. I did have a strategy."

Daniel chimed in. "No, you didn't. Cheetahs talk."

Alexandra moved next to Minotauro and sniffed him before moving on. "And you *do* stink."

Byron corrected her, "*Pheromone,* Alexandra."

Alexandra shook her head, "It doesn't work."

"Not on you!" Minotauro stood up, folding his letter into his pocket. "So what if I had no strategy. I didn't need one. I saw Lydia, I knew I was going to love her the rest of my life, and I pursued her. Lydia knew what she wanted, and she wanted me. Why wait to declare our love?" He looked at Daniel and Alexandra, "If I did, I would never be married...like you two."

Daniel was not amused. Diana took in the banter between the kings and queen, still reeling from her near-death experience after shouting at them and accusing them of being cannibals and villains.

Believe them...

Diana inhaled sharply, "I don't understand...how is it that you're so familiar with one another?"

"What's not to understand?" Minotauro draped his arm around Byron's shoulders. "We're soul mates."

"No, I meant...the stories I've heard are histories of war, tragedy and violence between your clans."

Minotauro's smile faded. He had a serious look on his face as he replied, "I told you...*we're soul mates.*"

Byron threw Minotauro's arm off of him. The bull king grinned widely. "Am I ruining your strategy?"

Daniel answered her instead, "The stories you heard, most of them are true...as much as we hate to be reminded of them. But Alexandra told you the truth about why we're here."

"Rain."

Help them...

She looked at the remnants, still listening to the wind. "Then, you seek the Element Fortress."

"Yes. Can you tell us how to get there?"

The horse queen paused.

Tell them...

Diana swallowed hard. She knew she could help, but part of her still was still uncertain if she should. Several moments passed before she said, "It can never be found. Only if they want you to find it."

"What do you mean?" It was Alexandra who asked.

Seeing the wolf queen's distraught face, she almost felt sorry for her — for all of them. Even in the moonlight she could see their distress and desperation.

Daniel continued, "Can you and your horses help us?"

"I don't see how."

Minotauro answered, "Don't send them after us." He leveled his eyes at her.

Daniel moved toward Diana, holding onto his satchel. "I need my maps. We're trying to get to the fortress. If I showed you the maps, could you tell us which way to go?"

She paused, "I burned them."

Daniel's face fell.

Alexandra, however, continued staring at Diana. "You don't need them, Daniel." He looked at her while Alexandra continued to stare at the other queen. "You said that Agoura shifts the landscape. How often?"

Daniel finally understood. "The maps…that's why there's so many. That's why they didn't match up."

Diana answered, "She does it any time she wants to. You could be in the same spot for weeks and think you traveled across the world."

Minotauro shook his head, "So how far have we really traveled? A foot?" He threw a stone into the pool, frustrated.

It was then that Tick-Tock's stone began to flicker. He swiveled his head and looked behind him.

Daniel looked at her, pleadingly, "But there has to be a way to get there."

Diana was about to reply when she spotted movement behind Daniel. It was Knight — one of her black stallion warriors. She saw him pull the string of his bow as he took aim…*directly at the lion king*.

Alexandra tilted her head to the side, having heard his movement and recognizing the sound. She whirled around, shouting, "*NO!!!*"

The stallion fired.

Daniel slowly turned…and right before the arrow plunged straight into his heart, wind violently exploded in front of him with a loud *SNAP!* forcing the arrow to move in an entirely new direction. Stunned that he had not been hit, he turned to find Diana clutching a bronze medallion hanging around her neck, her one arm spread wide. Wind had exploded from the horse queen's fingertips.

"*DANIEL!!!*" Alexandra was immediately on him.

Without missing a beat, Minotauro spotted Knight and another black stallion warrior beside him. He spun on his on his heel like one of his buffalo

55

soldiers, ripped two daggers from his sheaths and sprinted toward them keeping his body low to the ground. Before they knew what was about to hit them, the bull king raced alongside the black stallions, slicing their torsos with his daggers, leveling them to the ground. Diana watched hopelessly as her warriors dropped like flies, *"NO!!!"*

Alexandra, hearing the horse queen's shout, turned to attack her. Diana saw her coming and tried to get up just as Alexandra slammed into her. They collided into a tree. She had Diana pinned by the shoulders against the trunk. "You should have called them off! You saw them and said nothing! He's a *remnant!*"

"Alexandra! I'm all right." It was Daniel. He tried to calm her down by softly touching her arm, but she was so angry, she could not hear him.

Diana tried to fight her off. "You kidnapped me! They did what your pack would have done to protect you! It was too late by the time I saw them!" She threw Alexandra's hands off of her. "I saved him! No one was hurt!"

"Correction."

They turned to see Tick-Tock standing in front of Byron, the arrow embedded deep inside the gorilla king's chest. Diana's face went ashen.

"Byron!" Minotauro cleared the distance and was immediately at his friend's side. He was livid.

"It was the wind." Byron was breathing hard, turning his attention back to Diana. "To be as fast as your horses…" He looked at Minotauro as his eyes were closing. "I can't…feel my legs." He began to lose consciousness.

Minotauro roared, *"BYRON!!"* The gorilla king's body slipped to the ground; Minotauro caught him and turned to look at Diana. He shouted, *"HELP ME!!!"* He shouted at everyone, but no one knew what to do — no one…except for Tick-Tock.

His head swiveled to snow owl — the head of the past. In one swift movement, he pulled Minotauro off of Byron and ripped the arrow from the gorilla king's body.

Minotauro cried out, *"What are you doing?!?"*

But Daniel held him back as they watched the totem lower his head, focusing on the medallion around Byron's neck. Tick-Tock's eagle hand clasped the medallion, pushing it against Byron's gaping wound. Tick-Tock shook Byron awake, looking Byron dead in the eye. *"KING!!!!"* It was Rebekah's voice. Byron's eyes snapped open, focusing on Tick-Tock's face. *"Keep your eyes on me, Byron!"* Tick-Tock raised his raven hand to the moonlight while the eagle claw remained clutching the medallion.

SNAP!

A blinding white light exploded in the darkness, causing everyone to shield their eyes. When they finally opened them, they saw Byron staring at Tick-Tock. His breath was coming in fast breaths until it slowed into a steady rhythm. *"You must have your many sons…"* Tick-Tock stepped back from the gorilla king and crouched down by a nearby rock. His head swiveled to horned owl — the voice of the future, "Becoming…" The stone was no longer glowing.

Diana was stunned as she unconsciously clutched her own medallion, recognizing the same power summoned by Tick-Tock as he clutched the medallion with the golden sun that hung from Byron's neck.

No one spoke as they stood there in shock and awe as to the miracle they had just witnessed. It was Daniel who spoke first; his voice was barely a whisper, "What are you?"

Tick-Tock paused before answering, "Dark…and light."

Daniel felt a chill run down his spine. It was the exact same thing Cheetah had said to him only a few days before.

Minotauro dropped to his knees in front of his greatest friend in all the realm and rested his head against Byron's, clasping his hand around Byron's neck. "No…not you…it can never be you." He turned to Diana, "*Her* maybe."

Alexandra had recovered her senses and was beside herself. She glared at Diana, speaking through gritted teeth, "*Get out of here.* I told you we should've fled when we had the chance! I told you we should never have sought her help!"

Daniel wrapped his arms around her, trying to calm her. They were all staring at Diana.

Minotauro lowered his head, his voice was low and lethal as he spoke to the horse queen, "I'm glad our clans separated when they did."

The remnants were taken aback by his words — as was Diana.

Minotauro continued, "I, too, know the histories of the clans…especially yours. Yours was once kin to mine. The horses were banished to this forest centuries ago for one single crime." He stepped toward her so that they were eye to eye. "*Your warriors killed their children.*"

Diana's face went ashen. "That's not true."

"It *is*, queen!"

Diana's jaw clenched; her heart was hammering inside her chest. Her voice was barely a whisper as she said, "No…we would never…"

"*Mares!* Your horses trampled their newborn mares when they began to outnumber the stallions. *Stallions* are the champions of your clan." He looked back at her dead black stallions. "Aren't they, *queen?*" Diana stood there, speechless. "I never want to see you or another horse again in my lifetime." Minotauro's eyes suddenly burned red, *"GO!!!"*

His shout echoed so loudly, it caused Diana to jump as she turned and raced through the darkness of the trees. She did not know what to do other than to run. She ran from the waterfall and out toward the forest, running faster than she ever had before. Everything that had just happened was overwhelming. The cannibal remnants sought the Element Fortress. A medallion like hers. A creature made from old magic used it to save the king. Who were these people?

"Your warriors killed their children…"

In anger, she ran even faster. Her mind was reeling.

Liar! The king was lying! Her people were peaceful. Her people loved one another, lived for family…

She raced through the darkness, not knowing where she was going when Byron suddenly dropped down from the trees, stopping her dead in her tracks. He was aiming her sword directly at her heart. She backpedaled. There was nowhere she could run, it seemed, that he would not catch her. She could not see the look on his face as he kept aim.

"Please…" She lowered her eyes, unable to meet his stare. "I tried to save the lion king! I didn't mean to harm him…or you, king!"

Byron remained silent, watching the kaleidoscope of emotions swirling across her face. He lowered the sword. "Look at me, queen."

Diana slowly looked up; her jaw was clenched tightly — a defiant look on her face as she said, "The bull king is *lying!* My people would never commit the crimes he's accused us of."

"That's the same thing we said to you. It's up to you to decide what to believe." He extended his arm, holding her sword out to her.

She stepped toward him and took it. She slowly lifted her eyes and met his gaze.

Looking at the strong-willed queen in the moonlight, Byron knew he was going to love this woman forever.

"Why are you alone…without your warriors?"

"That's the way we were told it had to be done."

"By who?"

"An old chief from one of our clans."

She shook her head in disagreement. "You're all risking your deaths and your clans' destruction."

"Or the means to live and thrive, queen."

She pondered this.

"I did not know you and your clan existed. If there's anything that was gained from today's events, it's knowing that we're not as alone as we thought we were. You are always welcome in my jungle, Queen Diana."

"After I almost killed you."

"I almost died once before…"

Diana did not understand his meaning, only seeing the sad look behind his tired eyes. She lifted her hand and laid it gently against his chest where the arrow had found its mark. He was completely healed. She kept her hand there, feeling the beat of his heart; it was strong.

"How was the totem able to do this?"

Byron lifted his hand and laid it over hers. The moment their hands touched, she felt her heart jump. It was racing as his hand held onto hers.

"I don't know. The bird queen had this gift given to her…she honored the Sun."

The bird queen.

Diana looked up into Byron's dark eyes, hearing the tone in his voice change the moment he mentioned the other queen.

"You admired this queen."

Byron nodded, "Very much."

She tilted her head to the side, seeing that he may have more than just admired the bird queen. Her heart almost burst inside her chest as he continued to look at her. She had never reacted to a man like this before. She did not want this moment to end. She did not want him to go. But she knew he needed to, and she knew she had one more piece of knowledge to help him know how. Diana swallowed hard as she said, "The elements…they reside in the tallest mountain beyond my forest. Agoura changes the landscape so that outsiders can never find their way."

Byron narrowed his eyes, "How is it that you find yours?"

She lifted her head to the sky…*and the wind answered her.* A warm breeze blew gently through her long, raven hair; almost as if it were whispering ever so softly to her. As Byron witnessed this moment, his heart fell to his knees.

"You must listen, king, to what the Old Ones are telling you — you and all the others." She lowered her head so that they were looking at one another once more. "Tell the wolf queen to listen to the wind just before sunrise. It blows the same way every day…north. That is where their fortress lies." Diana reluctantly lowered her hand and stepped away from him. "I hope you find what you're looking for, king."

"Byron."

"I hope you get your rain, Byron."

And before he could say another word, Diana ran further into the forest, remembering her way. Byron watched her as she ran like the wind; her hair whipping through the trees like one of her stallions, until she disappeared into the darkness. Byron touched his chest where the arrow hit him and looked at the sky. He whispered softly, "Thank you, Rebekah."

XIV

Minotauro was seated on a rock when Byron returned. He could barely look his friend in the eye. "I didn't mean to tell her that way. I meant to say it differently. To shame her, the way we've been shamed...I shouldn't have done it. But it couldn't be helped." He looked at the gorilla king. "You're not allowed to go into the dark just yet, you know."

"I know." Byron sat down beside him. "I had no idea horses were kin to your clan."

"I heard the story once. I wasn't sure I really believed it...until today."

"There's so much to our histories, I often wonder what kind we are writing. Knowing our reputations have preceded us outside the realm, and how harried it sounds when spoken from another's lips, reminds me that the book being written about us had better be accurate. I'm still wondering how she had heard about us." He looked in the direction Diana had fled.

"A wonderment indeed." Minotauro was looking out into the vast forest.

"She's a lot like us, you know. We riot over the accusations, weep over the truths. And rally at the call to make greater change. She'll do the same."

Minotauro shifted his gaze back toward the gorilla king, "She's not like us, Byron. She's free."

Byron studied his friend's tense face. He could see the corner of one of Lydia's letters protruding from the bull king's pocket. He knew his friend was missing her.

The bull king shook his head, "What are we doing here, risking our lives? Elements shifting the land as they see fit when we need the crooked paths made straight."

"What other choice do we have? We're all going to die someday. I'm just hoping that when I do, I don't take down my entire clan."

"That's twice for you, Byron." He looked back out at the landscape once more. "I don't know how many lives you have when it's always been against us."

"What?"

"The world. Just another impossible mountain to climb…and a mudslide to follow."

"I thought you were the optimist in the group. That the universe was answering."

Minotauro shook his head. "Not tonight. I have my days too, Byron, when I cannot see the sun shining even when its rays are beaming down right over me." He exhaled deeply. "These Creators…if they are what they are supposed to be, why do we need to go on this trek? Wouldn't they know what we need already? Why not just give it to us?"

"Perhaps they don't mind the asking."

Minotauro turned and looked at him. "I ask all the time — even if it's just inside my own head. And the only answers I ever hear are the ones filled with silence."

"You're here, my friend, putting something good aside to do something great. For the ones back home. For the ones yet to be born. Even for ourselves…to know that we are going to leave this world better than the way we received it."

"But will it matter in the end?"

"I hope so. But even if it doesn't matter to those tomorrow, it matters to most today."

"So keep going?"

"Yeah. Keep going."

Daniel and Alexandra approached; Tick-Tock was at her side. "We may as well sleep here tonight," Alexandra said. "Agoura just shifted the waterfall away. And I'm glad she did. I had that feeling we had in my woods…that someone was watching us…but this time…through the water."

They turned and saw the rocks were bone dry. Instead of a waterfall, a large group of trees stood where it once was.

Byron suddenly smiled. "Good."

"What's good about that?"

"I was hoping for some sleep tonight. It's quiet now."

Minotauro grunted, "At least she answers one of us."

"Isn't one enough?"

"One queen for one sister. One king for each brother…not exactly the way the chief expected. Hopefully they answer each of us. We need all the help we can get."

"Thinking of Lydia?"

Minotauro chuckled. "Always. But I was actually thinking of Sebastian. He must have seen them go down. Like the last time we saw it. You have no idea what it's like, Byron, to see your warriors fall." Minotauro looked up at the moon. "I can only imagine what Sebastian is going through right now.

61

And I wouldn't wish it on my worst enemy...even the horses."

A myriad of emotions was pumping through Sebastian's veins as his hand rested over Rod's heart. The gorilla, baboon, and orangutan warriors covered the ground. Rod's massive chest slowly rose and fell, as if he were in a deep sleep.

"My king..." It was Chango. He was standing beside his king with a torch in his one remaining hand. "The bull queen is here."

Sebastian turned his head as Lydia approached. "I was out on my evening walk when I heard the commotion." Seeing the bodies of the sleeping gorillas, Lydia was deeply troubled. "I brought warriors to watch over them. There's stirring in the shadows." She rested her hand gently on Sebastian's shoulder and looked down at Rod's still form. Immediately, she placed her hands over her stomach. "He's moving." Sebastian looked at her belly. "Look!" Lydia lifted her hand and pointed, "They're all moving!"

Sebastian looked down at Rod and saw the gorilla warrior's eyes slowly open. Seeing the amphibian king staring down at him, the silverback warrior looked relieved. He closed his eyes and said, "My king lives..." His voice was barely a whisper. "It was her...I saw her in the light..."

"Who?"

He opened his eyes slightly. "The bird queen. She...was standing before the fire...standing in the light..." He fell back asleep. Sebastian's jaw was clenched tight. He lowered his head, struggling with the anger, sadness, helplessness and relief he felt. He did not know what to do with it. He looked up at the full moon and closed his eyes.

"The day I don't hear the sound of gorilla warriors anymore will be the day the last bit of light in this realm dies." He opened his eyes and said, "Chango, Amun, Ram...stand watch over the jungle tonight. Gather more warriors. The clan is vulnerable and need to recover."

They nodded and headed to Bull Valley and Amphibian Swamps.

Back at the den, a tiger warrior had just delivered the news to Chester that the gorilla clan had gone down but would soon recover. Chester took the news well, knowing the time would soon come when the den could strike and show the rest of the clans that it was the den, and no other, that ruled the realm.

XV

Diana walked the familiar lines that led to her kingdom. Wooden bridges connecting pockets of thatched houses wove through the land, connecting her people and its properties together — a colony built on protection and trust — simplicity. She stood in the shadows taking in the sight of all the children, watching as her warriors played with them, coddling them, disciplining them, loving them.

"Your warriors killed their children…"

She flinched, closing her eyes. She gritted her teeth trying to shut out Minotauro's words.

"Diana!"

The horse queen opened her eyes, happy to be torn away from the thoughts haunting her mind as her younger sister Mary approached. "Where have you been? I heard the cannibal clans were here! Everyone is talking about it!"

An old Clydesdale warrior named Victor approached. He bowed, "My queen…" As he rose to standing, she could see a look of trepidation behind his eyes. "Where are the stallions?"

She ran her fingers through her sister's long black hair. "Mary, I need to speak with Victor in private."

"Is it about the clans? Did they eat the stallions?"

"They did not eat the stallions. And I don't want to hear any rumor that they did. The clan kings and queen will not return here. They have no intent of harming anyone. They are trying to find the Element Fortress."

Mary's eyes went wide. "The Element Fortress! But why?"

"Their tale is theirs alone to tell. Now, you must promise me that this message is spread amongst the village as fast as possible. They are gone, they will not return, and they mean no harm. Do you understand?"

"Of course. But Diana, no one has ever found the fortress."

"I have a feeling these kings and this queen will."

Mary nodded, turning swiftly on her heels as she headed toward the center of the forest. Diana knew her sister would do as she had wished, rallying and calming the clan to the news. She knew her sister would be a formidable queen one day. She was already full of compassion, curiosity, wisdom, and a deep loyalty to those whom she loved and deemed worthy of her private circle. It was a relief to the horse queen to know that if anything happened to Diana, the clan would live on and thrive under Mary's rule. That was why she had lied to Byron about being a remnant — to protect the clan at all costs. Diana turned back to Victor. "Come with me."

He nodded and followed his queen into her chambers.

"My queen, I can feel the heaviness in your heart."

"The stallions are dead."

"Knight?" He immediately snorted and stomped his foot. "We must retaliate!"

"We will do no such thing!" The anger in her tone silenced him. "Our dealings with them on this matter are over. Is that understood?"

"If this is so, why are you so troubled?"

She paused. Images of Minotauro's face filled her mind. "Why are we here?"

He narrowed his large almond eyes. "I don't understand the question."

She exhaled slowly. "Our clan…how did we come to this place? Why this forest?"

Victor was taken aback, slow to answer as he said, "You know the history, my queen. It was to flee from the bulls. The bull king from the southern realm threatened to wage war with our clan."

"Why?"

Victor narrowed his eyes, studying his queen. "What is this about?"

"Truth. I want to know if the words I heard tonight from the bull king's mouth are true."

"The bull king…" He lowered his large head in anger. "I don't know what he revealed, my queen, but do not listen to the weaver of lies! The ruler of a clan who wished to keep us in bondage! We fled to this forest because we no longer wanted to be slaves to the bulls! Building their walls, hauling their supplies, chained to their plans without any freedom to form our own! We were their *slaves*! No tribe to claim with an identity to be proud of!"

"But there was no war, Victor."

Victor's entire body went still.

"We did not fight for our freedom. And if we were the slaves as you say we were, why would he ever let us go?"

The old Clydesdale remained silent. His silence was the loudest noise Diana had ever heard as the realization that what Minotauro had revealed was the truth. It hit her like a punch to the gut. She suddenly felt sick and needed to sit down. "It's true then. I see it written all over your face."

65

"What's true?!?"

"*Banished!* Banished out of shame!!!!"

Victor's face darkened, *"There is no shame!"*

"You're lying, horse! This clan was banished here for murdering our mares! *Mares*, Victor!"

Victor approached, kneeling at her feet. "My queen...it is the mares that *rule* this clan."

She turned away from him, barely able to look at him. What else had her counsellors and guides not revealed to her? What else did she not know...even now?

"My queen, what you speak of is from centuries ago! *Centuries!* The clan is at peace. It has been rectified! Bringing up the past changes none of that."

She touched her medallion, "No...it changes the heart of me." Her answer was a whisper as her thoughts were spoken aloud. She stood up. "The stallions are to guard the forest but not to venture beyond the village borders until I return. Watch over Mary for me. I'm going to be gone for a while."

Victor sighed deeply, knowing full well where she intended to go. "You must be careful, my queen. Very careful. They are a ruthless clan."

"Keys will be with me." She whistled sharply. Seconds later an Arabian stallion entered her chambers. He stood on his two hind legs, bowing to her. "My queen."

"We're going for a ride. A long one."

Diana grabbed her bow and satchel filled with arrows as Keys bowed and dropped to all fours, asking no further questions. She looked back at Victor. Their eyes locked and, with no other words spoken between them, Diana climbed on top of Keys and commanded, "Ride south."

XVI

Sebastian stood at the banks of Wolf Lake looking up at the midnight sky. He was anxious, tormented by his thoughts of rage and frustration as he searched for answers he had yet to find as images of the gorilla clan going down a second time filled his mind. And as he thought of this last episode, he could not help but be reminded of the first.

He was going down the rabbit hole of dark thoughts as to who or what would have caused one of his best friends to be attacked, leaving him close to dead and a clan annihilated.

Was it one of the element brothers?

Was it the creature Poe had revealed through Tick-Tock?

What was it?!?

Who *was it?*

His chest constricted tighter and tighter in the frustration and helplessness he felt while trying to keep his angst at bay. His fists were clenched tightly as he tried to figure it all out from the silence of the banks of Wolf Lake. The more Sebastian thought about the world he was living in and that, even as a king in the realm, he had no control over any single part of it, the angrier he became. He begrudged its entire design and the part he had to play within it.

Who decided that the realm should bind clans to the remnant kings and queens?

Who decided that an entire bloodline should cease to exist with the last remaining king or queen?

He felt hopeless. He felt useless. He had answers for nothing. He had no one to talk to about the relentless thoughts of doom inside his mind. And because he could vent to no one, he was suddenly consumed with the desire to do…*something!* But there was nothing he could do. His warrior Chango told him he all he could do was trust. Trust in Chief Netapheha's counsel. Trust that it was all going to work out. Trust that his friends would survive. Trust that somehow, they would make it home. Trust that they would succeed.

But what if they didn't? And who was he supposed to trust? In what? The Creators?

He still didn't even know if he believed in their existence, let alone that there really was a stone, or that they would give it to them even if it did exist. And if it did, would it really raise the waters in a forsaken sea? Sure, his own chief believed in all of it, but Sebastian didn't even know that the old toad was still alive until a few months ago. And who's to say that all prophecies were true and would come to pass...even if it was spoken from one of his own clan members?

It all seemed so impossible. So unbelievable.

But he was willing. He was willing to try to believe that there was hope in the realm. That his chief was right. That there were external forces that existed in the world that were those of the good, the beautiful and the true. And he was willing because he had witnessed the existence of miracles.

Because of her...

The first one came the day the bird queen had awakened, and after that, even more miracles followed: food for his clans, rain to end the drought, and the ceasing of cannibalism in the realm. Queen Rebekah was proof of hope, proof that impossible ideas could be made possible. And for that reason, Sebastian had been willing.

But today did not help his willingness to hope or believe. For if there truly were benevolent forces in the world, they did not show up today. Byron would not have been hurt. The gorilla clan would not have gone down. There would be...*less suffering.* There should be...*less pain.*

Sebastian shook his head in despair. He couldn't do it. Not today. There were no benevolent forces, never were. There was no stone. The sea would never rise. The rain was not going to come ever again.

All that was left to hope for or trust in was the idea that somehow, some way, Byron and Minotauro would make it home. And when they did, Byron would need an heir, and soon, or his clan would not survive. And he wasn't the only one....*Sebastian* needed an heir. The more he thought about Byron, he thought of himself. As king, how could he not? He was a remnant. If anything happened to Sebastian, there would be no more amphibians. Today was a blatant reminder of that simple fact. And until he had a son or daughter, he needed to ensure his life was never in danger. But how to do that when so exposed? How to accomplish it when needing to walk amongst the other clans and lead them all in building a dam that would never have a sea to contain anyway.

Lionsss cannot be trusted...

The thought suddenly sprang up inside his head. It seemed to come out of nowhere, but how many times had he heard that blasted saying? His thoughts suddenly drifted to Chester and the band of den warriors. They made him cringe. It was the lions who were the cause of most of his troubles throughout his lifetime. Even now, they were the reason his days were so hard. Why couldn't they just do what their king wanted? Why didn't they just do what *he* wanted?

Knowing he had to have bull and amphibian warriors stand watch over the gorilla clan warriors in their vulnerable state for protection against the den, he was beginning to believe the old saying. How could Daniel lead such a group of despicable characters and be deemed the Noble One? How was that even possible? Wasn't the reflection of a king his people? Why couldn't it be the lions that went down?

Sebastian had to stop his mind from spiraling downward once again. He knew better. Daniel *was* the Noble One. Sebastian respected Daniel. He knew the lion king would have been livid over how his warriors had been acting. He didn't want any of the clans to go down. He knew he had to stop his spiraling thoughts. He had no idea what he was supposed to do next.

Trust.

He didn't want to.

Believe.

There was no point.

The amphibian king exhaled deeply. "I don't like being watched — especially when there's nothing to see."

"Better it's me than the rest of my pack." Hood emerged from the shadows of the trees. "Why are you here?"

"I needed a place to think."

"You're foolish to think this was the place."

"Many things seem foolish lately."

Hood did not reply.

Sebastian continued to look north from Wolf Lake. "I've been thinking about them, trying to feel them — the kings and the queen. But I sense nothing. I see nothing. No sign from a single element being." Sebastian turned his head to Hood. "And you? Can you feel your queen? Can you see her? Do these Creators speak to you?"

Hood stepped up beside Sebastian and looked up at the moon. "You are a remnant. Your clan feels what you feel — your highs, your lows — joy, pain. I feel my queen...*always.* What you see is what you choose to...true or not. My visions are my own." Sebastian watched as the fur on Hood's body rose straight up.

"Is she in danger?"

"Yes." Hood almost winced in pain as he answered. "But she suffers, king. She is always suffering...by her own desire to remain in the shadows — of doubt, of fear. She does not know how to be strong, confident, even when her strength is there. She doubts when she should believe. She hesitates when she should leap...*far.* She holds us back when all we want is to run."

Sebastian listened to the wolf captain, feeling as if his own thoughts and doubts were laid bare. Seeing the reaction of the warrior as to how Alexandra's feelings affected her clan and warrior suddenly made him feel as foolish as Hood said he should as he thought of how his thoughts must be making his own warriors feel at this moment.

Hood continued, "I cannot stand it. None of us can. It's logical that the guardian is there."

"You blame your queen for that?"

Hood's eyes glowed silver, resenting Sebastian's tone. "Yes."

Sebastian studied the alpha's demeanor, "You're afraid. Afraid of your queen."

"She is nothing like our king."

"I heard otherwise. The gorillas told a story once of how your king was lost in his own self-pity and sorrow." Hood's lip curled into a slight snarl. "It was his pack who helped him rise from the ashes. It was his pack who did not allow him to stay down. It was Skoll, the alpha, who led them there — to be where the king was — to rally him into a better existence, was it not?"

Hood remained silent.

"I've been standing here at this lake thinking about many things. Listening to you, more thoughts come to mind. How did they know what to do? What drove the pack of old to venture into forbidden lands to drag their king from his hole of despair. How did they know to act? Did they feel it? Did he? Did they despise their king? How did they know? Was it the Elements that told them? Because I feel nothing. Whether the kings and queen are out there in pain or experiencing joy, I know not. I only see the result of what happens here if they're in pain. And it's driving me mad! But you…you don't seem to care. You simply despise that she suffers because of how it makes *you* feel. It should rouse you, should it not? Like the pack of old…to be driven to go out there, to find her and bring her home?" He stared deep into Hood's eyes. "What kind of alpha are you?"

"Not every king and queen born to the pack is meant to lead." He stepped closer to Sebastian, his eyes glowing silver. "As alpha, I recognize the hunger in others to be what I am, to have what I have been given, waiting for that moment, king, to take me down. My queen can be taken out at any moment, for she does not know who she is and who she can become."

"And you do?"

"I feel it, king." He pounded his paw into his chest. "Embrace it or race it…*it is she.*"

Sebastian's eyes narrowed, remembering the moment when Chief Netapheha said the exact same thing.

Hood continued, "Our queen has never embraced her authority, her power, her feminine genius. She has never stood before the fire. And until she does, it is *I* who must lead the pack to protect the lair, for she is too weak to do it."

Sebastian stared at him a long time. His earlier thoughts weighed more heavily on his mind now after hearing the warrior's perspective. He thought of his own warrior Chango and what he had told him earlier. His warrior was giving him the answer he needed — even if it wasn't the answer he wanted. His warrior was roused to aid his king. And there was only one reason for that…a reason he had not truly cherished or embraced until now.

"You don't love her."

Hood looked up at the moon. "How can one love a queen who does not love herself? All we can do, king, is protect ourselves — even if it's from our master. And yet, we are powerless, commanded to remain here with you…to build a dam to a sea that may never rise again."

Sebastian's heart stopped the moment he heard Hood speak his own thoughts out loud.

He watched as Hood looked out at the land beyond. "With or without that dam, she should know…she should know what it is to rule…"

"None of us do."

Hood turned his large head back toward Sebastian.

"We didn't have the best examples — at least not we three kings. We only hope that what we're doing is the right thing to do — whether from our choices or off the ones from those who came before us."

"For whom are the choices for?"

The amphibian king pondered the question before saying, "For my clan. For the realm."

The realm…" A low growl rumbled in Hood's chest as he looked out at the lake. "A harder push where others have sway. The realm is not what it once was. And it isn't meant to be what you kings envision."

"Why not?"

Hood turned his head toward the amphibian king, his eyes mirroring in the darkness. "Because there is no love here. No pride. No tradition. It died with the last generation. It was they who understood what the realm was and what it could become. You are all merely picking up the scraps of what they left behind so you can survive, but you do not understand the power of the realm and what you are meant to be within it. *You do not believe.*"

Sebastian swallowed hard.

"How to follow those with shallow passions…" He paused and looked out at the lake beyond. "This entire exercise of forced unity amongst the clans has amplified a single thought I alone desire." He closed his eyes, suddenly looking exhausted. "I long to be bound to an equal master. One whose will is in line with mine. Like our last king and the kings and queens of old." Sebastian watched Hood as he opened his eyes and stared out across the lake. "Do not step foot in our lair again, king. You walk too freely with your back to those who begrudge the following. Commands or not, the clans will survive the loss of you and yours." He turned his head to Sebastian, "This is your only warning."

Hood turned and walked back into the darkened forest. Sebastian watched him go, thinking about what the alpha had just said.

From the lake behind him, Sebastian's toad warriors rose from the darkened waters. He looked at Chango and Amun, reeling from his own self-pity and what it meant to his warriors, having heard Hood speak of how his queen's thoughts and emotions affected the pack.

Only moments before he had begrudged being a remnant and the binding of his blood to his warriors. He suddenly felt very ashamed, for in all his despair, he suddenly understood. They were bound to each other to keep balance in the realm, in the clan; to help one another, to give strength to one another, counsel to one another. To rouse one another to stay focused on the purpose of their time in life and the responsibility as king or queen to embrace their position in that history...*and thrive.*

He looked into his warriors' eyes and realized, for the first time in his life, that he was not alone. He never would be. Byron and Minotauro were his brothers, his family, but so were the warriors that stood before him. They knew the answers he needed to hear. Their wisdom was built for him and he for them.

He looked at Amun and Chango.

It was then that the wind blew and the ground beneath Sebastian began to shift. He looked out at Wolf Lake and saw the waves rising and falling as the moon shone brightly down over him and his warriors.

Amun and Chango moved toward their king. He was still looking up at the light as the wind swirled gently around him when he said, "I think...I'm starting to see."

He heard them ribbit in reply as Chango said, "Becoming..."

XVII

The toad soldier slammed his spear into the ground. The ground beneath Feyedor began to rumble until the gate slowly opened and the surrounding waters sank into an unseen hole as a spiral staircase emerged.

The wolf king looked up at the soldiers, wondering how the chief knew he would be here, but the soldier spoke no other word as Feyedor descended the coral steps and walked quietly across a bridge that led to the high staircase to Chief Netapheha.

He had debated about this trip, making his final decision after visiting the bird queen one morning. She was holding her son in her arms, still grieving over the loss of Palimus — the clan's most beloved king. Seeing them there, Feyedor was reminded once more of Palimus' vision in the fire, knowing that the bird king's betrayal of the lion king was rooted in his belief that he needed to protect the heirs of his clan from the Lion's Den. Knowing Palimus' vision had never come to pass was a weight on the wolf king's heart, unlike he had ever known. Thinking of his own son, he finally made a decision. He did not even tell Brock about it as he secretly gathered the items into the small satchel clutched in his hand.

"The wisest and strongest amongst us…"

And as he made his way to Chief Netapheha's abode, he knew that the ultimate guardian would have to be fierce. It would have to be cunning. And it had to be wise. The creature he imagined in his mind's eye would have the bloodline of the greatest predators amongst the clans.

Kin clans.

Feyedor made his way up the last set of stairs where he saw the flickering lights dancing across the rock walls. As he ascended the steps to the chief's abode, he stopped the moment their eyes met.

"King."

Chief Netapheha stood tall for one so short, wearing a headdress with a

73

ruby-colored borax stone in its center, his coral staff at his side. Feyedor knelt down in front of him and unwrapped the contents of his satchel. The moment the toad chief caught sight of the ruby red medallion bound by a platinum chain hanging from the king's neck, his bulbous eyes began to glow. He looked up at the wolf king in surprise and whispered, "Her chosen king. A sight unseen…"

"Chief, I've come…"

"To bind, to shield, to protect…yes, yes…like the kings and queens of old."

"So it is true, it has been done before."

"Once. Only once before."

As the old chief spoke the words, a shadow seemed to fill the cave. Feyedor noticed the atmosphere rapidly shifting; he was suddenly very cold. He watched as Chief Netapheha walked over to the pool in the center of the cave. He peered down into it, searching the clear water, looking deeper and deeper into its depths. "Strange that your heart would be stirred to such an act when there is nothing but still waters. What have you seen that I have not? What have you seen in the fire?"

Feyedor's jaw clenched tightly as he spoke, "Nothing." He lied. "Just a feeling that I can't quite shake."

Netapheha turned and looked at him, almost as if he was trying to study the king's heart to decipher his true intent. "More than a feeling, I'd say to come here this day." His eyes homed in on the satchel in the king's hand. "What have you brought me?"

Feyedor handed it to the chief. The moment Netapheha opened it and peered inside, his eyes dilated rapidly once more. "The dark and the light…the greatest guardian, king."

"Can you do it?"

Chief Netapheha held the satchel in his webbed hand, silently thinking before replying. "Yes, yes…but only with their consent."

"Whose?"

In reply, a strong wind blew through the cavern, followed by the aroma of roses. The pool of water started to glow as the wind grew stronger and stronger, moving swiftly around the toad chief and wolf king, knocking over several of the chief's books, until blowing out all the torches and candles in Netapheha's home. The cave began to rumble and quake.

Then the wind was gone.

The rumbling stopped.

The water was still.

Both Netapheha and Feyedor stood in silence, listening for any further sound. "Does that mean 'yes'?"

The torches and candles were ignited once more, illuminating the chief's abode with varying colors of flame. All around the rock walls, vines had appeared; they were covered in roses. At the base of one of the rocks was an emerald stone. Netapheha immediately saw it and scrambled to pick it up. He lifted it to his bulbous eyes, studying it while still clutching the satchel in his hands. The stone began to glow brightly. "Yes, king...it does."

"Only once before..."

Feyedor stared at the dancing flames of the large bonfire before him. He was perfectly still, thinking about what he had just done as he ventured into Amphibian Swamps, hoping that his vision would change now that he had done it.

But it hadn't.

Damon, the raven assassin, and a fleet of his ravens were beside him waiting for the wolf king to reveal his vision from the flames. But he revealed nothing. Instead, he remained in complete silence. He had been standing there for over an hour in the same position watching the flames as they moved against the darkness.

Then, with no further warning, Feyedor turned and walked swiftly back through the woods and toward Wolf Lake. Garm, leader of the pack, and Damon followed, keeping pace with the wolf king as they continued to walk in silence. The moment they reached the banks of the massive lake, Feyedor froze. They watched as he looked out past the darkened waters. He turned his gaze back in the direction of Mariner Sea; he was thinking.

Garm finally asked, "What did you see, my king? I can tell it troubles you."

Feyedor did not answer him but turned to stand in the direction of Mariner Tower. He closed his eyes, tilting his head, listening. "Write my words down. Spread it across the land...Whomever controls the sea, rules the realm." It was the first time the words had ever been spoken, and it was the vision Feyedor had seen when he looked into the fire.

"An enemy will come. Footsteps of the wicked. Warriors of the wretched. But not in our lifetime."

The fur on Garm's body rose straight up. He growled the words, "What menacing spirit do you speak of, king?"

Feyedor turned and looked at his alpha; his eyes seemed to glow silver as he said, "No spirit, but a man. One of the forsaken."

Garm stepped closer toward his king. "Not possible. The bridge to their exile was annihilated, severing any pathway from reaching the realm ever again. It was done *centuries* ago."

Feyedor looked him dead in the eye. "His heir will find a way through it from the north. And when he does, she will not be ready."

"Who?"

"The cornerstone." He clutched his medallion tight.

All the while, Damon stood abnormally quiet, absorbing the wolf king's words. *"Wasss it enough, king?"*

Feyedor turned his gaze to the raven assassin. Looking into the raven's eyes, the king knew the raven had known what he had done. "The greatest guardian…the dark and the light…it has to be. They must always remember. Remember…"

"What?"

"The lions cannot be trusted."

Damon tilted his head to the side, his eyes glowing scarlet, *"Tok…tok…tok…"* was his only reply.

XVIII

"This is not the most comfortable position, Byron."

"Diana didn't complain."

Alexandra scoffed. Byron was carrying Alexandra on his back as he climbed the tallest tree he could find. When they reached the top, they found a sturdy branch to sit on. They looked out and saw the peak of an enormous mountain in the foreground.

"Do you think that's it?"

"It has to be."

"It's so far."

He had to admit that from their position, it surely was. Time was not on their side. "Remember what Diana said. Agoura can shift the landscape any time."

Alexandra kept staring at the mountain. "Do you really think we can do this?" She sighed. "Do you think we can build a dam, unite the realm, and fill the sea again with a stone we don't even know exists, so no one starves ever again?"

Byron studied her expression. "The way you make it sound, it sounds impossible."

"It is."

"Then why are you here?"

"I don't know." Her voice was barely a whisper, "I really don't."

Byron could tell that her answer went deeper than just the flow of questions she had just posed. He watched her expression as she stared out at the Element Fortress and suddenly felt a wave of empathy for her. He had not realized until now how alone she must have been all those years when she was isolated from the rest of the realm with only her father and pack as friends and family. And now she was thrust alongside all the kings who had friendship as their bond. "Does Daniel know how you feel?"

"Daniel is an optimist. Even if I told him, he'd find a way to help me see

77

the positive in any situation — one of his many gifts. My father was like that. Sometimes optimism is exactly what I need, and sometimes it's just…annoying." She paused. "I heard you talking to Minotauro last night. I felt exactly as he did. I know we haven't been gone long and knew that this journey was not going to be easy." She shook her head. "I've been thinking about Rebekah and how she asked the Elements to protect her clan. And they did. Why can't we just ask the same?"

"She honored the Sun. We never have."

"Did your father?"

"I don't know."

"Did you love him?"

"My father?"

She nodded.

"Yes, I did. He wasn't here long, but what I remember of him, I loved."

"What was his name?"

"Brutus."

She smiled. "That's a good name."

"So is mine."

They smiled at one another before turning their attention back to the fortress beyond. Alexandra's smile slowly faded as she gazed at it. *So far…*she suddenly felt defeated. "I don't want history to repeat itself, Byron. It scares me to think that without food, it could."

He turned toward her. "It won't."

"Part of me has been thinking that, instead of the fortress, we should be looking for another place to migrate."

"Like the horses."

"If they can thrive somewhere else, maybe we could too. Perhaps that's why we came upon them — a sign to consider something different."

He could hear the despair in her voice. He reached out and grabbed her hand. "We can do this, Alexandra. You are not alone in this. Our goals are the same. If we don't find the fortress, perhaps migration is another alternative. But for now, let's focus on the primary task. One day at a time." She smiled faintly and nodded. "Now close your eyes, queen, and listen."

She closed her eyes. Nothing happened. She opened them and exhaled deeply. "I don't hear anything. I don't know what I'm supposed to be listening for. My head is filled with too many thoughts to focus. I can't shut out the noise thundering inside my head."

"It has mattered…"

Alexandra looked down at the ground and saw Tick-Tock staring up at her. *"It has mattered, queen…that you sought to go outside your comfort zone and do the impossible."*

"Reginald…"

"It is easy to give into the shadows of the heart, my queen. And it is common. Only a

rare few fight against the tide to turn it toward something good….you are not common. That is why you are queen."

He stopped talking.

Alexandra stared at him for several moments. What he had just said…*mattered*. She suddenly felt at peace, consoled by his words. Realizing that he spoke from the past, Alexandra knew his words originally spoken were for another. Knowing that he now meant them for her, filled her with a deep sense of resilience; the way she imagined it must have filled Rebekah. The noise inside her head suddenly quieted, all anxiousness leaving her. She closed her eyes.

She breathed in long and deep as the sun began to rise. The wind gently blew through the trees, swirling around her. Byron watched as her dark hair lifted in waves, almost as if the wind were speaking its whispers softly to her.

Like Diana.

She tilted her head to the side, listening. She slowly turned her head east. She opened her eyes and looked out at the landscape below. The mountain was no longer in front of her but east of her. "The horse was right." She turned and looked at Byron. "Let's go."

"Where are we going, my queen?"

They had camped near a spot just outside the border to their side of the realm. A small fire burned, keeping them warm as the temperature started to drop; they continued to head south.

She hesitated before blurting out, "To the Realm of the Six Kingdoms."

Keys was deafly silent. "I should say five now that the Bird Clan is gone."

"It was once more than even that."

"So, you know."

He nodded. He took a small stick to stoke the fire. "I always assumed you did too."

Diana continued to stare at him, feeling both foolish for her unknowingness as well as a bit embarrassed for her actions now. "I did and I didn't."

"And now that you do? What is your intent?"

"I…" She looked out at the darkened landscape beyond. "I don't know."

He stared at her for a few moments before he said, "You are looking for a connection to this world, my queen. But not one that will bring back the chains that once weighed us down. Nor one where we would be forced to apologize for an existence we hold no part in. Yet you feel the void anyway. We all do."

Diana was struck silent. She watched her warrior as he absently continued to stoke the fire. His words were true. It was how she had felt all her life but never really knew why. The feeling over the years came and went, only surfacing in certain moments in life that warranted the questions, What's next? What is this life all about?

There always seemed to be something missing, like a deep hole longing to be filled. It hit her hard in that moment as she watched the flames in the fire. Now that the remnants from another realm had found their way to her kingdom, impacting her life by simple knowledge angrily shared...what next?

Diana exhaled deeply before speaking. "What am I supposed to do with this knowledge now, Keys? Knowing that my ancestors did such harm? How is it to be rectified?"

"What makes you think it hasn't been?"

"Because others remember."

"Others who did not live during that epoch, my queen. What is it to those who never witnessed but only heard? What is it to them to see into the past instead of looking at the present? It only blinds. Darkness arises in such moments. You are not responsible for the choices of the past. You are only responsible for the footsteps ahead. Look to the untraveled path beyond."

"The way the bull king looked at me..."

"Do not focus on what he sees. Show him another vision. Do not retreat into what he holds onto but live as you always have: as queen of a clan that forged a better tomorrow."

She smiled faintly in appreciation. "You want to know something else? I envied them: the kings and queen."

He looked up at her with his large, almond eyes. "Why?"

Flashes of Byron, Minotauro, Daniel and Alexandra bantering with one another filled her mind. "There was a bond. A friendship they all had. It's not that I need friends or that our clan needs kinship or community with others, it's just...we are not as alone as I thought we were. And it was comforting. It opened my mind to an idea that I never knew I longed to have. Our clan was not meant to be so isolated — although, we stand together that way." She paused. "And here are these kings and queen from different clans standing together for a common purpose, daring to risk their own lives for something far greater than themselves...and I want to help them. They are *remnants,* Keys."

The hair in Keys' mane rose at her words, their impact rolling down his spine as the chills covered his massive body. He threw another piece of wood onto the fire.

"And we were once part of their realm; a clan amongst them." She was overwhelmed by all the thoughts swirling inside her head. "And on one hand, we're lucky to have been banished, to not have been a part of their tragedy. But on the other hand, we belong to their history and journey…so what if our part to play…aids in their triumph?

"I've been thinking about time, Keys, and the timing upon which knowledge and purpose is revealed. It's for a specific reason, meant for a larger design. And yet, I feel the need to move. To go. To see. Even when I see nothing and don't know why I'm really going. I just know…I must." She exhaled deeply, "I don't know. My heart is saying go and see. But when I get there, I don't know how I'll truly feel or what I'm really hoping to do once I arrive." She laughed. "I suppose I'm trying to say…I don't know what I'm doing."

"Neither do those remnants. No one has ever reached the Element Fortress. Neither of us knows what the next steps will be. I suppose that's the risk one takes when trying to be better than what we already are and do better than what we've already done before."

"Is that what we're doing, Keys?"

He turned his large eyes toward her, his eyes boring into hers. "It is in the doing that we become."

Hundreds of miles away, Rhodes — the lord of the sea — stood atop a ledge of the Element Fortress looking out across the forest. He could see the wind blowing through the leaves, causing the entire landscape to sway, as if it had a breath all its own. He narrowed his turquoise-colored eyes as the wind moved toward him, suddenly whipping wildly around him, forming a funnel that encircled him as it wove through his golden hair.

He spoke to it. "Your queen is about to cause a rumble throughout the realm and arouse the heartbeat once thought dead. And she just might be killed while trying to do it. Brave."

"Queens always are, brother."

"Not all of them."

"You could help her, you know — your chosen queen."

His turquoise-colored eyes glanced up at the wind. "She has yet to seek my help."

"Unnecessary suffering is beneath us, brother."

"Not if it can bring about change."

The wind swirled around him once more before moving back out across the land, and out toward the direction of the realm.

Rhodes was moved. He had not expected the horse queen to leave her domain in search of a haunted past with no other purpose than to simply understand. Another queen doing something unexpected. Even the bull queen surprised him, stepping forth with an army beside her to protect the vulnerable and the weak — just as her king would have done if he had been there.

He watched for moments like these. When someone did something so utterly unexpected, that their single choice shifted the course of history. Sometimes it was good, sometimes not. But these moments? It intrigued him. It almost gave him…hope. He had been disappointed so many times over the years in a lack of superb choices by independent minds and wills, that he forgot what it was to witness better moments. Even his chosen queen had yet to have one, for she had yet to do…*anything*.

Off that single thought, Rhodes suddenly stood, jolted into anger at the reminder that those gifted with the grace to do something remarkable in this world had yet to do it — and quite possibly — never would. Was it a waste of a choice in choosing her? Knowing what was coming, he hoped not. But thinking about the queens he had just seen shift the world toward something good, it angered him even more as the reminder that his own chosen queen had yet to do something selfless. To do something…*great*.

He knew only time would tell, but seeing the shadows moving in the trees down below, Rhodes knew time was running out.

Damn the raven. He was supposed to keep others out, not open the door widely to let others in. He was not supposed to slaughter those in the realm but finish what Palimus started…it was the north that was the path. It was the north that held no boundary. And it was the north from which the cunning king would come.

He plunged his fists into the rock wall beside him; snow forming a path all down the mountain. Rhodes stepped onto the white powder and traveled down the slope in lightning speed and out toward the shadows of the trees.

Another unexpected moment. Not from a queen, however, but from an extremely ruthless king.

XVIX

Alexandra led the men across the outer realm: a dizzying maze of movement and control as the landscape shifted all around them, almost as if the world was daring them to pay attention, challenging them to watch for the subtle signs of change all around them to see if they understood the silent message the universe was giving them. And with each shift of land, tree, and stream, Alexandra led them on, following the signs, listening to the whispers on the wind as they moved along with it. It was exhilarating. It was frightening.

How had she not seen? How had she not heard...all these things before?

As the wind blew through her hair, Alexandra felt it: the connection and realization that the power behind it was beyond this world. She felt, for the first time, a connection to something beyond herself. That Wind itself was beckoning to her. She could not help but long to follow it — this yielding would lead to something good wherever it led; she could feel the benevolence within it. And it was in that moment that Alexandra realized that this feeling of inspiration, motivation and excitement was one she had always felt when she heard Reginald speak, when she stood at her father's side, and when she had met Rebekah.

Alexandra was so focused on yielding to that power that was calling her to a higher purpose, that she suddenly recognized she was in a place and moment in time she had always wanted to be — *leading.*

Knowing the kings were behind her, trusting her to lead them to the place of their desire, she felt confident in her steps, powerful in her decisions as she traversed across the labyrinth of time and space that was bending to her movements. It was then that the Element Fortress finally came into view.

She slowed her steps and calmed her breaths as she stopped before a large lake that rested as the barrier between her and the fortress. Alexandra looked all around for an opening to cross but could find no further extension of nature or shift of motion in the landscape. Even the wind had ceased

83

blowing. In that moment, Alexandra knew that the next steps were a test of will, a freedom of choice to keep going or not — to give up or overcome as she stood before the banks of the Element Fortress.

Byron stared at it, "There it is."

Daniel arrived and looked at the monstrous edifice up ahead, "I guess we didn't need the maps after all. We just needed Alexandra."

They smiled at one another. They were almost there.

"I can see the top of the mountain," Daniel said.

"But how do we get there?" It was Minotauro.

Byron's eyes scanned the mountain, examining each crevice, searching each ledge. "We climb." He moved toward the lake's edge staring at the still water before him. A little too still. He turned and looked at Alexandra. "Can you swim across?"

"I can try." She turned to Tick-Tock. "I'm going to need your help."

Tick-Tock's head swiveled to snow owl as he spoke in Amun's voice, "Queen, you will be safe with me." He held out his raven hand. She grabbed hold.

Daniel nodded. "Let's go."

They entered the lake and began to swim across. Byron led the way. Alexandra clutched onto Tick-Tock's neck as he paddled across. Daniel glided underwater while Minotauro struggled to keep pace up top. When they were halfway across, Alexandra's heart skipped a beat; she had heard something — *movement in the water.* She looked all around but saw nothing but a shift in the waves. They were growing in height…but how? It was then she noticed her breath fogging on the air as well. It was getting colder.

Byron noticed it too. It was a moment of déjà vu; a piece of the memory to the nightmare he had forgotten.

"Tok…tok…tok…"

He heard Poe's voice inside his head…and all went black. He stopped mid-stroke as it all came back to him once. He remembered…Wolf Lake. He had fallen from the sky. He was swimming to shore when the water turned colder, and the water began to freeze. Byron immediately snapped out of his memory. *"MOVE!"* he swam faster, *"MOVE!!!"*

Tick-Tock's emerald stone was glowing vibrantly. He growled and immediately began to swim faster than even Alexandra realized he could. Minotauro picked up pace as best as he could. The ice was headed straight for them, forming directly behind them. If they did not move fast enough, they would be trapped underneath a sheet of it.

Tick-Tock's head swiveled around to face the way they had come. He was looking at something in the shadows of the woods behind them. He growled lowly in Reginald's voice, *"You do not belong here."*

Daniel was swimming rapidly underneath the current when he spotted the ice forming overhead. The temperature continued to drop. He had not come up for air in some time and needed to move faster. As he ascended to the water line, the sheet of ice had already formed overhead. He butted up against it, slamming his fist against it as he tried to break through. It was then he saw something odd. A man's foot appeared on top of the ice directly overhead. He narrowed his eyes and saw an athletic looking man standing on top…and then the man was gone. Daniel continued pushing forward, racing against the path of the ice but to no avail. He began to panic as he realized there was no opening. His lungs had begun to burn. He needed air, and he needed it fast.

Byron had reached the shore.

"Byron!"

He turned and saw Minotauro struggling in the water. He dove back in and swam as fast as he could to get to the bull king. The moment he reached him, he saw the ice extending toward them like a cloud covering the rays of the sun — and it was coming their way. "Kick! *Now!*" Grabbing hold of Minotauro, he lurched forward, focusing only on the view ahead. "Harder!" Minotauro kicked as hard as he could as Byron continued to swim. They reached the shoreline just as the ice froze over. It barely missed their feet as they watched the ice continue to harden.

Byron looked down shore and spotted Alexandra and Tick-Tock. They had reached it in time.

Minotauro asked, "Where's Daniel?"

Byron looked out at the frozen lake but saw nothing and no one.

Minotauro shouted at the lake, *"KING!!!"*

Alexandra heard their shouts and looked out across the frozen lake, seeing no one there. *"DANIEL!!!"* She dropped to her knees and continued shouting his name. *"DANIEL!!!"*

Byron and Minotauro could hear the fear in her voice. Byron looked at the thin ice quickly hardening. "We'll fall straight through if it doesn't harden fast enough."

Minotauro lowered his head, looking at the pattern of ice. "Not in all the spots. My body weight is too heavy. You'll have to walk across it. Bring Bane."

Byron clutched the scepter at his side and nodded. "We have to move fast." They suddenly realized Tick-Tock was beside them. He lowered to all fours on his wolf legs, motioning for Byron to climb on top; he did. As Tick-Tock raced onto the ice, sprinting across the lake, all three of his heads shifted and turned as they searched for the lion king. Byron scoured the ice for any sign or movement reflected underneath.

Nothing.

Minotauro and Alexandra watched from the shore. "They'll find him, Alexandra." But she was not listening to him. She was listening for Daniel instead. She instinctively reached for her silver medallion hidden under her shirt, clutching it tightly as she lowered her head, she whispered the word, "Please."

Upon reply, the frozen lake started to splinter and crack as the ice shifted.

Understanding the sounds and what they meant, Alexandra's head snapped up. "Go right!"

Tick-Tock shifted position off her command. Byron shouted, "I see him!" Byron jumped off Tick-Tock and skidded on his knees, sliding onto a thin patch of ice. He raised his bone scepter Bane high above his head and slammed it down, smashing the ice into pieces as Daniel's hand punched through. Tick-Tock immediately pulled Daniel up out of the water, wrapping his eagle and raven wings around Daniel to provide his body with heat.

Byron looked at Daniel's pale skin and blue lips as the lion king stared back at him, shivering violently. "Thanks." Byron simply nodded. He was staring at the raven claw, thrown back into his own forgotten memory.

"Get off the lake!" It was Minotauro.

Byron and Daniel looked down and saw the ice thinning. *"MOVE!"* Byron was immediately on his feet. Tick-Tock picked Daniel up and turned to shore. Byron began to run across the ice but slipped, going facedown. Tick-Tock immediately grabbed at his shirt, dragging Byron across the ice with his eagle claw while carrying Daniel with his raven arm.

Tick-Tock skated on his wolf legs across the ice as it continued cracking and splitting. The moment they reached shore, they turned and looked at the lake in disbelief — it had turned back to water once again.

Minotauro glared at the body of water. "Ice...is such a bastard."

All the while, Tick-Tock stared across the lake at the shadows of the trees. Not everything was as it seemed.

XX

Daniel was in a deep sleep, dreaming of a large bonfire. Rebekah was dancing before its flames as the eagle rose up on her right and the raven on her left.

"Remember...remember..."

His eyes snapped open. He turned his head and saw Tick-Tock staring at him with his large bulbous eyes. The rest of the remnants were fast asleep, only the remains of a small fire remained.

Daniel had fallen into a deep sleep after being pulled from the lake; his body heavy with exhaustion. The kings and queen were just as exhausted and fell asleep shortly after Daniel did. Like always, Tick-Tock was wide awake, never eating, never sleeping.

He studied the totem for a long while, taking in his form and the care upon which he seemed to be crafted. His eyes roamed to the green stone hanging around his neck, trying to determine what made it flicker to life at certain moments of danger while remaining dormant during others. He continued on, thinking about the moments when Tick-Tock spoke and how and by who. He started pondering the moments when he chose to act, and wondered about the times he stood still. What was the determining factor?

Tick-Tock's head slowly turned to horned owl — the head of the future. "Defend till the end, only then."

Daniel's eyes narrowed. "What is it I am supposed to remember?"

Tick-Tock remained silent.

"I know you hear them...the thoughts inside my head. Dreams are no different. You know what I see the moment I close my eyes. So tell me...what am I supposed to remember?"

His head slowly swiveled to snow owl as he spoke in Marcus' voice, "Your compass."

A wave of emotion washed over Daniel at the sound of his uncle's voice. He remembered the letter Marcus had left him. It was right before Marcus had left the den, never to return. A sick feeling filled Daniel as he swallowed hard and asked, "Why did Poe kill him?"

The moment he asked the question, he could see the raven claw clench into a tight ball as the bulbous eyes staring back at him suddenly closed. He watched as Tick-Tock's eyes scrunched together tightly as if he were struggling with something deep inside. His eyes suddenly snapped open. Daniel could see a red glow behind them — scarlet like Poe's. The lion king slowly sat up and stared the totem down.

"Tell me."

Out came Poe's voice, *"Tok...tok...tok...lionsss cannot be trusted."*

Daniel's eyes slit to a cat as he suddenly erupted, "Excuses!" His shouts echoed across the landscape, "Why did he have to die?!?"

"He would have found it."

"What?"

"The way..."

Daniel paused before saying, "Go on."

"Creaturesss from long ago...banished from the realm. Their bloodline wasss the darkest the kingsss and queensss had ever ssseen. They long to be found, king. They yearn to seek their revenge in order to rectify. Darkness within. Destruction isss their footstep. One of their kind found their way to my queen'sss domain. And where there isss one, othersss follow. He would have found them. He wanted to."

"*LIES!* He only sought to do what we have done! Find the rain!" Daniel was furious. He knew his uncle. "He was selfless! He was hopeful! He was not out to find a way to bring darkness to the realm or the den! *He wanted to find the stone!*"

"He feared my queen! Loved her as a boy, despised her as a man! He feared her. He feared our clan!"

Tick-Tock's head spun around three times before speaking in Marcus' voice again, *"If she is awakened, there's no telling what she'll do! Vengeance or mercy...she could annihilate us all with her army of birds! Stay away from that kingdom! Stay away from the queen!"*

Daniel remembered that moment. He remembered the look on his uncle's face when he shouted the words, but he still refused to believe the raven's tale.

"She doesn't find me noble!" It was a young boy's voice. *"Why won't she let me inside?"*

Tick-Tock's head quickly swiveled back to barn owl. His voice immediately shifted from a young boy to one that was low and lethal. "He knew the den was hated, king. He knew he needed to find a way to bring the rain — with or without the bird queen. With or without a stone. He had seen the waterfall before. He knew he would find it again. The waterfall is their gate. He had reached it when the raven found him." His head swiveled around three times before stopping once more on the snow owl.

"Whose gate?"

"*Othersss…*"

Another voice similar to Poe's spoke through Tick-Tock, *"We build for that moment. We grow for that time. We become…for what we need to be. In thisss, the ravensss will alwaysss defend."*

And there it was — his answer.

Tick-Tock's head swiveled slowly back to barn owl. He sat back down and said nothing more. He simply stared at the dying flames; his eyes no longer glowing. It was then that Daniel realized everyone was wide awake, looking at him in complete silence. Without looking at anyone, he stood and walked toward the trees. He needed to be alone.

XXI

Daniel stood in the shadows between a few small trees. He was angry. He had not been this enraged since the night he found Marcus' body in Wolf Lake. He could feel his muscles tensing as he shook in rage as images of Marcus' bloated form and mutilated body filled his mind.

Marcus had left the den to seek a stone to bring the rain! Not a gate to let others in! Anyone who understood his clan knew that seeking help was against everything the den stood for. They did not *need* any help! They *never* needed any help! And what did he mean, lions cannot be trusted?!? Just because his great-grandfather had tried to kill the bird queen didn't mean the rest of the den operated off sinister plots and actions.

The more Daniel thought about all that the totem had to say, the angrier he became. And he knew it was his fault. He had asked the question to the one being inside Tick-Tock who had the answer. What good he thought was going to come of it never crossed his mind before he engaged, but the peace and closure he was seeking was drowned out by the pain and anger he felt the moment he heard Poe's response.

"Are you all right?"

Daniel turned as Alexandra approached. "No." He looked away from her, still feeling the heat rising inside his body as his heart hammered away inside his chest. "Do you believe the totem's tale?"

She paused before replying. "I don't know. Hood told me about the creature's footprint they had found on Bird Clan soil out in the fields. Poe and a few golden eagle warriors discovered it. He told me the story after Tick-Tock mentioned it that day in your library."

He turned to look at her. When he did not say anything, she continued, "Hood said that Poe fled the realm in search of it. When he returned, he was changed. Whatever he found drove him mad."

Daniel glared at her, "*Whatever he found?* How about what he *did!* He was mad the moment he awoke from his slumber. I have the scars to prove it!"

Alexandra narrowed her eyes at his statement, completely unaware of Daniel's encounter with Poe. She was about to ask him about it when he said, "You said that the ravens protected the clans. Do you still believe that?" But he did not wait for her response as he continued, "Is that why Poe is built into Tick-Tock…our guardian?" But before Alexandra could reply, he continued, "What exactly was the raven protecting when he killed my uncle and dumped him in *your* lake! As if he were trash. Mere carnage, Alexandra! After he tried to kill us all? Poe wasn't protecting anyone! He was trying to start a war between the clans, and he used my uncle to do it!"

She spoke in soft tones, trying to calm him. "If you already had your answer for Poe's actions, why did you ask the question?"

Daniel did not respond.

"Tick-Tock is not Poe."

His eyes were slit to a cat. "Then what is he?"

Seeing his eyes change, she whispered her reply, "I don't know. But the more questions you ask him, the more he will tell you. But I don't know that having the answers to everything, especially the past, is anything good. It keeps you there."

"You would know."

She was taken aback by his response. "What's that supposed to mean?"

"You *live* in the past." He looked out at the trees, "Mourning your father while leaving the rest of us kings to start the work at the dam without you. We all wanted to grieve and hide away in our kingdoms. I still do. I'm allowed this moment, Alexandra."

Alexandra was stunned by what he had just said to her. She had never seen him this angry before. He had never spoken this way to her before, and he wasn't done.

"I try my best to be purposeful. I'm particular about the words I use when I speak. I take my time, weighing my options constantly before I act. It's a curse I've placed upon myself, that others count on me to be the calm in their storm. The king they can count on. And sometimes, I want to rage, to shout with the lightning, to run in the violence of the wind inside the storm and be the lightning itself. To simply be angry that someone I loved was taken out of this world. Angry that others did it and found it justified. Because that's all I'm hearing you and the totem say. Marcus' legacy is not remembered as it should be. The lions cannot be trusted." He almost spat the word. He looked down, closing his fist tightly. "*I miss him*, Alexandra. And I have every right to ask the question. I have every right to be angry with the totem's story. True, justified, understood or not, I have the right. I don't want to forget him and all he did for me. He mattered to me. They all mattered to me. The ruthless ones. The vicious ones. The forgotten ones. My family…the way they lived, the way they died…*matters*. Even if it only matters to me. And it matters more to me now because I almost saw them again today."

"Daniel…"

Daniel turned away from her. "I want to be alone."

Alexandra just stood there.

Looking back at her, he shouted, *"Go!"*

She jumped at his shout and swiftly walked back toward the campfire.

Daniel cringed the moment he saw her reaction at his shout. He did not mean to take it out on her. Marcus' death had nothing to do with her or her clan. But he was angry, and she was the easiest target to take it out on. He knew better. He knew she was only trying to help but did it anyway. He exhaled deeply in disappointment at himself and looked down at his tightly clenched fist, slowly opening it to reveal a tiny object in the palm of his hand.

It was the compass.

Minotauro was staring at Tick-Tock. He was not the only one disturbed by the story the totem had just told. Byron was standing watch for Daniel and Alexandra's return. Tick-Tock remained quiet, continuing to stare at the campfire in silence.

Byron sat down beside Minotauro and looked at Tick-Tock. "Do you believe him?"

"That the den is hated? Yes."

"I meant…"

"I know what you meant. Nothing surprises me anymore. There's another clan with a darkened bloodline, all the more reason to get to the fortress, get what we need and head home."

Alexandra returned and sat down by the campfire. The kings could see she had been crying. Neither knew what to say. It was a rare moment when they had seen Daniel get upset about anything, let alone seeing the wolf queen cry.

"How's Daniel?"

She looked down, trying to control her emotions. "Angry. I seem to have upset him more. I don't have…great words."

Minotauro replied, "You don't need great words, Alexandra. Sometimes it's enough to just know you're there."

She remained quiet.

"What is that?"

Alexandra shifted her gaze and looked at Byron, "What?"

He pointed to the silver medallion resting against her chest. He had caught a glimmer of its shining metal as she sat by the firelight. She reached up and touched it, not realizing it had been exposed from beneath her clothing. She looked down and reluctantly pulled her hand away.

The moment Byron and Minotauro saw its intricate design, their attention shifted from Tick-Tock to Alexandra. "Where did you get it?"

"*When* did you get it?"

"I found it." She placed the medallion back under her shirt. "It washed ashore at my lake just after I buried my father."

Minotauro narrowed his eyes. "It never occurred to you that it looks like Queen Rebekah's and the horse's?"

"*Queen* Diana" Byron replied.

Minotauro ignored him. "Rebekah honored the sun and could call the light down with her medallion. The horse commands the wind. Yours has a wave etched over it."

Alexandra laughed nervously. "You don't think I could command the waves?" The two kings looked at one another. "I can't even swim. I don't honor water or the moon. I've never honored any of the creators. I didn't even know they existed until recently."

"You honored your father. Perhaps, he honored the creators in some way."

"Or your other ancestors."

"Maybe."

"May I see it?"

She took it off and handed it to Minotauro. He studied it, clutching it in his strong fist. He looked up at the night sky, reaching his hand up, and said, "RAIN!"

Byron laughed.

Minotauro glared at him. "I wasn't trying to be funny, Byron. What if it worked?"

"Well, if it's meant to, it wouldn't be coming from you. It was given to Alexandra."

Minotauro turned and handed it back to Alexandra. "Try it."

She laughed nervously, "This is all so very strange."

"Why didn't you say anything about it?"

"I don't know." But she did know. It was a deeply personal gift given to her during one of her darkest moments. She did not want to share it with anyone. Yet, she knew they were right. The medallion was a gift from the Creators, meant to be used for the good of others. Now that it was out in the open, Alexandra held the medallion delicately in her hands. She looked over at Tick-Tock. "How do I use this?"

Minotauro answered, "Yell, *RAIN!*"

Byron hit him in the chest.

"What?"

Tick-Tock slowly turned his barn owl head toward her.,

"Call…his…name…"

XXII

Diana had reached the border to the realm. She could see the change in the landscape immediately: it was drier, withering, *dying*. She jumped off Keys and stood looking at the ground for quite some time. She studied the state of the trees, noticing their skeletal design. Even they appeared barren as their twisted branches reached out to her like beggars in the road. It was so unlike the thick green trees of her own home.

No wonder...

She suddenly felt a pinch of empathy for the remnants.

They began their trek through the deserted forest, walking silently amongst them until coming to a small lake. Diana stared at the body of water sensing no life inside it.

"OW...*WOOOOO!!!!!*"

A wolf howled in the distance.

"My queen, get on my back."

Diana did not hesitate as she mounted her warrior. They immediately took off in the opposite direction of the howl. They raced through the woods, weaving through the trees as they moved east. More howls sounded in the distance.

Diana looked up at the fading sunlight — *feeding time*. She clutched her medallion tight, closed her eyes and said a silent prayer. The wind picked up behind them, pushing them forward as Keys was propelled faster and faster as they raced over a hill. As the trees dissolved into open fields, the horse queen saw another change in landscape as they trampled over fields of dead vines covered with blackened roses over small gravestones. Diana's heart stilled the moment she realized the acres of gravestones formed a massive cemetery — it was Critter Country. On and on they rode, mile after mile, until it seemed the sight of gravestones would never cease.

"Where are we, queen?"

"I don't know."

"There is nothing but death here. A clan's downfall."

"We ride toward life, Keys. Keep going."

They rode on until a group of white mountains emerged in the distance. "There!" Keys rode faster as they climbed the hill toward Bird Kingdom. Unbeknownst to them, two members of the wolf pack followed from behind.

Daniel looked to Byron to take the lead as the gorilla king tested out his grip on the smooth rock. Finding his footing, he moved swiftly up the mountain. The rest of the group followed, matching his movements grip for grip, groove for groove. Tick-Tock brought up the rear as they moved to the first ledge. Minotauro was struggling and almost slipped. With a deep exhale of frustration, he looked down and saw Tick-Tock. "Can't you fly? Find an opening or something?"

Daniel looked down at Tick-Tock climbing up the mountain with ease. "Perhaps his torso weighs him down."

"I don't see how. Poe and Reginald were taller and more muscular than he is. Besides, he seemed to skate across the ice pretty easily."

"Perhaps it's his heads that are too heavy then. He does have three."

Daniel noticed Tick-Tock had stopped climbing and was staring up at them. Without any further sound, Tick-Tock lunged up the mountain, past Byron and onto the first overhang. He reached down with his raven claw, extending it to Byron. The moment he saw the ebony talon, the gorilla king's entire body broke out into a cold sweat. He tried to calm his breathing and slow the pounding in his chest. But no matter how hard he tried, he was reminded of Poe. It was almost as if Tick-Tock knew it too as he studied Byron's reaction. Tick-Tock's head swiveled to snow owl. *"'Protect' he said….protect like the ravens of old…"* It was Rebekah's voice. Then Poe's followed, *"Tok…tok…tok…"*

"Just grab it, Byron! We can't hang on forever!" It was Minotauro.

Byron slowly reached for Tick-Tock's hand. He was immediately lifted to the top of the ledge. The rest of the group followed until Tick-Tock had pulled them up onto the ledge.

"That's more like it." Minotauro patted Tick-Tock on the shoulder. "Work smarter not harder. Right, buddy?" Tick-Tock did not respond. He was busy looking down at the base of the mountain. He growled lowly just as the emerald stone began to glow.

Daniel stepped up beside him. "What is it?"

"I hear it too." It was Alexandra. It was then that she saw her breath fog on the air.

The mountain began to rumble and shake. Where the gray and brown colored rocks had been visible only moments before, they suddenly turned white as snow rapidly crystallized over them. Alexandra's eyes suddenly grew wide as she shouted, *"AVALANCHE!!!!"*

The remnants flattened against the side of the mountain as the snow pummeled down over them. Tick-Tock shielded Alexandra as the rest held on with every ounce of strength they had as the rocks, snow and boulders continued to fall all around them. She screamed.

Daniel shouted, *"HOLD ON!!!"*

The rocks smashed down all around them, breaking into shards. And just as fast as it had started, the avalanche suddenly stopped. Minotauro looked down at the devastation below. "Not a mudslide but an avalanche. Great."

The path they had just climbed had been completely wiped out. All that held them to the mountain was the narrow ledge they were standing on. He turned his head upward and said to Byron, "Ice is such an ass."

"Wrong clan."

Alexandra looked up and listened. She suddenly shouted, *"Move! Fast!"*

Byron swung up onto the ledge. Minotauro extended his hand and pulled Alexandra up. They swiftly climbed. Unbeknownst to anyone, Tick-Tock was looking down at the dismantled pathway; his emerald stone no longer glowing.

XXIII

"Keys...look at it."

Bird Kingdom.

It still stood tall in all its beauty, surrounded by the Great White Mountains. The horse queen was in awe, never having seen such architecture or craftsmanship before. It was so different than the thatched homes in her forest. Looking at the marble pillars, stained glass windows, pyres, towers and domes, the horse queen was overwhelmed. "This must have been some queen to have lived in a palace like this." She looked all around but saw no movement. She listened closer but heard no sound. "Do you think it's abandoned?"

Understanding her intent, Keys replied, "We must be on our guard no matter what, my queen. We are strangers here. We have enemies here."

They moved silently toward the large gates still covered in vines and roses. They crossed through and entered the clan gardens. It was massive. Trees and flowers that covered the grounds had begun to wither and die. Regardless of its current state, Diana could see the beauty it held. "Can you imagine waking up to this every morning?"

Keys said nothing as they moved closer toward the palace entrance. Diana looked up and saw a balcony overhead. She dismounted as Keys rose up onto his two hind legs. They pushed the doors open and stepped inside.

Keys gripped the hilt of his sword as they entered the palace. A long hallway stretched out before them. As they walked silently through the hall, the portraits of all the kings and queens of the clan came into view.

"I wonder which one she is?"

"Who?"

"The last bird queen."

They took in portrait after portrait. Diana looked back at all the paintings lining the long corridor. She walked slowly down the hall, taking in all the faces of the Bird Clan royalty. She stopped at one portrait in particular.

A gentle breeze blew past her, speaking the name of old.

"Palimus…"

Keys stepped up beside her. "I remember this king's name from the Old War."

Looking at the mischievous smile captured on the king's face and the joyful glow residing behind his knowing eyes, Diana tilted her head to the side. "Not all the kings and queens in this realm were fools." She saw the medallion hanging around his neck. "This king and his clan honored the Sun." Diana gently touched the medallion adorning her neck. "They were powerful, Keys."

They moved along, combing through the palace until reaching a set of golden doors. "Well, do we dare?"

Keys lowered his head, "You're asking me that now?"

She pushed them open. Sprawled out before them was a grand ballroom. It was covered in slate-colored marble with pillars that circulated around the room. Diana gasped as she looked up at the glass-domed ceiling that showcased the magnificent blue sky. Sunlight poured down upon them, hi-lighting the gold trim around the pillars, lighting them afire. Paintings of bird clan warriors covered the walls. Keys stepped in front of one of them, gazing up at the dark raven assassin — it was Damon. Seeing the lethal look of the warrior, he gripped his hilt even tighter. Warriors to be reckoned with indeed.

"Keys…"

He turned to find his queen slowly climbing a small group of stairs at the opposite end of the room. A large glass box rested at the top. The glass to its lid had been smashed. Shards of glass covered the floor.

"Be careful, my queen."

Diana saw the satin pillow and padded sheet that lay inside. "This is a coffin…" The realization suddenly hit her. She looked all around. "Where is the queen?"

A strong breeze blew the golden doors wide open, causing them to slam up against the walls, their sound echoing throughout the room. Keys pulled his sword as the sound of a stampede thundered from outside the garden. Diana and her warrior raced toward the courtyard. When they spotted the source of the stampede, they halted mid-stride, rapidly backtracking to hide amongst the shadows.

Bulls.

Keys shoved his queen back against the wall. "Inside!"

They watched, crouched behind a nearby window, as the bull, ram and buffalo soldiers moved out across the gardens to a field beyond. Diana turned and ran down the hallway.

"My queen!" Keys dropped to all fours and raced after her.

She ran up a staircase and down several hallways, following the sound of the stampede. She ran down another hall and burst through a set of doors that led to a bedchamber. Diana ran toward a large balcony at the other end of the room. When she got there, she crouched down and watched as the powerful beasts entered the fields. Keys was suddenly beside her.

"They're gathering food."

They watched in silence as the bull warriors gathered up the crop, loading it onto large carts before charging back in the direction from where they came.

"And they're doing it without their king to command them."

"That's just it, Keys. He's already given the order. The bull king's presence remains without him needing to fill it. They honor him in this act."

They continued to watch the muscular beasts working together as one solid force; their sheer strength and collective force was overwhelming. All Diana kept thinking about was the look behind Minotauro's eyes as he spoke to her — the hatred she saw behind them.

Banished.

A deep feeling of dread pitted itself in the bottom of her stomach. She shrank back from the balcony and into the bedchambers. Keys followed her in silence.

"You are pale, my queen." He quickly pulled a chair for her to sit in just in time before she collapsed.

"Maybe this wasn't such a good idea."

Keys knelt down beside her. "Look at whose house you're in." She finally looked around and realized where they were. "This is a queen's chamber." Diana remained silent, looking at all the beautiful items in the room. She had never seen anything like it before. She suddenly felt...poor, unworthy.

"If this queen could stand before lions, you can stand before bulls."

Banished. Ashamed.

"I don't know, Keys. Sitting in this room, seeing the size of this kingdom, it exudes power...authority. How could one not know that a queen resides here? Come to our forest, any tribe could exist there...but a queen? Those bull warriors out there will see right through me." A gentle breeze blew through the room. Diana lowered her head against Keys and touched the side of his face. She closed her eyes and said, "Sometimes, I wish I weren't queen, Keys."

"Then I'm glad it is a wish that you have never been granted, for I would follow no other..."

Down below, a bull slowed his step. Another bull followed suit grunting, "What is it?"

"Someone went inside."

The other bull turned and saw the doors to the palace; they were open. A bark sounded from the shadows of the garden trees. "The wolves...they sense it too."

In reply, two wolves emerged from the shadows and dropped to all fours. They raced through the kingdom gates. The bulls dropped down and immediately followed.

XXIV

"I don't see an entrance."

Night had fallen. The remnants were seated around a warm fire on one of the cliff ledges trying to come up with their next plan of action. Tick-Tock stood behind Alexandra, crouched silently in the shadows, watching for any sign of threat from down below.

"There has to be a way in. Some kind of door or pathway."

"The only way to know is to climb."

They had been climbing the mountain all day. Daniel led the group. Even after the avalanche, he and Alexandra had not really spoken to one another. It made the day awkward for the other kings, but Minotauro knew they would figure it out. If they planned on being married, they would have to.

Thinking about his own wife, Lydia, he felt a tinge of loneliness. He could tell that he was growing weary of this quest and longed to be home with his queen. He shut out thoughts of her, knowing full well he would only miss her more. And the more he missed her, the more irritable he knew he would become living another day without being beside her.

"Maybe we missed it. Perhaps we descend and go all the way around the mountain to see if there are doorways around the base?"

The ground began to rumble.

Minotauro looked back at the fortress, "What was that?"

Alexandra replied, "It came from inside the mountain."

All eyes turned toward the mountain. Everyone remained silent as the rumblings continued. The power from beyond could be felt amongst the remnants.

"Earth and Wind guided us here. Why not guide us inside?" Minotauro asked.

Alexandra replied, "I haven't heard or felt the wind all day. It's almost as if it's done speaking — at least for now."

Byron's brow furrowed as he as he said, "Ice seems to be the one taking

108

over now that we're here."

"But didn't Rhodes help the Bird Clan? He froze her kingdom."

"He wanted her to live, that's clear. But his actions to us seem to speak otherwise."

Tick-Tock turned his head to the conversation but said nothing.

Byron looked to the lion king, "Daniel, did you read anywhere else in your uncle's books where the elements helped other kings in the realm?"

"Earth tried to help the Critter Clan."

"When?"

Daniel paused. His voice was barely a whisper, "When the gorilla and bull clans invaded their land, capturing their people for food." The entire camp went silent.

Alexandra shivered at the thought as she shook her head. "Even if we get inside, what are we supposed to do? Ask them to ignore the last fifty years of cannibalism, war and slaughter…and help us to survive anyway?"

Daniel replied, "If they've seen the horrible acts from the past, they would have had to have seen all the good we are doing to rectify what our ancestors did in the present. That has to count for something…or why would Agoura and Zephyrus guide us to the fortress if we weren't supposed to be here?"

"To annihilate us once and for all. Slaughter us here, all of our clans die. All except Sebastian's clan anyway."

Alexandra was horrified by Minotauro's response. "But that would be evil if that was the Elements' intent. They would be no better than anyone in our clans if that were true."

Daniel stared at the fire. "Then I suppose we simply need to take our chances. Whether they listen or not, at least we tried. It's the trying that most people shy away from. I don't want an excuse keeping me from the attempt. I'd rather die trying to do something great, rather than dying over a complaint that others should have done it or be the complainer when I was the one who could have done it — and didn't." He paused deep in thought. "Marcus died trying. His intent was for the good regardless of what the totem had to say. And even then, he was not given the knowledge on which path to take. We have been. It wasn't my uncle's destiny. It's ours. They know why we've come. Our words may not be perfect in how we petition their help, but the intent behind them are. They will see it. They will know we're different than the kings and queens who came before us."

"And if they don't?"

"Then we go home and think of a new plan. And one after that…like our fathers did. Perhaps we think of an even better one they never thought of." He looked at all of them. "We won't let history repeat itself."

Tick-Tock moved closer.

Minotauro spoke, "I'll take watch first. Get some rest. We'll need it if we're going to climb the rest of the mountain."

Alexandra turned to Byron, "I wish Agoura could move the mountain for us."

"Maybe she will."

Another rumble followed. Byron shifted his eyes to Tick-Tock. His head was gazing up at the top of the mountain. "What is it?" His head swiveled to snow owl, the voice of the past. *"Fire will show usss when. Fire will show usss how."*

XXV

Diana had fallen into a deep sleep inside Rebekah's bedchamber. Keys had built a small fire in the hearth, having fallen asleep on the floor beside her.

Diana was dreaming.

She was walking through the woods in the lair. As she looked all around her, all she could see were barren trees. Crowded around her, their skeletal branches appeared to be reaching for her. She felt a breeze gently blow all around her, moving past her, as if beckoning her to follow.

The horse queen watched its path and followed it all the way toward a large lake. She slowed her step the moment she saw a hooded figure standing at its banks.

"Hello?"

The figure did not move. Diana continued moving forward, slowly approaching the cloaked being. That was when the horse queen heard the being speak. It was a woman's voice, "Whoever controls the sea, rules the realm…"

Diana followed the woman's gaze as she looked out across the lake. The horse queen replied, "An old saying." She turned and looked back at the woman, "But who can control the sea?"

"He is coming…the king is coming with his vicious horde…tyranny…nothing but death will follow…"

A chill ran down Diana's spine as the woman spoke. That was when she saw the medallion resting against the woman's chest; she immediately recognized it.

She gasped, "The bird queen…"

Rebekah slowly turned her head and looked Diana directly in the eyes. "How do you want to be remembered?" Rebekah looked back toward the lake as a fog began rolling in. Diana's breath started to fog as the temperature dropped all around her. "Better than this day…" Diana watched as the lake began to freeze over. "Wiser than the others….to do something great. To be someone unexpected."

It was then that Diana realized that Rebekah was looking directly at her. "Be the unexpected…resurrect your house." The wind swirled around them and began to blow

111

harder and harder until the bird queen whistled sharply to the sky. A loud shrill echoed across the forest. Diana looked skyward as the clouds parted and a large eagle warrior descended. As it approached, the bird queen turned and ran along the shoreline, jumping onto the warrior's back as he glided alongside her; they ascended to the sky, swallowed up by the clouds.

A cock crowed three times…

She heard Rebekah whisper, "Enemy."

Diana's eyes snapped open. She sat straight up and looked toward the closed door that led from the bedchambers and out toward the hallway beyond. She slowly climbed off the bed, never taking her eyes from the door. The horse queen shook Keys awake. He stirred as she crouched down beside him. He followed her gaze toward the door.

They looked at one another, knowing there were others on the opposite side of the door. Keys' voice was barely audible as he said, "Get on my back. We have only one shot at this."

He quietly lowered down to all fours just as the doorknob slowly began to turn. Diana climbed on top of her warrior. His eyes faced forward, a fierce determination on his face.

Get to the balcony.

Diana kept her eyes on the door, "Keys…"

He charged forth, racing for the balcony just as the wolves burst through. They immediately pounced on the bed, viciously attacking, shredding anything they could get their claws on.

Keys leapt off the balcony, crashing down to the garden below; he charged through the vine gate with ferocious speed.

The wolves, realizing their intended target had eluded them, turned from the bed and dove off the balcony. They charged after Diana and Keys, howling to other members of the Wolf Pack.

Hyenas, foxes, jackals and wolves stealing food from the fields dropped everything and raced toward the howl.

Diana and Keys rode hard and fast toward the Great White Mountains. The queen looked back and saw two lone wolves up on the hilltop. Within seconds, they were joined by more members of the pack. They descended as one.

"FASTER!!!"

He charged harder and faster than he ever had before. As the black stallion rode across the landscape, he jumped over small mounds of what appeared to be dirt. Little did they know that they were the decaying bodies of slaughtered ostrich warriors.

Diana watched as the wolves started to close the distance between them. She grabbed hold of her medallion, stretching her hand out toward the wolves.

SNAP!

A tornado descended from the sky and wound its way across the landscape and over toward the wolf pack, lifting and careening them across the hillside. They did not see it coming. It was just enough to allow Keys and Diana the escape they needed as they rode east…toward the lion's den.

The wolf packed slowly picked themselves up from the ground, searching for the force of the wind that had disappeared as quickly as it had appeared. They looked in the direction Keys had ridden.

A wolf named Igor, the head of the pack, looked skyward, "She called upon Wind."

"And he answered her."

The grey wolf barked to the pack. "We follow." They dropped to all fours and ran in the direction of the horse queen.

From the hilltop, the two bull warriors who had been following the wolves emerged. The Black Angus warrior's eyes glowed red as he lowered his head. "They have returned."

The other bull stomped his hoof in anger, "Ram must be told."

The Black Angus warrior snorted in reply. They dropped to all fours and charged toward Bull Valley.

XXVI

Tick-Tock and the remnants climbed as swiftly up the mountain as their skills could possibly take them. Snow and ice now covered every crack and crevice along the rock, making it harder for the remnants to climb as their limbs numbed and their bodies shivered the higher they rose. Alexandra's body shifted once again. She placed her hand and ear against the rock to listen closer. Alexandra pushed away from the rock and looked up.

Byron asked, "What is it?"

Tick-Tock, however, did not look up. He looked down. His emerald began to glow.

"Sounds like…"

"WATER!!!"

Daniel shouted, "LOOK OUT!!!" Daniel jumped up next to Alexandra and threw himself over her to shield her as water poured down from the top of the mountain. Minotauro and Byron grabbed for a branch extending from the cliff, holding on as tightly as they could; but the force of the water dislodged it. They were immediately rocketed down the mountain, being carried off the flow of water as a mudslide ensued just as the ledge Tick-Tock stood on gave way. He slid down the mountain after them.

The water kept pouring down on top of Daniel and Alexandra; the dirt and rocks pummeling down all around them. Alexandra lost her footing and slid down.

Daniel cried out, "Alexandra!!!" He dove off the mountain after her.

Minotauro, Tick-Tock and Byron slid down the rest of the mountain off the water's force. A river now formed at the base of the fortress. They were carried down the current, hurling over another cliff to the newly formed waterfall. They plummeted into the dark lake below.

Daniel landed in the pool of water at the base of the waterfall. Alexandra careened off the cliff above and slammed into the lake below.

They all rose to the surface and started swimming to shore. Tick-Tock's barn owl head, however, continued to stare in the direction of the waterfall.

Minotauro blurted out, "I hate this guy!" He was the last in line. He was swimming hard and fast underwater; his muscles were burning. With the lack of sleep and physical exertion from their climbing; his body was exhausted. He could feel his arms and legs getting heavier and heavier as he swam. His muscles were weighing him down. He thought of Lydia again, focusing on her smile, knowing she was waiting for him back home.

Home.

He felt a sudden burst of energy as he thought about the life waiting for him back in Bull Valley; one where he had, for the first time in his life, a love he had never known. He knew he was lucky. He knew that the universe had given him a gift he had always desired but never said a word about. It hit him then that he had been heard; his prayer had been answered — at least one of them. And it suddenly occurred to the bull king that it was the most important one.

Minotauro swam harder, trying to catch up to the rest of the group when he was jerked backward, feeling a sharp pull at his side. The hilt of his sword was caught on some sort of plant. He pulled at it, trying to break free, but it would not budge. He tugged harder, feeling his lungs beginning to burn. He needed air, and he needed it now. Minotauro looked ahead through the weeds but could no longer see Byron. He started to panic.

Minotauro felt for his belt buckle, but the weeds had somehow wound around it, making it impossible to undo it. He looped his thumbs under the belt and tried to push the leather down over his hips to wiggle himself free, but the harder he tried the more entangled he became.

Panic turned to fear as he tried to swim to the surface, but he was too tangled up in the weeds. Minotauro knew what his fate would be if he did not cut himself free, but he had no available weapon; it was tangled in his sheath amongst the weeds. Fear turned to terror.

Above water, Tick-Tock was swimming behind Alexandra pushing her along. He suddenly stopped. His heads swiveled quickly as the emerald stone began to glow. His main head turned back toward Alexandra's direction where he saw her begin to struggle in the water. He shifted his gaze over toward the waterfall — there was something there. A low growl escaped him, knowing that whatever it was intended harm. He looked between the waterfall and Alexandra before shifting his gaze back toward where he had last seen Minotauro. It had been too long since the bull king had risen from the water, and the emerald stone was now glowing vibrantly. *Where to go? Who to help?* He made his decision.

He shifted his body around and started swimming back toward the bull king.

But as soon as he began swimming forward, he felt a tug at his neck pulling him backward. The stone had risen to the top of the water. The chain around his neck was pulling him back toward Alexandra. He fought against the pull but to no avail. He looked back in Minotauro's direction; the bull king was nowhere to be found.

Choosing of his own free will, Tick-Tock was determined to fight against the force of the stone but lost out as the chain around his neck continued to pull him back toward the wolf queen.

Underwater, Minotauro continued to struggle as he kicked and ripped at the weeds. The bull king shouted in rage at the weeds as he fought to free himself. That was when he saw a man with turquoise-colored eyes watching him through the foliage.

Rhodes. It had to be.

The two men stared at one another. For a moment, Minotauro thought Rhodes was there to help him — an answer to another silent prayer. But Rhodes did not move a single muscle. Only a flicker of sadness seemed to flash across his face as he looked at the bull king. That was when the plants seemed to surround the element brother, swallowing him up as he faded away as quickly as he had emerged.

How could this be? Three kings for three brothers…isn't that what the old toad chief had said? Where was Rhodes going?

A great guttural shout erupted from Minotauro as he roared across the water at the lord of the sea and at the universe itself.

He waited for an answer.

And he received it. It was an answer to a question he never asked and had not expected to come this day.

He was going to die today.

He wasn't ready.

Minotauro's lungs burned even hotter, and his limbs became even heavier as his body began to jerk. A rapid wave of thoughts flooded his mind as his body fought for air.

Not yet. I'm not done just yet…I haven't finished what I just started.

But as he felt the burning in his lungs with no help in sight, he realized…his time was up — whether he thought it should be.

He reached for the letter in his pocket, the one closest to his heart. His life flashed before his eyes as he thought of his father, his friends, his family...*his wife...and their unborn child.*

His heart broke at that moment as he thought of the heir he would never see, the one he would never know.

"And where do you stand, bull king?" Netapheha's voice sounded in his ears just then.

He was not a man of many words. Most of the time, he could not articulate well the thoughts he had in his mind, the feelings he felt in his heart. But he had them now. And as Minotauro struggled to fight against his fading life, the one he longed to hold onto, he finally had an answer to the question the old toad chief asked him so long ago.

For family.
Protect them.
For his friends.
Champion them.
Do not stop. Do not hesitate.
Believe.
Keep going...

That's what he wanted to say to them all as his hand fell away from his chest where his letter rested near his heart...and all went dark.

Just.
Like.
That.

Daniel and Byron had just reached the shore when Tick-Tock pulled Alexandra out of the water. She had not heard a thing as she rung out her ears. Byron and Daniel were face down in the mud; they were exhausted.

"I'll bet you wish your muscle could float now, Minotauro." When he did not hear a response, Byron turned his head back toward the lake, He looked along the shoreline and only saw Daniel, Alexandra, and Tick-Tock. His heart dropped as he whispered, *"Minotauro..."* He scrambled out of the mud and to his feet. *"Minotauro!!!"*

Daniel and Alexandra whirled around as Byron raced back into the lake. *"MINOTAURO!!!"*

Daniel was right behind him. He was faster than Byron and swam rapidly down. Several moments passed before Daniel's head emerged.

"I can't find him!"

Byron dove under. Daniel took a deep breath and descended once more.

This could not be happening. *Not another one. Not this man. Not this king.* Even though she did not know Minotauro well, she liked him. She liked him very much. Alexandra stood helpless on shore; she got down on all fours, trying to listen closely, but she could not hear a sound. "Tick-Tock, do you see anything?"

And before he could reply, she whispered, "Oh my gawd…"

Daniel and Byron emerged; they were holding onto Minotauro's body.

She raced toward the kings as they swam to shore. Byron took Minotauro's body from Daniel's grasp and pulled him up alongside him and out of the water. He slipped in the mud, struggling as he continued to pull Minotauro out of the water. Byron held onto him as the bull king's lifeless body rested against his chest.

Byron shouted, *"TICK-TOCK!"* He took the medallion from his neck and placed the medal over the bull king's heart. Byron reached out for Tick-Tock's eagle hand and raged in desperation, *"Help me!* Use the medallion!"

But Tick-Tock did not move.

"Call down the light! *TICK-TOCK!"* It was then that Byron noticed that Tick-Tock's head had turned from snow owl to horned owl — the face of the future.

Alexandra's voice was a desperate whisper, "The clan…"

The wind blew rapidly across the landscape, barreling toward the realm. Sebastian was standing at the top of the dam on the amphibian side, when he felt it — the changing of the wind.

Hood stood straight up, his fur had risen. He and the rest of the pack looked north as the wind approached. The clouds collected in the sky blocking out the sun as the sky slowly darkened.

Chief Netapheha was rapidly writing in his book when he suddenly stopped. The quill fell from his hand, *"King…"*

Sebastian looked out at the clans surrounding the sea. Everyone was working and moving about like normal, until he caught sight of the wolves. Hood looked directly at the king just as the wind arrived. He watched as the alpha's gaze followed the path of the wind…it was headed straight toward the bull clan warriors.

There was a loud crash. Material began collapsing all around the dam. Sebastian looked down and watched in horror as the entire bull clan went down.

"GET OFF THE DAM!!!" The dam itself seemed to hear the pain in Sebastian's voice as it began to break and split apart on the bull clan side. Sebastian jumped off the dam just as the rest of the construction fell apart, crumbling to the ground. No one knew what to do. It was as if all the other clans were in shock as they watched the bull clan go down and the dam falling with them.

"HELP ME!" Sebastian was beside himself, scrambling to move debris away from the bull, buffalo, ram and goat bodies. As if coming out of a trance, the other clan members snapped out of their stunned horror and jumped into action. Hordes of gorilla and amphibian warriors worked to pull debris off of the bull clan warriors. Sebastian moved like a madman, careening rocks off their bodies, trying desperately to do…*something.*

Diana and Keys were still riding like lightning across the plains when they suddenly heard a man shouting, followed by a thunderous roar of clan warriors. The sounds were deafening.

"Follow it."

Keys shifted direction, racing toward the cacophony of sound. They had reached the top of a hill when Keys dropped to all fours and Diana dismounted. Crouched low, they peered over the hill as Mariner Sea came into view.

Diana took it all in, seeing the massive construction of the dam…and it was crumbling before her very eyes. She watched as the beasts she had seen — strong, vibrant — speeding across Bird Clan Fields a day before, now tumbling down like rotting trees. Her voice was barely a whisper as she said, "The bull king…" She heard a man shouting. "We have to help them!"

Keys put his hoof out in front of her to stop her from racing forth. He wrapped his arms around her, holding her back to protect her as she struggled against him. "There's nothing we can do, my queen."

"There has to be!"

He did not let go.

She watched as the warriors continued to drop like flies. The horse queen had never seen anything like it. Minotauro, the bull king, was gone.

Bodies of bull, ram, goat and buffalo warriors covered the landscape. Gorilla and toad warriors were pulling bull clan soldiers from the sea. And as the lesser clan warriors worked feverishly beside him, it was hopeless. Not a single bull clan member moved. Sebastian looked around at all the bodies, not knowing where to turn or what to do.

"King…"

He turned, barely hearing the warrior. "They're alive. King…they are alive." Sebastian looked at the collapsed bodies covering the grounds and saw their chests slowly rising and falling. He suddenly realized why…he looked toward the Lion's Den.

Lydia.

He immediately started running toward the den as amphibian and gorilla warriors followed.

All the while, the lion's den warriors just stood there and watched. Chester took in the sight before him and was smiling inside. Across the way, Hood and the pack studied the den captain's reaction, knowing full well what would be coming next.

XXVII

Netapheha was on his hands and knees staring down at the pool of water in his ancient abode. "Where is the reason...why in this season..." He looked deeper and deeper into the water. "Tick-Tock..." The old toad chief's voice seemed to echo across the water, and out toward the Element Fortress.

"Guardian of old...bound to this world and the one beyond, only when all will be lost, defend till the end...only then..."

The old chief shifted his eyes and saw the reflection of Feyedor looking back at him from the water. His image disappeared as quickly as it came before.

"Time is not now...trials alone...preparing for the day...he knows."

Across the realm, Tick-Tock was staring at the water, having heard Netapheha's voice as it echoed across time and space. He turned his head slowly to the remnants. Byron was beside himself, holding Minotauro's head in his lap.

Daniel reached out and grabbed Alexandra's hand. She immediately clung to him.

Byron lowered his head and laid Minotauro's head on the ground. As he looked at the lifeless face of his best friend, a low, guttural sound slowly erupted from deep inside of him. "*RHODES!!!!*" The gorilla king looked to the sky and roared in fury. He took his bone scepter, rose up and ran toward the mountainside, hammering away at the base of the mountain in utter rage. He swung with all his pain, all his resentment, all his woe — exerting his pent-up emotion onto the rock wall until it seemed the whole mountain quaked as he expended all his feelings upon it. He pounded away at the mountain with such force, Daniel was sure that Bane, his bone scepter, would snap in two; but it never did.

It was not until the gorilla king had exhausted himself that he finally stopped, collapsing in defeat. He was breathing hard, feeling so much at the same time while feeling nothing at all. He simply sat there staring out at the land beyond with a lost look of hopelessness. Alexandra recognized that look. It was the one she had seen reflected in her mirror day after day. She immediately went to his side, kneeling down and gently took his hand. He did not even move, barely noticing that anyone was beside him.

Daniel slowly turned his head in Tick-Tock's direction. The totem had moved to crouch down beside Alexandra. Byron suddenly felt the guardian's presence beside him. His face twisted into pain as he lunged for Tick-Tock, "*Why?!?* Why didn't you protect him?!? Why didn't you save him?!?" Tick-Tock did not move as Byron grabbed for him. The gorilla king released him from his grasp and grabbed for his bone scepter, lifting it to strike. The totem's head quickly swiveled to the past, and Reginald's voice came pouring out, "Loss…as unbearable as it is, is necessary….it is the great risk of truly living."

Byron slowly lowered his scepter.

"To engage in life, you encounter all its odds, all its chances, all its pain and miracles….and its tragedies."

Byron's face began to fall as Reginald's words resonated deep within.

"To never have what you thought you wanted, to never be what you dreamed you could be, to give everything you had and get nothing in return…it is a choice you have to make." Tick-Tock lowered his body so that he and the gorilla king were eye to eye. Reginald's voice spoke once more, "*Do you engage?*"

Byron remained silent.

"What you want demands great risk — *change always does.*"

Daniel watched as Tick-Tock extended his raven claw to the ground. The totem closed his eyes, almost as if he was listening to something in the depths of the earth. It reminded the lion king of the moment he witnessed Tick-Tock engaging in the same act when he saw the totem inside his den. That moment seemed so long ago. Even now, Daniel knew that action held purpose. He continued to watch as all three of the totem's heads began to slowly shift.

As the remnants watched Tick-Tock, a gentle breeze rose up all around them. But it was not just the wind that was moving. Daniel looked down and saw the ground shifting as well. He lifted his eyes and looked up at the surrounding trees. They were swaying and twisting in all directions, almost as if they were speaking to one another.

In reply, the grass, vines, and soil itself seemed to come alive and move as they gathered to one single point. Like a whirlpool, Daniel watched as the ground collected just beneath Minotauro's body. Byron suddenly felt the ground move underneath him. He lifted his head and watched as the grass underneath him moved past him and toward the bull king.

Underneath Minotauro, the ground swirled beneath his body, moving and shifting. Rising up from the ground, a woman arose. Her mouth hung open as if she were sobbing out loud, but no sound emitted from her grief-stricken face. Her long hair was the vibrant color of red roses, swirling in waves that resembled petals as they fell all around her face. Her pale skin was covered in dirt. Tears and streaks of blood marked her face as the signs of grief and mourning covered her like a shroud. The satin white dress that hung from her hauntingly pale form was stained in dirt and blood.

Agoura.

Byron fell to his knees before her. His face was a mirror of hers as he watched her look down at Minotauro's lifeless body. She spread her arms wide, sinking down to pick him up, holding him to her chest like a mother to a babe. Cradling him in her arms, she caressed his sleeping face, holding his head close to her heart as she silently wept. It was then that she looked up at the other remnants; her emerald-colored eyes boring into theirs. Agoura did not utter a single word as she looked at each of the kings and queen. Her grief-stricken face communicating to all.

Tick-Tock began to howl. It was long and mournful. Its chord struck something deep inside Alexandra's heart. The wolf queen lowered her head and began to cry. Another being to mourn for added to the list of names etched into her heart.

Byron, however, was not weeping. He simply stared at Agoura; an understanding of each other's grief reflected in each other's eyes as she held the bull king in her arms. And as Tick-Tock howled and Alexandra wept, Daniel could not help but think of Marcus. He thought of Nathan. He thought of the mother and father he never knew until his thoughts turned back to Minotauro. He suddenly felt like he was on the hilltop again, overlooking Bird Kingdom. But this time…the sun would not be rising on the horizon.

Seeing Minotauro's lifeless body underwater, entangled in the weeds, Byron and Daniel had both frantically tried to free him. But they knew. They knew it was too late. The bull king was dead. And with his death, it was a reminder to all of them how much they had endured during their lifetime. And that even when pursuing that of the good, no one was immune to what the world wanted…more for the taking, more for the enduring, more for just being alive — or so it felt.

He was reminded of what Cheetah had said, *"It is the good that perish first, my king. It is the honorable whose light is extinguished before the candle burns out. There is a specific time allowed for us all, and however long we think it may be, the world has other ideas…"*

Staring at the remnants in their silent grief, Agoura slowly lifted her hand and pointed to the fortress. In reply, rock walls slowly split open upon her silent command, as if the mountain itself had doors. An entrance formed, leading directly inside the mountain. Agoura looked at them, waiting for them to move toward it.

But none of them could move. Looking for a stone seemed like the last thing any of them wanted to do; instead, wishing to remain a little while longer in the wave of woe that kept them bound to no further movement as the hope they all shared seemed to die the moment Minotauro was pulled from the lake.

It was Tick-Tock who stared at them with his large bulbous eyes as he said, *"Keep going."*

It was Minotauro's voice.

Byron stared at the totem for a long while as tears streamed down his handsome face. He was looking at Tick-Tock as if the bull king himself were standing right in front of him. The gorilla king breathed in sharply, rallying himself to do what his best friend desired. He turned and silently walked toward the fortress.

Daniel and Alexandra followed his lead as they walked slowly toward the entryway. Just before crossing through the entrance, Byron looked back to see Agoura still holding onto Minotauro's body, cradling the bull king in her arms. She looked down at his sleeping face and swept her arm across the bull king's body over and over again. Each time she moved her arm over his body, Agoura covered it with her vines and roses; their bodies descending as she held him. By the time Byron had walked inside the fortress, they were buried in the ground, and all that remained was an earthly grave covered with rose petals and leaves.

124

Rhodes was crouched low on a ledge overlooking the riverbank below. He watched as his sister rose from the ashes to embrace the bull king. He looked solemn as he listened to the totem's howl. It was a song he was used to hearing for decades, and it never ceased to affect him — even now. He closed his eyes as he listened to the remnants weep until a different sound stirred amongst the sorrow. He let his turquoise-colored eyes wander past the base of the mountain and out toward the forest that surrounded the fortress beyond. He thought he had deterred them...*but they were still there.*

His eyes were locked on where they stood, but they made no further movement. It was a long time since they had traveled so close to the fortress. His brothers and sister knew they would one day return. Knowing it was during this period in time, all the cries of the past generations seemed to rise up suddenly like a chorus of thunder crying out for justice. Rhodes closed his eyes as the voices continued to amplify in his ears. He clenched his eyes harder as he tried to shut out the symphony of sorrows; his entire body constricting as it grew louder and louder until he could take it no more.

And then it was gone.

As the fortress shifted and closed, Rhodes saw the shadowed creatures move silently around the entrance and out toward the direction of a waterfall.

XXVIII

Sebastian climbed the coral steps that led to the old chief's abode. His footsteps were heavy. His body moved slow.

"King...my king..." He found Chief Netapheha in his familiar position writing in an old book by candlelight. The moment the chief saw his king, he jumped down from his seat, grabbed his staff and shuffled over. Taking in Sebastian's forlorn form and, seeing the sadness behind his eyes, Netapheha paused and lowered his head, "I'm sorry, my king."

Sebastian did not say anything. He was trying to keep his emotions in check.

Netapheha kept his head bowed, "What can I do?"

The king sat down and rested his head against his hand as he looked at his chief. He looked exhausted. "I need answers."

Netapheha lifted his head, "What are the questions?"

"Did you know King Minotauro was going to die?"

The old chief looked up at Sebastian, "No." The amphibian king stared at him for a long time. Netapheha continued, "This I did not see but knew was a possibility. It is still a possibility for all."

"Why was I chosen to stay behind?"

The old toad moved closer toward his king. "For you to lead and others to follow."

Sebastian rubbed his neck in frustration. "No more rhymes or riddles. Just a straight answer. I need to know what it is I'm supposed to do now."

"You're doing it."

"I don't mean about the dam! I mean about what's out there!" He stood and gestured toward the unknown as he began pacing the small cave. "The kings are rising and falling, and I'm stuck here to build a dam that may never need to be built if they don't come back to see it!"

Chief Netapheha looked at his king's angry face and said, "You must trust, my king."

"In what?!?"

"The things you don't see, in the things you imagine in your mind's eye." He moved closer toward Sebastian and studied his king's face, looking deep into his eyes. "To do what others have not and could not. It is there…yes, yes…deep within…the humble strength which defies ego and pride and separates the strong from the weak, keeping them apart. You are the binding the realm longs to seek."

Sebastian narrowed his eyes, "What do you mean?"

He waddled back to his desk and began writing again. "It was not I who chose you to stay…it was they…"

"The elements?"

Netapheha nodded.

"Why?"

"Once it was she…almost married to he…but she is no longer in this realm. Within but not in…all that remains is faith in the mirror. Yes, yes…the image which you see…until it is they you see…in you." The toad chief suddenly stopped speaking, whipping his head around as if he heard something.

Sebastian caught his look. "What is it?"

The chief's bulbous eyes rapidly dilated. He turned and looked at his king, "A queen is coming…riding on the path of the wind…for he answers her."

The amphibian king narrowed his eyes at this sudden revelation. He continued to watch the chief as he ran through the thoughts in his head. "How do you know this when you could not see…"

"Not everything can I see…this, my king, this was suddenly revealed to me." He looked at Sebastian and moved toward his king. "Do not be afraid…*listen*…challenge what they all fear." He looked out at the pool of water below. "This queen will help against the king from a clan of old…a destroyer, he is. Evil yet cunning. Cleverness the innocent won't be shielded against. He too is coming…" He looked back at Sebastian. "It was the bull king's voice who stirred her home…even though he was not meant to be here to open the doors…"

Sebastian's mind was reeling, "Did you just say there was an evil king? And another queen?"

"Yes, yes…you will see, but for now set aside and be…do not take long to grieve, for the realm needs your strength…they will all see who you were meant to be…"

The chief continued to stare at the pool of water.

"That's it?"

Netapheha turned his large bulbous eyes toward his king. "That was plenty. Listen and know…remember, remember…now go."

Sebastian watched as Netapheha continued to study the pool of water. He watched as the old toad chief took his coral staff, turning it into the water as he continued to search within its depths. "For every death there is a life. When it seems the darkest, the light will come…" The amphibian king slowly turned to move down the stairs, pondering all that Netapheha had said and didn't say.

Chango was standing guard near the bamboo gate. He turned upon hearing his king approach. "Did he have any answers, my king?"

"Not the one I was looking for." Sebastian looked back at the old toad chief's abode. "He had much to say but nothing that made sense. I don't know if he's mad or wise, Chango."

The frog warrior noticed the worried look on his king's face. "You look troubled, my king. What did he say we needed to do?"

He looked back at his warrior. "Pay attention."

"I don't understand."

Sebastian was deep in thought. "The wind is about to change. Keep watch — especially at the borders…to the north."

"Yes, my king."

XXIX

The moment Daniel, Byron and Alexandra stepped through the archway into the element fortress, the world seemed to change. It was almost as if they were transported into a different time and place; and they felt it. Not in a grand announcement or loud shift, but deep in their hearts — almost as if the door behind them had shut out all they had known to show them they were in a place where they would soon learn what it was to have one foot in the living and one foot in the world beyond.

The remnants could hear a loud rumbling behind them. They turned to see the rock wall to the mountain sealing itself shut. The fortress inside was massive, covered in a garden of pale green crystals at its base. Alexandra's eyes scaled up its sides. She could see the flickering light from the emeralds' glow causing the rock walls to glitter. It reminded her of the fireflies she would see each season out near Wolf Lake.

She continued to gaze upward to the top of the fortress. She could see various arches cut out from various pieces of rock that seemed to lead deeper inside the fortress. She could not, however, see to the very top.

The fortress exuded power and strength. Standing inside it, she suddenly felt small and insignificant. Beneath her feet, she felt the slightest vibration. Alexandra tilted her head to the side, hearing the faintest of sounds; she listened intently. They were voices — faint echoes of words being spoken that she could not quite make out.

Daniel grabbed Alexandra's hand, "What do you hear?"

"Whispers I can't understand." Her body was trembling. "Daniel, are we going to die?"

"Not today." He squeezed her hand tight.

A strong wind filled their cavern blowing all around them. *"Remnants of the realm…"*

Alexandra looked all around, attempting to follow the voice on the wind.

"The queen of wolves, keeper of the lair."

Daniel's eyes searched the cavern.

"King of lions, ruler of the den..."

Byron's heart was pounding inside his chest.

"And sovereign of gorillas, the king of the jungle...faces of chaos that shape the realm. We know why you're here."

"Who are you?" Alexandra asked.

"Spirit...inspiration...wisdom...truth..."

But just as quickly as the wind entered their cavern, it disappeared.

"Zephyrus..." Alexandra turned toward Daniel as he spoke the name. "This is more than a fortress."

Daniel reached for his compass. He looked down at the small instrument and found the arrow spinning rapidly — clockwise, then counterclockwise — never stopping, never knowing which direction it should take. He looked up and out at the rock walls surrounding him. "We're nowhere and everywhere at the same time."

Byron slowly turned his head and looked at the lion king. "This isn't the way it was supposed to be." He could hear the slight panic in Byron's voice. "We're never getting out of here."

Without looking at him, Daniel placed the tiny compass back inside his pocket. "She let us in. Agoura wants us here. We have nothing to fear." He said it with confidence, reminded of when he had been pulled through the vines at Bird Clan gates. They were *supposed* to be here.

"Wind did not attack. And fire is all around us." He moved forward, continuing to take in the glistening minerals and gems as they shimmered against the colorful firelight. He touched one of the rocks. "This is exactly what I pictured in my mind...to the last detail."

Alexandra asked, "What do you mean? Did you see this in one of your dreams?"

"No."

Byron replied, "Then it was in one of your books...your uncle's writing."

"No. He never found this place. No one has. Even Diana said the same thing." He continued examining the walls. "I imagined it would look like this though."

"I don't understand."

"Neither do I."

Byron turned his head to look at Tick-Tock. He watched as the totem gazed all around the cavern, shifting his eyes and heads all the way toward the height of the unseen peak. Byron's eyes fell on the emerald stone hanging from his neck; it matched the ones from inside the fortress. "Tick-Tock..."

Tick-Tock's barn head lowered as he shifted his gaze to the gorilla king.

"You know this place."

Tick-Tock tilted his head to the side, swiveling his head to horned owl, "I belong more to *this* world than the one left behind."

Byron moved toward him, gripping Bane, and hitting it against Tick-

Tock's chest, his voice angry and desperate, "But you're in *our* world! Until then, you help *us*! Protect us in *this* one! Whatever this place is! Be the guardian you're supposed to be! I don't want this fortress to be the gravestone of my death! Do you hear me?"

The sound of wind filled the cavern once more. Tick-Tock turned his head in Wind's direction.

The remnants could hear the wind blowing as it barreled through the archways above them. The wind dove down toward them, and like an invisible hand, the wind gathered around the remnants. It swirled violently around them, lifting all three from where they stood, splitting them apart.

Alexandra shouted, *"DANIEL!"* Alexandra and Daniel's hands were ripped apart from the force of the wind.

Daniel shouted back, "Alexandra!"

They reached for each other but to no avail. The wind pulled all three of them apart, lifting them up and away from each other. The rock walls began to grind and shift. Higher and higher they went, powerless to do anything as the wind forced them higher and higher toward the unseen peak. That was when Wind pulled each of them through a separate archway into different caverns, leaving each of them separated, alone, and in the dark.

The only one who remained anchored to where he stood was Tick-Tock. He was not looking skyward however, but up toward a ledge. The emerald stone around his neck began to glow. A low growl erupted from deep inside his chest. He leapt up the rock that led to another passageway and ran through.

The bull, buffalo and goat warriors were still comatose, vulnerable to attack as they slept wherever they had fallen the moment the bull king went down. The amphibians had been guarding the bull clan warriors incessantly by order of their king.

SNAP!

A toad warrior turned around, holding the torch in front of his bulbous eyes. He looked all around, unable to see very far in the darkness. Scanning the grounds, he could not see anything. Determining that the sound was the crackling flame from his torch, he moved on.

The moment the toad was out of sight, a small group of lion and tiger warriors crept toward the vulnerable bodies of bull, goat, and buffalo soldiers. They wove through their sleeping forms until reaching the strongest warriors in the group. Chester stood directly over Ram. He looked around and nodded to his band of warriors that had emerged from the shadows.

They pulled their swords from their sheaths and their battle axes from their sides, raising them high above their heads.

"HALT!"

Firelight lit up the landscape as Chester and his band of assassins froze mid-action. Sebastian stepped forward along with a large group of amphibian and gorilla clan warriors. Chester snarled viciously at the king as he slowly lowered his sword. "No longer hiding in your treehouse, are you, king?"

Sebastian held Chester's stare. The sight of the lion warrior disgusted and enraged him. When he spoke, his voice was low and lethal, "Rod, Amun, take this group of traitors and lock them up inside the prison in Gorilla Jungle." The smile on Chester's face slowly faded until a menacing sneer replaced it as a growl rose from deep inside the lion warrior's chest. His other warriors followed suit, shifting their positions to attack mode as they crouched low.

"Dare to take us down and we'll strike as many bull warriors along the way as our swords can reach." He took a second sword from behind his back.

"Not tonight."

The lion captain whipped his head around at the sound of Cheetah's voice. Beside him and behind him was a legion of cheetah and panther warriors. The tiger and lion warriors were beside themselves. *"TRAITORS!"*

By the look of rage on Chester's face, Sebastian did not know who the captain was going to kill first.

"Our king gave me the command to guard and protect his orders. What you and your men are about to do is not it. Lay down your weapons...*now.*"

The tiger and lion warriors watched for their captain's command. The moment they saw their commander's mane rise straight up; they knew what to do. They gripped their swords and axes tight. The cheetah and panther warriors growled back, armed and ready. The gorilla and amphibian warriors pulled their weapons as well.

Chester snapped at Cheetah, "Your tribe is shamed this day by you and your dissent!"

"It is you who shame the den!" Cheetah hissed back. "Lions and tigers may have powerful blows, but cheetahs and panthers are swifter in the attack. Our weapons will hit their mark. We know how to make the brutal go down!"

Behind the cheetah and panther warriors, the gorilla clan warriors began to beat their breasts, readying for battle. The growls and grunts were amplified across the terrain. An all-out brawl was about to go down when a horn sounded in the distance.

Diana and Keys were up on the hilltop watching all the action when they turned their heads to the sound of the horn. They saw a woman approaching with cheetah warriors behind her — and not just female beasts, but human women too. The women were dressed for battle — all except the main woman in front. Even from where they crouched, Diana could see the woman was the leader of the group — and she was pregnant.

As Lydia approached, she moved directly towards Chester. Sebastian moved to step closer to her, but her kinswomen stopped him. Lydia was toe to toe with Chester. The look on her face said it all. Her eyes were slit to a cat as she stared directly into the captain's eyes. Sebastian had never seen such a look on her face before; it froze him in his tracks. Several moments passed before Chester lowered his sword. His warriors followed suit.

Gorilla and toad warriors immediately surrounded them, binding the warriors' hands behind them.

"Cheetah isn't the only traitor to the den." Chester spat on the ground at Lydia's feet as he was led away. The bull queen watched him go.

"Cheetah, gather the lionesses and other cheetah warriors at the den — tiger and panther females too."

"Yes, queen."

It was then that Lydia caught the mirroring eyes watching from the darkness. "King…"

Sebastian turned and saw Hood and other members of the wolf pack approaching.

Hood looked straight at the bull queen. "We will guard the bull warriors, queen, alongside the gorillas and amphibians. For every lion, there are three hyenas. The bull clan warriors will not be harmed."

"Thank you, wolf." Lydia nodded at him in gratitude. She looked at Sebastian, "The kings would be dismayed by what was about to go down this day. The queen, however, would be proud." She suddenly lurched forward and cried out in pain.

"Lydia!"

Sebastian rushed to her side just as the bull queen fell to the ground.

XXX

Sebastian waited outside Lydia's chambers. He could hear her groaning with the sounds of labor as her cheetah kinswomen worked beside her. They were worried. She was not due for several more weeks, and the birth of the remnant was the last hope for the bull clan to survive.

Sebastian had been pacing the floor for hours not knowing what to do with himself as he waited. Everything depended on this moment. He looked up at the portrait of Minotauro hanging in the room and stared at it for a long while.

"The universe *will* answer, my friend!"

His thoughts were interrupted by the sound of Lydia's scream. He whirled around and faced her doors.

All went silent.

Sebastian's heart stilled as he listened for any sound from the queen's bedchamber. He heard women crying. His heart stopped as he looked back at Minotauro's portrait. He could not even breathe.

And then he heard it…a baby's cry. He was not even sure he heard it, but it grew louder and louder until the king could not do anything else but run. He raced toward the doors and threw them open. Lydia looked at him. She held a baby in her arms.

He crossed to her side and knelt beside her.

Lydia took Sebastian's hand in hers and squeezed it tightly, "Minotauro lives on. He has a son."

Sebastian could feel the tension in his muscles release; he was overcome. All he could do was nod back as tears filled his eyes. He nodded and whispered, "He has a son." Sebastian placed his finger in the tiny hand as it clasped automatically around his. The amphibian king smiled as tears streamed down his face.

He looked up and saw Lydia crying. He squeezed her hand tightly as she said, "Minotauro…" He cried silently with her as she held her son in her arms. "You know, he looks just like him. The cleft in his chin…the furrow in his brow as if he's already angry with the world…" She smiled softly as

135

she looked at the babe, "Yes, you are your father's son. His namesake is now yours." Her chin began to tremble as she tried to hold back the tears.

Looking down at the baby's face, he did look like Minotauro. Sebastian could see his friend's dimpled, strong chin in the son. He could see Lydia's nose and almond-shaped eyes etched in his features.

He thought of their treehouse then; the one place where he could hide from all the evil that never seemed to sleep. And evil was still out there. There were still things left undone. Seeing the little babe's finger wrapped around his own, he suddenly felt a shift in his purpose.

Innocent...

Sebastian vowed right then and there to dedicate the rest of his days to protecting his best friend's son — to be the treehouse — the shield, the sanctuary — for this little one.

Just.
Like.
That.

He had gone to see Chief Netapheha for answers, but it was through the face of Minotauro's son that he found them.

This is why you are here.
You are going to build that dam.
You will watch for the queen.
You will defend against this unknown king.

He would do it all — even if it meant losing his own life. For this was the first time in his life that Sebastian felt a true sense of purpose solidifying itself deep inside his heart as he looked down at the tiny human being.

"No evil shall come to your door. This, I promise you."

There was a loud commotion that suddenly sounded from the grounds below. Sebastian crossed the room to the balcony doors and threw them open. Rising up from their slumber one by one were the ram, buffalo, goat and bull warriors roused by the remnant's heart as he was birthed into the world.

They looked up at the balcony feeling the young babe within their blood; they knew he was there. The bulls snorted in triumph, spitting on the ground as if stamping out death itself beneath their hooves. The buffalos were turning on their heels. The goats were ramming their heads against one another's. Sebastian could feel the rage in their hearts at the death of their king and their near-death experience, as the pride came forth with every movement they made.

Sebastian shouted over the balcony, *"RAM!"* The Black Angus warrior stomped back at the king. "Are you whole?"

The bull commander shouted, pounding his large hoof into the ground. In reply, the rest of the bull clan warriors followed suit until the grounds below sounded like one thunderous drumbeat. The bedchamber vibrated and swayed as the clan roused itself back into the living, demanding that the shadow of death hear their thunderous roar alerting the universe that they were still here…and they were not going down this day. They were alive…and they were angry.

The bull clan warriors continued to shout, forming a mosh pit of rage as they pushed and butted their heads against one another; a retort to challenge death and show they there were still amongst the living.

Lydia approached the balcony windows carrying the heir in her arms. The moment they saw the remnant, a cacophony erupted from down below. Little Minotauro burst into tears. Sebastian could not help but laugh at the angry look on his face. Just like Minotauro.

Diana and Keys hid in the shadows just outside Bull Valley. They watched in awe as the bull clan rose once again.

"It's a miracle, Keys."

He snorted loudly as a shadow emerged from overhead.

Diana turned her head and saw the two gray wolves behind her. Their eyes glowed silver as they sneered, "*Enemies…*"

They growled lowly as Keys rose. Diana grabbed her medallion and reached her hand to the sky as the wolves crouched and pounced. She threw her hand up as the wind snapped down into her hands and out toward the wolves. The wolves careened off her wind-like shield and were knocked back into the hills. They tumbled as the wind hunted them down and hurled them back across the valley.

"We must go, my queen."

"Where?"

"To the forest beyond."

She nodded and followed Keys as they fled to the Old Forest in Bull Valley.

Amun entered the bull queen's chamber. He knelt in front of the bull queen. "Congratulations, queen."

"Thank you, Amun."

Amun rested his webbed hand on his king's shoulder. "Forgive me, my king, but you're needed at the dam."

Sebastian looked at his warrior, never having seen the look behind Amun's eyes that he was seeing now.

Haunted.
"What is it?"
"Mariner Sea."

XXXI

"Daniel!?!"

Silence.

"Daniel, are you there?" Alexandra could not see a thing.

"Byron!"

"Alexandra!"

"Byron! I can't see you!"

"I'm on the other side of the wall!"

She pushed up against the rock and listened.

Byron shouted, "King! Are you there?"

No response.

It was then that Alexandra noticed the temperature rapidly dropping as her body began to shake. "It's getting...colder..."

Byron could feel it too as his breath began to fog. He shouted through the rock, "Alexandra!" She did not reply. "*Listen!* Do you hear me, wolf? *Listen!*"

It was then that Alexandra understood. She lowered down to the ground and felt all around her, feeling all along the ledge upon which she stood. She sank down to her stomach and felt over the edge; it completely dropped off. She put her ear to the ground and could hear the faintest of hums. And then she heard it...a still, small voice. It was suddenly interrupted by a voice directly ahead of her.

"Queen..."

She quickly looked up but could see only darkness. She could feel the ground growing colder, harder. She knew he was there.

Rhodes.

"Why do you tense at the sound of my voice?"

She pursed her lips, refusing to answer.

"You have no need to fear me."

Alexandra remained silent.

His voice was almost a sigh as he said, *"You believe I mean to do you harm. Why?"*

Trying to keep her teeth from chattering, she replied, "You killed Minotauro."

"Did I?"

She paused, angered at his response. She felt a tinge of confidence as she said, "You drove the raven mad."

On the other side of the wall, Byron listened in.

"He was mad already. Mad from grief. Mad for vengeance. He had a choice on how to become."

"I can go on...you threw us off the mountain with a mudslide and an avalanche. You froze the lake over on top of us."

"Are you certain it was you I was trying to deter?"

She was taken aback by his response, feeling her anger rising, "Of course it was! There's no one else here!"

"Isn't there?"

Angry and annoyed by all his questions, she began to ask a few of her own. "Who are you?"

"You know who I am."

She could feel her medallion lifting from her chest. She barely glanced down at it as she said, "In name and substance only." She grabbed hold of her medallion and continued to look all around for him, still listening to the direction his voice was coming from.

"I am the wave of serenity when one lives in abandonment to the whims of the world. I am the hardness of heart when pain becomes unbearable to the suffering who have lost the desire to weep."

"You helped the bird queen."

"And other kings and queens who came before her. Even one who came after."

Alexandra homed in on the sound of his voice. "I don't recall you ever helping me."

"No?"

"No! Not ever! But if you want to help me now, prove it." She swallowed hard, not even believing the boldness she was now speaking to one so powerful. "Give me the stone to resurrect our sea. Give it to me so we can bring the rain."

Rhodes was silent.

"Well?"

"Simply because you exist and have a need does not mean you are entitled to that which you think you should get. You who have never looked to the sun, pondered the power of the sea or listened to the voice on the wind. You never once looked our way until now. And it's only because you want something. And I don't owe it to you, queen. None of us do."

His answer struck her as if he had slapped her across the face. "Then why let us in?"

"I didn't."

The wolf queen's eyes mirrored in the darkness. She was angry. "If you're not going to help us then your desire is clear. You wish us dead!"

"My desire, queen, is in line with the answer you seek but have yet to acknowledge. It's not the stone you're after. You desire something more. It lies deep inside your heart. Speak it. Say it out loud."

Alexandra swallowed hard, "Say what?"

"What is your greatest desire?"

Alexandra remained silent as Byron continued to listen in on the other side of the wall.

"Tell me, queen. Now's your chance. What...do you want?"

She refused to answer. No one had ever asked her that question before. Every fiber in her being seized, for she knew what it was, but she was unwilling to share it, terrified to speak it out loud. Almost as if, by doing so, would remove the barrier around her heart that she did not even know she had until Rhodes asked her the question. The longer she waited to respond, and the longer he waited, she could feel the words rising inside her as they fought against her terrified will until she said, "I want...to be a great queen."

And there it was. Her desire laid bare. Her fear that she was not and never would be, now out in the open. Her entire body relaxed as if she had been waiting to exhale for years. The shame she thought she would feel by admitting it out loud was not there. It surprised her. She felt peaceful, never having been so honest with herself before. But even in her reply, there was more she knew she wanted still.

"And what is a great queen?" His tone was gentle.

Her eyes started to adjust to the darkness. She could see him. He stood against the opposite wall, leaning against it with his arms folded across his muscular chest. His turquoise-colored eyes bored into hers. "One like Queen Rebekah."

The air was no longer freezing but had adjusted to a cooler, more tolerable temperature. *"And what did Queen Rebekah have that binds you to her memory and path that deters you from creating and walking upon your own?"*

"She was strong, confidant. Whatever she chose to do, she accomplished. She protected her clan. Whenever there was a problem, she had a solution. Whomever she loved...loved her in return."

"She was despised, queen."

"No, she wasn't!"

"She was despised in her lifetime by the other kings in the realm: Gunthar, Rom, Mar, Archer. She did not have all the answers, and those whom she loved were daggers to her heart to the point where she had lost hope for all that she had desired and dreamt for in this world...she was betrayed, abandoned..."

"But my father..."

"Your father was not a dagger but a sword and one of the most despised in all the realm."

This was not the answer she expected. Alexandra gritted her teeth and shouted, *"YOU LIE!!!* My father was a great man! He was the best of kings!"

The cavern rumbled and shook in reply, causing Alexandra to fall to the ground as Rhodes' voice thundered all around her. *"HE WAS NOT A GREAT MAN! It's because of him the critters are no more! That the reptiles are gone! It is because of your father, a king of the realm, that cannibalism began! It's because of him that my sister no longer speaks!"*

"LIAR!!!"

Rhodes stepped forward and crouched down to where Alexandra could clearly see him so that they were eye to eye; his turquoise-colored eyes were luminous as he said, "I don't lie. *Ever.*" His eyes roamed her face, almost as if he was searching for something deep inside her. "He did it *for you.*"

Her entire body shook. "My father never left the lair! My pack never hunted outside the woods!"

"Not after he brought you home. He ventured outside the lair many times...especially into Gorilla Jungle...where you were born."

His words sank in slowly, changing Alexandra's confidence to stunned silence. She felt as if her heart had plummeted to her stomach. Rhodes caught her reaction.

"Alexander should have told you." He slowly stood and moved away from her. "He should have told you many things. But he did not want you to suffer or endure that kind of pain. But pain is often necessary. For it is in the suffering that we become. Embrace the mirror." He faded back into the darkness leaving Alexandra all alone.

On the other side of the rock wall, Byron heard all.

Daniel was face first on the ground, having been carried off by the force of Wind to this very spot. He looked up and saw a warm glow up ahead. Pushing himself off the ground, he grabbed the hilt of his sword and walked slowly through the archway.

The lion king's eyes grew wide the moment he saw the fire. Flames of every color imaginable lit the enormous hall: violet, fuchsia, emerald, aqua. He had never seen anything like it before. And it did not escape Daniel that with all the fire burning in the room, it was not hot. It was warm...comforting.

"Noble One..."

Daniel stopped moving.

"We saw you coming. We've been waiting for you."

Daniel swallowed hard before answering, "You know why we're here."

"You seek a stone. One of pain. One to bring rain. But do you seek it in vain?"

Daniel almost winced at the question. "Why in vain?"

The flames around the hall grew brighter. *"Who do you say that I am?"*

The lion king's heart was thundering inside his chest. "Fire. One of the creators."

"Who do you *say that I am?"*

"I…I don't understand."

But Fire did not reply.

As the fires all around the lion king continued to burn in anticipation of his answer, the wheels in Daniel's head were spinning. He had not anticipated this question. He had never actually thought about it before. For all his reading and research into the Elements, he had never really thought about them as being…*real.*

And as Fire spoke to him in a personal way, Daniel realized this was the most real experience he had ever had. He longed to answer the powerful voice whose essence seemed to pierce all his senses at once and deep into his very soul. He knew the answer. It was a question he had contemplated as he stood atop the hill in Bull Valley day after day, simply to watch the sun rise. He looked at the flames and said, "You…you are the one the bird queen honored as she sought guidance at the dawn of each new day. You are the one my grandfather longed to know as he looked for the peace he yearned for and finally found. You are wisdom and strength. You are hope and peace. And as you protected the worthy, you are love and mercy."

"How do you know this?"

Daniel spoke from his heart; there were no barriers to his mind or soul as his voice filled with strength and confidence, "I, too, have stood on the hilltop before the dawn of each new day. This is what I have come to know."

"Do you desire to know me more?"

And by that simple question, something inside Daniel suddenly broke. He felt the tension in his body dissipate as the tightness in his shoulders loosened. He could feel them drop as he inhaled deeply, almost as if he had been holding his breath for years. He lowered his head as tears stung his eyes. "Yes. I have longed to know you since I saw…*change.* Impossible change. The queen who could have been vengeful was humble before you. My king was calmed by the light of your rising sun. And I have wanted to share in what they had, what they knew…when they stood in your light."

The flames danced before him, almost pondering what Daniel had just revealed. *"And do you feel what you imagined they felt?"*

He lifted his head as he looked at the fire. "No. I feel something more. I feel the urge to do, to move. But I don't know where or what it is that I'm supposed to do. Why is that?"

"You have yet to become. You have seen the top of the mountain but are not yet ready. It is the valley you must walk through. You are gold, lion, that will be tested in fire. You must trust me, Noble One, for my grace will be enough."

And with that, the flames in the hall were extinguished, leaving the lion king alone in the darkness.

XXXII

Sebastian arrived at the dam and saw various warriors from the Lion's Den, Wolf Pack and Gorilla Jungle gathered together, overlooking the bull clan's canal; it had completely collapsed and was in utter shambles. The entire dam was in shambles. It would take months for them to rebuild if they were lucky. They were silent as they looked at the pile of debris.

Amun directed Sebastian over to a group of frog and toad warriors. They were gathered around another frog warrior seated on a rock. The moment their king approached, the amphibian warriors separated and bowed.

"*King.*"

Sebastian took in the look on their faces. Amun motioned to the frog warrior that seemed to hold everyone's attention.

"My king…"

The warrior was completely soaked; his body was shaking violently. For one whose skin was so colorful, Sebastian could not help but notice how pale his warrior looked as he took in the bewildered look on his face.

"You look like you've seen a ghost."

The warrior looked back at the sea.

"My king, I was on top of the dam when the bull clan went down. I was about to dive into the sea when I saw something swimming in the water. It wasn't one of us."

Sebastian narrowed his eyes. "What was it?"

The warrior swallowed hard. "I didn't know…I dove in…"

"And?"

The frog warrior shook his head in disbelief.

"What did you see?"

"You won't believe me."

Sebastian crouched down and looked deep into the warrior's eyes. "Tell me."

"You must look for yourself, my king. It must be you who bears witness."

144

And with that, the amphibian king dove into Mariner Sea.

Tick-Tock was crouched low, deep in the shadows in front of a small waterfall inside a cavern in the fortress. His eyes never blinked as he watched for movement through the gushing water. He knew they were coming. He had sensed their presence since leaving the lair; they had been following the remnants ever since. He was sure of it. He had seen their large forms amongst the shadows and never lost sight of them, not until they had entered the fortress. The luxury of having three heads.

"Remember...remember..."

Netapheha's voice rose from the pool of water that rested at the base of the waterfall. Tick-Tock looked down and saw the old toad chief's image amidst the rippling water. It quickly faded away until Tick-Tock saw nothing but his own mage staring back at him. He tilted his horned owl head to the side and stretched out his raven claw to touch the image. He slowly swiveled his head to barn owl and then to snow owl, slowly taking in his appearance; almost as if it were the first time he were really seeing himself.

His eyes moved to his raven claw and then over to his eagle claw. He lifted both to his face, taking in the different nature of his talons. It was then that the emerald stone around Tick-Tock's neck began to glow.

The totem shifted his gaze back to the waterfall, carefully concealing the emerald beneath his fur to shield himself from being seen. He moved further away from the pool and into the shadows just as the tips of two spears slowly emerged through the shower of water.

After several moments, the paws holding the spears emerged, long black claws followed, until the rest of the creatures' forms came forth. Tick-Tock studied the size of the warriors as they slowly crept through the powerful flow of water. They cautiously stepped forward, searching for any sign of danger. They were over twelve feet tall.

XXXIII

Byron sat against the rock wall clutching onto Rebekah's medallion. "Alexandra? Are you alright?"

Several moments passed before she finally replied. "Is it true? Did my father start all the slaughter in the realm? Is he responsible for all the cannibalism? For all of this?"

Byron inhaled deeply. He knew this could not be easy for her, for he knew how much she revered her father. "Your father is the reason that Sebastian, Minotauro and I lived to be men. We owe our lives to him."

"Is he the reason?"

"I don't know. All I know is that he was part of why it ended." He paused, looking down at the medallion. "He told us about you. He said he didn't like to see you cry. I don't like to see it either. And I know Daniel cannot bear it."

"I'm not crying." She was silent for several moments before she finally said, "I'm not who I thought I was."

"You are your father's daughter. You are queen of the Wolf Pack. Ruler of the lair. And the best part...you have gorilla in you. Do you know how lucky you are to have gorilla in you?"

"He should have told me."

Byron leaned his head back against the rock wall. "Fathers do lots of things before they have their daughters and sons; things they don't want their children to know about — even mine." He let Rebekah's medallion fall against his chest. "Whatever your father did in the beginning, he changed it in the end. It's the last round that matters most."

She paused before saying, "If I'm part gorilla, why did your clan go down?"

"I thought about that. Your mother must not have been of the royal line."

"So, she was ordinary."

Byron was not sure where Alexandra was going with her thoughts, so he said nothing more. They sat in the dark in complete silence for a long time.

146

Alexandra sighed deeply, "How are we going to get out of here?"

Byron narrowed his eyes, unsure of what he was seeing through the darkness.

"Byron?"

"Fire will show us the way. Fire will show us how."

"What?"

A small flame high above the rock wall opposite Byron started to make its way down the wall. As it flowed down the edifice, it left a small trail a few feet at a time before disappearing as it moved forward. Byron was mesmerized, watching as the flames lit a path for him to follow. Byron slowly stood up. "Alexandra…I see a way out."

On the opposite side of the wall, she stood up. "Byron!" She started pounding on the rock.

He shouted back, "I'll find you, Alexandra!" He watched as the flame's path disappeared around a corner. He was desperate to follow it.

"Byron!"

"I'll find you!" He moved forward and followed the light.

Daniel moved swiftly through the rock-covered hallways of the fortress' domain, searching for Alexandra and Byron. His dialogue with Fire played over and over in his mind as he tried to decipher each part of their conversation.

Do you seek it in vain?

What did that mean? That such a stone did not exist? That the Creators would not give it to them? Or was it something more…

Daniel moved through the hallway and through another archway. He almost gasped the moment he stepped through. Markings covered the walls: pictures of kings, queens, and warriors from all the clans; some were clans he had never seen before. His eyes scaled up the wall to the top where it all seemed to begin. That is where he saw symbols that represented a sun, a rose, a wave, wind, and something else. It was a blacked-out symbol that he could not quite make out. He reached out to touch it, dusting away any debris to get a better look but to no avail. Whatever this last symbol was had been purposely damaged. He wondered what it was.

He followed the images beneath the element signs and saw carvings of twelve kings and queens followed by warriors — animal warriors. He realized that it was the story of the realm's creation. As he studied the graphics of man and beast, he saw where the twelve, not eight, began to split apart.

Twelve clans…

Graphics of battles and wars were drawn along the rocks, showing the rise and fall of many. Even the horses were there: a drawing of their banishment from the bull king. He saw petroglyphs of ravens, eagles, and wolves before a large bonfire. There was a man standing before its flame; it was a man with dark hair and olive skin. Daniel followed the story, seeing the next one follow: the split between the kingdoms.

"The Old War..."

He followed the petroglyphs along the wall until coming to an image of the realm on fire. The only clan left standing were the lions. As he stood there looking at the illustration, he was bewildered. He did not remember this story. He backtracked to follow the storyline through the pictures.

Impossible.

"*Lionsss cannot be trusted...*"

Daniel whirled around having heard Poe's voice. "Tick-Tock?"

No reply.

He went back to the image, touching the flames drawn on the wall. He could not see where in the hierarchy this image landed, only that it was there...just like Palimus had said.

"*I know what you're thinking...*"

This was a different voice. It was soothing — melodious. As the gentle breeze blew all around him, Daniel had heard it before. It was the voice he had heard when they first entered the fortress.

Wind.

"*Is it the making of his vision...or is it a future yet to come?*"

Daniel followed the voice as it moved through the cavern. "Which is it?"

"*Hard to say. The doer has yet to decide.*"

There were only so many doers in the den and only one king. "The future I intend to build does not result in burning it all to the ground. Not under my rule."

Silence.

The lack of response bothered Daniel as he continued to stand there before an illustration of fire.

"*Pain destroys the intent of the good. Suffering dismantles the will and turns the tide...*"

"It didn't with Queen Rebekah."

The wind suddenly stopped blowing.

"*Her intentions laid the path for the true of heart to follow — even through all her pain.*"

"You forget about the shockwave. Firing the realm would be no different if one is in pain and needs the suffering to stop to protect the ones you hold most dear. She did that to survive."

"*As could another if threatened.*"

The wheels in Daniel's head were spinning. "But the kings and queen and I are united. We are no longer enemies."

"*That does not mean there is no enemy.*"

148

The wind blew past him until it was no more. Daniel turned back to the wall filled with pictures, but he saw no other images that told a different story than the one he was seeing.

He thought about what Tick-Tock had said a few nights before.

"Their bloodline wasss the darkest the kingsss and queensss had ever ssseen. They long to be found, king. They yearn to seek their revenge in order to rectify. Darkness within. Destruction isss their footstep. One of their kind found their way to my queen'sss domain. And where there isss one, otherss follow."

Daniel continued to study the storyline, searching for the image of the darkened clan, but all he found was the scratched-out symbol up above.

Around the corner there were more drawings — signs and symbols of what he was looking for — drawings of clans beyond the realm. But Daniel did not see them as he followed the petroglyphs that wound around another archway.

Byron continued to follow the flames as they led him through multiple caverns. It was not until the gorilla king passed through one archway in particular that the flames completely died out. He stopped jogging, slowing his step as he took in his surroundings. It was a large hall surrounded by walls lit afire in different color flame. Byron had never seen anything so beautiful as the violet, crimson, emerald and fuchsia flames dancing before him, almost as if seducing him into a trance. He was mesmerized by their choreography.

He moved toward a wall covered in white flames and slowly extended his hand to touch it when a slight breeze blew through the halls.

"Fire calms you."

Byron whirled around at the sound of the voice. He looked all around but could see nothing. "This fire does."

"Your voice does the same for my sister. It comforts her."

The gorilla king continued to search the halls as a gentle breeze surrounded him and Zephyrus' voice sounded all around him, moving with the wind's path.

"It's the conviction in your tone. The honesty. The purity of intention. You are true, king."

"How do you know Agoura feels this way?"

"Agoura is my twin. I am sky and she is earth, born on the same day. Although she has been silent for decades, I can still hear her voice through her silent screams and cries. Even through her grief, I know her meaning. She sings in silent whispers when you are near. The sound of your voice calms her. I haven't heard her sing in a long time, king. When she is calm, so are we."

He swallowed hard, unsure of how bold or humble he needed to be at this moment. He took a chance, "Then…help me get the stone so we can get out of here and Agoura can sing on."

Silence.

"It's not for me alone to decide."

"You are Wind, are you not?"

Silence once more.

Byron could feel the disappointment in the pit of his stomach as he contemplated the silence between his challenging replies. He continued to look all around until the realization hit him as he said, "You have not found us worthy."

"Son of the father, why are you here?"

It was almost the exact same question he heard Rhodes ask Alexandra. He knew the question was meant to be personal, thoughtful…deeper than answering with the finding of a mere stone. Byron clutched Bane tightly. Why was he here?

"To stop the pain."

"Pain. The pain of your people or your own?"

Now it was Byron who was silent.

"Pain is often necessary, king…in order to become."

"Become what?"

"Free."

Byron's shoulders fell slightly, remembering what Minotauro had said when they last sat at the waterfall. His jaw clenched, not knowing which way to turn or look as the voice in the wind seemed to be everywhere all at once. Coming to this fortress to have this kind of conversation was not what he had anticipated.

"Without a mountain to climb, there is no peak to reach. Without loss, there is nothing found. Without a problem, there is no solution. Without darkness, there is no light. Why come to a fortress?"

Byron's heart was pounding. "To live. To find a means for the clans to live on. We cannot survive another drought."

"Couldn't you?"

"No!"

"Food will not make you whole. Rain in a forgotten sea is not the final answer. What is it that you seek…from me?"

And with that simple question, Byron spoke his deepest of thoughts out loud for the first time, "I want…to live without pain, without constant suffering. Not just for my people…but for me. I cannot bear anymore." The emotions he constantly held back began to rise. "There are too many blows that keep breaking me…that keep breaking my heart."

Wind remained silent for several moments before replying, *"King, there is no life without pain…without suffering…even when there's love…great love in the midst."*

"What love?"

"The kind that you desire most in this world. That is what you truly want in this life, isn't it, king?"

Byron did not reply; his mind was reeling.

"You envied him."

Byron's entire body froze as the image of Minotauro flooded his mind. "I…he deserved his season."

"You yearn for yours. You have always sought the mountain when there are easier steps to follow, other paths to take. Yet you thrive on the road less traveled. You do not want just a woman to love. You desire a queen. Time requires such a match. Purpose demands the discipline to hold out for the top of the mountain. Easy it is to love any woman, harder to hold out for The One." The wind blew gently around Byron. *"Easy to speak words to your people that there will be a better tomorrow. Harder to show them. Easier to imagine the life others have built than be the builder. Pain is the risk of truly living, king. Suffering in the steps of those who can become. They make it look easy, don't they? The courageous ones. The wise ones. The successful ones. Those that sacrifice. Those that risk. The ones who seem to have it all…"* The wind seemed to stand still before him. *"You are not afraid to love, are you, king? Just to lose that which consumes your heart. You did not need to come here to know my words are true. So, I ask you again, Why are you here?"*

Byron swallowed hard before saying, "For the stone." He almost felt foolish saying it, for it seemed so trivial yet so outrageous when speaking to a powerful element. Even in Wind's midst, Byron could feel the power of the element brother. It seemed too small a gift when standing in his presence, for the gorilla king knew that this element brother could do much, much more than gift a stone to bring the rain. He felt small in his imagination as he asked, "Does it even exist…the one the lion prince searched for? The one the lion king believes in?"

"The Noble One…"

Byron waited for an answer.

"It exists."

Byron exhaled, not even realizing he had been holding his breath.

"Because he believes it does. And because he does, so do they."

"Who?"

"The ones you don't see coming."

Byron clenched his jaw, reaching for Bane out of reflex. And with that, the wind blew loudly, forming a small tornado in the middle of the room, extinguishing all the flames, leaving Byron alone in darkness.

XXXIV

Sebastian dove down into the depths of the sea, swimming deeper and deeper into the darkened water. Everywhere his eyes roamed he saw rotting metal — weapons of old — chunks of marble gathered on the seabed floor from when Mariner Tower collapsed. Bones of the dead: warriors, women, children.

Amun, Chango and other warriors were on edge. They did not like being here one bit. If there was anything alive in this sea, they were vulnerable to its existence — especially their king.

They were relieved the moment they saw their king turn to swim up and away from this haunted tower of the dead as he rose to the surface. The moment Sebastian broke through the water, he swam toward the anxious amphibian, gorilla and bull clan warriors standing watch over the sea from the busted canals. He even noticed Hood and members of the Wolf Pack gathered beside them.

"Nothing but ghosts down there. A kingdom wrecked."

Everyone turned to look at the frog warrior who had been haunted by what he had seen earlier. "I swear to you, my king, there is something down there. Even if you did not see it, I know you can feel it."

Sebastian could see the sincerity and fear behind his warrior's eyes. He looked back at the center of the sea — the darkest part of the water. He had felt...*something*.

"If there is anything down there, I need a better set of eyes to see in the darkness." He turned to his warriors still wading in the water. "We will need to see the chief. Perhaps he has something we can use."

"A spectral light."

The amphibian king looked at the frog warrior once more. "What *did* you see?"

He was shaking his head, reliving his memory, "It was fast...so fast..."

Sebastian looked up and saw that Cheetah and a few lion's den warriors had joined the rest of the clan warriors near the demolished canal. They were unnaturally silent. He watched as they stared out at the center of the sea. He could only imagine what they had been thinking, knowing the part their clan had played in its demise. He followed Cheetah's stare, seeing the warrior's mane standing on end. As he turned back to look at the darkened waters, Sebastian could not help the chills that suddenly ran all down his spine.

Alexandra sat alone, unable to move from her ledge. Although her eyes had adjusted slightly to the dark, she still had trouble making anything out around her. She had been listening for any sound of movement — including any sound from Byron or Daniel.

But she was all alone.

It reminded her of all the nights leading up to this one where she sat alone in the dark thinking about all her misery. Alexandra had been thinking about what Rhodes had asked her earlier, *"What is your greatest desire…"*

She had responded only partially. She had not shared her deepest one. It was as if, by doing so, a deep, dark secret brought into the light would brand her in some way that would only do her more harm. But what she wanted was not a harmful motivation or submission. It was really quite simple. It wasn't just to be a powerful and good queen. She wanted to be valued. She wanted…*to be loved.*

She felt embarrassed, weak, by such an admission. She was already loved, wasn't she? Her father loved her. She believed Reginald had loved her. And of course, Daniel loved her. There was no doubt in her mind that he loved her. But her pack? Questionable. So, was it that she sought the love of her pack? Maybe. She wanted their respect, but their love? Did their love matter?

To most, probably not. But as queen it did. Never had there been a queen in the lair that had not been loved by the pack — at least, none that Alexandra knew of. And why was that? What was it about her that kept their hearts guarded against their queen? Was she that unlovable?

She looked down at her hands and touched the ends of her dark hair.

The gorilla clan.

An ordinary woman.

She had no idea her father had been there, thinking that she was born on her side of the realm. Alexandra had asked about her mother once, but all Alexander had ever told her was that she had died giving birth to her. She had even asked Reginald once if he had known her. All she ever saw in his response was a saddened look behind his grey-colored eyes. That was when she began to think it was Rebekah. Rebekah with her raven-colored hair. A queen.

The gorilla clan.

153

An ordinary woman.

And her father had started the cannibalism in the realm. No wonder he kept her inside the lair. Never knowing what was beyond her kingdom walls. Never knowing the other kings on the other side of the realm.

He was responsible for it all.

And now she was inside the fortress — not just for a stone to resurrect the life of the realm, but to rectify her father's part in causing its slow death.

Her head began to hurt, and her heart felt heavy. What else didn't she know? What other tales would she soon discover? And what part was she going to play beyond the one she was trying to figure out already?

She sighed, finally fed up with even her own self-pity as she willed herself to stand and feel her way out. She was tired of just sitting there waiting to be found.

Alexandra felt all around the rock wall as she thought about what it was she truly desired, when her hand felt an open space. She almost fell forward but caught herself as she nervously placed one foot in front of the other, carefully sliding her foot across the ground, feeling for any sudden drop-offs. She held onto the rock wall with one hand feeling all around when the wall suddenly shifted. Alexandra screamed as she fell through another archway.

The wolf queen landed on the ground. The wall behind her shifted again and sealed her into what appeared to be another cavern. Alexandra looked up and was pleasantly surprised she could actually see. She pushed herself up and brushed herself off as she took in her new surroundings. It was a cavern filled with snow.

XXXV

Byron ran through various archways, hallways and caves as he wound his way through the element fortress. He had no idea where he was going as he continued running, rounding another corner.

BAM!

He slammed right into Daniel. They butted heads, landing flat on their backs.

"Ow."

Neither of them moved. "I take it you didn't find the stone."

"Nope. If I had, I'd have left you here and headed back to the realm already."

"Not possible. It goes against your nature, lion. You're the best of us."

"Push the wrong button, you might change your mind." Daniel slowly sat up, "I don't even know if there is a stone."

Byron rubbed his head, slowly sitting up. "What are you saying?"

"It was something Fire said."

"They're speaking to you too."

"I haven't come across Rhodes yet."

"Alexandra has. He seems to lean her way. Apparently, you haven't seen her medallion. I think she's Ice's chosen queen."

Daniel's eyes slit to a cat.

Byron sat up, seeing the sudden change in the lion king's eyes. "Hang on there, king. It's not a bad thing if she has a protector. Diana and Rebekah never seemed to be in any danger with Wind or Fire."

"Rhodes is different. He is much more active than the others, and I have yet to see him gesture toward any act of grace or mercy."

Byron thought about what Rhodes had said to Alexandra earlier. "Perhaps, he is not what he seems." He paused before continuing, "I ran into Zephyrus and asked for the stone. I figured it could save us time."

155

"What did he say?"

"It's not for him alone to decide."

"Fire said something about us seeking it in vain."

Byron narrowed his eyes, "What's that supposed to mean?"

"I don't know."

The blood in Byron's veins suddenly began to boil. "We didn't risk our lives to be turned away! Minotauro's *life* taken for nothing! I don't know what game these element brothers are playing, king, but Ice told Alexandra it *did* exist!'

"But do you deserve it?"

Byron and Daniel's heads snapped up at the sound of another voice.

It was Rahelio...*Fire.*

They could not see anything but felt Fire's warmth all around them all the same. It was Byron who replied with a loud shout, *"YES!"*

"Words mean nothing. It is action that speaks to the heart of any matter...especially this one, kings. There are certain things you must fight for. You must say to the world, 'I desire this one thing. I am meant for it.' You have merely walked the steps, but you have not laid the path."

Byron answered with, "The path for what?"

"Others to follow."

Daniel asked, "What do we have to do?"

"Only the pure of heart can use the stone."

Byron narrowed his eyes in confusion but somehow Daniel understood. "So anyone can find it."

"Whoever rules the sea, rules the realm..."

Daniel slowly looked all around the cavern, listening to what Fire was really telling him. He whispered to Byron, "We're not alone in here."

"You're never alone." And with that, Fire left the cavern as the warmth the kings had just felt evaporated.

Byron was gripping Bane tightly as Daniel continued thinking. "What's going on here, king?"

Daniel was deciphering the conversation they had just had with Fire when another thought came to his mind. He clenched his jaw tightly, "Follow me."

Diana and Keys slowed down the moment the trees came into view. They had reached the Old Forest in Bull Valley. She did not know what she expected, but the horse queen did not expect this.

Diana dismounted Keys as he rose on his two hind legs and walked alongside her. His bow was out; he reached up for an arrow. They slowly walked through the desolate forest. There was nothing but an eerie silence.

156

Keys was on edge.

"I feel them, my queen...spirits of old. They are sad, lost. What is this place?"

"Our forgotten kingdom."

Keys lowered his weapon. They looked at one another and continued on in silence as they made their way through the thickest part of the trees. The moment they were in the center of the forest, they stopped moving; they were stunned by what they saw.

The layout...the same.

The bridges...the same.

The thatched homes...the same.

"Impossible."

Diana was in shock as she took in the sight of the abandoned homes, remembering her own. "It's all true..."

"My queen..."

Diana turned and moved toward an ancient-looking tree. She followed Keys' gaze, looking up to where his eyes rested.

A treehouse.

She began to climb. She opened the hatch and maneuvered inside. She saw names etched into the wood: Minotauro, Byron. "This was theirs."

Then she saw the last name.

Sebastian.

The other king. The other friend.

She sat there for several moments, staring at their names. She looked out of one of the treehouse windows and saw the dilapidated remains of her ancestry.

Banished.

Diana's heart felt heavy. She peered out one of the windows to the forsaken kingdom below. Lowering her head, she touched her medallion as she spoke to her warriors below, "Keys..."

"What is it, my queen?"

"We're home."

XXXVI

"I need a spectral light."

Netapheha ignored Sebastian, completely lost and distracted in his own thoughts, as he moved about his abode.

"Chief."

He continued to move toward his desk, flipping through books of his own writing, searching for something.

"Did you hear what I said?"

"No, no...not the time."

Amun and Chango looked at each other sideways, knowing how it could be when trying to communicate to the old toad.

"*CHIEF!*"

Netapheha stopped flipping through the pages of his book and stared at Sebastian.

"I *need*..."

"Those are for deep waters..." The chief's bulbous eyes dilated; he was thinking. "What did the warrior see?"

"He will not say...other than it was something fast."

"In Mariner Sea!" The chief dropped the book, almost as if it had been smacked out of his hands, finally giving the king his full attention. He looked down at his pile of books on his desk and then toward the Tablet of Destinies on his shelf. He looked exacerbated. Sebastian had never seen him so frazzled. Looking at the mess in the chief's abode, he asked, "What's wrong?"

"Scales, scales on my eyes!" Netapheha continued to look all around his room, thinking. The bulge in his neck revealed the quickening of his breath. "So many things unseen..." Netapheha froze, staring at the pool of water down below. "The bull king..."

Sebastian immediately clenched his jaw, trying to gather his emotions at the mention of Minotauro. But before he could say what he was about to say, Netapheha continued, "What holds your attention shifts all others and all else in this world. Know that what you control is what you choose to have hold your attention....what you choose amongst the chosen." The chief continued to stare at the pool, as if he were listening. "Let go. Trust in what you don't know…that is which is beyond you. 'Go weaponless' he said…it's the only way to take care of them."

"Who said?"

"The bull king…your shield in the treehouse."

Sebastian narrowed his eyes.

"No, no, not a spectral light…you have need for something much more powerful." He moved quickly to the pool of water down below. Dipping his coral staff into the water, he slowly turned it counterclockwise as he searched its depths for an answer to a question only Netapheha was apt to seek.

Sebastian collected himself as he, Amun and Chango watched the pool as it began to illuminate.

"Yes, yes…come to our aid…make haste to help us…"

The amphibian king watched as tiny little fish rose to the surface setting the pool aglow. They were strange fish, unlike any Sebastian had ever seen before.

"The little ones shall light the way for you, my king. They live in the deepest, darkest depths of the sea. You went below but you must go much deeper. Follow their bio-luminescent glow…their light will show you the way."

"What's down there?"

Netapheha turned and looked at Sebastian. "I do not know. So many things unforeseen…but the warrior…too afraid to show. When something is buried so deep for so long, it does not always long to be found. Go, go…my king…listen to the bull king's voice. He is speaking."

"What's he saying?"

"Keep going."

Sebastian watched as the old toad chief waddled back to his desk as he began searching through his books once more. He turned and looked down at the tiny fish. "What do you think, Amun?"

"I don't know how there could be any life in that forsaken sea. But although our chief said for you to go weaponless and without a light, he did not speak his command to me."

Chango was beside him, "Nor to me."

Sebastian saw that Chango had grabbed a spectral light from the choral staircase down below. He looked back at Netapheha to see if he had witnessed anything, but the old toad chief was too frazzled in his current state to notice anything.

The amphibian king nodded his approval to his warriors and looked back at the tiny luminescent fish swirling in the pool of water waiting for him. He dove into the pool of water after them. The fish immediately took off ahead of him, swifter than he thought they could. He followed them till he came to end of the swamps. The fish had disappeared, but Sebastian knew that once he was in Mariner Sea, he would find them again.

XXXVII

Tick-Tock had been making his way all throughout the Element Fortress following the creatures that had emerged from the waterfall. They were fast. More agile than he had anticipated given their size. They had been moving swiftly between the caverns inside the fortress — almost as if they were familiar with all its routes and pathways — forcing the totem to move even faster so as not to lose sight of them. But he eventually did.

He continued to search for them, knowing the threat they brought to the remaining kings and queen — with or without foreknowledge of their will or intent. Tick-Tock found himself inside another cavern that led him to a ledge that overlooked the center of the mountain. He stopped the moment he reached the edge and slowly looked at the surrounding light up above; a rainbow of flames flickered across the midnight-colored rock. His eyes watched the kaleidoscope of flames as they danced across his eyes, almost as if he were studying their rhythmic dance as they swayed and moved. All three of his heads were looking up at the same time, memorizing and absorbing the energy that surrounded him.

Tick-Tock moved slowly up a small incline and knelt on one knee, extending his eagle claw to the ground. The moment his talon met the earth, the fortress seemed to answer. All three owl heads closed their eyes and listened. He listened to the fire dancing all around him; he listened as a slight breeze suddenly blew gently past him; he listened to the shifting of the earth moving between his claws; and he felt the cold breath of another being watching him from the shadows. As the lights and embers from the fire fell all around him like snowflakes, the emerald stone around his neck began to glow.

Rhodes was crouched down, watching the totem from a ledge up above, witnessing the power of the moment down below.

Wind funneled inside the cavern and spun like a tornado on the opposite ledge from Rhodes.

A line of fire descended from up above and burned silently along the rock walls on either side of Rhodes and Zephyrus.

All three element brothers watched Tick-Tock's movements below.

No ordinary totem.

Rhodes had been summoned only once before to create a guardian. But the one before was nothing like this one. When Feyedor willed the existence of Tick-Tock, he had created a masterpiece of thought, intent, purpose — and something more. No totem before this one had been made of what this one was.

He remembered the night the wolf king Feyedor had crossed the realm to summon the old toad chief. It was Rhodes' face the king had seen in the swamp's reflection. He was curious as to what his sister's chosen king was up to, for he had felt the shift...the rumble of change over a single choice for a time that could be long in the coming. Staring down at Tick-Tock now, he was curious at what the totem would ultimately do knowing what he was meant to become.

And as the remaining embers fell to the ground, all that remained was the emerald glow emanating from the stone. The soft glow began to flicker rapidly until a fierce, sharp blinding light lit up the entire cavern.

Rhodes' head whipped around to an archway behind him; he was immediately on his feet.

Tick-Tock's eyes snapped open in response. He immediately stood, clutching the stone with his raven claw. *"Queen."*

With ferocious speed, Rhodes burst forth, skating through the archway.

Leaping to the upper cliff, Tick-Tock raced behind him, disappearing into the shadows as the wind and fire dissipated and extinguished behind him.

Alexandra looked all around the cavern and saw snow as far as the eye could see. A frozen pond lay ahead of her filling the grounds to the other side; crossing it was the only way out. "Of course there would be a frozen pond."

She sighed, testing her weight as she gently stepped onto it. The ice cracked slightly. She heard a strange sound, whipping her head upward as she saw Rhodes skate past through an archway above. Alexandra watched as he shifted directions, skiing and sliding down toward her cavern. She backed up, attempting to find a place to hide. She did not know why she was hiding from him. All she knew was that she did not want to face him.

Looking around frantically, she raced toward a far corner of the cavern where a large pile of snow was stacked high. She crouched low, backing into the corner, burying herself in the snow just as Rhodes entered the cavern. Alexandra looked out and saw Rhodes coming through the archway at the other end of the frozen pond on the other side of the cavern. He switched from skiing down the passageways, to skating across the frozen lake.

Rhodes looked all around the cavern searching for something — little did she know it was her. Alexandra ducked her head down just as his eyes landed on the pile of snow behind her. Rhodes slowed down, pausing to stare in Alexandra's direction. The wolf queen's heart was thundering inside her chest. She was sure he could hear it.

Rhodes stared at the pile of snow for what seemed like an eternity. She could see the tiniest glimpse of hope and expectation on his face, almost as if he could see her, willing her to speak to him, to call upon him. But when she did not, his face seemed to fall a bit as he suddenly lowered onto his knees and spun slowly around, catching all angles of the cavern, using his hands to move him across the ice until he moved toward a rock wall. It shifted and opened; he moved through it; the wall closing behind him once again.

Alexandra lifted her head and decided it was time to move. She remembered the path Rhodes had taken as he moved across the ice. Realizing he had not fallen through, she decided to do the same. She stepped onto the ice to follow...when she heard movement behind her.

XXXVIII

Daniel and Byron were inside the cavern filled with petroglyphs. Byron was taking in all the illustrations on the wall as Daniel followed the story's path with great precision.

Byron's voice was barely a whisper, "There is no recording of this kind of history in my library."

"Nor mine."

Byron's eyes roamed the drawings until coming to the large fire drawing with the lion warrior. His eyes shifted to Daniel as the thoughts behind its meaning flooded his mind. He had heard the phrase many times over his lifetime but never gave it credence until he saw the illustrations on the wall. This image had not yet come to pass, and the gorilla king knew if it was written in stone inside an element fortress, this was no mere vision in a fire.

The gorilla king looked up at the symbols for the Elements; his eyes narrowed as he tried to decipher what looked to be a fifth symbol. He focused his eyes, attempting to make out the shape of the blackened symbol. It had been scratched out.

Daniel continued to follow the path of the story at the bottom of the wall when he turned the corner. There were several rocks piled up along the adjoining wall. And as the lion king moved the rocks and other debris away from it, he paused the moment more drawings emerged; they were covered in blood.

"Banished from the realm….they long to be found, king."

Daniel's heart stopped as he took in the violence of the illustrations of what had been etched onto this wall.

"Byron…"

Byron rounded the corner and paused the moment he saw the new markings. The look on his face was grave. "What is this?"

Daniel was speechless. He merely shook his head continuing to study the drawings. None of them made sense. They were warriors of varying breed, differing sizes. Some had large tusks and snouts, some resembled the wolves, while others were full-bodied warriors of differing animals with other fur-covered beasts roaming the snow-covered tundra.

It was then that Byron saw a darkened figure with, what looked like, the fifth symbol etched onto his chest.

"What clan is this…"

"The darkest one that's ever existed. I think it's the one Tick-Tock mentioned."

A low growl rumbled behind them.

Daniel and Byron's heads spun around at the sound of the growl, but no one was there.

"I don't think that was Tick-Tock."

"Nope."

"We'd better hurry up and get out of here."

Byron gripped his bone scepter tight. He moved to the front of the pathway, while Daniel turned back to the wall to continue rapidly studying the markings of the mixed clan, following the story of their descent. He had missed it the first time, having walked past the rounded corner that held this clan's tale. As his eyes followed their history, he saw where the last graphic led: to a land of snow and ice. There was a boundary between this land and what looked like the realm — *a waterfall.*

Byron stood there uneasily, listening for any further sound. He narrowed his eyes, searching for any movement when he saw a pair of eyes mirroring in the darkness in front of him. He squinted, unsure of what he was seeing.

"King…" Byron backed into the cavern where Daniel was. "Run…"

Daniel looked up.

Byron turned and rammed his way toward Daniel, *"RUN!!!"*

A loud roar erupted from around the corner, causing the rocks around them to vibrate.

Daniel turned and raced over the piles of rocks alongside Byron. Whatever it was the gorilla king had seen, Daniel was unwilling to wait to find out. They moved fast and furious until they reached a dead end.

"There's no way out!"

They quickly felt all around the surrounding walls, feeling for any opening they could work off of to barrel through.

Roars thundered from around the corner.

Both kings turned to face their pursuer — Byron gripped his bone scepter; Daniel clutched his sword. They waited, hearing the sharp snorts of whatever was coming around the corner. They could see the shadow of movement forming against the torches surrounding the cavern. They could hear its heavy footsteps.

Whatever it was, it was big.

Byron clutched Bane even tighter, sending out a silent prayer.

And it was answered.

The walls behind Daniel and Byron shifted and the two kings fell through. The wall began to close but did not shut completely, barred open by boulders that blocked its closure.

Long black claws suddenly appeared, gripping the wall, trying to pry it open.

They scrambled and moved quickly, running through various halls and under multiple archways, not paying attention to where they were going. Byron saw a ledge up ahead.

"JUMP!!!"

Without hesitating, both kings leapt into the unknown and came crashing down onto another ledge further down the mountain. Daniel rolled and flipped over the cliff.

"KING!" Byron dove over the ledge after him, catching Daniel's hand before he plunged into the darkness. Byron pulled hard, using all the strength he could muster to lift Daniel back onto the ledge but to no avail.

Daniel was gripping so tightly onto Byron's hand that Byron thought his skin would rip off.

"Hang on, lion!"

Over Byron's shoulder, the lion king caught sight of a pair of eyes mirroring in the darkness.

"BEHIND YOU!"

Byron's head spun around; his eyes grew wide as a pair of black claws swiped at his jugular. He leapt off the ledge before the blow struck its mark, pulling Daniel along with him as they plunged further down the mountain. They crashed onto another ledge, colliding into each other.

Daniel rolled onto his back trying to catch his breath as the wind was knocked out of him. His entire body ached. "King..." He was breathing hard. "What was that thing?"

Silence.

Daniel's entire body froze as he waited for a reply, listening for any sound of movement. He slowly reached his hand out to feel for anything beside him. All he gathered in his fingertips was rocks and dirt. "Byron..." He turned his head, waiting for his eyes to adjust to the darkness, when he saw that he was completely alone. He rolled over and pushed himself up, reaching all around him. "Byron!" He moved forward slowly, continuing to feel all around him when he felt another ledge. His heart almost stopped the moment he realized Byron had gone over it. His eyes slit to a cat as he roared, *"KING!!!"*

"Out of your element, aren't you, wolf?"

166

Alexandra was on top of the ice when she heard the unknown, gravelly voice behind her.

A loud cracking sound erupted behind her and, before she could turn, she was plunged headfirst into the freezing water. As the shock of the ice-cold water seized her system, her initial reaction was to scream. She frantically attempted to swim to the surface but was immediately shoved back down by something up above her. Her body moved further underneath the sheet of ice, pulled by its drag. She pounded on it, trying to break through.

Above her, she could see rapid movement atop the ice. Whatever was happening, it was swift and vicious. She could hear yelling and roaring, followed by a thunderous collision of rocks. And as she continued to pound on the ice, everything began to get blurry. She could not breathe. She was panicking, inhaling large amounts of ice-cold water. She began choking, feeling her entire body jerking just as a vibrant green light illuminated the frozen water above her head.

The vibrant light was growing dimmer and dimmer as Alexandra began to lose consciousness. And as everything turned black, the wolf queen's only thoughts were of Minotauro and that she would soon see him again.

Hood and the rest of the pack were standing atop one of the canals, watching for the amphibian king's emergence from the sea. That was when he felt it.

"*Queen…*"

The entire wolf pack lifted their heads in unison and turned toward the north.

Hood's voice was barely a whisper as he said, "Its breath is cold on my neck…protect my queen, lion…"

And then it happened.

Hood and the rest of the pack dropped to the ground all around the dismantled dam, while some warriors fell straight into the sea.

XXXIX

Sebastian glided through Mariner Sea, going deeper and deeper as he followed the tiny, luminescent fish. They had emerged out of nowhere the moment he had reached the center of the sea. The temperature continued to drop as he followed their path going further and further down. It was completely black all around him; not even the darkest night had ever been colored in such a shade. He looked to his right and his left, seeing his warriors beside him. They were on edge, clutching their spears tight as they silently swam beside their king.

Whatever the frog warrior had seen had not been this far down. He wondered what it was that had been stirred from deep within this cavern of the dead. The fish in front of him were weaving their way into the depths of the sea, when they suddenly split and dashed away faster than Sebastian thought they could swim. His warriors immediately surrounded him as they stopped their descent. Chango gripped the spectral light tightly and handed it to his king.

Sebastian lifted the choral staff as the spectral light illuminated their surroundings. The amphibian king moved it all around, searching for movement up ahead. He turned his head slightly right when something in front of him dashed straight for him, ripping the light from his hands. His warriors immediately grabbed for him and pulled him rapidly to the surface. They were not taking any more chances.

As they rose to the surface, Sebastian could not make out what he was seeing. Bodies were descending in the water, while others seemed to be floating above it. He focused his eyes as he was being pulled upward. His eyes went wide as he saw the bodies of wolves, coyotes, and hyenas filling the sea. He kicked harder, fighting with his own soldiers to get to the top faster. And then he saw more bodies — *wolves.*

As his head burst through to the surface, he shouted, *"GET THEM OUT OF THE WATER!!!"*

Amphibian, gorilla, bull and even lion's den warriors dove into the sea.

They worked furiously to pull the bodies of the wolves out of the water. Sebastian dove down again and again, grabbing onto as many of them that he could. His only thoughts were the ones that had sunk deeper. The tiny fish guiding them were scared off; he had no light to see. He had no idea what to do next. He dove down once more.

Sebastian kicked hard and fast to descend to the sea's depths when he felt multiple forces swimming past him and up toward the surface. Whatever they were, they were fast. He saw wolf pack warriors rocketing to the surface. He reversed course and followed.

The moment Sebastian's head emerged from the water, he watched as bodies of wolf pack warriors were hurled from the sea and onto dry land.

"KING! GET OUT OF THE WATER!!!" Kingston, a tiger warrior, was shouting to him from the edge of one of the wrecked canals.

Sebastian swam rapidly toward him. As he reached shore, Kingston reached out his hand to help the amphibian king out of the sea when two spears landed on either side of Sebastian's head. The amphibian, lion, gorilla and bull clan warriors went berserk, immediately pulling their weapons to defend against the unknown warrior hiding in the sea.

Amun and Chango vaulted out from the water, dragging Sebastian with them. They all turned toward the sea, searching its waters for any sign of movement. Sebastian, however, was staring at the spears. They were made of pure ivory. He turned his gaze back toward the darkened waters. His heart was racing as they stared at the stillness of the sea.

The frog warrior who started their hunt in the sea was suddenly beside him. Sebastian could see his neck bulging rapidly, knowing full well it matched the pace of his own heartbeat as they stared down into the darkened waters. He studied the waves, searching for any further movement as the wolf pack warriors lay unconscious at the foot of the dam. He narrowed his eyes trying to see what no others could see.

"LOOK OUT!"

He jumped back just as two creatures vaulted up and out of the sea. They landed on dry ground amongst a throng of lion, amphibian, gorilla, and bull clan warriors. Everyone was dumbstruck as they took in the sight of the eight-foot-tall warriors.

Cheetah was standing beside the amphibian king when he said, "Impossible…"

They all stood there, thunderstruck, as they stared into the black eyes of a shark warrior.

No one said a word for several moments. And before anyone could digest what was happening, mariner warriors soared over the shambles of the dam: eel, octopus, and devil ray soldiers. They landed all around the other clan warriors.

The rest of the clan soldiers gripped their weapons tight, readying for battle. Growls and uneasy roars rumbled across the camp; everyone's eyes were on Sebastian as to how to act. He stepped toward, what appeared to be, their captain. It was a great white shark warrior.

Sebastian swallowed hard as he watched the gills on the warrior's neck rise and fall. The warrior spoke in a deep, gravelly voice, "King of Amphibians...I am Stab."

Stab waited for Sebastian to speak, staring at the king with his dead, black, doll-like eyes. Sebastian had no idea what to say; he was in complete and utter shock. Somehow, he was able to spit out a word, "How?"

Stab replied, "We live on through the lion king."

Cheetah, Kingston and other members of the den measured his words. Stab looked directly at the lion's den warriors. "Your king is our king...the grandson of our princess...Lara." At the sound of her name, the mariner warriors bowed their heads in deep respect. "It was she who sent us to the bottom of the sea...so that we would survive King Nathan's slaughter. It was time, amphibian king, to make ourselves known. You seek to resurrect our sea, our home. We will help."

Diana and Keys felt the rumble and the shift beneath their feet as they moved about the Old Forest.

"What is it, my queen?"

"Change."

Across the realm, Rhodes extended his palm over the ground inside the element fortress. His eyes were closed as he listened to the rumbling across the realm. He had heard the sea move. He had felt the heartbeats of old rise up. He had felt the summoning of hope amongst the clans who stood near his sea. He could hear the mournful cries of old mounting from Mariner Sea. The wave of memories from that time flooded his mind as he thought of the lion king and the death of the people in his sea.

A vine emerged from the ground beneath his hand and gently draped itself over his skin. It wound around his hand, holding it.

Rhodes' entire demeanor changed by that small gesture. "Sister..." He lowered his head, clenching his jaw, and silently wept as he remembered the day the lion king annihilated members of the sea...

XL

Nathan stood over the bloodied Mariner Sea. He watched as his lion guard slaughtered every mariner in sight, tossing their bodies into the fire as the remaining bits of Mariner Tower burned in the center of the sea. An eel warrior leapt out of the water and tried to escape. Nathan took the sword of a dead hammerhead warrior laying at his feet and hurled it out at the eel. The sword slammed through the being's heart, rocketing him back into the sea.

Die. All of you.

A tiger guard approached. "My king..." Nathan's catlike eyes turned to the guard; they almost seemed to glow. "The queen is in labor."

Without a single reply, Nathan turned and raced toward the den.

Nathan threw the doors open. A Cheetah clanswoman held the heir in her arms. Nathan saw her but did not approach the baby; he did not even glance its way.

Nathan entered Lara's bedchamber. She was surrounded by den clanswomen. They were weeping silently as they looked upon the lion queen.

Nathan commanded, "Everyone out."

They immediately scattered at the sound of his voice. Nathan looked at Lara's pale face; her eyes were closed. He moved slowly toward her and knelt by her side. He gently took her hand. "Lara..."

She barely opened her eyes. "We have a son..." She smiled weakly. "I know you wanted a child with her...your one true love. I, too, wanted to bear the child of my love. But it was not meant to be...for either of us." She was breathing shallowly. "Our son...was born out of both our sorrow. Do not...take it out on him. Do not shut him out. He is all that is left of me...that

171

I lived in this world." It was then that her eyes opened as she locked eyes with Nathan; he could feel her grip on his hand tighten as she said, "I have watched you destroy my home and the people of my heart."

With the last of the strength she could muster, she lifted her head from the pillow. "*You owe me, lion*...if there's one thing you do from this moment on, you let me live on...through my son. Rule as if *she* were beside you. Live as you once wanted to. And do it with our son at your side." Lara lowered her head back onto the pillow. She closed her eyes and breathed her last breath.

Outside her bedchamber, he heard the baby cry.

King Nathan walked through the courtyard. He looked up and saw torches burning inside the Great Library. SinJin stood beside him.

"Marcus is up late again."

SinJin replied, "He is obsessed with his books."

"He's been that way since the treaty was signed."

SinJin looked up at the library. "I think it was spurned by something the bird queen said to him once before."

Nathan looked at him. SinJin lowered his gaze, unable to meet his king's stare at the mention of Queen Rebekah.

"You may go."

SinJin bowed his head. Nathan headed to the library as the lynx warrior cowled and charged across the plains.

Nathan opened the library doors only to find the room in complete shambles. Books and scrolls were scattered everywhere, but Prince Marcus was nowhere to be found. Nathan moved across the room and over to the desk. He sifted through the papers, glancing through all that his little brother was working on.

Nathan looked down at one of Marcus' drawing. It was a rose. Nathan immediately shouted, "*GUARD!!!*"

The roar of lions, tigers and jackal warriors answered their king in reply. The Lion Guard immediately appeared in the doorway.

Chester, captain of the guard, bowed, "King!"

"The prince is missing! Cover the grounds of the den and out toward the borders near Gorilla Jungle. You!" He pointed to SinJin. "Come with me."

172

Marcus sprinted toward the vine gates, ramming against them, attempting to break inside as Nathan and the lion guard approached.

"Marcus..."

Marcus ignored him. He backed up from the gate, gathered speed, and raced toward it once again. He smashed against it and bounced off it and onto the ground. His arms, head and sides were bleeding from the thorns on the vines. Nathan watched him back up again and run toward the gate. Before he collided into it, Nathan wrapped his arm around Marcus' waist and lifted him up. Marcus fought viciously with him.

"Let me go!"

Nathan dropped him. Marcus hit the ground and growled at his older brother. His eyes slit to a cat. He jumped up and charged at Nathan, pummeling him as hard and as fast as he could, growling as he did so. Nathan held him off and crouched down.

"Stop it...stop fighting me, Marcus!"

"It's all your fault! Everybody's dead!"

Nathan lowered his guard and allowed Marcus to expend his rage on him. Marcus lowered his head in exhaustion. "Mother! Father!" Tears streamed down Marcus' face. "She won't let me in. I killed that critter warrior. That's why she won't let me in! That's why she doesn't find me noble!"

Nathan's face looked pained. "Marcus...you are noble."

"Then why won't she let me inside?"

Nathan took his brother's shoulders in his strong hands. "I think she's..." He swallowed hard, trying to contain his emotions as he looked at her gate. "Because Queen Rebekah knew that if she let you in, you would use your brave and noble heart for this purpose and not for a more important one."

"What do you mean?"

"Perhaps she didn't want you wasting your strength running against her doors but using it to barge your way opening others. What's behind these walls has nothing to do with you, Marcus." Nathan looked out to the plains beyond. "It's what's out there...beyond them."

"Is that why she doesn't let you in?"

Nathan was hit hard by the question; like a punch to the gut. "She already opened the doors for me. And I walked through different ones."

"But you loved Queen Rebekah."

He stared at his little brother before replying, "I still do. I always will." He looked down, trying to collect himself. "My heart...I left it here with her...behind these doors."

"But you can't live without your heart. You'll die."

Nathan looked at the prince, trying to control his emotions. "Tell you what...I'll live off yours instead." He stood up. "Come on. I want to go home. There's someone I want you to meet."

Marcus nodded and wrapped his arms around his older brother's waist; they started walking. Nathan picked him up and placed him on his shoulders.

Marcus held onto his bothers strong neck. "I didn't mean what I said. It's not your fault."

"I don't know, Marcus. With all the things I've done, I think maybe it is."

XLI

Daniel had climbed over the ledge and down the mountain desperate to get to Byron. But by the time he reached the bottom, the gorilla king was nowhere to be found. On one hand, Daniel was relieved, as he was not looking forward to another blow of another king — and friend — perishing inside the fortress. On the other hand, he was hoping to find him and soon — not so much if he was hurt — but in case whatever had been chasing them found him first. Seeing the massively long black claws on the creature, for a split-second Daniel wondered if it was Tick-Tock. But the violence upon which they were pursued and the sound of the roar coming from their pursuer did not match Tick-Tock's other voices.

This entire experience was nothing like what Daniel had imagined in his mind's eyes.

He paused, realizing what he had just thought.

What he had imagined...

Daniel stopped mid-step and looked all around the fortress. His eyes roamed the foundation, the look, the feel...everything about it was familiar. He had imagined it to be this way...and it was. Down to the colors, the caverns, the archways — even the color of fire. The only thing that differed was the experience of being in this place.

"Remember...remember..."

Daniel listened closely to the voice on the wind. "It's you." A slight breeze blew past Daniel's face. "It's your voice I've always heard in my dreams."

"Yes...I have spoken many times...to you, to many kings and many queens, but only a few have truly listened."

Daniel's heart was racing. "Is this place even real?"

"It's what you have needed it to be."

"For what?"

"To become..."

Daniel paused before asking, "What was that creature hunting us?"

The cavern began to quake in reply, almost as if recognizing their existence

175

stirred the fortress to anger.

"A beast from a clan that fears no other masters. A warrior that honors no code. A spirit who lives in shadow. A bear warrior."

"I didn't imagine him here."

"Yet they are here all the same."

Daniel could not help but notice he said, *they.* "What is it I'm supposed to remember?"

"Whomever controls the sea, rules the realm…follow your compass…"

Daniel exhaled deeply, suddenly realizing he had been holding his breath in fear and anticipation the entire time. The wind began blowing harder and faster until a funnel of wind wound around Daniel and the image of a man appeared. From his head to his waist, the lion king could see Zephyrus' form, but the lower half of his body was vapor. Zephyrus' hair was copper in color, his skin dark, his body perfectly sculpted. Daniel was awestruck by the strangeness of his appearance.

"Noble One, your honest heart beats strong inside our fortress. They hear it too. It's a drumbeat they cannot stand. They will seek you out to destroy you…for lions cannot be trusted."

Daniel's heart seemed to stop; he swallowed hard. "Tell me what I need to do."

Zephyrus crossed his muscular arms over his lean chest, tilting his head to the side with an almost amused look on his face. "There are many questions in that single one. I will answer the most immediate reference to your underlying need. Your stone…one of pain…one for your rain." Wind studied Daniel for what seemed like an eternity before he continued, "It's the heart of suffering. You will find it there…unless they find it first. It matters, king, to have faith, belief in the unknown…to embrace the signs and symbols. Matters more who finds them, contemplates them and how."

The fortress rumbled once more. Daniel watched Zephyrus' eyes look above and around, listening to the sound of the small quake. His eyes suddenly shifted back to Daniel's; his look was severe. "Seek and ye shall find." His lower body began to spin like a small tornado as Zephyrus rose above Daniel. "The cornerstone will crack, the vine will soon break. The dead sea can only rise if you remember the wisdom given to you by those who came before…"

And with that, Zephyrus' upper torso evaporated until his entire form was wind once more. He blew past Daniel and out of the corridor, leaving the lion king baffled and confused.

"Seek and ye shall find…" He tried to decipher Wind's meaning. "Where is the heart of suffering?" He had encountered Rhodes outside the fortress. He had heard Fire's voice within and spoke to Wind directly throughout. Where was the heart? Daniel did not know. All he knew was that he needed to find Byron, Alexandra and Tick-Tock before the other creatures found them first.

Alexandra…

Something gave him pause; a feeling of dread. His eyes slit to a cat. He ran on.

A black talon punched through the ice and ripped Alexandra from the frozen pond and pulled her onto the snow-covered shore. A low growl sounded from Tick-Tock's mouth as he began chest compressions on Alexandra. His head had swiveled to snow owl as Alexander's voice raged from the totem's beak, *"Demolition of my house is not so easily done!"*

He worked hard and fast on her until Alexandra began coughing up water. She rolled onto her side and opened her eyes. Tick-Tock scooped her up and wrapped his winged arms around her shivering body.

Alexandra could barely speak through her blue-colored lips, "Tick-Tock…" She closed her eyes and fell unconscious.

Unbeknownst to the wolf queen, Rhodes was standing behind Tick-Tock. Looking down at the queen's pale form, a myriad of thoughts ran through his mind. His jaw was set; his body tight from frustration. "You will die one day, queen, but not today." He moved in front of Tick-Tock, crouching down in front of Alexandra. His turquoise-colored eyes boring into Tick-Tock's as he said, "You're in there, aren't you, wolf?"

Tick-Tock stared at him for several moments before replying in Alexander's voice, *"She is the cornerstone of my house…"* Tick-Tock began to howl mournfully and softly.

Rhodes looked at the silver medallion hanging around Alexandra's neck. "King, you have seen what I have seen when you looked into the fire long ago with the bird queen. You must teach her how to use this, totem. It is my gift to her. I ache to help her through her pain. I long to ease her suffering. That is why I gave it to her…so she could commune with me and invite me in that I might give her grace. She is not alone in this world — even if you are not in it, Alexander. Embrace it or race it, it is she…" He reached out and moved a strand from Alexandra's sleeping face. He looked at Tick-Tock, "You are Agoura's masterpiece of pain and remembrance." He slowly stood, "Do what you came to do and then go rest in peace. *All* of you."

XLII

Sebastian stared up at the moonlit sky. He was exhausted, and not just physically. His head was pounding, his muscles ached, but he knew he would not be able to sleep this night.

"Today was quite a day..."

He turned and saw the bull queen approaching. He did not even have the energy to respond as he weighed the events of the day. Lydia stepped up beside him and looked up at the stars.

"The wolves go down and then rise up again, and a clan thought to be extinct rose from the dead. I would say it was quite a day indeed." She looked at Sebastian for any reaction, but he continued to remain silent. She could see the weight of the world on his shoulders.

"When Minotauro and I first met, he didn't talk very much. He wrote me letters instead. I think, for him, it was the only way he could articulate his emotions and thoughts, as it seemed that his emotions would rise up so swiftly sometimes that he could not find the words to speak what it was he felt so deeply."

"You shouldn't be out here. Minotauro would be beside himself if he knew you were wandering the realm at this hour."

"I'm hardly wandering. It's called a nighttime walk, Sebastian. And Minotauro knew I took one every night — with or without him." She studied his tired and anxious face. "I think he'd be more concerned about you. I can't imagine how you must be feeling or what you're thinking, having gone through what you did today — and what you've been going through all along."

"That's the thing...I don't feel anything. I'm too tired to feel, but I know I'm supposed to do something. And I don't know what. No one has any answers for me. Not even my own chief."

"So you came to King Nathan's hilltop."

Sebastian finally turned and looked at her. "Right now, it seems like the only thing to do." He looked out at Bird Kingdom. "I just keep thinking about them out there, wondering what's happening that keeps making them

178

go down." He gritted his teeth. "And why the totem isn't doing its job?"

"And what job is that?"

"*Protecting*, Lydia! He's supposed to be the guardian of the kings and queen!"

"Perhaps, we do not understand what the totem guards…"

"Minotauro is gone. And every time I turn, the clans are dropping like flies all around me — especially Byron's. I can't take it anymore. One blow to my heart almost ended me, but I can't take two, Lydia. Not two. And now the Mariners are alive…do I trust them? Do they seek vengeance? Are they true? I can't do this on my own."

They stood there in silence for some time until Lydia spoke. "Minotauro told me how his father beat him when he was a child." Sebastian slowly turned his head toward her. She was looking up at the stars. "There were moments, he said, when the pain and anticipation of another beating was so intolerable that he thought he was going to die…many times. Pain and suffering in life were expectations rather than a hurdle." She paused, looking at the universe beyond. "Even when he got sick. Very sick from being forced to eat rotted meat — the decomposing flesh of the critter clan. Do you remember it?" Sebastian nodded. "Minotauro said the pain in his body was so crippling, he knew he would never live past his childhood. He wanted to die. But it was then, he said, that he looked out at the stars one night through the window in your treehouse. He asked the maker of the stars to make his illness go away, promising that he if he lived to be king, he would be better than his own. To give him time to do it. Time to rectify all that had been done for the next generation to live on." She looked back at the sky. "His prayer has been answered. Someone out there watches from above and knows when the limits are met, Sebastian."

Sebastian took in her words.

She continued, "After he told me that story, I started going on my nighttime walks to thank the maker of the stars for answering Minotauro's prayer, for giving me the gift of knowing him and joining my life with his as co-champion of his heart — to protect the innocent, the helpless, the hopeless — as his queen. And now, when I go on these walks, looking up at the same stars, I can feel Minotauro looking down at me, strengthening me on my path as I lead the clan and look to raise our son as king. As queen of the bull clan, my responsibility is to help you build that dam. You are not alone, king." She looked up at the stars. "Nor am I."

She looked down at her wedding ring, "I miss him too, Sebastian, but the totem is not responsible for whatever happened to Minotauro. Perhaps, Tick-Tock had protected him, or tried to, in ways we will never know. With the Mariners, only time will tell whether their intent is true and where their hearts lie. What I'm trying to say…is that this hilltop is not where you need to be."

"What do you mean?"

"King Nathan and King Daniel stood here because they did not have what you had when looking for solace amongst the noise." Sebastian narrowed his eyes. "The treehouse, Sebastian. That is your hilltop. Yours, Minotauro's, Byron's…you will find your answers there. You will find peace there. Not here."

Sebastian looked out at the stars and exhaled deeply. "I don't know that there are any answers, Lydia, no matter where I stand — just reactions to whatever the day decides to hurl at us and hoping it forgets about us once in a while. And I don't know that I will ever have peace."

"I would agree with you if you were a mere man, Sebastian. But you are a king. A king who has survived great suffering and endured much pain. A king like that is a man to be reckoned with indeed."

"I don't know how much more I can endure, king or not. I can't help thinking that there is no stone to resurrect that sea; that everything we're doing is all for naught."

"The clans hope for it. Even the Mariners believe in it." Lydia took his hand in hers and squeezed it tight. "Do it anyway. Build it anyway. Miracles are born from the belief that the impossible isn't always so."

"And the universe will answer."

Lydia smiled softly. "Minotauro would be proud. And as much as we don't like what is hurled at us, there are many things hurled at us we can't help but embrace: my son being born, the mariners being alive…" She suddenly stopped talking and whirled around, looking back toward Bull Valley.

"What is it?"

"I don't know…the wind…it changed suddenly…"

Sebastian looked out toward the Old Forest. "I'll walk you home."

"There's no need. Cheetah, Kingston…" The two warriors emerged silently from the shadows. Sebastian had no idea they were even there. Lydia turned and looked at him. "Be careful." She descended the hill with the warriors at her side.

Sebastian looked back toward the Old Forest, suddenly filled with the single thought, *Get to the treehouse.*

XLIII

Alexandra was dreaming. She was back in the lair playing a game of chess with her father. The fire in the hearth was glowing warmly as they sat opposite one another deep in thought; they had been playing for hours. Alexander suddenly shifted in his chair and looked out across the room toward his balcony.

A wolf was howling in the distance.

Alexandra followed her father's gaze. He was looking up at the portrait he had painted of Rebekah dancing before the fire.

"What is it?"

He reached for his cane and slowly rose from his seat and moved to the edge of the balcony. He peered out and looked at the woods beyond. Alexandra made her way across his bedchambers and stood beside him. There was an orange glow illuminating the night sky; it was coming from deep inside their woods.

"A bonfire." He was deep in thought.

"A bonfire?"

"Alexandra, there's a very old ritual between the wolves and the ravens. It's sacred, only conducted when a king or queen is giving thanks or is seeking wisdom and guidance to benefit the clan. It's done with a dance; a dance before a large bonfire." Alexander's gaze never left the direction of the glow. "Fire is powerful. Beautiful." He was lost in his own thoughts. "But it does not comfort you when you are afraid or when you are filled with sorrow. It's life is short when you are lonely, for it only burns for a time. I have forgotten what it feels like, what it looks like, to stand in its presence. When I danced before it...when I honored it." He was lost in whatever memory this represented, saying nothing more. Alexandra watched his face as he relived his memory; she had no idea what he was talking about. She had neither heard him speak in such a way before nor seen him look so serious; it bothered her.

She gently touched Alexander's shoulder. "Father, you're tired. We've been playing for hours. Let's get you back inside and get you something to

181

eat."

But Alexander turned and looked at her with anger; his eyes glowed silver. Alexandra was startled by his reaction. "You're not listening, Alexandra!" He took her by the shoulders, "There will come a time when you will not see the light you always lived in. It will go dark. You will lose your way. You have never stood before the fire, tested by its flame! The darkness inside will devour you because you have never seen! You have not heard! And it's my fault! You will not be ready!"

"Ready for what?!?"

"The world, Alexandra." He let go of her and looked back out at the orange glow lighting up the sky. "She told me…that if I had a daughter…you would not be ready." He exhaled slowly, "It will be harder for you." He turned and looked back at her, his face softening. "I didn't mean to frighten you, but that bonfire is a reminder to me, staring me in the face, that I have never asked you about your dreams, your happiness. I never told you how much you can be loved or hated. I never told you…" His voice drifted off as he looked down at his hands; they were old, withered. "I should have told you many things…"

Alexandra touched her father's cheek; a look of tenderness and love passed between them. He placed his hand over hers. "My daughter, if there is one thing I could say to you that you could carry with you long after I'm gone, aside from all the love I have for you…" He paused, catching himself as his eyes filled with tears. "Is that when you are most hesitant, most afraid but feel the need to move…do not be afraid. Leap…and leap far…"

"**D**on't go into the dark just yet, queen…"

Alexandra slowly opened her eyes to find Tick-Tock looking down at her with his large, bulbous eyes. She was wrapped in his embrace, feeling the warmth of his body heat as it warmed hers. She could barely lift her head, feeling like a huge weight rested on top of it. The muscles in her body were just as heavy. She could barely move; she was exhausted.

"Tick-Tock…" Her voice was raspy. "What happened?"

Tick-Tock remained silent.

"All I remember was stepping onto the ice and someone pushing me under. Was it Rhodes?"

Tick-Tock did not answer.

"I thought he was supposed to help me, his chosen queen." Alexandra's throat hurt. She slowly sat up and looked all around the cavern. "I don't understand any of this. Why don't the ones who are supposed to help, do so…"

"*Queen*…"

Tick-Tock looked up at the sound of the voice. Alexandra followed his gaze; there was a small trail of fire descending from the wall, making its way toward where they sat.

"*You misunderstand our nature. We desire nothing more than to see creation thrive. You think of us in mortal terms, not as we really are.*"

The fire stopped right in front of Alexandra.

"I don't know you. I had never even heard of you before Daniel read his book. If you want to be honored, why not make yourself known? If you want creation to thrive, why have you all allowed so much suffering? So much…"

"*Pain?*"

She did not reply.

"*Again, you misunderstand our nature and the order of things. You live in this world, you rule your realm, you command your pack, do you not?*"

She nodded.

"*And what do you expect to get out of it? A world of straight lines and calm seas? Is this the nature of the pack you lead?*"

Alexandra remained silent.

"*There is no life without pain, queen. We are not the ones who bring it. We are the ones who help you through it…*"

The wolf queen narrowed her eyes by Rahelio's unexpected answer. "Rhodes killed Minotauro. He tried to kill me."

"*He did not kill Minotauro.*"

"Then why didn't he help him?"

"*Mortality has a select timeline to existence. It was his time to transition from mortal to immortal in order to become. And my brother did not try to kill you. Understand our nature, queen…*"

Alexandra's heart began to beat faster and harder inside her chest. Tick-Tock sat beside her in silence, absorbing her reactions to the discourse. She was angry and confused; she did not understand all the things Rahelio was revealing to her. He watched as her eyes turned to a flashing silver. "Then why are we here?!? Why did you let us in?!? Why not just give us the stone or resurrect the sea?!? If we are all to die one day, what is the point of seeking your help if you won't do it?!?"

The small fire turned dark blue. "*To understand us…to know us more…to understand we are here to help you, but not in the way you think you want but in how you need.*"

Alexandra's shoulders fell at his reply. All anger and energy leaving her as she said, "You won't give us the stone."

"*Wolf, you have not been listening.*" He said it in a gently tone, almost the way her father did when he was trying to teach her something and wound up being disappointed that she did not understand. "*Embrace it or race it, it is she.*"

Tick-Tock swiveled his head to barn owl, staring at the fire.

"You have ownership in the things of this world. You have a responsibility to it — how it is shaped, what tradition becomes new, how the rules are written. When you look in the mirror, queen, what questions do you ask? Help from current fate? Guidance in your will? Discernment from the darkness and the light? We do not influence your choices or our will over yours but are always present — especially when options abound."

"I'm here, aren't I? Even if I haven't asked before or knew to do so, I'm here now. I believe."

"In what, queen?"

"In the autumn tint of gold." Tick-Tock's head swiveled to snow owl as he looked at her. "That as a queen, there really is something I can do for my pack. Help me! Help me show my pack that they can believe too." She hesitated and then finally said, "In me."

The flames in the fire continued to move in a dance of calming beauty.

Alexandra stood up and slowly moved closer to the fire. "My father..." Tick-Tock's eyes followed her. "He should have told me. He should have told me many things...I don't feel ready to be queen. I never have. I don't see bad things coming. I don't recognize the next steps to take. My mind refuses to birth new ideas. Help me take the steps I need in order to become."

And with that, the flames went out.

Alexandra's head fell to her chest in defeat. She did not know what to do. And as she sat there with her chin against her chest, she felt the metal against it. She looked down at the silver medallion and grabbed hold of it. Alexandra sat back near Tick-Tock and continued to stare at its design. She shifted her gaze to the totem, lifting her medallion in his direction as she said, "Show me."

His head swiveled back to barn owl. "I told you." Tick-Tock took one of Alexandra's hands and moved it toward the direction of the frozen pond, while leaving her other hand over her medallion. *"Call...his...name..."*

XLIV

Byron was walking through a thick set of trees. He could barely see his hands in front of his face as he groped his way through the forest. He could not even see the night sky up above as he tried to decipher where he was and where he was going.

A woman's laughter sounded up ahead; it seemed familiar. He followed the sound until making his way toward a large bonfire burning in the middle of the woods. He suddenly recognized the trees; he was in the lair.

"Does Reginald know?" It was a man.

"You know he doesn't. He'd kill me if he knew I was here."

Rebekah.

"Eaglesss do not understand the importance of the dance..."

Byron stopped dead in his tracks the moment he heard the raven assassin's voice. He hid behind one of the trees and looked out. Standing beside the large pyre was Rebekah and a strikingly handsome, athletic-looking man. They were both dressed in black. Surrounding them were wolves from the pack and a legion of ravens.

"That's a good point, Poe."

Alexander. He had forgotten what he had looked like; only having seen him once so long ago when he came to their treehouse. It suddenly became very clear to Byron as to why the wolf king was so popular amongst the women in Gorilla Jungle in his day.

Alexander turned toward Rebekah. "You'd better not screw this up. You'd be the first queen to do so." He lifted her medallion from her chest. "Fire just might take this back."

"Stop that." She swatted his hand away. "Poe's clan has been teaching me the steps since I was a young girl. I'd focus on yourself, *wolf.* You might get confused with a dance from Gorilla Jungle. Mixing the steps...thinking of other beats..."

Alexander was not amused. He crossed his arms over his lean chest and glared at her. Rebekah could see the slightest tightening of his jaw. "Well, Skoll? Freki? Did you teach it to him?"

185

Skoll, the alpha, barked a laugh while Freki joined him.

"I'll have you know, *bird*, my father taught it to me."

"Ah, yes, but did you *learn* it?"

Without taking his eyes off her, he commanded his wolves, "Throw more wood into the fire!"

The gauntlet had been thrown.

The wolves and ravens tossed more logs into the fire. Rebekah raised an eyebrow as she watched the flames grow higher and higher. "Ready?"

"Waiting."

The ravens and the wolves had already taken their positions forming a circle around the pyre. They held drums and other musical instruments, starting to play them as a low drumbeat sounded. Byron thought it sounded like a heartbeat as the wolves and ravens played as one. Alexander was on one side of the fire while Rebekah stood opposite him on the other side. Their warriors were further back, giving the prince and queen enough room to move.

Rebekah took her position and readied herself for the dance as she listened to the beat; her face grew serious as she focused all her attention on the movement of the flames.

"Don't screw it…ow." Skoll hit him from behind.

"Focus, my prince."

Alexander shook it off and positioned himself in front of the fire.

The last drumbeat struck…and the Fire Dance began.

Alexander watched Rebekah through the flames as she danced in perfect beat; she was not lying. She knew the dance — and she knew it well. He could feel the pride and desire rising up inside his chest as they danced opposite one another. Byron watched in awe as the prince and queen moved their bodies in unison with the flames.

The dance was passionate. Tribal.

And then…Rebekah turned. There was a large flash off her movement and the fire exploded. Byron jumped even further back from where he hid as the bird queen spun rapidly, faster than anyone could possibly move. And in reply, the flames shot higher and higher, changing different colors as Rebekah moved with the flames. Even Alexander was taken aback, continuing to dance, but looking around at the reaction from the wolves and the ravens as to what was happening as Rebekah danced not just before the fire, but what seemed to be…*with* Fire.

Byron was spellbound as he watched her move all around the fire, reaching for it, bending toward it, swaying with the flames as they rose higher and higher, shifting in color from orange to green to blue, finally burning brightest in its center…*violet.*

The ravens and wolves were moving in almost hypnotic-like unison as they swayed and continued to beat their drums as the flames rose higher and higher. Only Poe was watching his queen. His scarlet-colored eyes illuminated against the flames.

Rebekah continued to spin and move, making her way over to Alexander for the next part of the dance. They moved together in unison, as if they were one body and one spirit as they faced the pyre. And Fire…*was answering.*

Byron was mesmerized, seeing something deep within its center. The violet color started to take form when…

"King…"

Byron snapped out if his trance and noticed that the music had stopped. All was still.

Rebekah was staring at him, as were Alexander and the entire wolf pack and a legion of ravens.

"Tok…tok…tok…"

Even Poe was staring at him with those scarlet-colored eyes of his; they were all looking at him as if he had intruded upon them and their territory. He felt like the most uninvited guest.

"Why are you here?" It was Alexander.

Byron stared at him, dumbfounded.

Rebekah looked at him and said…

"Byron…"

Byron was lying unconscious on the floor in an unknown cavern inside the fortress. He had fallen several feet as he and Daniel were attempting to allude their unknown pursuer. He had hit his head on a rock below as he landed and had been dreaming in his unconscious state ever since. An eagle's talon gently touched Byron's head.

"You're fond of him." It was Reginald's voice.

Rebekah's voice answered in reply, *"Very much. As are you…"*

Alexander's voice interrupted, *"Enough about the baboon already…"*

Byron twitched, answering them unconsciously, "Byron…call me…Byron…"

"Byron…"

Byron opened his eyes and saw Tick-Tock crouched and leaning over him. It took him a few moments to realize where he was. The dream of Rebekah and Alexander dancing before the fire filled his mind. He looked down at Tick-Tock's raven claw, remembering Poe.

"You are more than just a totem, aren't you, Tick-Tock?"

His large owl eyes blinked. "Becoming…" His head tilted to the side as Netapheha's voice answered, *"You have the voice of a true king…call to the earth…she is the most powerful element of all."*

Byron slowly sat up. He winced as a sharp pain shot through his head. He looked all around, realizing they were in some sort of mine. He reached for his scepter and panicked the moment he realized it was gone. He looked all around, feeling for it, until finally looking up at the ledge he had fallen from. "Tick-Tock, I need to climb. My scepter is my crown. I need to find it."

Tick-Tock looked up at the ledge; it was an impossible climb. There was no way to do it. Instead, the totem stood and started jogging outside the mine and on toward another archway.

"Hey, wait!" Byron stood and had no other choice but to follow.

XLV

Sebastian was in the Old Forest. Although the place had a look of desolation, it was a place of great consolation to him. He found solace here — peace. He knew every tree, every path, noticing every sign of change — especially the one he saw now.

He crouched down and studied the hoof marks in the dirt and the small boot marks in the dirt beside it. His violet-colored eyes followed their path as it led to his treehouse.

He whispered, "Amun, Chango…"

They followed their king's gaze toward the ancient tree. They silently moved in to surround the treehouse. They waited. Sebastian lifted his hand and counted with gestures…one…two…three!

The toad and frog warriors leapt up the tree just as they heard a loud *SNAP!* The wind exploded from the treehouse and moved down upon his warriors just as Sebastian heard a shout, *"QUEEN!"*

From the treehouse, he saw a woman leap through the window, landing atop a black creature that was hidden in the shadows. He watched as they took off like lightning, riding fast, weaving through the trees as if they already knew the roads and pathways.

Sebastian, too, had been knocked to the ground by the wind's force. He slowly sat up.

"King, what and who was that?"

He suddenly remembered Chief Netapheha's words, *"She is coming…a queen is coming…riding on the path of the wind…for he answers her."*

It had to be her.

He looked up at the treehouse; queen or no queen, he was angry. She had invaded, not only their realm, but his private sanctuary. He stood and climbed the tree, entering the treehouse. His eyes searched for any sign of change. And then he saw it: etched into the wood beside his, Byron's and Minotauro's names was a new one. *Diana.* And it had today's date.

The queen.

189

He had heard the shout. A queen...but from where? And why would she come here with a single warrior alone? Or...were there others?

A wolf barked down below.

Sebastian looked down and saw Hood with Igor beside him. "King, we will find the invaders. My pack picked up their scent the moment they crossed into Bird Kingdom several days ago."

And with that, the wolf pack raced toward the darkened path after the unknown queen and her beast.

"Diana..."

Sebastian touched his fingers over her name. The last time he had seen the pack in these woods was when Alexander was inside his treehouse. But instead of following their king to engage in battle, the pack was on their own with no queen in their midst. He looked out at the forest and thought of Alexandra as his fingers felt the marked etching of this new queen.

From the forest below, he saw the buffalo warriors moving from the shadows of their domain. They moved silently through the trees, following Hood and Igor.

Diana and Keys rode hard and fast, winding through the shadows of the trees. Wolves howled in the distance. Diana looked all around, trying to think of where they should go when...

BAM!

Diana and Keys were lifted straight up into the air, suspended in a make-shift net fifty feet off the ground, swinging helplessly.

"Are you all right, my queen?"

Diana did not answer. She was looking down at the ground instead...and straight into the eyes of Kingston and Cheetah.

XLVI

"ALEXANDRA!"

He was running fast through each cavern; his eyes were slit to a cat as he searched for any sign of her. He moved inside a cavern filled with ice and snow. He slowed his step the moment he saw the frozen pond up ahead and a large mound of snow at its base. He looked all around the cavern for any other way across to the next archway, but he quickly realized this was the only way out. Even with the ledge above that led to a second archway beyond, he would still have to cross the frozen pond to access it.

It was then he heard the faintest sound of Alexandra's voice. It was coming from the ledge above.

"ALEXANDRA!!!"

No response.

He keeled over, trying to catch his breath as he rested his hands on his knees. He felt a sense of relief, having heard Alexandra's voice. He knew he needed to find her quickly — including Byron. He looked out at the frozen pond to inspect its depth when he saw something beneath the ice. It moved quickly underneath; too fast for Daniel to catch its form.

He crouched down to survey the pond when something behind him moved and hit him from behind. All went dark as the lion king went down.

Diana and Keys were led straight to Bull Valley and to the rock fortress that was their kingdom. As they moved through the various caves, Diana could see the various clan members: some with looks of rage on their faces, some with curiosity, others with fear and amazement. Not so much for her but for Keys.

191

Cheetah and Kingston led them to a throne room filled with bull, buffalo, and goat warriors as well as cheetah clan warriors. They were being guided toward a woman Diana had seen before — the bull queen.

Lydia was holding a baby in her arms, rocking him, and humming a tune as Diana and Keys approached. Cheetah and Kingston bowed to the queen upon approach. "Queen."

She did not lift her head but continued to smile and cradle the remnant in her arms. Diana and Keys continued to stand there until the bull queen finally spoke, "Who are you and why are you here?"

"My name is Queen Diana...of the horse clan."

The bull warriors began to snort and stomp their hooves in anger. Lydia, however, continued to rock her son, never once lifting her eyes to the intruders. "And the answer to my other questions?"

"I'm here because of your husband...the bull king Minotauro."

Lydia finally looked at Diana. The entire room went silent. Everyone was staring at Diana and Keys. The bull queen handed her son to one of her kinswomen as she rose from her throne and stepped toward the horse queen. Her eyes were slit to a cat. "And what of my husband, *queen*?"

Diana could see the bull clan warriors gripping their weapons tight as they lowered their heads in a challenge.

"Neither I nor any member of my clan killed him, queen. I only spoke with him briefly as he and the other kings and queen made their to the Element Fortress."

She had the clan's full attention as this was the first news any of them had had of their kings and queen.

"They were alive and well when I saw them last."

"I don't believe you."

Everyone turned as a handsome man with a band of frog and toad warriors made his way toward Lydia. He stepped up beside the bull queen and stared at Diana with his violet-colored eyes.

The other king.

"You wouldn't be here if there wasn't more you had seen or said than just a brief conversation with the kings and queen." He continued to look deep into her dark eyes when he asked, "What happened to the gorilla king? He went down...*several* times."

Diana's body tensed at the question.

Several times...that could only mean one thing.

The horse queen could barely breathe, weighing her words very carefully before she said, "I only know of one. He was shot. An arrow in the chest."

The room gasped as Sebastian's eyes began to glow. "How did it happen, queen?"

Keys moved closer toward his queen.

"One of my warriors."

The entire room erupted. The bull clan warriors were ready to charge as the buffalo soldiers turned on their heels. All the while, Sebastian and Diana never took their eyes off one another. He was angry. Lydia watched them both as the horse queen stood before the clan with a formidable confidence and yet…there was something more.

Lydia spoke above the cacophony, "The gorilla king lives, queen. How is this so?"

The warriors quieted down.

Diana kept her eyes on Sebastian. "The guardian healed him."

Cheetah's fur shot straight up at the very mention of Tick-Tock.

Diana could see Sebastian's shoulders lower in relief. She shifted her gaze to the bull queen. "The last I saw of the kings and queen, they were whole. I commanded my clan to leave them in peace so that they could find the stone to resurrect your sea."

"And what does my husband have to do with your arrival here?"

Diana swallowed hard, feeling the well of emotion rising to the surface as she looked at the bull clan warriors surrounding her and Keys. "King Minotauro revealed to me the horror of my clan's history. He told me of our banishment from the Old Forest here in your realm. That we were once kin to the bull clan, exiled for our crimes…" She could hear her voice begin to crack as she confessed the truth to the clan who drove them out. "Our warriors killed our mares at birth in order to champion the strength of the stallions."

The bull clan warriors were silent.

Diana's eyes were filled with tears as she looked at Lydia and the warriors surrounding her. "I have much to rectify for what my clan had done. As queen…" She gathered her confidence once more as she spoke, "I am here to reclaim my kingdom…" The bull warriors began to retort. Keys slowly turned his head and looked at his queen as the room erupted in a cacophony of thunderous protest. She spoke even louder, "I AM HERE…*TO REJOIN THE REALM!*"

Cheetah was standing beside Kingston, taking in all that had been said. He could feel his heart hammering inside his chest. It was almost as if he had just run the race of his life although he was standing perfectly still. He shifted his gaze to find the horse warrior watching him, recognizing that the horse warrior could see the slightest change in the cheetah warrior's demeanor.

They locked eyes with one another as the light began to dim and Cheetah collapsed to the ground.

XLVII

"*Noble One…*"

Daniel heard a voice calling to him, but it was muffled.

"*Lion…*"

Daniel slowly opened his eyes to find Rhodes looking up at him from the ground below. He slowly lifted his head and found that he was still inside the cavern filled with snow and ice. He tried to move and wound up crying out in pain. He turned his head to the side and found that he was hanging on the rock wall, nailed to it by two icicles embedded into both his shoulders. Daniel cried out in pain. They were embedded in the same spot as where Poe's talons had ripped him from the ground and into the sky. His shouts echoed throughout the cavern. He was breathing hard. His head was pounding.

"Did you do this to me?"

"No. Your death, king, would be an unnecessary kill. But not every creature or king in this world agrees." He caught Daniel's reaction. "Are you surprised?" Daniel remained silent. "I've heard many cries of those in the realm. Those who wish you dead, your clan annihilated. If it were so, they pray, no more mistakes would need to be rectified. No more suffering to ease. No more wars shifting power amongst the clans anymore. Do you agree?"

Daniel was shivering; he continued to remain silent.

"Have you ever really thought about, king, what cannibalism truly was? What your den had done?" Rhodes studied the lion king before continuing, "Sometimes the lions would keep the bulls alive by hacking their limbs off piece by piece. They learned from the old bull king that the meat spoils quickly. It was brutal. Painful. Terrifying."

Daniel swallowed hard.

"The fear…the helplessness…the other clans still remember it all when they see your den. And my brothers and sister and I have heard their questions, Why have we allowed so many to suffer so? Why allow all this

194

pain? We did not bring it. The wolves and lions did. Uniting them all to build the dam is a good start to rectify what your forefathers have done before you, but more will be needed, king, for the realm to truly live again. More than a stone. I know you of all understand. Your will is hard to break. You refuse to dishonor anyone or anything. That is why you are what we know you to be."

Even from where Rhodes stood, he could see the blood stains on the king's clothes and reddish tint in his hair from the blow to his head.

"It grieves me that they did this to you. It angers me that you're even here. You never needed to be, you know. Mercy does not live here. All you ever need, you already have. It is the choice within that moves a mountain. You have only to realize the commands you can make with us at your side when our wills are united as one."

He started to climb the wall to move closer toward Daniel. Whatever had nailed him there was tall. "How easily the world forgets the forces that can change this world in an instant." Rhodes leaned in to examine the icicles. "I know how badly you and your clans have wanted their rain. And for a time, I tried to help bring it. But Rahelio kept melting my ice and drying it out. So, I stopped helping, for his reasoning was one I slowly came to understand. And then your famine came...and the realm shifted once more. But not the way it did before."

Daniel's entire body shook.

"When the bird queen awoke, it was her raven that I summoned in order to rouse his nature." Rhodes pounded on the rock wall three times and continued. "But he didn't listen. He only heard what he wanted to hear."

Daniel looked at Rhodes. "You...told him..." his teeth were chattering, "To finish what Palimus started..."

Whatever reaction the lion king expected, it was not the one he now saw on Rhodes' face. His entire face seemed to darken as his turquoise-colored eyes began to glow. Daniel waited for what he was going to say next, but Rhodes did not say a word. Instead, the Lord of the Sea pounded even harder against the rock wall. He hit the wall with his fist so hard, the entire cavern shook. Whatever Daniel had just said to Rhodes made him furious.

Daniel could barely feel his limbs, but his mind was reeling. It was then that the realization hit Daniel, "It wasn't you..." Rhodes continued to pound on the wall. "Who...who...was it?"

But Rhodes did not answer the question. Instead, he looked the lion king dead in the eye as he said, "She is going to break you, lion." Daniel's eyes narrowed. "You are good. You are true. That is why you are noble. That is why you have always been worthy. That is why I am telling you this now. So that you do not forget." Rhodes stopped pounding. "There is a king who is coming. One who listens to the voice of the shadow in the dark. He wants three things and three things alone — wealth, power, and domination. There are those who will hand it over. There are those that want him to have it.

And there are those who want to be slave to a higher master. He is cunning. He is ruthless. And you, king, are his rival in the light. An heir is needed for you both."

Rhodes looked up just as a trail of fire descended from up above. It was moving quickly down toward Daniel.

Daniel was so cold he was having a hard time concentrating. Regardless, he asked, "Who has claimed him?" Rhodes shifted his eyes to Daniel. "Who?!?"

Rhodes remained silent as the flames surrounded the wall, enveloping the icicles. They slowly began to melt as the heat from the flames warmed the ice. It was then he said, "The darkest element that has ever existed, king. *My other brother.*"

The flames went through his shoulders as Daniel cried out. His body dropped as he hit a pile of snow down below. Rhodes, however, climbed the wall to the upper ledge as the trail of fire followed him. Rhodes stopped and turned to look back down at the lion king before moving through the archway. "Go get your stone, king…before they do."

He moved through the archway just as the wall Daniel hung to moments before shifted and an opening for the lion king emerged.

XLVIII

"*Call...his...name...*"

Not a chance.

There was no way she was going to call Rhodes' name. As a matter of fact, she had almost thrown the medallion down into the pool of water when Tick-Tock stopped her.

The moment he did, the rock wall shifted creating an opening. The wolf queen was immediately on her feet and ran through.

Alexandra tried to run hard and fast but found that almost drowning fatigued her. It was probably a good thing she was not moving so quickly throughout endless caverns and mines, or she would have missed the one she just walked into — it was a cavern filled with petroglyphs.

"Tick-Tock...look at this." She was mesmerized. Her eyes went from the top down, following all the drawings on the wall from the beginning. She saw the marking of the wolves in Gorilla Jungle. She touched the wall and followed the story all the way towards the gravestones of critter warriors and on toward the barren lands of Reptile Desert. She thought of her father then as she gently rested her hand on the clans of old.

Her heart was beating rapidly as she followed the storyline. She paused on the illustration of the lion king amidst the fire. It did not escape Alexandra's notice that the fire consumed the entire realm. She reached out and gently touched it.

"Daniel...Tick-Tock, we need to find Daniel." She turned, "Tick-Tock?"

Alexandra had no idea when she had lost him. She had not paid any attention to him from the moment she left the cavern filled with snow.

"Now, where did he go?"

That was when she heard the sound of rushing water coming from somewhere nearby. She followed the sound, climbing over the rubble of rocks that covered most of the petroglyphs. The sound of water led her away from the corner and into the cavern with the story of the unknown king.

197

The wolf queen went through an opening between the rock walls and found herself in a cave that contained a powerful waterfall. She looked all around, trying to see if there was any other way in or out, wondering where the source of the font was coming from. She moved toward the bank of the waterfall where a small pool of water resided. Alexandra got down on her hands and knees and looked into it, trying to decipher how deep it went. She had no desire to find out by swimming in it after her own experience moments before.

Her own...

Alexandra whipped her head around, listening for any other sound of movement. She had suddenly remembered hearing the slightest sound behind her before falling into the pool of ice, but she could not make anyone or anything out.

"Queen..."

Alexandra scattered back away from the water. The voice had come from the pool.

"Do not be afraid."

It was a man's voice — deep, sultry. The wolf queen slowly crawled back toward the pool. She looked into the waters and saw the image of the most handsome man she had ever seen in her life. His eyes were dark, glistening. His jaw was strong and muscular; his hair jet-black.

"I didn't mean for them to harm you..."

It finally dawned on Alexandra that she *had* been attacked — and it was not by Rhodes.

"Who are you?"

"My name is Decimus."

The moment he said his name, Alexandra's body seemed to ignite like wildfire. There was something about the way he said his name, something about the way he was looking at her through the water when he said it that affected the wolf queen in a way she had never felt before. She leaned in closer.

"You are beautiful, queen."

She could barely breathe. Decimus smiled softly and lifted his hand, almost as if he were about to reach up out of the water and touch Alexandra's face. And if that was his intent, everything within her body wanted him to. She closed her eyes just as his hand emerged from the pool of water. It was then she felt the temperature drop rapidly. Her eyes snapped open realizing the reason.

Rhodes.

Alexandra whirled around just as the cavern started to freeze over. Snow emerged on the rock walls surrounding her. She turned and found the waterfall freezing over and into the pool.

She dropped down onto her knees to move the snow from the sheet of ice that had moments before been a pool of calm water. He was still there.

She felt her body exhale in relief. He lifted his hand and rested it up against the ice. She reached her hand out and laid it over his. He drifted down back into the pool of water, disappearing from view.

Alexandra was bewildered. She was intrigued. She was no longer thinking about the stone. She was no longer thinking about how to get out of the fortress. She was not thinking about her pack. All her thoughts were suddenly consumed by one thought…the man in the water…*Decimus*…

XLIX

Daniel was on his hands and knees thinking about what had just happened to him and what Rhodes had just said…*and what he didn't say*. His shoulders were numb, shielding him from the full force of the pain he would feel the moment the cold wore off. He looked all around the cavern trying to recall what had happened before he was attacked. He saw nothing but flat snow.

The snow.

He remembered that there was a mound there before — and something that moved in the water.

Clever.

One of the creatures must have distracted him while the other attacked him from behind. The one from behind must have had white fur allowing it to be camouflaged by the snow. There was no doubt in Daniel's mind that their claws were long and black as flashes of his and Byron's previous encounter with one of the beasts flooded his mind.

How many were there?

He sat back on his legs and looked up, attempting to find a means out of the cavern. He saw a few ledges above and knew he would have to climb. He attempted to raise his arms and immediately cried out in pain. He looked down at each shoulder to examine where the icicles had pierced through.

Daniel looked at his wounds to assess the damage when he suddenly realized what Fire had done. Not only had Rahelio melted the icicles, but he had cauterized his wounds in the process. As painful as it was to move his arms, he knew he would eventually be able to do it.

"She is going to break you, lion."

He tried to shake off Rhodes' words. He slowly began moving one of his arms to get the muscle warm.

"That is why I am telling you this now. So you do not forget."

Somehow, he knew he wouldn't.

"There is a king who is coming…"

He moved the other arm, pondering what Rhodes had revealed to him.

200

"And you, king, are his rival in the light. An heir is needed for you both."

He knew Rhodes had not lied about the unknown king. Tick-Tock had even alluded to the man's existence. What bothered him more, however, was what Rhodes had alluded to about Alexandra; he refused to believe it, yet Ice's words settled deep inside his heart.

"She is going to break you, lion..."

He stopped moving his arms. He sat there for several more moments taking it all in.

Another king.

Another clan.

And then it hit him. *"It wasn't you..."*

Another brother. Another element...the fifth symbol.

And all at once the pieces were coming together. The elements were taking their time with them inside this fortress. The remnants had come for a stone, but the elements were giving them something more.

Daniel's eyes slit to a cat as he stood. Whatever pain he was feeling was completely wiped out by the rage and determination he felt brewing in his heart over who this new king was and what he was up to. He was a king who reveled in shadow, claimed by the darkest element of them all...and he wanted their stone.

The lion king backed up, looking at the rock wall and the ledge above. He took several short breaths, focusing his mind as he sprinted toward the rock wall, scaling it quickly as he ascended toward the ledge. He needed to find Alexandra and Byron — but Tick-Tock most of all. For in all his pondering as to what had been revealed to him inside this fortress from the moment he stepped inside, Daniel suddenly realized... he knew where the stone was. And if this new king's warriors had been listening to the discourse between him and the element brothers while hiding amongst the caverns, they knew it too.

L

Byron had been roaming the fortress. He was looking for one cavern in particular — he had remembered it when they had first stepped inside the fortress. He knew that was where he needed to go, but he was lost. He had no idea where he was or which direction he was going. He was determined yet frustrated, knowing that he would eventually find it. He had realized that the medallion hanging around his neck was helping him search as well. It would grow cold and hot depending on if the presence of fire was nearby. It had grown colder and colder for some time, but he had no idea how to get back on track. He rounded another corner and ploughed straight into Daniel. They collided into one another and fell to the ground.

Daniel was flat out on his back. "We need to stop doing that."

Byron was overjoyed; he sat straight up, "Lion!"

"Done with your nap?"

"Now I see why you lions do it."

His smile slowly faded when he took in the blood on Daniel's shoulders and the crusted blood in his hair. "What happened?"

Daniel slowly sat up, wincing in pain as he touched one of his shoulders. "I got knocked out and was nailed to a wall with icicles."

"Geez. I missed all that?"

"I think it was the creature that chased us through the cavern." Daniel studied him. "You seem to be all right."

Byron's face darkened. "I am now. We need to find Alexandra, get the stone and get out of here."

"What about Tick-Tock?"

"What about him? One minute he's beside me, the next minute he vanishes into thin air. I don't know why he's even with us. I have yet to see him protect anything or anyone. He seems to be built for defense versus offense."

"I think he's meant for one thing…and it hasn't happened yet."

"Well, whatever it is, I wish he had done something to shield you. Your den must have gone down when you were attacked."

Daniel paused, "I hadn't thought about that."

"No doubt Sebastian is at his wits end not knowing what is happening here." He looked down at Daniel and saw him lost in his own thoughts. "Your lions will be fine, king. When Poe tried to murder me, the moment Rebekah healed me, they were healed as well."

"That's not it. It was something Rhodes said…"

"He spoke to you."

Daniel nodded. "It was about Poe."

Byron's body went rigid at the sound of the raven's name. Daniel could see the gorilla king's jaw clench tightly.

"*Tok…tok…tok…*"

Byron immediately reacted and jumped at the sound of Poe's voice. He reached for his bone scepter and remembered he still did not have it.

Daniel, however, was not bothered. He looked around for Tick-Tock, finally finding him crouched amongst the shadows. "Ravens were the protectors of the clan. That was what Rhodes was rousing in Poe. Not just to protect his kingdom…but the realm. Alexandra was right…but not completely. Poe did not listen…"

Byron swallowed hard, still searching the cavern. He saw Daniel staring at a mark up ahead. He followed his gaze and saw Tick-Tock.

"Who was it, Poe, that spoke to you?"

Tick-Tock's head swiveled to snow owl; his eyes glowed red but the totem said nothing more.

"You said that Marcus was going to the waterfall."

He watched as the totem's raven claw clenched into a tight fist.

Daniel shifted his gaze, thinking. "There was a waterfall outside the fortress. There was a waterfall near Horse Clan Village."

Byron asked, "Is there a waterfall inside here?"

Tick-Tock's head swiveled to horned owl — the voice of the future, "Yes. They came through, king. He is coming…"

It was a maze, and she had no idea where she was going. The more she thought about Decimus, the more she began to feel embarrassed, guilty. As if the very thought of him was somehow a betrayal to Daniel — and it was. The moment she realized that all she wanted was to see the handsome man's face again, to hear his voice, she understood that her focus had shifted — and in the wrong direction. She was relishing in her thoughts instead of ignoring them. All she knew now was that she wanted to find Daniel and Byron as fast as possible, get the stone and get home.

Alexandra slowed her step as she reached a dead end. The only way out was to either go back the way she had just come or climb to the upper ledge that led to another archway up above. She was in some sort of mine.

She wished Tick-Tock was with her to help her climb quickly to the top.

How was she going to get up there?

Alexandra looked down at the medallion but immediately rejected the idea of calling for *his* help. She still was not ready to do it. As if that simple act of going outside herself were a surrendering that she had given in to the idea that she could not do all things by herself. In reality, she still did not understand the nature of the elements. She still believed the only reason to commune with them was if she needed something. And right now, she did not.

She looked at the rock wall for a path to climb. She backed up and ran toward the wall; she jumped.

Alexandra grabbed for a rock and missed. She slammed back onto the ground. She picked herself up and decided to take smaller steps; she slowly climbed. She slipped several times but continued on. She looked down to see how far she had come and looked up to see how far she had to go. She tried to pull herself up again but lost her grip; she hung on by one hand. Alexandra reached up with the other hand for the ledge and missed. She swung backward, shifting her weight like a pendulum. Her body swung; she reached out and caught the ledge.

Alexandra looked at the next ledge across from her. She tried again and swung. She did it again, moving across the wall just as she had seen Byron do. It felt...natural.

One more ledge to go...

At the bottom of the mine, Tick-Tock, Byron, and Daniel raced inside. They slowed their step as they took in all the illuminated crystal rocks surrounding them — it was mesmerizing.

Byron asked, "How many stones are there?"

"Too many."

Byron was overwhelmed, "Do you think it's one of these?"

"No."

"How do you know?"

Daniel looked at him, "It wouldn't be common, and it wouldn't be in a pile."

Small amounts of rubble fell onto Daniel's shoulders. He brushed it off, looking up to see where it was coming from. Byron touched Daniel's arm. Daniel looked at Byron and saw him staring up at the top of the mine. Daniel followed his gaze and saw Alexandra.

Byron said, "Either Alexandra really is part gorilla, or I've stirred something deep within your woman to inspire this."

"Choose a different verb. And what do you mean, 'part gorilla'?"

"I'll tell you later."

Alexandra was almost to the ledge. It was several yards across from her. She swung back and forth several times trying to gain enough momentum. Tick-Tock watched her intently from down below, but he made no further movement to help her. She swung backward one last time and lunged for the ledge with all her might. She caught it with both hands.

Daniel shouted, "Alexandra!"

She looked down and saw Daniel and Byron below.

Alexandra shouted back, relieved to see them. "Daniel! Hold on while I pull myself up!"

Bryon looked all around the mine, suddenly realizing Tick-Tock had disappeared. He gritted his teeth in anger, "That totem…"

Alexandra pulled her body up with both hands. Her head cleared the ledge when she saw a large black snout and grizzly teeth at her head. She screamed as the creature grabbed her hands and ripped her up from the ledge as if she weighed nothing more than a piece of straw.

Seeing Alexandra dangling up above, Daniel roared; his eyes slit to a cat. He vaulted across the rock wall and raced up its sides as Byron seethed, running up alongside the rock, swinging as fast as he could to get to Alexandra.

Alexandra swung her right leg back and slammed the top of her foot into the creature's groin. It wailed in pain, releasing her as it keeled over in agony. Alexandra kneed the creature in the face. Its head snapped back causing it to reel backwards just as she ripped her dagger from her sheath and plunged it into the creature's chest.

The creature cried out and grabbed at the dagger, pulling it from his fur-covered body. He hurled it down below and dropped down on all fours, letting out the most ferocious roar Alexandra had ever heard. She did not know what was going to happen next.

The creature roared again, rearing up on its hind legs. Alexandra gasped as it rose to over twelve feet tall. It fell down again onto all fours and came face to face with her. Its eyes were jet black; its fur was pure white. She could not help but notice its long, dark claws itching to swipe at her face, ending her life right then and there.

"*Stop.*"

It was Decimus' voice. Alexandra looked all around for it but did not find the source of where it was coming from.

The creature's growl became low and lethal as his snarl revealed grizzly teeth and fangs as it said, "*Queen…*"

The warrior slowly backed up and into the shadows of the rocks behind him, until the wall shifted, and the creature disappeared. Alexandra was still staring at the shadows when Byron swung to the ledge.

"Are you alright?"

She nodded, completely bewildered. The creature could have attacked her…but didn't. He had listened to Decimus' command.

"I didn't mean for them to harm you…"

She remembered his words.

Byron was breathing hard as he stared at Alexandra. He took her hand and turned her palm over. "You *are* part gorilla." Byron brought her hand to his lips. "Welcome to the clan, queen."

Byron was still holding her hand when Daniel leapt across the ledge to join them. He strode toward them, took Alexandra's hand from Byron. "That's mine, thank you."

He pulled Alexandra through the passageway without once breaking stride. He took both of her hands in his, "Are you alright?"

She dove into his arms. "I'm so glad you found me."

He held her even tighter. "What happened to the warrior?"

"He went through another archway."

Alexandra lifted her head, finally noticing the deep gash on his head. She touched his wound gently, "What happened?"

"One of those creatures attacked me."

Her jaw clenched in anger, "How many are there?"

"I don't know."

Byron made his way over to them. "Where is that totem?"

Daniel looked at Byron. "He only seems to be around when we are in life-threatening danger."

"That wasn't life threatening?"

"Apparently not." He looked at Alexandra, "The creature didn't attack you. He just tried to grab for you. I wonder why."

Alexandra suddenly realized they had not heard Decimus' voice. "Probably because he already attacked me. I almost drowned."

"What?"

She looked at Byron, "And Tick-Tock did help me."

"I'd feel a lot better if I had my scepter. I don't like roaming this fortress without my weapon — especially with those creatures running around attacking us. They seem to know everywhere we go without us ever seeing them. How is that possible?"

"We didn't see them coming. We didn't know they'd be here."

Alexandra asked, "Why are they here?"

"For our stone."

"What for?"

Daniel looked at both the gorilla king and wolf queen. "Whoever rules the sea, rules the realm…"

Byron looked as if a shadow had cast itself across his face. "The king…"

The lion king nodded.

Alexandra remained silent.

Daniel said, "I think I know where the stone is."

The gorilla king looked all around the halls, lowering his voice. "They don't. They're following us in order to find it."

"I'm not so sure." Daniel looked at the wolf queen, "Alexandra, I need you to listen and listen hard." He looked at Byron. "You're going to have to move fast. You're faster than me above water. Wherever Alexandra says to go, when she says to move, do it."

He nodded. "I don't have Bane. These creatures are swift and clever. We don't know what they'll do to us once we have it. All I know is that we have to find our way out once we do."

Alexandra shook her head, "How do we do that?"

"Lion, any ideas?"

Daniel was thinking, "He said…mercy does not live here."

The wolf queen and gorilla king remained silent as Daniel continued to filter through his thoughts. "Not here…"

"You have only to realize the commands you can make with us at your side when our wills are united as one."

Realization suddenly hit the lion king full force as he whispered to himself, "It's everywhere." The lion king began to walk through the cavern, touching all the walls that surrounded them. "We haven't been listening. We've only heard. They've been telling us what to do this entire time." He looked at Alexandra's medallion. His eyes drifted from hers to Rebekah's hanging around Byron's neck. Daniel put his ear to the rock once more. Instead of answering Alexandra, he whispered to the rock instead, "I trust you."

Upon reply, the rocks began to rumble. Daniel smiled softly. He nodded to himself. He had found his answer.

"We'll find the way out."

"How?"

He turned and looked at Byron and Alexandra, resting his hands on both of their medallions. "Call their names…"

LI

Diana and Keys were inside a bedchamber in Bull Valley. The bull queen had offered a room, welcoming her to stay the night, but no invitation was offered beyond that.

Keys was staring at his queen, waiting for her to explain herself. When she remained silent, he pressed her, "That was a bold statement to make in the sight of our former brethren and masters."

"Were you really that surprised?"

"No. But our people will be. I don't think they will desire to uproot themselves and leave life in the forest to return here. This is not their home. It is not my home, my queen."

There was a knock at the door. Keys gripped his weapon tight and moved swiftly toward it.

"You need not fear me, queen. I want to talk to you." It was the bull queen.

Diana nodded and Keys opened the door. Lydia stepped inside and glanced at Keys. "Alone."

Keys waited for his queen's approval before exiting the room. He stepped into the hallway to guard the door, only to find two Black Angus warriors opposite him. They sized each other up but remained in silence.

Lydia moved inside the room and sat on top of the bed. "I can tell Minotauro did not offer you an invitation here. If he had, you would not have come alone to creep inside the realm without a band of warriors at your side. Which tells me two things. One, you are not here for ill intent…and two, you are not a remnant." Diana did not respond. "No doubt my husband's words were harsh in his reveal of what he perceived your clan's history to be. I know…*knew*…" Her voice caught but she continued, "His emotions well and the kind of effect they could have when he spoke from his heart…and from his anger."

Diana relaxed a bit and moved to sit beside the bull queen. "I didn't see it coming. I had no idea what we had done or that we were a part of your realm. I grew up never having heard the tale."

"And now you have. I've been trying to think about what should be done, knowing how unforgiving and harsh this clan can be. The Old Forest…"

"I have a right to it."

"Do you? When the doors close behind you, shutting you out, do you have a right to be let back in when the lock has been changed? Queen Diana, as hard as this clan is, there is one thing they champion that keeps their hearts pure — family. They cherish children. Minotauro wanted an entire herd of them." Her voice trailed off as the queen caught herself.

"I understand." Diana looked at Lydia — queen to queen. "The past has shaped our present. You need to know that our clan has learned the lesson of cherishing family above all. As their queen, I'm also their mother. My whole existence revolves around caring for each and every one of them; to be the best of what they can be to leave a better world for the rest of those that come long after any of us are gone. I cannot bear the idea of knowing they live in a forest second best to the one whose roots bore them from the beginning. I cannot leave a hole that will never be filled. I want to bring my people back into the fold of this realm. It is where we were born. It is where we belong." She paused, "Will you help me?"

Lydia stood and began to slowly pace the room. "Is there a horse king?"

Diana almost blushed, "None that I have chosen."

The bull queen tilted her head to the side as she looked at Diana. "I see. And is this what your people would want? To leave the only home they have ever known and return to a land now foreign and unwelcoming to them?"

Diana looked down at her hands resting in her lap. "No." She looked up at Lydia. "They would rather remain where they are, comfortable in the place they are now."

"So why not leave it alone? I don't mean to sound cruel, but we don't need you or your clan here. You are better off where you can survive. Our realm is dying, queen. And my husband died…" Her voice cracked, "He died trying to keep it alive. Living here, there is so much we have sacrificed and continue to so that we can keep order and balance amongst those of us who remain. Another clan will make it that much harder…for all of us. Go home, queen. Go back to where you can live and thrive." Lydia moved toward the door.

Diana stood up. "And if they succeed?"

Lydia turned.

"King Daniel, King Byron and Queen Alexandra. If they succeed, you will need my help. My clan can help build that dam. They know how to farm. They can teach the others to cultivate the land like the bird queen's fields."

"You've been to Bird Kingdom."

"Yes."

"And your clan knows how to do this?"

Diana's heart felt like it was going to burst in excitement as she heard the shift in Lydia's tone. She nodded.

Lydia thought for several moments before replying, "If the other kings and queen return, they will need to weigh in on the matter. We all must decide."

Diana moved toward Lydia. "Then we must ensure that we can."

"How do you mean?"

Diana gently touched her medallion as she weighed the thoughts swirling in her head. "How did the kings and queen know to seek a stone? How did they know to seek the Creators inside the Element Fortress?"

Lydia thought for a moment. "Prince Marcus. He had maps…journals…"

"May I see them?"

Lydia paused.

"Please."

The bull queen nodded, leading the horse queen to the last place either queen thought they would be going. They headed toward the den.

LII

Tick-Tock was inside the cavern with the petroglyphs. He was looking for something in particular; and the moment he came across the cavern, he knew he was going to find it. He had been studying the illustrations as his heads spun round and round. His heads finally stopped as it swiveled to horned owl.

Tick-Tock followed the story all the way back to the top where he saw the symbols for the elements. His large, bulbous eyes zeroed in on the blackened symbol that had been scratched out. His head swiveled to barn owl just as a lethal growl erupted from his body.

Tick-Tock scanned the petroglyphs, studying them, memorizing them. His heads began to swivel between past, present and future once again. Tick-Tock crouched and rose following the pictures all the way around the corner to where Daniel had found the storyline of the land filled with snow and ice. His eyes stopped the moment he saw the fifth symbol once more. That was where the story ended. Or was it?

Tick-Tock's head rapidly spun to horned owl once more — the head of the future. His black taloned hand curled into a tight fist as he looked at the rocks beneath the last illustration. He raised his arm and drove his fist straight into the ground. The entire cavern shook. He did it again, plunging it over and over like a hammer until more rock gave way.

Tick-Tock crouched down, hurling rocks out of the way to clear his view. There were more petroglyphs. He continued reading the symbols. And whatever it was that the totem saw in these new illustrations, caused every feather and piece of fur on his body to stand on end. He was staring at a creature with the long tusks and a cat-like body; *he recognized it.*

Tick-Tock's body went rigid as he rose to his full height. He lifted his head toward the top of the mountain. From his beak came the mighty cry of an eagle.

Deep inside the fortress, the remnants heard Tick-Tock's cry. They covered their ears as the totem's shout raged through the element fortress. His shout was so loud, the rock walls surrounding the remnants began to vibrate and quake. Rocks began falling all around them.

Daniel shouted, "ALEXANDRA! WHERE IS HE?"

Without answering, she turned — still covering her ears — and raced through the fortress. The kings followed.

Both Tick-Tock's raven and eagle claws were clenched tightly as he expunged whatever anger the sight of this creature had provoked deep within him. The entire cavern shook in reply...and it did not stop shaking.

The kings and queen had reached the archway to the cavern. Byron shielded them from entering.

Daniel's eyes slit to a cat as he shouted, *"TICK-TOCK!!!!"*

But Tick-Tock wasn't listening.

Daniel shoved the gorilla king aside and ran through the cavern, rounding the corner as he tried to grab for the totem. More rocks descended upon them as the cavern continued to quake.

Alexandra shouted from around the corner, *"DANIEL!"*

"KING! GET OUT OF THERE!"

Byron ran through, rounding the corner. He saw Tick-Tock raging at the rock wall. He looked down and saw the new illustrations. He caught sight of the new creature. He looked up as the rocks continued to fall. The ceiling was going to collapse.

Daniel was dodging the debris as he shouted, *"TICK-TOCK!!!"* He lunged to grab for the totem when Byron grabbed hold of him, pulling him back through the archway just as the ceiling caved in...with Tick-Tock still inside.

Alexandra, Daniel and Byron shouted as they watched the remaining debris seal off the archway leading to the cavern. They were breathing hard, speechless as to what had just occurred.

Daniel scrambled toward the debris and placed his ear against the rock.

Alexandra stood, "Can you hear anything?"

Daniel shook his head. "Can you?"

She placed her head against the rock. "No. What made him react like that?"

Byron jumped up onto the wall to see if there was a ledge up above that would lead them out. "Whatever it was, Tick-Tock clearly didn't like it." He moved like a spider all across the rock. Daniel watched him maneuver as the gorilla king swung across the rock walls. He thought of Rhodes.

Alexandra leaned against the wall to listen again for any sound from Tick-Tock. "Do you think he's dead?"

Byron shook his head, "I don't think so. I agree with Daniel. That totem was created for a single purpose…and he will only cease to exist once it is done. He is still amongst the living. I'm sure of it." The gorilla king slid back down to Daniel and Alexandra; he could not see a way in.

Alexandra asked, "Do you think those creatures heard him?"

"I think everybody heard him." Byron sighed, "What do we do now?"

The lion king looked at sealed off wall. "We continue on like we had been." He turned and looked at Byron, "We get that stone."

"Well, all right then."

Diana and Keys stood in awe as they stared up at the ceiling of the Great Library. Their eyes roamed every corner of the room as they took in all the mismatching maps.

"The sister did not want them to find the fortress."

"Not the uncle, anyway. Not before now."

Lydia was standing over Daniel's desk trying to find the book Prince Marcus had written. Diana and Keys moved further inside the library, taking in its massive size with its myriad of books. She scanned the walls until her gaze fell on the stack of portraits. "He's very handsome."

Lydia looked over at the painting and smiled. "Yes, he was. Even in his old age."

"Who was he?"

"King Nathan — King Daniel's grandfather. He was the most sought-after king in the realm."

"I can see why."

"Hmmm…" Lydia stared at the painting as memories flooded her mind. "So many women inside the den wished to be his queen, but there was none who could claim his heart but one."

"The mariner."

The bull queen looked at her curiously. Diana smiled sheepishly, "Keys and I were at the dam the day the mariner warriors revealed themselves. I overheard the leader tell King Sebastian they still lived on through the lion."

"Ah. Well…" She sat down in Daniel's chair. "Although King Nathan married the Mariner Princess Lara, it was a loveless marriage; a mere contract. The mariner princess was in love with the wolf prince Alexander

— Queen Alexandra's father. King Nathan…his heart belonged to another…the bird queen…Queen Rebekah."

Diana slowly sat down opposite Lydia. Something about the look on Lydia's face as she spoke of the lion king and bird queen made her want to hear more of the story. "What happened to them?"

The bull queen suddenly looked sad; her voice was barely a whisper, "So many things you do not know….so many things have come about that I don't know what I truly believe anymore…" The bull queen studied Diana, "Do you believe in these creators…these beings that reside inside this element fortress?"

The horse queen narrowed her eyes. "How can anyone live in this world and not?"

"I suppose I've never seen the world painted the way others have. The colors I see aren't that vibrant." She smiled to herself. "Minotauro believed that there was something beyond this world. He would look at the stars and see dreams within them. He taught me to look up. He taught me to believe. I don't know that it what necessarily in these creators, but I'm willing to consider the idea that they might be real. The bird queen seemed to think so. She believed in these beings just like you do. It's been said that they protected her and her clan."

Diana shifted her eyes to Keys. His mane stood on end.

"Their shield is why our realm is in the shambles it is now."

"I don't understand."

"The bird queen was frozen in time."

Ice.

"But before she was, she sent a shockwave across the realm to destroy her enemies."

Diana touched her medallion.

"The way it was told to me, wind and fire pulverized the dam at Mariner Sea, flooding the valley, demolishing Mariner Tower, destroying the dam."

Diana was stunned.

"Our realm fell into a deep drought, and the only food we had…" Lydia's face turned white as she tried to find the words, "Were warriors from each other's clans."

Keys lowered down to all fours.

Lydia looked over at the portrait of King Nathan. "For seventy-five years, we lived like that until Prince…" She smiled, catching herself. "*King* Daniel awoke the bird queen. Her gates had been guarded by massive vines. They were the only things that seemed to grow."

Diana exhaled slowly, remembering the massive gates when she had ventured inside bird kingdom.

Sister Earth.

"There were roses that never ceased to bloom. They wove the words, 'Only the Noble'."

214

"King Daniel."

Lydia looked at her and smiled. "He's an extraordinary person, queen."

Diana thought about when she had discovered him and the other remnants inside her forest. She had told Alexandra he had honor. She had sensed it. Looking around the library at all his efforts and hearing this tale, now she knew why. "How long ago did all of this happen?"

"Two years ago."

Diana looked confused. "Then…what happened to the lion king and bird queen?"

The bull queen's smile vanished. "I don't know how to explain it." She looked off in the distance. "You see, all of these happenings have been a bit of a jolt to those of us who have lived inside the den. We did not grow up with the knowledge or the notion that there were other forces at work in our realm aside from our warriors and kinsmen. A king in our line banished all belief in invisible forces, thinking it absurd and the illusion of illiterate minds…no offense. We have all lived under the belief that our value was based on the work of our own two hands and the desires of our own will — not others. That our existence begins and ends here. That our time is meant to aid in the flourishing of our clan under our king and queen alone. That is where our lives find value…that all changed with Queen Rebekah. Suddenly there was the idea that there were unseen forces at work. Ones you could call upon. Ones that you could not see but would stand at your side and help make the impossible…possible. Ones that could give you a different kind of hope, knowing that your value had some greater purpose — and it wasn't just to serve your master in the realm."

Diana and Keys continued to listen in silence.

"When the bird queen awakened, so did her warriors. Beings that had not forgotten what and who were responsible for trying to annihilate them."

The horse queen remembered the paintings on the walls representing the bird clan warriors.

"They attacked the den against their queen's knowledge. King Nathan perished…" Lydia suddenly stood and turned toward the windows, looking out at the starry sky beyond. "After the bird queen took her own life."

The horse queen let out a small gasp.

Lydia turned back around. "They say she did it to save the realm." The bull queen sat back down and found the emerald green book she had been looking for. "Without the queen's birds, we have had no rain. And so, King Daniel, King Byron, King Sebastian, Queen Alexandra and King Minotauro picked up where she left off. They united the realm. King Daniel studied Prince Marcus' writings and now believes that there is a stone that could help bring the rain." She handed Diana Marcus' book. "King Sebastian stayed behind to rebuild the dam should the kings and queen succeed in finding the stone to bring it."

Diana took the book and gently laid it in her lap. She suddenly felt ashamed for having burned the lion king's maps and attempting to thwart the remnants' mission. She cringed as the memory of her stallion firing his arrow at King Daniel filled her mind. She looked up at Lydia and asked, "And what do you believe?"

"That not everything and *everyone* is as they seem."

Diana felt her full meaning.

"So, you see, queen, I understand your desire in trying to rectify the past. We all do." Lydia smiled kindly at her. "The library is yours to explore. I'm going to see my son." Lydia stood. "I hope to believe one day in what and whom you have already come to know, but I'm not there just yet."

Diana followed the bull queen's stare. She was looking at the queen's medallion. Lydia walked outside the library and shut the doors.

Keys stared at his queen for quite some time. "What do you intend to do now, my queen?"

Diana stared at him. She looked up at all the maps on the ceiling and stood while holding Marcus' book close to her chest. She moved around the room and stopped the moment she came to King Nathan's portrait.

"Before you make any more decisions, queen…" Diana turned and saw Sebastian standing in the doorway with a few of his toad warriors. "Come with me."

LIII

Alexandra was listening for every bit of sound as she, Daniel and Byron made their way through the various caverns and archways. She was listening, not just for the creatures' footsteps, but for the voice of their king — Decimus. She knew he was the king Daniel was referring to when he mentioned it to them. She knew she should have said something about him to both kings, but every ounce in her body did not want to. She remembered Decimus' eyes. They were dark but welcoming. She thought of his smile as he looked at her. He seemed...*curious*...not dark or evil. Besides, he had stopped his warriors from harming her a second time, so what if he did not really mean harm? As remnants, they had all been misunderstood, hadn't they? Diana thought they were ruthless cannibals. So, what if what they had heard of this king was just as inaccurate? She was willing to give this king the benefit of the doubt if he ever made his intentions known. But for now, she agreed that no one — neither this king nor his beasts — was going to get their stone.

Alexandra's hand shot straight up. Byron and Daniel froze to the spot, waiting for further command. She motioned for them to move back into the shadows of the rock to hide from view; she had heard something. They quickly and silently obeyed.

Several moments passed without any sign from the creatures. Byron started to wonder if Alexandra had misheard, but the moment he saw two shadows coming their way, he knew she was spot on.

Daniel could not believe how quiet the beasts were for being as large as they were. They came forth, creeping on their two hind legs, each standing over twelve feet tall. They held their spears tightly in their large paws as they methodically scanned and searched their surroundings; one of the beasts was carrying something under his arm but Daniel could not make it out. He wondered how Alexandra even heard them, suddenly realizing how sharp her sense of sound must surely be. And if she had such a gift as this, there was no doubt in Daniel's mind as to what her pack must hear. He knew they

217

had to have heard Byron being attacked by Poe. He knew now they must have also heard Marcus' brutal attack by Poe before he was dropped into their lake. Which meant that they had also heard who was following them in the forest when they first began their trek to the element fortress. Something the lion king was not going to forget if they ever returned home.

Byron was bewildered by the strength these warriors exuded as they continued to move closer toward where they were hiding. That was when he saw it: Bane. His scepter was hanging from the belt of one of the warriors. His jaw clenched in anger. Every muscle in his body contracted as he yearned to grab for it. He was almost about to when he suddenly felt Daniel's hand on his chest holding him back. They locked eyes. The creatures stopped right in front of them.

Alexandra's heart was hammering inside her chest.

One of the warriors sniffed the air rapidly.

Daniel could barely breathe.

The other creature was looking at the ground. It was then the remnants realized their mistake — footsteps marked the gravel. The warrior followed where they led and slowly lifted his head, turning his body in the direction the remnants hid. Simultaneously, the other warrior stopped sniffing and looked in their direction as well.

Daniel slowly moved his hand toward the hilt of his sword. He handed the one he was clutching in his hand to Byron just as Alexandra reached for hers.

The warriors were facing their direction, still gripping their spears tight when they both erupted in loud roars. They remnants braced themselves as the warriors dropped to all fours. And just as the creatures were about to pounce, a large ball of fire erupted from behind the creatures. They turned toward the flames as the fireball blew over the creatures' heads.

The remnants dove backward to avoid the flames just as the rock wall shifted the remnants into another cavern. Daniel landed on the ground beside Byron. The gorilla king cried out in pain. He had landed on a rock; its sharpened edge cutting deep into his thigh. He tried to move it but winced in pain. The cut was deep.

Alexandra cringed as she looked at the gash. "Do you think you can walk?"

"I don't have much choice."

"Come on." Daniel bent down, looping Byron's arm over his shoulder, picking him up. "If you can survive Poe, an arrow in the chest, and falling from a cliff, you can survive this."

The lion king turned toward a large glow coming from one of the archways up ahead. The remnants headed straight for it.

It was Rahelio's Halls.

"The stone is in the largest fire in this hall."

Alexandra looked at the gorilla king, "How do you know?"

"A dream...I saw Alexander and Rebekah dancing before a large bonfire.

A violet stone rested within its flames."

Daniel added, "He's right. It's here."

"They're all kind of big. Where is the largest one?"

Their voices were barely audible as they whispered between them. They looked out at the darkened halls, cautious not to move too quickly in case the creatures were hiding in the shadows.

Daniel whispered to Byron, "How's your leg?"

"It hurts. But I can move."

"Can you move fast?"

"Don't worry, lion, there's more than the ground to use for moving swiftly. Once you get the stone, I won't hold you back."

Daniel turned to Alexandra. "Do you hear anything?"

She shook her head.

Byron leaned in, "You're the one who's going to have to retrieve the stone, king."

"Easy for you to say. I don't see anything in these fires. Just a lot of flames."

"It's there."

"Yeah, but what am I supposed to do to get it out of the fire? Drive my hands in there before getting burned to a crisp?"

"What did you do when you were in front of Rebekah's gate?"

Daniel thought about it. "Nothing. Agoura's vines pulled me through."

"Perhaps Rahelio will do something similar. Maybe all you need to do is stand there. Either that or shove your hands in the fire and hope you *don't* get burned. Besides, you are the Noble One. And Zephyrus did say, 'Only the pure of heart can use the stone'."

"Yeah, but anyone can find it and obtain it." As he stayed in the shadows, he found the largest fire in the center of the hall. "There it is." He stared at the fire for a few moments. "I can't see anything in its flames."

"You have to get closer, king."

He inhaled deeply and looked at Alexandra. He was not looking forward to this. She nodded that it was clear for him to go. He swallowed hard, taking a deep breath before slowly stepping out into the darkened halls.

All he could see were the various flickering flames dancing in the shadows across the walls. He looked all around, taking in his surroundings, determined that the only way on was forward. Through the darkened shadows, his body hugged the wall, keeping himself free from view in case the creatures were crouched somewhere nearby. Although they had shifted away from them only moments before, he had a feeling the warriors would soon find their way inside.

Byron watched intently as the lion king moved throughout the halls, creeping along the wall toward the largest fire in the room. Alexandra was holding her breath, listening for any other sound that could put Daniel in danger. She did not hear a thing.

Daniel had the largest fire in the center of the room in his sights. All he had to do now was step out from the shadows and move toward it. His eyes searched high and low for any sign of movement. He saw nothing. He reached for the hilt of his sword and slowly pulled it from his sheath; he wasn't taking any chances. His entire body tensed as he recognized this test of will. He knew the creatures had to be near, watching, waiting for him to pull the stone free.

Byron began to climb the rock wall so that he could be closer toward the fire to help Daniel in case he was attacked. Alexandra held her sword tight, ready to race forward as well. From where the three of them were positioned, they covered all areas of the halls. Byron was clutching the ledge of the rock wall so tight, he thought the rock would crumble within his clenched fist.

Daniel's eyes roamed his surroundings, searching for any further movement.

Nothing.

They all looked at one another. Daniel nodded. He was ready.

A violet stone…one of pain…one for rain…

The lion king moved swiftly toward the center of the room. He rapidly looked all around him. The flickering shadows of the flames dancing along the walls unnerved him, as it made it harder and harder to see into the shadows. But it wasn't the shadows that he needed to look at but the flames. The moment the lion king peered into the fire, his eyes slit to a cat…*and his entire world faded to black.*

Chief Netapheha was staring down at the pool of water. He had not moved in several hours as the image of the long-toothed creature had appeared as a reflection in the water the moment Tick-Tock had seen it.

The sabretooth…

Like Chief Netapheha, this creature was ancient, granted the role of being oracle to his clan. The old toad thought back to the claw that had punched through the ice in his pool of water. He now knew who it was.

His sworn enemy…

How long had the sabretooth been using the pools, the water, to see inside his realm, to understand the players, to hear their plans to understand their designs, to read the signs of the times? How was he even doing it? It took tremendous power to do such a thing. Even Netapheha knew his knowledge was limited to the reach he had been granted by the elements. But the sabretooth? His reach extended far beyond the chief's.

There was more to this than met the eye and Netapheha was determined to solve this puzzle, for he did not take such intrusion into his territory lightly. He was the amphibian chief, born for the task of giving counsel, sharing wisdom, granting understanding to his king and any kings or queens inside the realm. He had always read the signs, but these last few cycles of the moon he had not seen such dark events coming. It was almost as if they were hidden on purpose, so that he could not see.

Scales over my eyes…

It troubled him.

He pulled the crown from his head and looked at the borax stone wedged in its center — the one the sister had given him. It was different than the one he had used to cure the bird queen after she had been poisoned, but its power was the same.

Looking at the stone, he wondered…

"Chief Netapheha…"

He turned to find his king standing at the base of the pool with a beautiful woman beside him. He narrowed his bulbous eyes to study the woman's features. "Queen of horses…you've come home." He bowed to them both. When he rose, he noticed a change in his king. It was his eyes. It was his stance. There was a strength there that was not there before. There was a fierceness there that exuded from his king's frame, a confidence. Netapheha recognized the change. His king stood before him with a focus he had never seen in him before. It was then that it occurred to him what he was seeing deep within his king…*no fear.*

Becoming…

"King, my king…"

"Chief Netapheha, this is Queen Diana."

The old toad continued to size her up, catching something hidden behind her dark doe-shaped eyes.

Yes, yes…formidable. Strong. Powerful. Underestimated.

It was then he saw the medallion around her neck. He hobbled quickly over to her; his bulbous eyes zeroing in on it. "Closer, closer, queen."

She looked at him curiously before crouching down to him. He took his coral staff and lifted the chain gently to examine the medallion's intricate design. Diana watched as the pupils behind his large bulbous eyes enlarged and shrunk as he studied it.

"What do you see?"

"More than what you want shown." He glanced up at her to find an amused smile on her face. "Keep it hidden till it's time."

The smile on her face slowly faded.

Netapheha turned and looked at his king. "You have your answer."

"I haven't asked the question."

"You don't need to. Do what you must…it is time you learned to trust."

Diana looked between Netapheha and Sebastian.

"He does that a lot." But it was Sebastian who was now studying his chief. "What is it? You look troubled."

The chief closed his eyes, "My king…"

Sebastian stepped closer to him. "Forget why I came here, what have you seen?"

Netapheha scrunched his eyes together, resting his head against his staff. "An enemy of old…long foretold…" He opened his eyes and looked deep into Sebastian's. "The sabretooth."

Diana gasped.

Sebastian quickly shifted his gaze to her. "You know of this creature?"

She crouched down to the chief and touched his webbed hand, "Impossible."

"Keep it hidden, queen…until your wisdom must be seen…"

She nodded in complete understanding and quickly stood. Diana turned her attention to Sebastian, "King, I need to speak with my warrior."

He stood, "I want to know what's going on."

"We will tell you everything, but you must come with me. The answer lies with Keys."

The amphibian king looked at his chief one last time. Chief Netapheha spoke before his king did, "I know what you aim to do. You need not have asked. Trust the mirror…"

And with that, the amphibian king led the horse queen to the surface, leaving Netapheha alone with his thoughts. He peered into the pool of water once more, stirring it with his coral staff. "It is time, it is time, time to go, Tick- Tock… scatter the enemies…time to bring the remnants home before the dark one comes, and all grows cold…"

It was then that the pool froze over.

LIV

"*DANIEL!!!*"

"Easy there, Alexandra..."

"What happened?"

Byron had no idea what happened. All he knew was the moment Daniel looked into the fire, the lion king's body went rigid. He had seen Daniel's eyes slit to a cat before the flames rose higher and higher, almost enveloping him, keeping him from view. When the flames simmered down, he caught sight of Daniel on the ground violently shaking; he was having a seizure.

Creatures or not, Alexandra had raced right for him, turning him on his side as Byron scaled down the wall, limping to join them. He was still on guard, searching all around for any sign of the warrior beasts. He seemed fairly confident they were nowhere in the halls, knowing full well they would have attacked had they been there. The fact they were nowhere in sight disturbed him even more. He looked down at the lion king, only to find Daniel's eyes wide open. But the lion king had not blinked. He only had a frozen, far-off stare, as if he were in some kind of trance. There was no doubt in Byron's mind that whatever he had seen in the fire, was not anything good.

The fire...

Byron stood and looked in the center of the dancing flames.

Nothing.

"It's not here."

"What?"

"The stone."

"But you said..."

He turned and looked at Alexandra. "It's not here."

"No, I don't believe it. It *has* to be here! It must be in another fire! You said you saw it in your dreams!"

223

"It *was* in the fire!" He shook his head, talking to himself as he said, "They must have taken it before we got here."

"How? How did they beat us here? How could they have taken it?"

"I don't know."

"I didn't see them with it!"

"We don't know how many warriors there are in here!"

Alexandra's voice fell into a whisper, "What are we supposed to do now?" She looked down at Daniel. "I don't know what I'm supposed to do." She rested her hand on Daniel's chest. "Speak to me, Daniel." Alexandra continued to shake him gently, but he did not stir. His eyes continued to remain in their frozen state, staring at nothing.

Byron looked all around the room, taking in all the different colored fires. The elements had been silent in their voices, but Rahelio had clearly spoken to Daniel when he looked into the fire. The fact that Daniel was in his comatose state told Byron that whatever it was the lion king had seen, was worse than anything the Bird King Palimus had ever seen, for there was nothing in any of the clan histories that relayed a king or queen collapsing after having a vision in the fire. Then again, there had never been a member of the lion's den who had looked into the fire before. Perhaps, they were never meant to.

Unseen by the wolf queen and gorilla king, Daniel shifted his stare. He looked up toward the peak of the fortress and saw Agoura, Rhodes, and Zephyrus staring down at him. He saw a powerful, dark-haired man looking intently at him; his eyes were ablaze. *Rahelio*. Each stood on separate ledges encircling the peak. All were looking down at him with a serious expression on their face. They knew what he had seen.

Staring at him, it seemed as if the look behind their stoic faces was one where they had been waiting for the moment of the lion king's deep awakening. And now that Daniel had seen the vision in the fire, they continued to stare at him in silence; their expression changing from statuesque to one of a deep challenge. As if to say to him, *What are you going to do now? Now that you have seen? Now that you know?*

The element brothers and sister did not wait for an answer but slowly disappeared into the shadows of the fortress. Daniel slowly sat up just as Byron said, "Alexandra, we need to find those beasts. I need you to listen for them as we head through the caverns. We have to get the stone before they find their way out."

"There is no way out."

"Yes, there is."

They both turned to find Daniel sitting straight up. He was still staring off in the distance as he spoke. And without another word, he suddenly stood up and started walking swiftly through an archway without looking back.

They paused in their conversation until Alexandra said, "Daniel!" But he did not turn. He continued to move swiftly ahead until breaking into an all-out run. Alexandra scrambled to get up to follow him as Byron limped quickly from behind.

The lion king was in his own zone, hearing nothing, knowing more than he did moments ago, and feeling the need to run and run fast. Daniel ran from cavern to cavern, as if he suddenly knew the way. There was purpose beneath his footsteps; there was strength in his stride. Neither Alexandra nor Byron knew what to say or think as they sprinted to keep up with him.

Daniel continued racing through the caverns until coming to the pile of rubble that led to the wall of petroglyphs. He dropped to his knees, lowered his head and waited.

Show me.

Alexandra and Byron finally arrived, breathless and confused as to what they were doing there, but neither said a word.

Show me.

And with that silent thought, his request was answered. The remnants watched as Agoura's vines rose from the ground, winding through the rubble like snakes, grabbing hold of various boulders and rocks, moving them away from the main wall. The walls surrounding the remnants began to shake until they shifted repeatedly, almost as if they were sliding doors, until the petroglyphs revealing the history of the clans came into view. The shifting and rumbling ceased, and all went silent.

Daniel stared at the pictures; his eyes focused on the bottom of the wall. There were claw marks on the final symbol; it was scratched out. The moment he saw it, his eyes slit to a cat and a humming sound began to fill his ears. The final symbol was all that mattered.

"There's more. Show me what Tick-Tock saw."

Byron and Alexandra looked at one another as Daniel continued speaking to what appeared to be no one. They continued to remain in silence as Agoura's vines rose straight up in reply, all in unison, slamming straight down and into the ground, pulverizing boulders and remaining rubble, hammering away at what remained hidden.

Alexandra and Byron jumped back at the forcefulness and power the vines brought forth and the damage they were creating. But Daniel remained on his knees, never moving, as his eyes watched for what was about to give way. And then he saw it…

He fell forward, almost reaching for the images that came into view, when the vines rose up once more. They hammered into the ground before the wolf queen and gorilla king could see what Daniel had seen. The wall crumbled and fell straight down into a crevice below.

Dust filled the cavern as Daniel watched the images fall into the shadows beneath him. His thoughts were dark yet focused. "We have to get to the waterfall." He closed his eyes and barely glanced over at Alexandra as he said, "Call his name."

"I…"

"DO IT!!!"

His shout was amplified in the small cavern, as anger filled its undertone. Byron studied the lion king closely, recognizing a change in his friend —ever so slight.

Byron whispered to Alexandra, "Do it, queen."

She reached for her medallion. Byron could see her hand shaking slightly, bothered by Daniel's sudden shout. She took a deep breath and said, *"Rhodes…"*

Immediately, a loud quake filled the cavern as water emerged from the crevice below. Daniel suddenly stood as the water gushed forth, pummeling over his feet. The water glowed, illuminated by an unseen light, revealing a bright turquoise color — the color of Rhodes' eyes.

Daniel squatted down and plunged his head into the water. He could see that there was no barrier underneath blocking his path beyond the small cavern. He rose from the pool, took his sword from his sheath, and turned to Byron.

"You can swing from trees swiftly. You can scale walls. Skating across ice will be no different." He extended his sword to the gorilla king, as Byron narrowed his eyes, not understanding what Daniel intended. "Take it. I'm going to need you to go before me. You don't have Bane. I'm going to need air."

Before Byron could reply, Daniel turned back toward the water just as it began to freeze over. Byron looked at Alexandra to see if she had made the request. She shook her head. Off her look, Byron knew that something was amiss between the command the wolf queen gave, and the ice that seemed to follow.

He knew he needed to remember this moment.

Without looking back at Alexandra, Daniel said to her, "Keep to the sides of the frozen path. Listen closely and let Byron know if they are near."

And with that, the lion king dove into the water, just as the top froze over. Byron watched as Daniel jettied rapidly forth, disappearing under the wall.

Byron looked at the wolf queen. "How do we follow him?"

"Call *her* name?"

Byron nodded and said a silent prayer. Immediately, Agoura moved all the walls blocking the frozen path, creating a clear passage for the gorilla king and wolf queen to follow.

"Nice, queen."

Byron was immediately on the ice. He started to skate forward, the way he had seen Tick-Tock do when they searched for Daniel in the exterior lake. He slipped and wavered a few times before catching his balance.

Like the trees. Like the walls.

He pivoted, changing his body motion as he pushed forward, swinging his arms from side to side as he glided across the ice. He winced as he moved faster and faster, trying to catch up to Daniel; his wound in his thigh still stinging with each stride, but he pressed on. It was then that he felt the wind behind him, pushing him forward, accelerating his pace. It was then he saw Daniel's form up ahead. With the wind on his back combined with his own momentum, he burst forward. He raced past Daniel and struck the butt of his sword down over the ice. He did it with such force, that an opening was created, and Daniel rose from below and lifted his head above the opening to catch his breath. And as soon as the lion king had inhaled, he was underwater once more, racing ahead.

Byron moved even faster, following the pattern of creating openings in the ice with Daniel's sword as they moved from cavern to cavern. All the while, Alexandra ran along the rock pathway, following closely behind; the wind helping her along as well.

They continued their pace as Byron followed the illuminated path of ice, hammering down upon it at various spots for Daniel to emerge. He suddenly came to a halt. There was a rock wall at the end of his path. He looked down and saw Daniel swim past him and underneath the wall just as Alexandra arrived.

Byron said another silent prayer, but this time, Agoura did not answer.

'What do we do now?"

The gorilla king looked up. "We climb."

LV

Daniel rose to the surface, only to find himself inside another cavern. He could hear the powerful force of water up ahead as he emerged from the pool. He headed toward the source of the sound.

The waterfall.

He had reached it.

He continued to climb until realizing that he was *behind* the waterfall. Through the falls on the other side, he could see the familiar setting of snow; the same snow-filled cavern he had been attacked in earlier. He realized this must have been the pathway the creatures took to enter the fortress. And there was no doubt in Daniel's mind that this was the path the warriors would take to get out of the fortress.

Daniel looked behind him but could not see where the rock pathway had led to the outside. All he could see was the pool of water ahead that led back into the deepest part of the fortress. Behind him was the pathway back toward Rahelio's halls.

How had they done it? Had Agoura helped?

It did not seem likely. He remembered the scratched-out symbol — what did it mean? He looked all around the cavern for a way out. There wasn't one. He turned his gaze from the pathway behind him and toward the falls, only to come face to face with Tick-Tock.

They stared at one another for several moments. Tick-Tock tilted his head to the side, almost as if he recognized the slightest change in the lion king's demeanor. His three heads began to slowly turn, each face looking back at Daniel with their large bulbous eyes, as if trying to decipher who and what was before them. The three heads kept turning and turning as a slight breeze began to swirl all around them.

Tick-Tock's heads finally stopped spinning as it landed on the head of the barn owl — the head of the present. "Time to get what you came for, king."

Daniel looked deep into the totem's eyes. He caught a glimpse of what he

228

thought was Rebekah and Alexander behind them. He turned and looked out through the waterfall. He could see two large mounds of snow amidst the white landscape beyond.

He waited and watched, staring at the mounds of snow. That was when he caught sight of movement up above.

Alexandra.

She was climbing down the wall, landing between the two mounds of snow. She looked all around until focusing her attention on the pool of water on her side of the waterfall. Byron was slowly scaling down the wall behind her.

He could hear her say, "I ran through here before…this is where I was attacked."

"Are we going in circles?"

"Only if Agoura wants us to."

"If that's true, there's something in here she wants us to see…"

Alexandra looked across the cavern and narrowed her eyes as she stared at the far wall. She slowly moved toward it, trying to make out what she was seeing. She stopped dead in her tracks. She looked down at the pool of water, remembering what she had seen when she was plunged into its depths. "The waterfall. It wasn't here before."

She crouched down to the pool of water and peered down before looking up at the waterfall once more. The direction of her gaze made it appear as if she were staring straight through the falls and into Daniel's eyes.

"Queen…"

Alexandra immediately shifted her gaze. She looked down and into the pool of water, tilting her head at the sound of a man's voice.

Byron was almost to the base of the cavern; Alexandra's position was blocking the gorilla king's view from the pool of water. He did not seem to hear the voice calling to the wolf queen.

But Daniel did.

He watched Alexandra's reaction; she was neither alarmed nor shocked at the sound of the man's voice. It appeared to Daniel as if she almost smiled. He continued to watch her just as the mounds behind her began to move. Alexandra was staring at the pool of water when Daniel saw the mounds of snow begin to rise.

And before Daniel could make a move, a green light illuminated the cavern and Tick-Tock rocketed through the waterfall. He headed straight for Alexandra with a speed faster than Daniel knew he could possibly move. Tick-Tock grabbed her, almost tackling her to the ground as he shoved her behind him as he spun around to face the two warriors camouflaged in white.

The cavern was illuminated in the emerald glow of Tick-Tock's stone as the totem belted out the shrill sound of an eagle. The warriors stood to their full height of over twelve feet tall.

Bear warriors.

Daniel lowered his head as his eyes slit to a cat. He could see their sneer as they bared their teeth, turning to face Tick-Tock. One of them held the violet stone under its massive arm. Daniel felt his chest begin to burn. *He had to get that stone.*

One of the warriors pulled his spear, while the other remained weaponless as he clutched the stone tight.

The armed warrior shouted to the other, "Through the waterfall!" It was then that Daniel saw Byron's bone scepter, Bane, at the other warrior's side. It was that warrior, the one with the stone, that turned and ran toward the waterfall and launched his massive body straight through. He barreled straight into Daniel, colliding into him. The lion king slammed into the rock wall behind him as the bear warrior trampled over him and raced toward the back of the cave.

Daniel could not believe his eyes the moment ebony-colored vines sprouted up from the surrounding rock. They rapidly wound around one another, until a solid black stalk was created. It slammed against the rock wall, hammering at it like a drum until the rock crumbled.

As the wall was pulverized, Daniel saw Agoura's green vines burst through.

The black vines immediately separated and grabbed hold of all sides of the rock wall, attempting to keep the pathway open for the bear warrior to run through.

Agoura's vines grabbed hold of the debris and began hurling them against the opening to close the pathway once more. The black vines fought against her green ones, trying stop them from rebuilding the rock wall, but Agoura's vines were stronger. Her vines wound around the ebony ones and ripped them apart, severing their grip on the open pathway — but not fast enough.

The bear had gone through.

The ebony vines gave way and immediately vanished underground, and the rock wall crumbled. But Agoura was not done. She moved the ground below, swallowing the rubble whole until the opening appeared once more.

There was another cavern beyond the opening.

Daniel shouted behind him, "Alexandra! Byron! He has the stone!" Without waiting for them, he ran through. Alexandra and Byron burst through the waterfall and followed suit, leaving Tick-Tock to fight with the other warrior.

The lion king was charging as fast as he could after the bear warrior who had their stone, but he could not seem to close the distance.

As if reading his thoughts, a gush of wind picked up behind him, thrusting him forward. Byron was struggling on his wounded leg, pushing himself as hard as he could. Alexandra was only slightly ahead of him. Wind suddenly surrounded them, forcing them faster along. They were catching up to Daniel. And up ahead, they were catching up to the bear.

Alexandra could see Bane at the warrior's side. She yelled to Byron, "He's got your scepter!"

Byron gritted his teeth in anger and ran even faster.

The bear warrior raced through the dark cavern; there was light up ahead. The kings and queen could see it as well.

Daniel shouted, "He's going to leap!"

The wind pushed them faster.

And just as the bear was about to jump, a rock wall shifted and the bear slammed straight into it, careening backward just as Daniel grabbed the stone from the bear's grasp. Byron was immediately beside him, ripping Bane from the warrior's sheath as the rock wall shifted again and the opening to the outside of the fortress reappeared. Wind hurled them through.

Alexandra screamed as they plummeted down the exterior of the fortress, over another waterfall, and down into the lake below. They immediately shot to the surface by the water's force. They continued to move forward by a single wave and were spit out onto shore. They were exhausted. Byron rolled onto his back to catch his breath while Daniel got to his feet. Alexandra's head was in the sand.

Daniel shouted, *"RUN!"*

Alexandra looked back at the fortress. She saw the rock wall moving and shifting above, pulled apart by black vines as another opening emerged, and the bear warrior dove down. She scrambled to her feet. Byron used his scepter to help boost himself back up.

"GO! GO!"

They raced toward the trees. The bear had reached the beach and charged after the remnants with unnatural speed. Byron limped in pain as he ran on his wounded leg.

Alexandra looked back, *"HE'S COMING!"*

Daniel looked back — a royal mistake. He tripped over a fallen branch and hit the ground hard. The stone rolled out from his grasp. He yelled to Byron. *"King! The stone!"*

The gorilla king raced toward the stone, grabbing for it as he clutched it to his chest. He was holding it so tight, it was going to take a legion of warriors to remove it from his grasp. No one was getting the stone. *No one.* That's all Byron needed to tell himself as he found the strength to charge forward.

Daniel saw the bear burst past him, zeroing in on Byron, as he pushed himself back up from the ground. He was about to run forward when he sensed a bright light emanating from behind him.

He turned around and saw what appeared to be a ball of fire blazing behind the waterfall. He suddenly felt the ground moving underneath him. He looked down and saw the ground shifting, but it was different from when Agoura moved across it before she opened the fortress for them. Agoura's movements were fluid; these were not.

Daniel continued to watch as the ground moved in a severed pattern, almost as if the force behind the momentum forward was met with resistance against it, pushing it back.

Like the vines…

Agoura was fighting against this unseen force that was trying to mirror her likeness and movements.

And now a fire…

The lion king looked back across the lake at the waterfall where the fire was growing brighter and brighter behind it. But it was no ordinary fire…

The flames were black, and the hottest part of its center was not blue but a strange shade of grayish white. *What did it mean? Dark vines, dark flames…*

But before Daniel could decipher any more of this mystery, two dark figures slowly emerged from the fire. One appeared to be in the form of a man. He was hooded and cloaked in shadow. Beside him was the outline of the largest creature Daniel had ever seen; he immediately recognized it. It was the same image he had seen in the cavern filled with petroglyphs; the one Agoura had shown him; the one Tick-Tock had seen.

The sabretooth.

The black flames moved from behind the figures, alongside them and out in front of them as it guided them through the waterfall. Both beings were completely unscathed as they walked through the fire. Daniel continued to watch in disbelief as the water in the lake began to rise and fall until a large wave ignited in black fire. The moment the fire lit the wave, it turned the wave into a sheet of black ice, creating a pathway for the two beings.

Daniel was stunned.

The two figures walked with even steps across the darkened ice and toward the banks of the lake. Their footsteps were purposeful, confident.

No fear.

Daniel crouched back in the shadows of the trees. He took in the sabretooth warrior, never having seen such a creature like this one before. Its eyes were yellow, its fangs long and sharp. Its body was perfectly formed. Even from where the lion king hid, he could see the muscles beneath the warrior's dark fur. It was powerful. It reminded him of Poe.

The hooded man stopped and looked out at the forest beyond, assessing the movement of the trees as they swayed, twisted, and turned.

"Wind is helping them."

Daniel recognized his voice. It was the same one he heard call to Alexandra in the cavern. He immediately felt his body tense as his eyes slit to a cat.

The sabretooth did not immediately respond. Instead, he was looking directly into the shadows where Daniel was crouched. The lion king held his breath, hoping he had not been seen. It was then that the sabretooth responded, "She asked him to."

"The horse queen."

"No…the *other* one."

The hooded man shifted his gaze to his warrior.

"Impossible."

In reply, a cold wind moved through the trees and out toward the two beings. It was an unnatural cold — freezing. It was different than the wind that caused the trees to sway, twist and turn. Daniel felt a chill run down his spine as the cold moved over him and all around him, seeping into his bones; the wind was painful.

Not Zephyrus.

The sabretooth warrior turned his large head, following the path of the chilling wind and back toward the black fire. It was still blazing behind the waterfall.

The moment the sabretooth's eyes rested on the flames, his fur shot straight up. He immediately growled and moved in front of the man. He ripped a huge battle axe from his back and wielded it as he crouched low, facing the fire, protecting the man.

Daniel watched as a fiery red flame erupted from the grayish-white ones, devouring the lighter flames, swallowing the darker ones until a crimson color shone through.

The lion king recognized the color. And then...*he saw her.*

Rising up from the red flames was Rebekah. On her right was Reginald and on her left was Poe.

His dream...

But Rebekah was not dancing in the fire. She was looking at the man and his warrior. Her gaze was both a challenge and a warning.

Daniel shifted his eyes toward the man and his beast. He could see the sabretooth trembling as he bared his teeth. Even from this distance, the lion king could see her eyes...they were as black as the raven. He remembered the first time he had seen those eyes; he knew she was angry.

The cold wind blew even harder, attempting to snuff out the crimson fire but to no avail.

The black ice broke apart and melted against the heat of the red fire as the flames grew hotter and brighter.

The ground rumbled but was unable to shift.

It was as if all dark element forces were attempting to attack the queen but could not.

How was Rebekah doing this?

Daniel could barely breathe. His body was paralyzed as he watched the dead bird queen and her champions come to life, standing amidst the burning flames.

The sabretooth roared as Rebekah lifted her arms, raising them to the sky as she shouted, *"Fire! Wind! Ice! Earth!"*

Reginald and Poe let out piercing, thunderous shrieks.

The man yelled to his warrior, but Daniel could not make out his shouts over the sound of the roaring fire and Rebekah's voice.

"Protect the realm!"

And with that, Rebekah wound her arms down and slammed her hands together.

A lightning bolt shot out from her hands and out toward the man and his beast. But before it collided into them, there was a loud *SNAP!* And black fire shot forth from the man, swallowing the lightning bolt whole.

Rebekah, Reginald, Poe, and the crimson fire were gone.

The black fire was gone.

The freezing cold wind was gone.

All that remained was silence.

The man was breathing hard, glaring at the spot where Rebekah had stood moments before. His warrior was in the same position as his master, breathing just as hard.

Daniel immediately recognized the effect.

A remnant.

The lion king narrowed his eyes, looking for it. And then he saw it…an onyx-colored medallion hung from the man's neck.

The man could barely spit out the words, "Impossible…"

Daniel slowly rose from the shadows.

The moment he did, the sabretooth's head spun around as he rapidly sniffed the air. He growled as the man turned to follow his warrior's gaze.

Daniel immediately turned and raced into the forest just as the man said, *"Kill him."*

The sabretooth burst toward the trees.

Byron's leg was burning and cramping, the injured muscle slowing him down. He grabbed for Bane, using it for leverage to help propel him on.

The bear warrior burst alongside Alexandra. It swiped its massive paw at the back of her leg, taking her down as it passed her and headed toward Byron.

"KING!!!"

Byron looked back only to find that the bear was inches from him. He braced himself for impact, raising his scepter to swipe, when he was ripped from the ground and into the treetops. The bear's black claws missed his jugular by less than an inch as the gorilla king was pulled to safety. The bear pivoted and turned, skidding into a tree trunk. But it was determined.

The bear roared viciously, keeping its eyes on its target. It charged forward, gunning straight for Byron when Ram, the bull warrior, collided into the bear. A vicious attack ensued.

Byron was hurled across the treetops as strong hands caught him and flung him from tree to tree.

It was his gorilla warriors.

Rod was the last to catch him as he launched his king into the sky. Byron landed on the ground, rolling across it only to be picked up again by another hand. He was thrown onto the back of a horse.

"KING!" It was Diana. *"HOLD ON!"*

Alexandra was running after them when a beast ran up between her legs so that she was immediately riding it — it was Igor. The wolf warrior howled to the sky and other howls replied.

From nowhere and everywhere clan warriors emerged, surrounding the king and queen.

As they raced across the land, Alexandra could see the ground moving in odd shifts. It was then she saw black vines moving alongside her and then on in front of her like slithering snakes. They were pulling the ground apart in an attempt to shift the landscape. The ground rumbled and quaked. The wolf queen could hear a noise that came from deep underground. Her eyes went wide; she shouted to Byron and Diana, *"LOOK OUT!"*

A massive rock wall burst forth from underground, several yards in front of Diana. Keys skidded and began sliding toward the wall. He pivoted and raced alongside it, trying to find an opening. The further he rode, the more rock walls erupted, blocking their path, attempting to keep them from traveling further south.

Diana shouted, *"FASTER!"*

Keys charged harder but could not beat the pace of the rock walls. They were rising up one after the other, creating a border so high and so long, it seemed that no one would be able to pass through; that is, until they heard the rumble of a powerful stampede.

Bull warriors — buffaloes, rams, bulls, goats — appeared out of nowhere. They charged directly into the rock border, hammering away at the walls like a drill as warrior after warrior butted into it. The rock walls began to splinter, crumbling to the ground as the bull warriors crashed through the border, demolishing it. The horse queen raced through.

Two bear warriors immediately followed.

Daniel was running faster than he ever had in his life. The freezing cold wind had emerged once more; it continued to surround him as he bounded through the trees. As he rushed forth, he saw a flash of green light resonating from behind him, followed by the sound of a loud, thunderous crash. There were vicious roars until all went silent. He pressed on, not about to make the same mistake he had before by looking back.

Tick-Tock was suddenly beside him. *"ON MY BACK, KING!"*

Daniel jumped onto the totem's back as Tick-Tock dropped to all fours. They raced on.

The sabretooth was nowhere in sight.

As they sped across the terrain, Agoura shifted the landscape. Daniel was bowled over at how quickly she was doing it as all the mountains, rivers, forests, and valleys they had crossed over and through to get to the Element Fortress moved and flashed in front of his eyes. He caught a glimpse of an unfamiliar territory where another waterfall resided; he did not remember it from before.

Then came horse territory.

The Wolf Lair.

Critter Country.

And on to Mariner Sea…

Diana looked behind her and saw the warriors closing in. She clutched her medallion. There was a loud *SNAP!* as she commanded, *"FASTER!"*

Keys charged harder, the wind aiding his every step, but the bear warriors were still gaining speed. Diana narrowed her eyes, not comprehending what she was seeing. *How was this possible?*

Byron shouted, *"The Lair!"*

He could see the crooked, desolate forest up ahead. The moment Wolf Lake came into view, Byron knew they had crossed over into the realm. Hood could be seen at the banks of the lake. He barked and howled loudly as Wolf Pack warriors surrounded him.

Alexandra shouted to Diana, *"FOLLOW HIM!"*

Keys obeyed her command as Hood ran through the trees, guiding them through. They came to the open ground of Critter Country, hurdling the graves as they raced forth.

Crossing Critter Country, the dam came into view. Diana shouted to Byron, *"KING! YOU'RE GOING TO HAVE TO HURL IT INTO THE SEA! GET READY!"*

Diana looked to her right and saw one of the bears coming up alongside her. Byron looked to his left and saw the other one. The bears were closing in on both sides. Diana and Byron braced themselves for impact.

Out of nowhere, another warrior slammed into the bear on Diana's right. The creature picked up the bear warrior, vaulted over Diana and Byron and slammed the bear's body down onto the other bear warrior.

It was Cheetah.

All around Byron and Diana, lion den warriors emerged to protect them as the horse queen rode on just as the clouds began to gather.

Alexandra rode past them while Hood, Kingston, and Ram joined Cheetah in battling it out with the bears. It did not take long before the bear warriors were annihilated. As soon as the bears went down, two more bears raced past the Wolf Pack and other clan warriors.

The captains of each of the clans roared and raged, immediately chasing after them.

Byron looked behind him and saw the new arrivals.

Where were they coming from?

Byron and Diana reached the dam; it was in shambles. Byron jumped off Keys and raced toward the rubble and collapsed bamboo. He struggled to sprint over the debris, crying out in pain as the wound in his thigh caused his leg to seize; he fell.

"KING!" It was Diana. She dismounted Keys just as Byron looked behind him.

The bears were charging straight for him.

He looked back to the top of the dam, rapidly assessing the distance he would have to clear to get there.

He wasn't going to make it.

That was when he heard their ribbiting.

All around him, amphibian warriors suddenly surrounded him. Amun reached down and pulled him up, placing his lanky arm under the king as the frog warrior jumped over the debris, carrying the king to the top of the dam. Diana and Keys followed.

When they reached the top, Byron could see Sebastian.

"BYRON!"

Sebastian pulled his sword, having seen the bear warriors rapidly approaching. He shouted to Diana, *"QUEEN! BEHIND YOU!"*

Diana turned and ripped her sword from her sheath. But there was no need. They were not headed for her...only the gorilla king. They bounded past Diana and Keys and continued charging up to the top of the dam.

Byron wasted no more time. He shoved his scepter into his sheath. With every ounce of strength and determination he had within him, he gripped the stone, and spun. He gathered momentum, and with a loud guttural shout, he hurled the violet stone into the center of the sea.

"BYRON!"

The gorilla king turned just as the bear warriors were about to collide into Sebastian and him. They braced themselves for impact but were suddenly blinded by a bright emerald light as Tick-Tock shouted, *"GET DOWN!"*

Byron and Sebastian dropped just as Tick-Tock grabbed hold of the warriors by the napes of their enormous necks with both his talons; he tackled them both into the sea.

Sebastian's eyes went wide, "Was that *Tick-Tock?!?*"

"And a few bear warriors."

"Bear warriors?"

"We have a lot to catch up on."

Sebastian shook his head. "You have no idea."

The gorilla king was on all fours facing the dead sea. He was breathing hard as his heart hammered inside his chest. He had thrown the stone as far as he could. He didn't even know if that was what he was supposed to do, but the moment Diana shouted the command moments before, he knew it made sense.

Diana was suddenly between him and Sebastian. Byron turned and saw her narrow her eyes, searching for any sign from within the sea.

"Queen…"

She turned and smiled at him. "Nice throw. I could've thrown it farther."

Sebastian, "So could I."

He looked at Sebastian. "You wish." He shifted his gaze to Diana. "And you would have cheated. It must be nice to have a medallion to use when needed."

"You have one too."

"Not one that I can use." He looked back at the sea, seeing it in the same state as it always was, "What now?"

Overhead, the clouds continued to gather, and the sound of thunder rumbled across the sky. The wind began to blow as more realm warriors arrived, gathering around the demolished dam.

Alexandra and Daniel joined the other kings and queen — along with their warriors.

Knowing that there were two bear warriors that had been tackled into the sea, Byron hoped that whatever was supposed to happen, happened soon…before the stone was seized once more.

Underwater, Tick-Tock wrestled with the bears, until one warrior broke free. It had spotted the stone. He headed toward it, descending rapidly towards it before it sank into the darkened waters at the bottom of the sea. The bear was fast. He was closing in quickly as he reached for the stone.

Almost there…

Its large black claws extended.

Just within reach.

It was then that the bear warrior saw movement out of the corner of his eye. And before he knew what hit him, a shark warrior chomped down on the warrior's arm, severing the limb from its owner.

It was Stab.

The bear never saw the shark warrior coming. But he did see the school of mariner warriors jettying towards him as he roared in pain from the assault; he was bleeding out from his wound. And before he could blink an eye, shark warriors were on him.

Stab dove down, grabbed the stone, and rapidly took it down to the bottom of the sea.

Tick-Tock was still battling it out with the other bear warrior when the bear was suddenly jerked free from his grasp. It disappeared, having been dragged down into its depths below. Blood filled the surrounding waters…and the bear was no more.

LVI

As Stab continued to rapidly descend, he could see the outline of an athletic-looking man at the bottom of the sea. His dark, doll-like eyes zeroed in on the powerful being anchored to the sand below.

The Lord of the Sea.

The heart inside the great white warrior's chest beat rapidly. He swam faster the moment he saw the element brother extending his hand upward toward him.

Reaching his fin-like hand out to Rhodes, Stab gave the violet stone to the element brother. The moment the stone was in Rhodes' hand, it exploded in a violet ray of light. Stab shielded his eyes from the blinding glare as Rhodes brought the stone down toward his chest, cradling it as if it were a small babe.

Rhodes stared at it for a long while, almost as if he was still deciding what he should do with it. The mariner warrior watched him, wondering what it was the element brother was pondering. His heart continued to beat rapidly — not just in anticipation but in fear. Rhodes continued to stare intently at the stone.

Do they deserve this grace? Are they worthy of this mercy?

Mariner Sea was the lifeline of the realm — the domain he claimed as his own. He looked at the bones piled up at the bottom of the sea; he could still see them. Feeling the tension in his body constrict as he was reminded of the dead and all the rubble of war that brought this mighty sea to its knees, he waited.

"They pierced the heart of my queen brother. They have severed her heart in two."

"Then let them rot for all they've done....and all they have failed to do."

"How could they have not guessed? How is it they don't know? It is true of what the old ones say, 'You will reap what you sow'."

"Reaping and weeping, its song is the same. They forgot about us, the Creators of the game."

241

"Then let us remind them, my brother, who dominates this land. For even our sister weeps at the works of their hand."

"Come Fire."

"Come Ice."

"Come Wind and the Earth."

"Entwined altogether, dismantle hope of new birth."

"The Lion."

"The Wolf."

"Gorilla and Bull."

"These kings and their sons will no longer rule."

"Only the noble can summon the queen's return."

"Until that day comes, dear brother…we shall let the realm burn."

And it had.

Knowing the nature of the kings, queens and beasts of the realm, Rhodes was still deciding.

Whomever rules the sea…rules the realm.

The dark king was coming.

His chosen queen would not be ready.

The lion king was going to break.

The clans were united but still separate all the same.

Should he do it?

At the top of the dam, the entire realm was in attendance. The kings and queens were staring down at the darkened sea below, seeing only the slightest bit of light coming from the sea.

"Why is there no change?" It was Sebastian.

Byron shook his head, his gaze still focused on the center of the sea. His voice was barely a whisper, "I don't know."

"They have to decide together." It was Daniel. "That is the only way it can be done."

Byron looked up at the sky; the clouds were still rolling in. Thunder continued to rumble across it, speaking to the realm below. The wind was blowing harder, causing the water to rise and fall. Even Agoura's rose petals had sprouted up, bordering the dam.

"It's Rhodes." Byron looked back at the sea. He swallowed hard as he asked, "What's he waiting for?"

But Daniel knew. He had seen the reasons when he looked into the fire. He understood why this moment must be weighed. And he knew that as lion king, he alone was the reason.

Alexandra was beside him, clutching her medallion tight. She was willing the Lord of the Sea to hear her as she waited for the waters to rise.

Sebastian, however, was looking at Daniel. He studied him, seeing the slightest change. He was not the same lion king that had left the realm in search of the stone. He suddenly looked quite different. He watched as Daniel stared into the center of the sea with a distant, far-off look; he almost appeared sad.

Rhodes could hear the wolf queen's plea coming from above. But the answer to this prayer was not meant for a lone queen. It was not even meant for any beast or being inside the realm. It was only for his brothers and his sister to decide.

Cradling the stone, hearing the echo of the voices of dead generations within, he remembered the raven. He pondered the lion king. He wondered at his chosen queen.

He and his siblings had allowed the lion king to see the vision in the fire.

What would the Noble One decide?

The lion king...king of the den...king of the sea.

What would the lion king decide, indeed.

He slowly lifted his head and saw the great white warrior looking him dead in the eye. The shark captain was surrounded by a multitude of mariner warriors floating all around their leader in anticipation of Rhodes' next move.

Rhodes studied each of their faces. They had the eyes of the forgotten; the eyes of fear; they were also the eyes of hope.

In unison, the mariner warriors bowed their heads before him.

And the Lord of the Sea finally made his decision.

His turquoise-colored eyes illuminated against the light emanating from the violet stone. He held the stone close to his chest, closed his eyes, and began to turn.

Lightning exploded across the sky, electrifying it. The wind funneled like a cyclone around the entire dam, whipping wildly around the clans. Agoura's vines sprouted from underground. Like arms and hands, they pushed all the clan members back and away from the sea.

The kings and queens stood witness as the vines multiplied. They looked like arms and hands as they moved over the debris, gathering the collapsed bamboo and material from all around the dam.

The entire realm watched in awe as Agoura gathered the boulders that had collapsed when the bull clan had gone down. She began stacking them in rapid succession. Her vines lifted the bamboo and edified them against the stone walls to reconstruct the irrigation system that Sebastian had begun building so long ago.

It was bewildering to watch Wind work with Earth to assist in the build. Within moments, the dam was complete.

The entire realm was dumbstruck.

Daniel immediately thought of what Rhodes had said, *"You have only to realize the commands you can make with us at your side when our wills are united as one."*

Up above, the clouds slightly parted, revealing the warm glow of the sun. A bolt of lightning struck down from the sky...*and into the center of the sea.*

Rhodes, still holding the stone close to his heart, began to spin even faster. Like a tornado, he gained momentum, causing the sea to rise...higher and higher.

From above, the lightning bolt shot down through the water and hit the stone, igniting it, unleashing the power from within. The stone exploded in light, illuminating the entire sea as the waves rose higher and higher.

From behind Agoura's vines, the remnants and clan warriors witnessed the sea level rising until it spilt over the top of the dam and down into the bamboo canals. And as the thunder roared, the wind howled and the lightning continued to electrify the sky, the rain began to fall.

From the center of the sea, Rhodes stopped spinning. He looked all around him, feeling the heartbeat of the sea as it came to life. Still cradling the stone under his arm, he gently raised it high above his head. He spiked it straight down into the ground below; a plume of sand erupted, clouding the surrounding waters. The ground shifted and quaked as Agoura shifted the sands and devoured the stone.

Rhodes looked up once more and saw the mariner warriors staring at him. Stab nodded his head in gratitude to the Lord of the Sea. Through the sandy plume, Rhodes slowly disappeared from view, leaving the mariner warriors alone in the resurrected sea.

"Daniel…you've made me a believer…and if you dream a bigger dream than this one…tell me."

Daniel turned and watched Sebastian relishing in the raindrops that were falling all over his face. He thought of his grandfather.

"It would take a miracle to resurrect that sea, Daniel…"

And the miracle just happened.

They had gone on an impossible quest to seek a stone they weren't even sure existed, risking their lives and the lives of their clans for this single moment. He looked at all the clan warriors gathered at the dam. They stood together, warriors mixing with other warriors. Clans working together to build the dam. Clans working together to venture outside the realm to bring their kings and queen home. *But not all of them…*

Seeing the bull clan warriors in their mosh pit celebration, he felt a tightening in his chest. Minotauro was not here to see that the universe had truly answered.

Although the rain was pouring down all over them, no one seemed to notice that the Elements, the Old Ones, the Creators had granted this mercy. All that held their attention was the rhythm of the powerful waves of Mariner Sea. Only Daniel truly understood what Rhodes had done.

Daniel reached his hand up and rested it against his chest. It was still there. His compass. He closed his eyes, breathing in slowly, relieved to find it there. He was going to need it now more than ever. He had seen what was coming.

He turned his gaze back to the center of the sea. He thought of the stone — an unnecessary object — but one they all needed in order to believe. That is what Rhodes had said anyway. And looking at the joy, shock, and awe of all the clan members rejoicing at the resurrection of Mariner Sea, drenched in pouring rain, he understood that the tangible gift had been necessary — not just for him, but for the entire realm. Miracles were real. Prayers could be answered. Grace paved the way for mercy to abound.

But wasn't that the way it was intended to be from the beginning?

Daniel felt a sense of joy and sadness all at the once as he continued to stare at the power of the roaring sea. He was grateful that Rhodes had decided to gift this grace, but he was deeply troubled.

Why had he been the one to think that there was such a stone? To imagine what it looked like? What the fortress looked like? What the creators looked like? He knew he had created their appearance inside the imaginings of his own mind. And they took on his dreamt-up forms. Which made him wonder, what did these powerful beings *really* look like? What were they *really* capable of? If they could form a mountain, shift the realm, resurrect a sea, rebuild a dam, freeze a queen in time...what more could they do if the realm actually gave them homage?

That was when he saw the shark fins. They were circling in the center of the sea.

For a moment, Daniel thought he was imagining it. He looked at Sebastian. It was as if the amphibian king was reading his mind, "You're not dreaming, king."

He looked back at the sea just as the shark fins disappeared from view. Looking at the spot where they had descended, on impulse, Daniel climbed over the vines and dove in.

Alexandra shouted, *"Daniel!"*

The rejoicing quelched the moment the den warriors realized what their king had done. They erupted in a cacophony of thunderous roars; Cheetah's, however, was the loudest. *"MY KING!!!"* The den warriors did not know what to do or which way to turn as their frenzied state caused the entire dam to quake. They vaulted over Agoura's vines and charged straight through. But they did not dive in, for as powerful as the den warriors were, they could not swim into the depths of the sea.

Byron was stunned.

Sebastian could not believe what Daniel had just done. He did not know what to do. So the amphibian king climbed over the vines and dove in after him.

Daniel jettied forth, swimming faster and faster into the depths of the mighty sea. He did not know where he was going; he just knew that the warriors were waiting for him.

Swimming down into its depths was different than the swamps and the lake at the Element Fortress. Daniel could feel the power of the sea and the pull of the tide as he swam harder and faster.

And as Daniel swam deeper into the sea, he realized...he was not struggling to breathe.

It was the sea...it was his sea...king of the mariners.

He had reached the bottom and was immediately surrounded by tiny fish. They moved right in front of him before quickly swimming away, almost as if they were studying him. It was through their luminescent glow that he saw the mariner warriors.

Daniel shifted his gaze, sensing their eyes on him. He looked all around and found a school of mariner warriors surrounding him. He could see Stab's dark, doll-like eyes staring back at him. Stab moved in front of the mariner legion, aiming a long coral spear directly at the lion king's heart.

LVII

"He's been down there too long." Alexandra was on all fours, clutching the edge of the dam. Her knuckles were as white as snow; her body was trembling. "Can you see anything?"

Cheetah could barely blink let alone breathe as he searched the powerful waves for his king. "No."

"Hood! Do you hear anything?"

"Nothing, my queen."

Images of Minotauro filled her mind. Byron and Daniel pulling his lifeless body from the lake. Byron trying desperately to grab Tick-Tock's talon to call Fire down.

Tick-Tock.

He had not risen from the sea since taking the bears down.

Alexandra began to panic even more. She reached for her medallion hanging from her neck. It was the first time Hood had glimpsed its existence. His entire body froze the moment he saw the silver moon with a wave etched across it. He immediately barked to the pack.

In unison, the wolf pack turned their heads toward their queen; their eyes zeroing in on the medallion. They began to growl lowly, attempting to understand what this gift from the element brother could possibly mean.

Hood studied his queen, sensing the slightest difference in her countenance. He knelt beside her, still staring at her face as she searched the sea for the lion king.

Queen...

An element brother had claimed his queen and marked her for protection. But it was the one element that had never claimed a king or queen from his clan before. He looked out at the power of the sea, not understanding what such claiming could mean and what kind of protection the element brother intended to offer. For the only reason an element claimed a king or queen in each era was for the protection of a great challenge that king or queen would face. One that could not be overcome without the help of those beyond this

248

world.

Hood's heart was thundering inside his chest as he tried to decipher what this seeming gift could mean. He stared at the power of Mariner Sea. The wolf clan hated water. *Hated it*...yet he wondered.

Whoever rules the sea, rules the realm...

The great Wolf King Feyedor had spoken the words ages ago when he had his vision in the fire. And now the sea was brought back to life and the mariner warriors were in it. *Whoever rules the sea*...the king to the forgotten kingdom was the lion.

The fur on his body stood on end as he pondered this great reveal.

Was his queen in danger because of the lion king, the king that was now master of the sea? Is that why she had been claimed by the Lord of the Sea himself? Or was she to aid the lion king as queen of the realm should she choose to marry him? With the element brother protecting her, did it mean that her power would grow along with the lion king as rulers of the realm? Hood did not know which one was the answer.

Igor growled to him, as it seemed his thoughts were the same. Hood stared at him as he thought of what the old ravens had claimed time and time again...*the lionsss cannot be trusted*...

Sebastian saw Stab down below, aiming his spear at the lion king. He swam even faster until wedging himself between the lion king and the mariner warrior. Not the brightest move, as the amphibian king did not know if the shark warrior would attack him — remnant king or not. But he made the move anyway, more concerned about what the mariners would do to the lion king. Sebastian stared straight into the shark warrior's lifeless eyes, conveying a warning to the mariner captain to that he had better think hard about his next move.

But Stab did not lower his spear. He continued to keep his eyes and aim on the lion king.

Sebastian's amphibian warriors had arrived, immediately surrounding the mariners. But just as soon as they did, more mariners arrived. Sebastian had no idea there were so many; he and his warriors were outnumbered but he refused to budge. He pulled his sword from his sheath. That was when he felt Daniel's hand on his shoulder. Daniel pulled Sebastian back and moved forward so that he could face the great white warrior.

Sebastian, however, still clutching his sword, readied himself for whatever was coming next. But then he saw Daniel do something he had not anticipated. The lion king began to unbutton his shirt.

Sebastian narrowed his eyes, not understanding what Daniel was doing until the lion king opened his shirt wide, exposing his chest, laying his heart bare. Daniel moved forward so that the edge of Stab's spear was touching his chest.

Sebastian moved forward to stop him, but Chango held his king back.

The lion king could see the shark warrior's gills moving in and out. He was staring directly into Daniel's eyes. All the mariners waited to see what their mighty captain would do. The longer they waited, the more anxious Sebastian became.

An eternity seemed to pass until the shark warrior lowered his spear. Stab slowly backed away from the lion king and swam away from the center of the sea and the rest of the mariner warriors followed.

Too long...

Alexandra could barely breathe as she continued to clutch her medallion, still staring helplessly into the sea.

Byron watched her, knowing exactly what she was feeling and thinking. But for some reason, he was unafraid. He was witnessing something he had not anticipated. The den warriors...*were not going down.*

All the lion, tiger, cheetah, lynx, and panther warriors were strong and whole. Had Daniel been in any danger of drowning, they would be experiencing his pain and fear. The only fear he could see on any of their faces was the one that waited for their king to resurface.

He shifted his gaze back to the powerful waves that continued to rise and fall.

Mariner Sea...*the lion king was king of the sea.*

Alexandra closed her eyes clutching her medallion tightly. She tried to summon Rhodes one more time...and this time...*he answered her.*

From below, there was a loud *SNAP!* and Daniel was immediately pulled up by a powerful movement of water — almost as if an invisible hand had grabbed him from behind — dragging him rapidly to the surface.

Sebastian and the amphibian warriors followed.

Daniel was pushed upward by a powerful wave. It carried him rapidly toward the dam where Alexandra awaited.

The moment his head hit the surface, Cheetah and the rest of the den erupted in roars. Alexandra opened her eyes and searched the waters for the lion king.

"DANIEL!"

She watched as he swam toward the dam and climbed onto its ledge. It had not escaped her notice that the waters had now risen to the height of the dam walls.

Sebastian and his warriors had reached the surface. They could see that Daniel had already reached the side of the dam.

"He's fast, my king. Faster than you."

They were swimming toward the edge of the dam. "Don't remind me."

Amun added, "And he did not drown."

Sebastian stopped midstride.

"Like you, my king."

They floated in the water as Sebastian thought about what his warrior had just said. As they bobbed up and down for several moments, the amphibian king looked all around at the newly risen waters. "No wonder he wasn't afraid."

"They would never have harmed him, my king. Kill their king, they all die."

Sebastian suddenly felt very foolish. "Yeah…yeah. I keep forgetting he's part Mariner."

Sebastian stared at the lion king; he seemed older. Distant yet stronger. It was then that the words flooded his mind, *Whoever rules the sea, rules the realm.* The lion king, even after all they agreed to make equal, was now the most powerful king of them all. He did not know why, but something about that knowledge began to make Sebastian's blood turn cold.

Alexandra rushed toward Daniel the moment he was on the ledge. She

251

wrapped her arms around him as tears streamed down her face. "How is this possible? I was so scared…I thought I'd lost you."

He lifted his arms to wrap them around her as she rested her head in the crook of his neck. He started to close his eyes, just to feel her heart beating against his, when he decided to keep them open. He lowered his arms just as his den warriors were upon him.

They were rallying to surround their king. Seeing his queen surrounded by a frenzied rioting of lion den warriors, Hood barked viciously to the sky. The pack immediately moved in, weaving, and wrestling with the den warriors to move through their crowded celebration, trying to get to their queen.

Alexandra and Daniel were separated as the den warriors moved to relish in their king's return — not just from the sea, but from his quest. Hood had grabbed hold of his queen, wrapping his arms around her, and pulling her through to safety.

"Daniel!"

She was reaching out to him, but her pack kept pulling her back from the throng. Daniel could not hear her over the rioting shouts of the den.

Hood and the wolf pack surrounded their queen like a shield, carrying her away from the den warriors. They were not taking any chances. Against her protests, Hood picked her up and began racing toward the lair.

Daniel never looked back.

Sebastian had finally reached the edge of the dam. He could barely hear himself think as the cacophony of lion's den roars thundered across the dam. He looked up just as Byron crouched down to him and extended his hand. "You did it, brother! You built the dam!" He helped pull Sebastian up from the sea.

Both kings looked at the den warriors as they steered their king back toward the den.

"It was in shambles!"

"What?!?"

"IT WAS IN SHAMBLES!"

"Not anymore!"

Both kings stood side by side — brothers, friends, family. Sebastian was suddenly overcome. There was one person missing amongst their trio. "It's about time you came back!"

"Yeah, but not all of us."

As the den warriors vacated the dam, a baby's cry could finally be heard. Byron turned his head and saw Lydia.

The moment he saw the babe in her arms, his knees buckled beneath him. He caught his breath as he made his way over to the bull queen.

Lydia smiled softly at him, "King."

They held each other's gaze as a rush of emotions rose inside both their chests. Byron reached out to the little king and gently touched the top of his tiny head. "Don't cry, little one."

"Minotauro."

Byron looked at Lydia.

"I named him Minotauro."

Byron's eyes filled with tears.

"I'm sorry, queen. I didn't think I'd be coming home without him."

Lydia smiled sadly and grabbed his hand, clutching it tight. "You didn't."

Byron narrowed his eyes in confusion.

"You carry him with you."

The gorilla king clenched his jaw, trying to hold the emotions deep within. He suddenly realized that the little king was no longer crying. Byron looked down at Little Minotauro and saw a tiny smile on the young king's face. His eyes were twinkling as he gazed up at the gorilla king.

"He never smiles, king. He loves you already."

Byron smiled back just as his breath began to fog on the air. The smile slowly faded. He turned in search of Alexandra. But the wolf queen and her pack were nowhere in sight.

Netapheha was frantically searching through various scrolls inside his tiny cavern. They were spilled out across the floor and desk as his webbed fingers scanned and searched. He froze immediately the moment the cold wind blew the scrolls across his desk. He turned his bulbous eyes toward the pool of water just as it began to illuminate, drowning out the candlelight in his tiny abode.

Cheetahs' fur was standing straight up as the cold wind swirled around the den warriors. He turned slowly and looked toward the north.

The breeze blew across Mariner Sea, causing the waves to rise and fall. Shark fins emerged from the depths below as mariner warriors lifted their heads above the water and looked North.

All around the dam the wind blew colder and harder. The sky darkened as the gorilla and amphibian kings, bull queen and clan warriors turned to face the oncoming north wind. They all watched the storm brewing as it loomed, announcing to the skies that it was coming their way.

Sebastian asked, "What's happening?"

"He's coming..."

The kings and bull queen turned their gaze to Diana. The horse queen and her warrior, Keys, were standing beside them; they were looking north.

Keys spoke softly to his queen, "He's crossed over into the realm."

Clutching her medallion, Diana replied, "We must go."

He immediately dropped to all fours as his queen mounted him.

Byron moved closer to her, "Wait."

She looked down at him.

And for all the gorilla king's talking, he could not think of a single word to say.

Diana smiled. "I'm glad you got what you wanted, king. I hope your invitation still stands."

Before he could respond, the horse queen rode off. Lydia caught the gorilla king's look as she watched his eyes follow the horse queen as she rode away.

Sebastian looked at Byron. "Who's coming? What invitation? What did I miss?"

Byron turned to look for Daniel, but the lion king was nowhere to be seen. "Where's Tick-Tock?"

Lydia's eyes went wide as she gazed back at the sea. "You don't think..."

Byron replied, "No. He is still with us; he has yet to become." He continued to watch Diana ride off in the distance.

"Yet to become..." Sebastian nodded his head. "I like that." He turned and looked at Byron. "What does that mean exactly?"

"I need to talk to Daniel."

"Does *he* know what that means?"

Byron turned away from the dam; Lydia followed.

"Does Daniel know who's coming? And seriously, what about the invitation?"

But no one replied to him as they headed to the den without him.

Sebastian threw his arms into the air, "Oh, come on!"

Chango and Amun moved passed him to follow the gorilla king and bull queen.

"Well, all right then."

LVIII

Daniel sat in silence, staring out at the windows of the Great Library as the rain continued to fall. He remembered the first time he ever heard thunder. The first time he ever saw lightning. He thought it was mesmerizing — magical. He had stood in the rain feeling the drops against his skin as he raised his head to the sky as it poured down upon him. He had relished in it, as if it were the longest banquet feast after a long fast.

Daniel had danced; he had rejoiced in the rain. He had sprinted down the long halls of the den until bursting inside the Great Library in search of his uncle. And now, here he was, sitting in Marcus' chair in the silence of the dark just as he found his uncle so long ago. Only a fire burning in the hearth lit the room, keeping the rest of it shrouded in darkness. His eyes were glued to the flames from the fire in his hearth reflecting off the glass in front of him. He dared not face the actual flames, remembering the last time he had looked into them.

"What did you see, king?"

Daniel did not turn his head but kept staring out at the falling rain. "Things I don't understand."

Byron moved closer to the windows, crossing his arms over his chest as he looked out at the rain. "Tell me."

Daniel shifted his gaze to the gorilla king. Daniel's eyes were slit to a cat; they seemed to glow, causing a shiver to run down Byron's spine. "What did Palimus see?"

Byron narrowed his eyes, *"Palimus?"* The wheels in Byron's head were spinning. "I don't know."

Daniel turned his gaze back to the reflection of the flames flickering across the glass. "She's going to love him."

"Who?"

"THE KING!" Daniel rose suddenly and spun on his heel, storming over to the massive bookshelves in his library. "A KING WE KNOW NOTHING ABOUT! All these books! All this knowledge! All this history and thought and philosophy! But not a *single* word written on this king or his

clan!" He looked at Byron. *"How is that possible?""*

The gorilla king looked at the lion king with a sudden understanding. "Prophecies don't always come to pass, Daniel. The vision in the fire. Symbols on a tablet. Foretelling in a book…they only tell of an option in the timeline of events in a history that has yet to be written. We have choices, king. So does Alexandra."

Daniel glared at Byron.

"You don't know for certain that she will choose to love this other king in the end. Her will may always only to be to choose you."

Daniel shook his head. "I *saw* her. I saw her through the waterfall. She saw him in the pool of water. He was speaking to her." He clenched his jaw in pain, remembering the moment. "And she was looking back at him with wonderment and awe. A curiosity that I had never seen before. A look of desire that flashed across her eyes the moment he came into view. She's never looked at me that way. And somehow, it seemed to be that she had seen him before…"

"How?"

"I don't know. Perhaps, somewhere else inside the fortress."

"She never said a word."

"There's many things I'm finding she does not say."

Byron thought of Alexandra's medallion.

She had never said a word to them.

Then he remembered their conversation in the treetops. She yet to share her thoughts with Daniel on what she was truly thinking or feeling. Looking at his friend in such as state, he felt a deep empathy for him. Daniel was not wrong to think or feel what he was currently expressing. Yet, the gorilla king was not satisfied.

"Our future, even Alexandra's choices, have yet to be written." He paused to collect his thoughts before continuing. "You asked me what Palimus saw? I don't know. I only know what Palimus *thought* he saw. And he was wrong. He was *wrong*, Daniel, and the entire realm paid for it. We're still paying for it. Don't do what Palimus did in mistaking his assumptions with reality. His is a path you must never follow."

He paused, waiting for any reaction from Daniel. There was none.

"That's not all you saw."

He watched as the lion king's body tensed. "Do you trust me?"

"Yes."

Daniel turned and looked at him, a little surprised by how swiftly he answered. "Why?"

Byron looked him dead in the eye. "You don't lie. You right wrongs. And you don't back away from a fight…even when you can't see who you're fighting. You seem to know that when you do, it's only because it's an enemy to your people, to your friends, and to the realm."

Daniel did not know what to say, yet Byron could see that his body still held its stiff and tense form.

"You, lion, *can* be trusted…"

The lion king's body finally loosened a bit. He knew that must have been what it was by Daniel's question. And it was true. Everything Byron just said was exactly what he felt and believed — and he was not the only one. He, Sebastian and Minotauro had had many conversations about the young lion king…how it was that he was the noble heart, how he stopped his grandfather, King Nathan, from slaughtering the gorilla clan and burning down his jungle…how he brought them all together to unite the realm with the new treaty and a new purpose.

But Byron also knew that Daniel rarely shared what lay deep within his heart and mind. He had always wanted to ask Daniel what it was he saw and thought about when he went to the hilltop in Bull Valley; they all had. And now, with everything they had been through together, he felt as if Daniel was one of his closest friends. And he did not like seeing his friend's demeanor as he studied him at this moment. It bothered him to see Daniel so distraught.

Daniel looked up at the portraits in the library. "Do you remember the petroglyphs in the fortress?"

"Yes."

"Then you saw the ones with the man, the man from the lion's den, commanding fire? A fire that set the realm on fire?"

Byron swallowed hard.

Daniel looked at him.

The gorilla king nodded.

"That's what I saw."

The gorilla king remained silent.

"I saw Alexandra enraptured with the dark king. I saw the fire engulfing the realm. And it wasn't just a man from the lion's den wielding it." His voice grew to despair. "It was me. I saw *me*, Byron. Not an unknown being…*me!*"

Byron could barely breathe.

"Lions cannot be trusted…"

The gorilla king's jaw clenched tightly. "I don't believe it."

"I SAW IT!"

"And what was the reason?!?!"

Daniel had no answer.

"You listen to me, king, visions in the fire are possibilities not finalities. If there was ever reason you'd set fire to our realm, you'd have a damn good reason for doing it." He moved closer to Daniel until they were toe to toe. "I'd trust whatever reason you had. And there's not one ounce of reason within me that would think it would be over a woman — even if it is Alexandra."

Daniel held his gaze.

"Fire is wielded by no man. If Fire answers your command, it is for that of the good. It is for that of the righteous, king — to make all things pure." He stepped back a little from the lion king. "And if I'm not mistaken, Fire has not claimed you, king. Not yet."

Daniel remained silent.

"Alexandra loves you."

The lion king looked away from him.

"She loves you, Daniel. Go to her." Still no reaction from the lion king. "You are king of the den and the sea. You are a guardian of the realm. This other king, whatever he is, only exists to seek that which continues to make great kings fall. He will not win. He will not reign here. Not ever. We kings will never allow that to happen. And should Alexandra fall in love with a man of this nature, she is not worthy of her crown. She is not worthy to stand beside you as your queen. She is not worthy of your heart, noble one. Nor is she worthy to be queen of her pack or of our realm."

"But I *want* her to be. I've always wanted her to be; since the moment I saw her. I knew it was her…"

"Then go. Remind her why it is she fell in love with you. Keep reminding her. And marry her, king. Rebuild the den. Revive the realm. What are you waiting for?"

But Daniel did not move. He did not know what he was waiting for. All he knew was that it was the first time he wanted to remain exactly where he was — and so he did.

Unbeknownst to Daniel, Sebastian was standing in the doorway of the Great Library, having heard the last bit of their conversation. He had never seen Daniel like this before. He had never heard him speak like this before. Looking at the lion king in his distraught state, something deep within the amphibian king rose up…it was a feeling he had never had before when standing in the lion king's presence. It was dread.

LIX

The cold wind began to howl as it blew through the surrounding trees. Shadows seemed to devour every shred of light as the army of darkness moved through the forest and down into Critter Country.

The sabretooth warrior stepped behind his king as the dark warriors followed. Decimus stopped in his tracks the moment he reached the largest grave in the field. He silently read the name on the headstone.

Chief Rayford.

His eyes roamed the desolate landscape; as far as the eye could see were abandoned graves of a forgotten cemetery.

They moved on.

With every step they took, a drop in temperature followed. Rainfall turned to snowfall as they made their way up a small hill.

"There it is." Decimus was looking out over the hilltop in Bull Valley. "Bird Kingdom." He smiled to himself as he surveyed the massive kingdom, taking in Queen Rebekah's domain. "This was all hers...Palimus' heir."

"You do not belong here..."

Decimus' warriors whirled around at the sound of the voice. Only the king and sabretooth were unmoved as Decimus barely turned his head in recognition of the words that had just been spoken. He lifted his eyebrow in amusement, almost as if daring the speaker of the words to show its face. He spoke softly to his sabretooth warrior, "Thorne, who is it?"

The fierce warrior looked to the sky and sniffed the air. "One who lives no more."

Decimus lost his arrogant smile. "The dead do not speak."

The sabretooth lowered his massive head, "Where do you think we are my, king? This is the realm of the dead."

This was not the answer the dark king had expected. It brought him no comfort as he noticed his warriors shifting in uneasy anticipation. They were armed, ready to attack and defend at all costs. But who can fight the dead?

259

As if hearing his silent thought, a warm wind blew through the army. The snowfall turned to mist, causing the warriors to shift nervously. The sabretooth growled lowly, and all went still.

"There is nothing to fear from a dead queen. She appears only as a reminder."

"Or a warning."

"Of what?"

When the sabretooth did not answer, Decimus turned his attention back toward Queen Rebekah's gates, "Time to go inside."

And as he was about to step toward Bird Kingdom, the ground quaked and shifted under his feet. Green vines immediately burst forth from the ground below and shot straight up. They rapidly wound around each other, gathering together to form a massive gate, barring the dark king from taking any further steps. The dark army could see these were no ordinary vines. Decimus' eyes narrowed.

The Sister...

Decimus' jaw clenched tightly. Thorne barked to the warriors behind him.

Off his command, the dark army roared and raced toward the gate. Some attempted to climb, while others grabbed their weapons: axes, spears, swords. Arrows were ignited and released, but just as soon as they hit their mark, the flames were extinguished by a warm breeze that melted the falling snow, creating a mist that snuffed out the flames. With every swipe of their sharpened weapons, more vines emerged, solidifying the gate into a massive wall of impenetrable design.

Those that climbed the wall were immediately hurled back onto the ground by the swat of Agoura's vines. The wall grew thicker as vine after vine wound around each other, continuing to sprout from the ground below.

Decimus' eyes seemed to darken behind his hooded shroud. He reached for his sword, pulling it slowly from its sheath; it was long and sharp, crafted in a shiny black metal. He held it firmly, gripping it tight. He took a step back to gain momentum and hurled the sword at the gate. It landed at its base, wedged firmly into the ground. He grasped the onyx-colored medallion from around his neck and whispered a command.

SNAP!

The ground quaked and vibrated in reply. The ground suddenly shifted, and ebony-colored vines sprouted from beneath the king's weapon. They slithered toward the gate, winding around Agoura's vines. They rapidly ascended, grabbing hold of her vines as if they were attempting to strangle them. The black vines continued to attack the green ones until the entire wall Agoura had built was covered in ebony vines.

Warriors began to climb the blackened gate, but they were hurled off the gate once more. Agoura's vines emerged from the stronghold of the black ones, breaking through them, and growing thicker over them, swallowing them whole until the wall itself was over ten feet thick.

But the dark unseen force was not done.

The black vines would not stop. They continued to shoot up from the ground below like a multitude of geysers, as they burst forth from the ground at the base of the massive wall.

"Give it time, my king. We'll eventually get through."

"How long?"

"Hard to say. She's very determined to keep us out."

Decimus looked up at the massive wall as the vines battled it out with each other. It was then that he saw Agoura's vines gripping a set of ebony ones, winding over them, twisting around them until ripping them apart. Roses started to bloom across the gate; they formed the words, *"Only the noble."* The red roses were so vibrant in color, they seemed to glow. And no matter how hard the black vines attempted to reach for the roses, they could not.

Decimus clenched his jaw even tighter as the sabretooth lowered his head at the challenge.

"Thorne, I thought the dead queen only honored Fire. Why is the sister here?"

The sabretooth kept his lethal glare focused on the center of the gate. "She's not the only one."

Decimus followed Thorne's stare.

On the other side of the gate, Rhodes, Agoura, Zephyrus, and Tick-Tock stood. Rhodes had his muscular arms crossed over his chest. He could feel the ground trying to shift beneath his feet as the dark force attempted to work its way under the gate and onto their side.

Agoura, however, did not move. Her emerald-colored eyes simply gazed at the ground as she kept the dark force at bay.

It was Zephyrus who spoke, "Our brother appears to have grown stronger."

Rhodes moved toward the wall and placed his hand against it. He pulled his arm back and punched straight through the wall, grabbing hold of an ebony vine on the other side, pulling it through. The hole he created was immediately sealed by green vines. He looked down at the ebony one in his hand; he studied it. Rhodes clenched it in his powerful fist and crushed it, causing the entire vine to disintegrate into dust.

His turquoise-colored eyes looked back at the wall. "The old wolf king made a single request." He looked at the guardian.

Tick-Tock's three heads began to spin until stopping on the snow owl — the head of the past.

"Only then do you become."

261

"We will know the moment, my king. Fire will show usss. The sssign will come...from the Sun...tok...tok...tok..."

Rhodes looked up at the darkened sky above.

"Yes, guardian, from the sun."

Tick-Tock let out a loud cry that echoed across over the wall and out across the hilltop, causing Decimus and his army to look all around for the source of the sound. It seemed to be everywhere and nowhere all at once.

The sabretooth seethed, begrudging the guardian's existence. He could sense Tick-Tock sanding on the other side of the wall. It was Tick-Tock who had taken down the sabretooth when it tried to hunt down and kill the lion king. No one had ever been able to overpower Thorne before, and the warrior vowed it would never happen again. He continued to hold his immobile stare at the gate as the ebony-colored vines continued to relentlessly work against the gate. "Not so easily done."

"Only one thing is."

Thorne shifted his yellow eyes to his king.

"To the lair."

LX

"To Minotauro."

"To Minotauro."

Sebastian and Byron were seated inside gorilla clan library, toasting to the memory of their dearest friend. Sebastian had joined the gorilla king as he returned to his jungle after leaving Daniel in the den. They had not spoken about Byron's conversation with the lion king, for Sebastian knew there would be time to do so — amongst all the other things they needed to talk about.

For now, however, it was time for the gorilla king to return to his jungle where his band of gorilla warriors had been waiting to celebrate their king's return. It had been a glorious feast filled with joy and merriment...and a lot of drinking; one where Sebastian and Byron had continued their binge inside the gorilla king's favorite place — his library. They were drunk.

Byron tried to focus himself, "Daniel should be here with us."

"Here, here!" Sebastian took a long gulp before stating, "Daniel seemed pretty pissed off in the library."

"He was pissed."

"Why? He just raised Mariner Sea with a purple rock from an element fortress nobody believed in only to become the most powerful king in all the realm in a single day. How can that not make somebody happy?"

"Daniel had a vision in the fire."

Sebastian gulped down his drink before setting the goblet down, thinking about the portions of conversation he heard Byron and Daniel talking about in the library. "When?"

"In the fortress."

The amphibian king pondered this for a while until he said, "I didn't know lions could do that."

"Neither did I."

"What did he see?"

263

"I think he should be the one to tell you. He has…"

"Great words."

"Yes!" They clinked goblets. "Great words!"

"Jealous?"

"Of what?"

"That it wasn't you."

"No…well, kind of. I did see Rebekah, though…and King Alexander in a dream. They were dancing before a large bonfire in the lair. Does that count?"

"I don't know. It might. Continue."

He remembered it. "Rebekah…she…it was like she became one with fire."

"Huh…did she…did she catch fire?"

"No. She moved with it and it with her. Like waves. It was mesmerizing." As he started to recall the vision, Byron began to sway.

"What was Alexander doing?"

He caught himself before he fell over. "Dancing…to the beat of the drum, but he was watching her dance with the fire."

"I can't dance. Amphibians have no rhythm."

"Agreed."

Sebastian took another large gulp of wine from his goblet. "You know what I don't get?"

"No."

"How that purple rock resurrected the sea. Who knew it would do that?"

"Apparently, Daniel's uncle Marcus."

"How? Where is this information written?" He looked all around the library at the shelves filled with books. "I mean, you have an entire library filled with books that have no meaning. No substance." He stared at the rows of books. "What are these books about anyway?"

Byron tried to focus his eyes as he looked at the books. "Histories."

"Where's the one on rocks? Where's the one on the elements and their fortress? Where's the one on dancing before fires? I want to do that…"

"You're amphibian. It'll never happen."

"That hurt my heart, Byron."

Byron looked all around the room. He stood and teetered a bit, trying to catch his balance. "Let's see if I have any." He moved to the shelves, searching through the titles.

"What?"

"Books…on rocks…"

Sebastian slapped his hands down onto the table. "Well, all right then. You look for the books on rocks and fire, and I'll look for the ones on horses."

"Hm?" Byron spotted a purple, velvet-colored book from a secluded shelf in the corner of one of his bookshelves. Intrigued by its appearance, he immediately grabbed for it and started flipping through it.

"Horses. How did we not know about the horses? All these years…our treetop was in their kingdom. How did we not know it? How did she?"

Byron looked up. "Diana?"

"Yes, Diana."

"Minotauro seemed to know."

Sebastian paused, "He did? How?"

Byron shrugged his shoulders, still flipping through the book.

"You know, she had the audacity of etching her initials in our treehouse!"

Byron started laughing. "What!"

"With the date!"

His smile widened.

"She's beautiful, isn't she?"

Byron looked at his friend. "She's…"

"She's beautiful. You know it and so do I. I can tell you're interested. Lydia can see it too." Byron blushed in embarrassment. "If your desire is for her to be your queen, you're going to have to make a move. Use Minotauro's strategy. He had one, you know…when he wooed Lydia." He took another gulp from his goblet.

As Sebastian continued to drink, Byron was trying to focus on the words written on the pages of the book he had selected. The amphibian king stood, crouching down to look at the books on the shelf behind him. He planted his palms on his knees and pulled one from the shelf. "And this other king…where did he come from? Is that why Daniel is going to burn down the realm?"

The gorilla king turned and looked at Sebastian.

"Yeah, yeah…I heard some of what he said. Alexandra's going to fall in love with this guy and Daniel is going to burn down the realm. Just like love to do something like that."

"Daniel is not going to burn down the realm." He went back to reading the book."

"But you didn't correct me about Alexandra."

Byron could not believe what he was reading. "No way…"

Sebastian turned, "What?" He began to read the book he had pulled from the bookshelf. He could barely focus his eyes as he brought the book directly up to his nose. "I knew it!"

"What?"

"You need to read this."

"I'm reading this one."

Sebastian looked up at the remaining bookshelves. "I need to start reading more. If I can find a book on Palimus, I can find a book on that other king."

Byron's head popped up. "Palimus!" He reached for Sebastian's book. Sebastian narrowed his eyes and grabbed the book Byron had. They both sat back down. "Where's the one on horses?"

"Quiet. I'm trying to focus."

Sebastian slithered out of his chair and landed on the floor. He crawled back over to the bookshelves. He never made it. He passed out right then and there; his face planted into the floor.

Byron reached for the purple book once more and began to read. As he absorbed the words, he was immediately sober. "The greatest guardian…"

Daniel was still sitting inside the Great Library as the rain continued to fall. He was reading a book he had not read in a long time.

"I am giving you a gift — it is one of the many books I have written about my most beloved queen. I have written down all my memories of her, including the things she felt and thoughts she once shared. I believe you will find what you are looking for. Keep it beside you always. Learn from it. See past the words itself for the things she was truly saying as she said them. For there will come a day when I shall ask for it back, but today is not that day."

He was looking for answers. He was reading the book Reginald had written about Queen Rebekah, hoping he could find where he had written about Rebekah's thoughts or actions when she had found out that his grandfather, King Nathan, had married his grandmother — Princess Lara. He had hoped there was something in there that would inspire him or bring him peace. But all that he found was what he had already known.

He was searching for *great words…*

"What did you see, king?"

Too many things. Horrible things. Images he could not get out of his head. The vision in the fire was too fresh in his mind; he was struggling to concentrate. No matter how hard he tried, his thoughts kept returning to the vision in the fire. Rhodes' words were still echoing in his ears. And the memory of Alexandra reaching for the king…

He slammed Reginald's book closed and forced himself up and out of Marcus' chair.

Daniel turned around to face all the portraits hanging in the room. All the lion kings of former eras were staring back at him. Each king before him had a challenge they had to face. Each one had difficult choices they had to make as ruler of the den. And what would they do with this one?

A dark king was coming.

His eyes combed the portraits feeling a wave of emotions as he looked at all their faces. Each and every one of them.

His eyes fell on his grandfather, King Nathan.

They all mattered to me

Then onto Prince Marcus.

The forgotten ones…

King Gunthar.

The ruthless ones…

Daniel's gaze fell on the last portrait he was looking for. It was then he felt the presence in the shadows of the corner of the library. How long he had been there, Daniel did not know, but he was glad.

"Tick-Tock, I need you to do something for me."

The totem came forth.

The vicious ones.

"Tell me about the Old War."

The last portrait was that of King Luther.

Tick-Tock's head spun to snow owl as the rain continued to fall.

LXI

Alexandra was staring up at the painting her father had created ages ago; it was of Rebekah dancing before the fire. She studied it for a long time, looking at it as if she had never seen it before. She was thinking of Daniel, wondering desperately what he had seen when he looked into the fire. She had sent him several letters since the day Hood and the pack skirted her away from the dam, but she had not heard a single word from him in reply.

She told herself it was because he was busy. Busy at the den. Busy catching up with Sebastian. Busy with the Mariner Clan. But she knew that was not it.

Alexandra had seen him through the waterfall. She had just passed the mounds of snow and was about to call to him when she heard Decimus' voice. She knew he had seen her reaching for the king in the water. He was not just being distant for distance's sake; she was remaining distant too.

Hood and the pack did not want her to leave the lair now that she had returned. And Alexandra did not put up a fight over it. She was not ready to see Daniel. Remembering his distant gaze after he had awoken from his comatose state, knowing how he barely glanced at her then, how he had not held her as she wrapped her arms around him at the dam, she knew there was something he had seen that had to do with her.

It made her feel even more guilty and afraid of what he had thought when he saw her reach for Decimus in the water. She clutched her medallion tightly, wondering if Rhodes was disappointed in her too.

She should go to see Daniel. She knew she should. The rain had stopped falling and the routine of regular days had now begun its predictable rhythm. She had nothing stopping her from going. So she made up her mind — tomorrow, resistance from her pack or not, she was going to go.

A wolf suddenly howled in the distance.

Alexandra moved toward the edge of her balcony. She saw her pack racing forth from the forest and out toward Wolf Lake.

Something was wrong.

Alexandra was beside Hood, hiding in the shadows of the trees that led to Wolf Lake.

"Do you hear them?"

Hood nodded. "They are many." He was crouched in the darkness. His eyes were set, staring out past the lake. "They're coming from the north. Unknown beings…yet you are calm, my queen. I can feel the even beats of your heart. You know who approaches."

Her silence was her answer. Hood could feel the agitation in his blood as it pumped through his veins. It always did that when danger was near.

The air temperature suddenly dropped. Hood could see his breath fogging on the air when Alexandra said, *"He's here."*

The fur all over his body began to rise just as a man's deep, sultry voice shouted from across the lake, *"QUEEN!"*

He could feel her excitement, the heat of her body temperature rising. A low growl rumbled deep inside Hood's chest. The same growls responded from the warrior pack behind him. They all sensed it — in their bones, in the chilling air around them, in the sound of the man's voice. Hood dropped to all fours as did the other pack warriors. They were barking and growling viciously; the cacophony of warning echoing across the lake.

On the other side of the darkened waters, Decimus smiled as he took in the warning from the Wolf Pack. He could see their mirroring eyes glimmering through the trees. "QUEEN! I can only cross by your command!"

Hood's heart was thundering inside his chest. The fur on his body stood on end as the heat from his body rose. Even Alexandra could feel it as she stood beside him. All Hood kept thinking was that King Alexander would have already given the order to attack.

What was she waiting for?

269

He could feel the pounding of her heart and the rush of her adrenalin. She was excited, not fearful. It was then he realized, she was going to invite him in. *"NO, MY QUEEN!"*

But Alexandra was not listening to her warrior. All she could hear and all she wanted to hear was the sound of the dark king's voice.

Hood was about lunge to stop his queen when he heard a loud *SNAP!*

Black vines immediately shot up from the ground beneath him, attacking him and the other members of the pack. The wolves, hyenas and coyotes erupted as the ebony vines wrapped around them and bound them to the ground as the biting cold wind whipped viciously across their domain.

Hood seethed as he looked to his queen as she shouted, *"I COMMAND YOU TO COME!"*

The pack erupted even louder as black fire rolled across Wolf Lake, and a black sheet of ice emerged as the dark army descended.

Chief Netapheha was staring down into the pool of water, stirring his coral staff around and around, looking deep into its depths. "Fire will show us when...Fire will show us how..." He stopped and crouched down, his webbed hands gripping the ledge as he looked down below. "Remember...remember..." His bulbous eyes narrowed as he said, "The lion king...only he will know...it is into the fire once more he must go...he must go...for all to see, for him to show the very thing they all know...*the lions cannot be trusted."*

Crouched in the corner of Netapheha's abode was Tick-Tock. He merely stared at the old toad chief, remaining in silence as his head spun from snow owl to barn owl to horned owl — the head of the future. *"It is in the suffering that he will become."*

270

ABOUT THE AUTHOR

Corina Zurcher is the author of the Christmas books *Growing Up Claus* and *Snow Falls*. She is also the author of the epic fantasy books *Archangels, The Father of Lights, Legacy* and *Nobility*.

For more information, visit: www.nevermorepublications.com.

ABOUT THE ILLUSTRATOR

Scott Edward is a freelance illustrator specializing in concept art and storybook illustrations. Trained in traditional art techniques, Scott converted his skillset to include digital art and uses Procreate and watercolor scans to bring his original style and artwork to life. Scott illustrates novels, graphic novels, and storyboards.

Freelance and aspiring writers are encouraged to contact Scott to conceptualize their projects on Instagram @Edwardartwork.